"Stout impresses with his second Carter Archives novel, drawing readers further into the gritty urban fantasy hellscape of the city of Titanshade while adding depth and complexity to his scarred, cynical hero. . . . Stout's detailed, impeccable worldbuilding and subtle characterizations are sure to captivate returning fans and new readers alike."

—*Publishers Weekly* (starred)

"*Titanshade* introduced readers to a compelling new world. The second book in the Carter Archives takes readers on a deep dive into its culture: politics and crime, social conflicts, fear and intolerance, local versus national interests, and especially the workings of manna and magic. It broadens readers' understanding of how the characters relate to each other and maintains a wonderful sense of discovery. Stout proves once again to be a master of retro sf noir."

—*Booklist*

"If you like rollicking detective stories with some action-adventure and alien culture to overlay the mystery, you should give this one a look. I can almost guarantee it won't be what you expect." —*SFRevu*

"Dan Stout's debut novel is flawless. *Titanshade* is set in an original, gritty fantasy world, like enough to ours to take you by the throat as the detective noir plot roars along, yet filled with intriguing other beings and moments of remarkable magic."

—Julie E. Czerneda, author of *The Gossamer Mage*

"It's a fascinating world, so different with its magic and mixed humanoid races, yet steeped in a familiar '80s ambiance, and a classic jaded detective who still manages to care about his city and its people." —*Locus*

DAW Books proudly presents
the novels of Dan Stout

THE CARTER ARCHIVES
TITANSHADE
TITAN'S DAY
TITAN SONG*

*Coming soon from DAW

TITAN'S DAY

DAN STOUT

DAW BOOKS, INC.

DONALD A. WOLLHEIM, FOUNDER

1745 Broadway, New York, NY 10019

ELIZABETH R. WOLLHEIM
SHEILA E. GILBERT
PUBLISHERS

www.dawbooks.com

First Mass Market Printing, April 2021
1 2 3 4 5 6 7 8 9

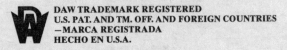

To my breath, my fuel and my fire.

Mandy Fox

SIX WEEKS SINCE THE WORLD had changed, and it was still the same old shit.

The news cycle was a nonstop parade of talking heads and pundits dissecting the discovery of manna beneath the ice plains. But for all the arguing in barbershops and noodle stands over how best to exploit our newfound resource, the city itself was unchanged. Titanshade still crouched in the arms of the Mount, its buildings of stone and glass coated in filth while the usual array of predators and drunks stumbled down cobblestone streets; every morning winds howled in from the ice plains as millions of residents woke up to find their life was a little worse off than the day before. And me? I was kneeling over another corpse.

The body on the ground had been a beautiful woman, once. Before the city claimed and corrupted her; before a killer added the final blow to her temple. She was Mollenkampi, with an unusually delicate red and black coloring to the thick plates that lined her scalp in place of hair. She also had a fierce set of bony jaws erupting from her face, flanked by a pair of spindly mandibles, though those traits were shared by all members of her species. Including my partner.

Ajax stood to my right, on the far side of the victim. His mandibles flexed and released as he studied the scene. To our backs a pair of patrol cops flanked the mouth of the alley, the dark crimson of their uniforms a match for the crime scene tape separating us from curious passersby. Not that there were any. The early morning foot traffic continued on with barely a hitch, residents too wrapped up in their own affairs to care about one more statistic in an alley.

I stood, pulling my overcoat tight to guard against the chill air. We were far enough from the Mount that the thermal vents didn't fully protect us from the frozen tundra surrounding the city. Still, I wouldn't have traded it. It was our first day back on the streets after six weeks of desk duty. Thirty full days of paper cuts and office politics. It was good to be back, even if the streets were as grim and unrelenting as ever. Someone had died, and I had a chance to help bring them justice. I did my best not to wonder why it took someone's death to feel good about myself.

"Detective Carter?" My name was underscored by the pop and sizzle of a flashbulb.

I shoved aside my doubts and turned my attention to the pair of crime scene techs circling the alley. Both human, both looking tired and unhappy to be there. One held a clipboard, making notes on carbon-paper forms, the first of many that would document the life of the investigation. Her partner swapped out a new flashbulb and hefted his camera to eye height.

"We're moving to the body," said the notetaker. "You can touch the surrounding items." She was doing her job well, even if she stole glances at Jax and me when she thought we wouldn't notice. We'd become accustomed to that mixture of interest and suspicion in the six weeks we'd been off the streets. I hoped the stares would fade when some new distraction claimed the city's attention.

That attention was why this case, this victim, had been selected for us. Training wheels for a pair of detectives with instructions to stay out of the limelight. In Titanshade, a dead candy in an alley was low profile: not flashy enough to garner press attention, and common enough that if we didn't clear the case, it wouldn't be considered an issue. It had fallen to us to find justice for this girl who was so disposable.

Sprawled on one side, the victim's arms and legs were askew, and the right side of her face was exposed, the wound in her temple on gruesome display. Her natural golden complexion was fading, growing paler by the hour. Her T-shirt had been pulled up, revealing more red and black coloration tracing her hip bones, before disappearing behind low-cut denim shorts. Her bra had been disturbed, but not the shorts. The medical examiner would confirm it, but I doubted she'd been sexually assaulted.

"Looks like a candy," I said. "Got herself killed and had her emergency cash plucked from her cleavage." The women and men who worked the streets often had a roll of bills discreetly tucked away, payment for pimps and something to hand out in case of a mugging or shakedown.

Ajax grunted a low note of assent, the deep nasal tones of his biting mouth harmonizing with the higher pitched tinkling of the speaking mouth in his throat, directly above the crisp knot of his tie. "Looks like," he said. "But looks lie, don't they?"

I smiled. He was right, of course. Fashion sense doesn't always indicate a vocation. Hells, I'm a cop and I wear a suit.

My partner stooped to press the sensitive skin of his wrist against the victim's exposed belly, below her crumpled T-shirt. Enough of the design was visible to make out that it read *Disco Sucks*. I liked her immediately.

"Body's cold," said Jax.

"Not ready to touch, Detective," the tech warned him away. Jax pulled his hand back, rocking the body slightly, which provoked an annoyed grunt from the photographer.

Jax pointed a thumb at the movement of the limbs. Mollenkampi went stiff slower than humans. That, combined with a chill skin, meant—

"Probably happened early in the night," Jax said, implying she wouldn't have had much cash. Maybe not enough to kill for. Definitely not enough to die over.

"It's the big city, kid," I said. "Candies work the streets at all hours." Ajax was still a relative newcomer to Titanshade, and on occasion he made the mistake of thinking there was any real civilization here. The city had grown on the back of the oil industry, and a large part of it still catered to the vices of rig workers blowing off steam after a months-long work detail.

Near the victim's feet lay a purple backpack, the kind a kid might use to lug around school books. The sides were cluttered with buttons and ironed-on patches, a mix of political slogans and dirty jokes. It looked like the kind of thing my step-daughter would carry. Truth was, Talena had a lot in common with the young woman sprawled on the ground. Age, attitude, even availability—Talena spent many days and most of her nights on the streets, leaving her vulnerable to the monsters who stalked the shadows. One more thought to push out of my mind as I refocused on the scene in front of me.

The pack was open, its contents dumped on the ground beside it. The pile was topped by a paperback novel and a black-bound journal. The bottom of the bag held a thick thermal bodysuit. A popular item with those staying on the very fringes of town, where the rent was cheap, the thermal vents sparse, and questions nonexistent.

"Looks old." Jax held up a corner of the suit. "But clean."

I nudged the other end with the toe of my shoe. It had several visible patches.

"Secondhand," I said.

Jax had already moved on to the journal, flipping through its pages before holding it up like a teacher reading to a roomful of kids at story time. There was a color sketch on one page, a caricature of Mayor Walcott, focusing on his lengthy nose and prominent front teeth, while still conveying a sense of authority. It had been done in some kind of chalk or pastels, and the excess had smudged into the blank page opposite, creating a blurry, reversed image.

A slip of paper fell from the journal, and Jax plucked it from the air before it joined the trash littering the alley. He read out the details. A single ticket stub for the bus line that ran between Titanshade and more civilized locales to the south.

"She's only been here a couple weeks," he said. "If it's hers."

"Another newcomer." It was the notetaker, a bit of disdain creeping into her voice.

Countless arrivals had flocked to Titanshade in the last six weeks, hoping to make their fortune on a new boomtown and straining the resources of the city. Rents had skyrocketed, leaving some longtime residents homeless, and even staples like food and drink had gotten more expensive. But none of that changed the fact that I was still a cop, the dead still demanded justice, and the city didn't give a damn about any of it.

Eyes on the victim, I drew my notepad out of my pocket. "She was stabbed in—" I fumbled the pad. I tried to grab it in the remaining two fingers and thumb of my left hand, but it slipped away. Ajax took one smooth step and snatched the pad as easily as he'd caught the bus ticket. He pressed it back into my hand without comment.

I was grateful for the silence. Over the last month I'd mostly adapted to my missing digits, but still struggled from time to time, as if my brain wanted to believe the pinky and ring fingers were still there, that they'd never been severed in the snap of a Mollenkampi's powerful jaws, that I hadn't been present to witness dozens of innocents lose their lives as part of a madman's scheme to find new resources in Titanshade's oil wells. His wild plan had succeeded, but not in the way he'd anticipated. He'd missed oil, but struck a source of manna, the raw material of magic. Now the city sat on what might be the greatest source of energy and wealth the world had ever known. The question was whether the rest of the world would decide to strip it away from us.

All of that had led to our time on desk duty. Our names were tied to the rediscovery of manna, and the brass wanted us hidden from the press and the public before we could cause more headaches. But now we were back, and we had a chance to get it right. We were there to help bring justice to this woman in an alley. We owed it to her, and we owed it to ourselves.

Standing by the body, I took a deep breath and struggled to refocus. To my right, Jax had begun an orderly, outward spiral from the body. Textbook as always. For my part, I concentrated on my breathing. But instead of seeking calm I imagined myself panicked, a killer with blood on my hands and adrenaline in my veins.

"She was stabbed in the right side of her throat," I said, and mimed holding a pencil-sized weapon in my left hand, then in my right, using a backhand strike. "Either way, the most natural place to discard the weapon was . . ."

I turned and walked two paces to the rust-eaten dumpster, heavily tagged with spray-painted phrases elaborate in their obscenity. The freshest was a stylized fist, stenciled wrist lines straddling the words "Titan First." I ignored the empty slogans and scanned the ground debris. The alley was on the small side, no more than four paces across. Narrow enough that the dumpster would have to be rolled to the curb for collection, the kind of unpleasant task that was often neglected by a building's tenants and managers. Which explained the buildup of trash in the alley, and the resultant stink. The glare from the streetlights was faint, but I had enough visibility to make out a set of skid marks where the dumpster had been recently pushed to the street. More surprising were marks leading away in the opposite direction, as if someone had also rolled it farther into the alley. That was strange, but not as interesting as the gleaming steel implement nestled among the fast food wrappers and soiled rags. It had a triangular blade the size of my thumbnail on one end, and a similarly sized blunt paddle on the other. Both blade and handle were covered with a congealed red liquid.

"Possible weapon," I called.

Ajax joined me, shining the beam of a flashlight on the unfamiliar item. The techs followed behind, tagging and bagging the item for posterity.

"Not likely to get prints off the surface," said the notetaker. "Not with a textured grip like that."

The notetaker was right, but I was already refocused on the victim.

"She came back here," I said. "Maybe for break, maybe for business." I pointed behind the dumpster. "Might have disturbed someone sleeping off a high, or maybe things went bad with the customer." I turned, leather soles scraping across the filthy cobblestones. "She didn't get out alive." It occurred to me that I'd regained a sense of calm as I stepped through the killing. I shut off that train of thought as soon as it surfaced. I wasn't there to analyze myself. I had a job to do.

The beam from Jax's light moved along the brick walls of the buildings flanking the alley. "I think I know what she was doing."

The walls held tags similar to those covering the dumpster, but there was also something extraordinary. A mural twice my height stretched deep along the alley wall, going as far back as the skid marks led, near the raised stairs of the fire escape. The mural featured skillful caricatures of politicians and celebrities, with a special emphasis on the local Ward's political bigwigs, a pair of twins. All the figures were larger than life, drawn in muted pastels with vibrant highlights, done in what appeared to be chalk rather than spray paint. It was a match for the work Jax had displayed in the sketch book.

Jax looked from the mural to the broken body abandoned amid the alley debris. "She wasn't a candy."

"Candies can draw," I said. "Just like anyone else. Anyway, if she was in the life, chances are her prints will be in the system, ours or someone else's. We get a name and we'll be able to track her pimp."

Another pop, and the alley was bathed in harsh, fleeting light. The photographer, a beefy guy with watery eyes and a mustard stain on his lapel, waved us over. "We're good to move the body."

"Can I get an ID check?" asked the one taking notes. Her lips were in a permanent pucker, as if she'd gone through life biting down on something sour.

Jax and I squatted and did the honors. We patted the victim's pockets and the collars of her boots, anywhere a wallet or ID might be tucked away; we came up empty. The tech grunted.

"Jane Doe it is," she said, and the scritch of pen on paper entered it into record.

We rolled our Jane Doe onto her back and revealed the other side of her head, the side that should have been untouched by the attack. Instead, we were faced with a violent mutilation.

There was the pencil-width hole in the side of her neck, and evidence of blunt force to her temple. But even more disturbing was what wasn't there. Where her left mandible should have been was only an empty void at the bend of her jaw. The back teeth were missing as well, along with a chunk of the jaw itself. What remained was a jagged hole, exposing the inside of her biting mouth and the spongy cross-section of her jawbone. I rocked back on my heels, stunned by the violence but also by the strength it had required. Whatever had been done, it had been brutal, happening fast and with great force.

"Side roads," Jax swore, and shined his flashlight onto the wound. I reached past him and shut Jane's eyes.

People describe death by saying that the spark has left someone's eyes. What they really mean is that the dozens of small muscles around the eye stop moving. We communicate with glances and furrowed brows. Even in sleep our eyes twitch and dart side to side. When those countless tiny movements are absent the eyes lose their spark, becoming as lifeless as the face of a discarded doll.

As we shifted her body, wet slips of paper came into view. Sticky with blood, an assortment of cash fanned away from the small of her exposed back, dropping to the ground in soggy clumps. An assortment of eights and twenties, the kind of cash a junkie or casual mugger would never leave behind. The techs documented and collected the cash, revealing something else on the ground beneath the blood-soaked bills. Something that sparkled.

Wedged between the cobblestones, half covered by the pale gray muck that collects near dumpsters, were broken shards of a glass vial. I waved over the tech and indicated that we'd need a photo. After the pop and fizz of the flash-bulb, Jax scooped the shards into an evidence bag, sealing and initialing it. There was the faintest glimmer of liquid on the fragments.

We returned the body to her original position, and I reached for the evidence bag. But Jax extended his arm, keeping the bag out of my grasp as he inspected it.

"There's no chance this is real," he said.

He was almost certainly right. That iridescent shimmer was distinctive, but most people had never actually laid eyes on manna, let alone had the means to carry a vial of it.

The mystical liquid that fueled the first industrial revolution had long been thought depleted. The few manna stockpiles that remained were the provenance of the ultra-rich and government-funded sorcerers. At least it had been, until six weeks earlier, when a reserve was discovered outside of Titanshade. Rumor and speculation still swirled around the manna strike, with different theories about how much it might contain, and whether or not there might be more reserves under the ice plains. I did my best to avoid thinking about it: it had also cost me two fingers and the life of a friend.

"Gotta be fake," I said. Since the manna strike the streets were teeming with knock-offs, hucksters trying to take advantage of the poor and desperate who hoped to grab a small piece of magic for themselves. The real stuff was on lockdown, and access limited to highly vetted workers. The military had seized control of the site, a move that the Assembly of Free States assured the good people of Titanshade was only a temporary step.

The notetaker called out, "Fingernails have some material under them. You want to double-check before we wrap her hands?" The tech popped open a pair of paper bags to be slipped over Jane's hands and secured with rubber bands.

"Hold on," I said. There was a glimmer of glass on the cobblestones. I borrowed a pair of tweezers from the techs and stooped to snag another glass shard. "Might as well be thorough." Jax held an evidence bag open as I navigated the fingernail-sized chunk of glass toward it. I fumbled the tweezers at the last moment, and the shard fell free. My left hand shot forward and the shard plopped into my palm. I expected to feel a slight prick at the most, but instead there was an uncomfortable, intense cold combined with a tingle that buzzed across my hand, as if I'd pressed my palm against a sheet of ice covering a fast-flowing river.

I snatched my hand away, letting the shard drop to the ground. Jax rolled his eyes, but picked it up without complaint. He probably thought I'd bungled the catch the way I'd fumbled my notepad earlier. I blinked, averting my eyes as Jax handed the bag to the notetaker.

I'd never encountered anything like that, not even when I stood in the spray of the manna strike. Manna on flesh simply felt like a pinch followed by numbness. But this also wasn't phantom pain. A cloud settled in the back of my head. If it was imagined, that meant another trip in front of the department shrinks, and maybe more time behind a desk. Best to shove it inside, back with the guilt for feeling at home as I stood beside a corpse in an alley. The best I could do was to promise myself that I'd be thorough in finding the killer.

The tech noted on the tag that I'd touched the shard

directly and put the bag with the others. If it was narcotics, that would at least tell us something. Something besides the fact that a woman was dead.

I looked at the alley opening and the city that lay beyond. Buildings and sidewalks crowded with occupants either waking up or stumbling home. Families and friends, young lovers trying to make time, hustlers trying to make a quick buck. All of them trying to scrape and scheme enough to make it to another day. Walking among them were more killers than a sane mind could comprehend. It was our job to reduce that number by one.

2

WE LEFT THE TECHS TO bag and tag the rest of the items, giving them instructions to have us paged if they found anything unusual while we worked the neighborhood. At the mouth of the alley scarlet crime scene tape stretched from one building to another like an exposed tendon. We pressed it aside as we reached the street. The phrase "red tape" supposedly comes from that material, a comment about the many levels of bureaucracy involved in police procedure. I wasn't sure if it was true, but it sure as Hells echoed my experience.

On the far side of the barrier, two patrol cops assigned to scene control leaned against their cruiser, thumbs hitched in their belts, eyes on the pedestrians streaming past in the morning darkness. One of them, a shorthaired blonde named Bells, squinted at us as we approached.

"Not much to go on, huh?" She was the one who'd spotted Jane's body, and called it in. We'd debriefed her as soon as we'd arrived.

"Not yet," said Jax. "We'll see what we turn up."

"Too bad," said Bells, with all the concern I might show a loose thread on a new shirt. "There'll be another dead candy in an alley tomorrow. Better luck with that one."

I kept walking. "Keep your eyes open," I told her. "And be careful out there. Hate to see you sprain a finger the next time you phone it in."

Bells responded with a malicious chuckle and an obscene gesture that proved her fingers were plenty limber.

I seethed, and felt Ajax side-eyeing me as we walked. When we had a bit of distance, he told me I should let it go.

"A woman's dead." I shot the alley a look over my shoulder. "Doesn't that count for something?"

"Of course it does," he said, his sigh accompanied by the tinkling of countless small teeth lining his eating mouth. "It just doesn't count for everything."

He was right. It takes a certain amount of compartmentalization to stay sane dealing with tragedy every day, and some of us have to make a show of it in order to get to bed at night. It was something most cops struggle with. I know I did. Maybe I could have talked to Jax about that. Instead I changed the subject. It's something I'm good at.

"I'm freezing." I pulled my overcoat tighter to ward off the chill. "I could use a hot drink." I craned my neck, taking in the neighboring buildings. Sturdy-built things of brick and steel, crowned with dilapidated storage sheds and water towers ready to be topped off by ice trucks. Each one was full of potential witnesses. "You want to grab coffee before we knock on doors?"

"Sure," he said. "Give them time to wake up."

I headed toward our car. Early morning fog twined among the alleys and parking meters, and the winter sun still hid far below the horizon. This season held only brief hours of daylight. In two weeks we'd hit Titan's Day, the moment when the days would start getting longer and the brightness of the sun stronger. But to get there we'd have to live through the longest night of the year. I merged with the crowd, finding some comfort in the anonymous bustle of the city street, only glancing backward when I realized I'd left Ajax behind.

I found my partner paused by a newspaper stand, digging in his pocket for loose change.

"Let's go, Jax!" I yelled. "Your partner needs coffee."

He ignored me and fed a few arcs into the coin slot of each vending machine. He caught up with me a moment later, several papers tucked under his arm.

"Alright," he said. "Let's have our drink and meet the neighbors."

We grabbed a couple steaming cups of caffeine from a street vendor and settled into our car, an unmarked unit from Hasam Motors. The Dash models were the choice of the TPD because of the balance they provided: small enough to maneuver the tight streets of Titanshade, cheap enough to be easy on the city's budget.

Ignoring the useless fold-out waxed paper handles, I gripped my coffee cup between my palms, enjoying the warmth against the stubs of my missing fingers. Unlike most cups in Titanshade, the coffee lids weren't tapered, making it more difficult for Ajax to use. He popped the lid and pinched the lip into a spout. With a handkerchief tucked into his collar to allow for any drips, he poured the drink into the smaller, more discreet mouth in his throat used for eating and speaking.

It was a nice moment of peace and quiet. Until Ajax ruined it.

He spread out the newspapers and flipped through them like a kid looking for the funny pages. I asked what he was doing.

"Catching up on the news." The newsprint rattled as he turned the pages.

I returned to my coffee. Jax and I had come a long way. Jax had barely made detective when we were paired up, a college-educated newcomer, whose primary task had been to make sure I didn't do anything stupid on a high-profile case. But he'd proven himself to be a good cop and a better partner than I deserved. Now I trusted him as much as anyone in a city full of predators and thieves. Still, he was a small-town kid struggling with the learning curve that came from patrolling one of the most densely populated cities on the planet. If the papers helped get him there, I was all in favor.

I should have known it was a lie.

Ajax tossed me one of the local rags, *The Titanshade Union Record*. "Looks like the hero of the hour is at it again."

Mollenkampis' dual mouths allow them to fill their speech with undertones and trills, enriching each word with subtle nuance. Absolutely none of which was present in Jax's tinkling chuckle, and I could guess why he'd really gotten the papers.

I flattened the *Union Record* across the steering wheel. There was a photo of me stalking out of the Bunker in shirtsleeves, holding what appeared to be a large evidence bag. The headline proclaimed HERO COP TAKES OUT THE TRASH. The article conveniently failed to point out that it was no metaphor; I was on desk duty at the time, and the photo was of me literally taking out the trash after our lunch had started to smell.

For most of my career, keeping my job had hinged on never attracting press attention. But since the manna strike, I couldn't walk out of my apartment building without getting a write-up. The city's economic landscape had turned upside down with a single well strike, and I'd become the face of that change. It had taken six weeks before things calmed down enough for the two of us to return to active duty.

I scanned the article.

"At least this time they got the details right," I muttered.

Mandible twitching, Ajax snatched the paper away. "*Detective Carter continues to right the wrongs of a city at war with itself,*" he read.

I shrugged, doing my best to seem embarrassed.

"*Strong jaw*?" he said. "*Stubble-laced cheeks*?"

"Sounds right." I scratched the day's growth of whiskers decorating my chin.

"Uh-huh." Jax scanned further. "*The look of a leader.* Who wrote this garbage?"

"Garbage seems a bit judgmental . . ."

He found the byline. "Taran Glouchester." He blinked. "Isn't that—"

"The asshole who did the smear piece on us during the Haberdine case." At the time it'd caused a major headache.

"After you ran into him with the Hasam."

"Bumped him," I corrected.

Jax hummed a low note. "Well, if it says something about

a full head of hair, then we'll know he's blind as well as incompetent."

I snorted and unfolded one of the other papers. While *The Union Record* may have latched on to those of us at the manna strike as popular heroes, other outlets had different agendas. *The Daily Saber's* front page featured a photo of Ambassador Paulus, our representative from the Assembly of Free States, making some kind of proclamation about the military presence. She managed to look dignified, even though the photo showed a sea of protesters waving signs declaring "Open the Wells" and "Titanshade for Titanshaders." Sharing the dais with Paulus was Colonel Marbury, the head of the AFS military encampment. Behind them, slightly out of focus, was Paulus's deputy, Gellica. The grainy black and white didn't do Gellica justice, or give enough weight to the impossible secrets behind her smile, but still, I found my eyes lingering.

Ajax drained the last of his coffee and crumpled the waxed paper cup into a ball.

"Are we doing this or not?"

I rubbed at my ear, which seemed to have developed a mild ring. One more health issue to worry about. I chucked the newspapers into the back of the Hasam and we got to work.

We canvassed the buildings on either side of the alley, as well as the two across the street. All were apartment buildings about five stories tall and packed full of people who didn't seem particularly concerned that someone had been killed within earshot. We knocked on every door, introducing ourselves and asking if the locals had seen or heard anything in the night. Not surprisingly, nobody had anything useful to share, but they all had an opinion on what had happened. There's this idea that when cops ask questions the neighbors clam up. It happens sometimes, but more often they're eager to talk, even if it's only to try and pry details out of us. Murder makes for juicy gossip.

The residents were mostly human and Mollenkampi, with a few Gillmyn thrown in the mix as well. The bulk of the city's population was made up of these three Families, as the remaining five either rarely came this far north or had physical properties that made it more difficult to co-habitate with their sibling species.

The interviews were slow going. The tingles I'd felt in the alley preyed on my mind, and the chill in the air made every moment uncomfortable. Ajax, on the other hand, seemed perfectly relaxed. Which was good, since there were more people at home than I expected—one more side effect of the manna strike. Some oil rigs had ceased operations by AFS order, others had halted production in order to search for manna wells on their property, hoping for a magical strike of their own. Either way, the result was rig workers sitting on their hands at home, while their bank accounts dwindled and their bored uncertainty turned to anger.

After a few hours, we came to a top-floor apartment where the door had so many layers of flaking paint that it almost looked cheerfully purposeful. Jax knocked while I tugged my earlobe, trying to release the pressure. I still heard a ringing echo, as if I'd clamped my hands over my ears. He knocked again, louder, but got no response, despite the sound of a television emerging from inside.

Finally giving it up for a lost cause, we started down the hall only to be greeted at the top of the stairs by a wild-eyed human lurching a sloppy zigzag toward us. She stopped a few steps away, pulling up short as if shocked to see two men who'd been standing in plain sight. Stepping back, she teetered on one heel, wobbling on the brink of a multi-floor tumble.

Jax shot forward and grabbed her arm. He pulled her away from the stairs and she staggered into me, head falling against my chest. She had an expensive haircut allowed to fall into disarray, light brown curls growing wild. Her breathing was heavy, but carried no smell of alcohol. Her perfume was dainty. Rose petals and honey.

As I helped her balance she gripped my arm tight—very tight. I registered her strength with surprise, even as the tingle I'd encountered in the alley returned, now racing from elbow to fingertip. I tried not to think what it meant if the severed nerves were more damaged than the doctors thought.

"Where you headed?" She had long strands of hair or thread over her jacket. I could feel them but they were too fine to see. I pulled them away, trying to get my hand free. This wasn't how I wanted to spend my morning—the hallway seemed dimmer and the chill in the air more intense than it had when we arrived.

"Up," she said, her tongue working at the corner of her mouth like she'd just discovered her lips. "I wanna see, you know . . ." A slight hiccup. "Starshine."

"Sure you do." No one in Titanshade saw stars unless they got to the ice plains, well outside the light pollution of the city. Jax fished the woman's wallet out of her back pocket.

"This says you live here," said Jax. "6F." The door we'd just been knocking on. "Is that right," he checked her ID again, "Sherri?"

The woman protested. "I live everywhere," she slurred. "And the mind's eye sees all things."

"Alright," I said. "Focus your mind's eye on me." I snapped my fingers to catch her attention. "Here's the deal. We're gonna walk you to your apartment, and if you can get inside and close the door on your own, we're not gonna drag your drunk ass down to a holding cell. You understand me?"

Sherri nodded, turning the motion into a whole-body expression. Jax released her, and she stumbled up the rest of the way, a muttered "whoosh!" accompanying each step, as if she were hearing an internal soundtrack of roaring winds. She fumbled her keys at the door, but she didn't even have her hand on the latch before it was pulled open from the inside.

Standing in the doorway was a kid no older than fourteen. He wore jeans and a ratty zip-up hooded sweatshirt over a faded T-shirt, and his eyes sparked, first with anger, directed at the woman, then changing to fear as he noticed us.

The woman skated her fingernails over the face of the door. "Ronnie!" she cooed, reaching out to cradle his cheeks. "Hey, honey!"

The kid craned his neck, avoiding her touch even as he slid between her and us. A protective gesture.

Jax flashed his badge, and that calmed the kid a little, but he still wasn't happy to find a pair of cops at the door.

"Were the two of you home earlier this evening, Ronnie?" I asked.

The kid's eyes narrowed. "Name's Ronald." He had the same tangle of curls and sharp nose as the woman. I guessed mother and son.

Sherri rubbed her chin and said, "I gotta get to bed. Got work in morning. Have fun talking to your friends, honey . . . ." She leaned in and attempted to kiss his cheek, a wet smack that seemed to contain more drool than affection. Then she shambled down the hall, one hand outstretched, fingers grazing either side of the hallway. Halfway down, she toppled a pair of framed photos from the wall and busied herself collecting them.

Ronald eyed my partner's intimidating biting jaws and began the conversation with an eloquent, "What?"

The kid had the lean limbs that came with a teenage metabolism and unhealthy living. We ran over the situation again, keeping details as minimal as possible, and asked what kind of activity he'd noticed on the street last night.

"Nothing."

"There wasn't anyone on the street at all?" In a town with the population of Titanshade, empty streets were a rarity.

The kid rubbed one arm, hugging it across his chest as he looked down, pouting. "I didn't say that."

"Who did you see?" Fishing around in my overcoat pocket, I pulled out the scarf I kept there for trips to neighborhoods farther away from the Mount. I slipped it around my neck to help ward off the surprisingly chill air.

The kid hesitated. Behind him, the TV still blared, occasionally interspersed with static as the reception faded in and out. A wire hanger had been shoved into its back, replacing the rabbit ear antenna.

"Nobody I knew," he said.

"Ronnie!" The kid's mother snapped, her voice loud in my ear. I hadn't seen her coming down the hall.

Sherri reached for her son's ear, clearly intending to perform the kind of ear twist that mothers have been practicing down through the ages. But she muffed it, and Ronald shifted to the side, letting her stumble past him, only catching her at the last moment.

Gathering her balance, she said, "Imp's blade, Ronnie. You saw something, you tell them!" Having either given up or forgotten about reaching for his ear, she wandered back down the hall. Ronald shot daggers over his shoulder, the kind of look that only a mother could tolerate.

"I already said," Ronald turned his glare back on us, "I didn't see nothing."

Jax grunted and snapped his heavy biting jaws shut with a cringe-inducing crack. Twenty years my junior, Jax didn't like to see killers walk free any more than I did. We were both running low on patience.

The kid shifted, and I got a good view of what he wore beneath the sweatshirt. It was a Viral Lode tour shirt that must have been a thrift store find or a family hand-me-down. The thing was older than him. I pointed my pencil at the worn fabric of the screen-printed logo.

"You actually listen to them, or just wear the merch?"

His chin jutted out. "I listen."

I tipped my head, as if showing respect. "I saw them live."

"Bull."

"At the Rosa Pavilion, back before it was shut down. They opened for The Daizey Chainz."

The kid uncrossed his arms. "Serious? Viral Lode *and* the Chainz?"

I couldn't help a smug smile. I'd snuck past the gate with my friend Hanford when we were kids, too excited to see the bands to care what happened if we were caught.

My hand rose. "Swear. I was twenty paces from a stack of amps so loud my ears rang for a week."

His cool broke, and a goofy grin replaced the sneer. For the first time since he'd come to the door, he looked his age. "Nice!"

I asked again what he'd seen.

"Where?" he said. "It's a big street."

"Down there." I jerked a thumb at the stairwell window and its view of scarlet police tape sagging across an alley mouth. "You notice anyone hanging across the way?"

He stared for too long, his eyes widening before he backed away and crossed his arms tight over his chest. "No."

I peered out the window, to see if something had spooked him. The scene was still intact, Bells and her partner no longer there. The coroner's wagon had already whisked away Jane's remains. From this angle there was something else, something I hadn't seen from the ground. A security camera over the wall-mounted streetlight at the mouth of the alley. Anyone coming in or out of that building would be caught on tape.

"Kid," I said. "Don't bullshit us. Who'd you see?"

He shot a glance back inside, at his mother. A look of concern, rather than a request for help.

"This is a confidential conversation," I said, and it was true—I wasn't about to put a kid in jeopardy. The question was whether he'd believe me.

I was silent, and Jax followed my lead. After a beat, the kid said, "There's a guy used to come round, stuff to sell."

"Stuff?" Likely cheap street drugs like angel tears or chono, but I didn't want to put words in the kid's mouth.

Ronald dug a thumbnail into the flaking paint of the doorframe. "Magic."

"You mean manna?" The pressure behind my eyes built a little more. "Kid, no one selling drugs on a street corner's got real manna."

"Whatever." He tapped his chest. "I don't get involved." But he couldn't resist a brief glance down the hall where his mother still struggled to rehang the family photos. He may not get involved, but I'd bet my paycheck Sherri did.

"This guy," I said. "He from around here?"

"Nah. Never seen him before."

I blinked at that. The neighborhood was gang territory, and local bosses rarely gave their blessing to outside operators.

"You sure?"

"Course I'm sure. He got two different colored eyes. Stood out from the crowd that way." Ronald bit his lip. "But that guy don't come around anymore. He got a permanent setup someplace else."

"You didn't actually spot anyone down there last night?"

Ronald shrugged again. It seemed like his go-to gesture for defiant indifference. "Nah. I was at Full Tilt most of the night."

Jax glanced up from his notepad. "What is that? Store? An arcade?"

The kid's sneer returned.

"The *best* arcade." He scratched his nose and added, "I made third round in the Moon Diver tournament."

Ajax's eyes crinkled, the equivalent of a smile for a guy whose lower face consisted of skinless jaws and tusks.

"How long did you stay?" I asked.

More feigned indifference. "Pretty much all night."

"Alright. You think of anything else, you call us, okay?" I motioned to Ajax, and he produced a calling card with his name and contact number on it.

The kid's mother was suddenly between us, snatching the card from the kid's hand, eyes widening.

"Wait a minute," she said. "You're *cops*?"

I stared at her. Something was off, but I couldn't identify precisely what.

Jax nodded. "Yes, ma'am. As we mentioned—"

"You get away from my boy!"

Sherri pressed forward and I reached to restrain her. When I grabbed her shoulder something danced across my hand, tickling and tingling. She shoved me, and I slammed into the wall, feeling as if I'd been hit by a delivery truck. I managed to hold on to her jacket and pulled her along with me. She fell into my chest, and I had another whiff of her perfume as invisible strands stuck to my hands, as if her entire body was wrapped in cobwebs. I batted at them, the same way I would if I walked through a spiderweb, and they dissolved like cotton candy in water. She stepped toward Ajax, easily breaking my grip.

Breathing heavy, the roaring in my ears growing into something like a distant windstorm, I kept waving my cobweb-covered hands while shouting, "Dammit, dammit, dammit! Just calm *down*!"

There was sudden release of pressure behind my eyes and I grew warm and lightheaded. Maybe I *had* been behind a desk too long.

But even as I pulled back, my words had the desired effect. Sherri paused, face scrunched up in confusion. For a moment, her legs buckled, and she wavered. That hesitation was all the opening my partner needed. He stepped forward and grabbed her, turning her away and dropping her to the floor.

"What are you doing? Get off her!" Ronald leaned into my partner and punched Ajax in the side. My head was clearing and I grabbed the hood of his sweatshirt, twisting his shoulders while he kept screaming. "Get off of her!"

"She's strung out on something." I thought of the rose petals and honey. There was no stink of liquor, but she was clearly out of control. I'd spent three years working Vice, and had dealt with people under the influence of almost anything imaginable. I'd never encountered anything quite like that.

"What the Hells did you do to her?"

"Nothing, kid, we—"

"Bullshit!" He shook the woman's shoulder. "Mom?"

She groaned, muttering, "So good. So strong." She was out of her mind but unharmed, even smiling. But Ronald didn't see that.

The kid snaked free, leaving the now empty sweatshirt in my hand as he planted another kick to Ajax's back. My partner reared around and bellowed, a loud, eerily plaintive rumble accompanied by a spray of hot mucus from the gaping maw of his biting mouth. Before that display of jagged tusks and grinding ridges Ronald fell to his knees, hands raised defensively, voice cracking even as he found the bravado to scream, "I won't let you take her away!"

Jax relaxed his biting jaws and looked away, mandibles twitching uncomfortably. It wasn't fair to put a kid in that position.

Fair didn't always ride along with justice.

With the kid calming down and the mother subdued, we had to decide what to do with her. Before either of us could speak, Ajax's pager went off, immediately followed by mine.

Jax nodded toward the interior of the apartment. "Help me get her on the couch."

We set the woman down, and Ronald tucked a pillow beneath her head with the same blend of concern and resentment I'd seen a hundred times before, in a hundred different kids' faces. It wasn't easy watching a parent struggle with addiction.

Jax yanked his pager from a pocket. "Code 187," he said. Homicide.

I glanced at the green on green of my display. "Same."

Ajax slipped past Ronald, asking, "May I use your phone?" The kid nodded absently.

While Jax dialed I slipped out of my scarf and overcoat. Maybe it was the adrenaline burst, but I was feeling much better. I gave the kid and his mother a little space, moving a few steps closer to my partner.

He rattled off his badge number to Dispatch, jotted a couple quick notes and gave a startled shake of his head. "Confirm that address, Dispatch." A pause, and I listened as he recited it back to the dispatcher.

I walked to the window and pushed aside the broken blinds that hid Ronald and his mother from the world. I stared at the address of the apartments across the street. 5150 Ringsridge Road. The building we'd just left.

WE LEFT THE KID TO tend to his mother and headed to the new crime scene. We were still a while out from noon's brief window of winter daylight but the neighborhood already had a different feel, the city having lurched its way into a new day. There were more signs of life, with people shouting at their kids or one another, only sparing the occasional glance at a pair of cops patrolling the shadows.

"We already covered this building," Jax said as we walked. "You think someone got killed between then and now?"

I took in our surroundings. Early Titan's Day decorations were already appearing in apartment windows, and in one of the first-floor storefronts an elderly Mollenkampi man climbed a stepstool to string up a sign wishing potential shoppers the traditional season's greeting: *Good Day's Dawning!*

"I don't hear sirens," I said, as we hesitated on the curb, waiting for an opportunity to cross the street. "More likely it's a cold body." We started across, cutting through slowed traffic. I carried my overcoat in the crook of my arm. I hoped the seesawing body temperature wasn't a sign I was getting sick. "What do you think that lady was on? She had full-on junkie strength."

"Didn't notice," he said.

I watched his face, assuming he was joking. "She planted me in the wall pretty good."

"Now *that* I noticed."

I wasn't about to ask him if he'd seen the cobwebs or hair or whatever it was I'd felt wrapped around her.

5150 Ringsridge was one of the first buildings we'd worked, knocking on every apartment door without finding anything out of the ordinary. I glanced at the streetlight as we approached the alley where Jane had been found. Like most streetlights in Titanshade, it was mounted to the building exterior, sidewalk space being too precious to surrender to safety concerns. Above the light I could barely make out the rectangular shape of the camera I'd spotted while talking to Ronald. My pace slowed, and I pointed it out to my partner.

"Strange place for a landlord to set a camera," I said.

Jax slowed as well. "Not much point in a deterrent that can't be seen."

"I don't know about you," I said, "but I'd like to know if its feed was recorded."

We stood for a moment, silently staring at the place where Jane's life had ended only hours before. Scarlet crime scene tape drooped at the alley's mouth, pulled or fallen loose, crime and victim already fading into background noise. Then we moved on. After all, we had one more homicide on our morning schedule.

Dispatch had informed us the body had been found on the top floor, so for the second time that day, we hiked the stairs.

Like many apartment buildings, the uppermost level of 5150 Ringsridge was occupied by storage and laundry facilities. When we'd door-knocked that morning we hadn't bothered to walk those areas. Why would we? Our victim had been on the street, four stories below us.

A pair of patrol cops had cordoned off the laundry room. We greeted them with a nod and a flash of our badges.

"What's the story?" I peered past them, not yet willing to cross the threshold.

The laundry was a simple thing, a relatively clean place lined with washers and dryers that were scratch and dent specials. Locked storage spaces lined the far wall, no doubt rented out to the tenants who lived in the apartments below.

The shorter, leaner of the two patrol cops rubbed the back of his neck.

"One of the tenants came up to do his laundry, and found the body. We arrived, and confirmed that it was . . ." he glanced at his partner, but she didn't offer any assistance. "Definitely deceased."

Ajax pulled out his notepad. "Where's the tenant now?"

"Down in his apartment. Looked like he might pass out."

"Okay," I said. "Tech team's on its way. Where's the body?"

He pointed at an area near the water supply lines. A red stain marked the vinyl tiles, but there was no corpse in sight.

I turned back to him. "Well?"

The patrol cop was pale, and when he grinned, it was the kind of sickly thing a man might wear to convince you he wasn't queasy. It was armor I'd worn more than once.

"See for yourself," he said.

Careful to watch our steps, we walked in. We were about halfway through the room when a voice called out.

"Sorry, pal. This is a strict no celebrity zone."

I turned to find another cop standing in the doorway. He wore dress pants and shirt topped by a burgundy windbreaker, the kind with white vinyl piping around the pocket lines and elastic on the sleeve cuffs. A checkered leather driving cap pressed down on his mass of dark curls, looking like it might slide off at any time. His badge dangled on a chain lanyard, half covered by the fabric of his windbreaker.

His name was Matt Dungan, and while he'd added some gray in his hair and wrinkles around his eyes, he also had the same gap-toothed smile he'd worn every day in the years we'd spent working Vice.

I suppressed a grin of my own and addressed Ajax. "That explains the lack of red carpet. Definitely a small-time operation."

Jax flexed his biting jaws, confused but playing along.

"And no craft services," he added. "You'd think the TPD could spring for some catering."

Dungan grunted.

"Glad to see fame hasn't gone to your head," he said.

We shook hands, and his eyes lit up even more as he tried to squeeze my hand into a pulp. He always did push everything too far, and a joke was no exception.

I made the introductions between my current partner and old colleague. Dungan was a barrel-chested guy, and his bulk stood in sharp contrast to Jax's lean build. He didn't give Jax the same squeeze treatment, probably wanting to make a good first impression, or maybe he just didn't care about pissing on my partner's territory.

"Dungan left Vice around the same time I did. He's OCU, now."

Jax grunted, impressed but not letting it show. "You're the guys in the papers." A high-profile group that worked separately from most other divisions, the Organized Crime Unit focused on entire organizations rather than individuals.

"Look who's talking." Dungan fished in a pocket of his nylon windbreaker and came out with a hard candy, the kind they gave away at banks and hotels. "I heard you Homicide guys got paired up," he said to my partner. "Guess you got asked to take one for the team, huh?" He peeled the candy from its wrapper before popping it between his teeth. "Can't say as I ever approved of arranged marriages."

"Just 'cause you can't get anyone to tolerate your ugly mug," I told Dungan, "doesn't mean marriage is a failed institution."

Dungan flashed his little-kid grin. "Ask my ex-wives," he said. "They'll tell you how failed it is."

His smile wavered when his eyes drifted down to my left hand and the manna-cauterized stumps of two fingers. He didn't meet my eyes immediately after that, looking instead at the far wall and the vending machines filled with single-serving dryer sheets and detergent packs.

"Why are you here?" I straightened the lapels of my suit jacket, using the movement to hide my fingers behind the fabric. "Nice to catch up and all, but if you're here then OCU must be interested for some reason."

What I didn't ask was whether he was about to dismiss us from the scene. The Organized Crime Unit could take control of damn near any investigation if it served their interests, and small cases had a tendency to get gobbled up and forgotten in favor of bigger fish. Some cops hated that because it could reflect poorly on them when it came time for promotions or transfers. Others just wanted to see bad guys go to jail.

"I'm here because I got a call," Dungan said. "Same as you." He passed us, walking a half-dozen strides to the laundry machine and nodding toward the top-load lid.

The fluorescent glare of the overhead lights revealed the watery pink smears on the inside of the lid, obscuring the instructions for a proper wash.

Ajax flipped his notebook open. "The victim was on the washing machine?"

"Not on." Dungan's child-like grin returned. "In."

Ajax and I stepped forward. The smell of bleach pinched my sinuses. The dingy, discolored water obscured the contents, until something shifted, and the rounded end of a severed thigh floated to the surface of the water. The flesh was hairless, with a pale green tint that, combined with its size, marked the victim as a Gillmyn. The thigh bobbed in the washer, an obscene buoy in a tub of bleach and bloody water.

Dungan moved beside us, light on his feet for a big guy. "Meet Cetus St. Beisht. A real son-of-a-bitch who's been scrubbing funds for several operations run by the Harlq Syndicate." Dungan said the name of the gang with a better pronunciation than I could muster. I said *Har-lek*, while Dungan got it out in a single syllable. Though Ajax said it best, with a gurgle in the back of his speaking mouth. Like he was gagging on swamp water.

"I've had him under surveillance for a while now," said Dungan. "He went missing a day ago and I asked—"

"A day ago?" I said. "That's some top-notch surveillance you guys run."

I crouched down, examining the area around the washer. There were no bloody fingerprints, nor was there a mess on the white painted steel of the exterior. "How'd you know it's him?"

"The nice thing about Carter is the positive feedback."
Dungan addressed Ajax, but I could feel his eyes on me as
I peered along the washer's side. "He's all about being a
team player."

I rose slowly. "I skipped the team sports days in phys
ed." I jerked a thumb at the washer and asked again,
"How'd you know this was your guy?"

The bigger man snorted. "His car's on the street. Wallet
and clothes are in the back seat. Call it a deductive leap."
A team of techs filed into the room, led by a heavy-set human
with a bristly mustache. Dungan gave them a lazy wave.
"We'll know for sure when they fish him out."

I didn't recognize the tech crew, which meant they were
OCU. Dungan wasn't wasting any time asserting his authority. I looked from the stain on the floor to the bleached
and blood-drained body. There was surprisingly little mess
from one to the other.

"You already like someone for this?"

"Wouldn't be much of a gang-breaker if I didn't," he
said. "I'd heard he was on the shit list of the local Harlq
boss, a nasty piece of work named Anders."

Jax sucked in a breath and jotted a note. I wondered if
that name meant anything to him. Dungan changed the
subject.

"I rolled down when St. Beisht's car was found," he said.
"Wasn't expecting to see you here. Aren't you on mental
rest or something?"

"Post-trauma interventional assessment," said Jax, still
writing in his notebook. "You think Anders did this as an
internal Harlq hit?"

Dungan showed his palms, as if apologizing for any offense.

"Post intervention thingamajig," he amended. "How did
you two get here so fast?"

"We were in the neighborhood," I said. "Already picked
up one today."

"The candy in the alley?" Dungan clicked his snack
against his teeth.

"We don't know she's a candy," said Jax.

"How'd you hear about her?" I asked Dungan.

He sighed, as if burdened by the questioning.

"Crime scene tape on the alley," he said. "And a pair of redbacks sitting in their cruiser. So I asked them the story." The sweet tumbled from one side of his mouth to the other with a clatter. "By the way, the blonde with short hair? Not your biggest fan, buddy."

Dungan stuck his hands in his back pockets and pivoted, looking around the laundry area.

"I'll get the paperwork started for the case reassignment to OCU." He paused, as if considering something. "I'll take the one in the alley as well. That way we won't be stepping on each other's toes."

"No," I said, and maybe it was because of the echo in the laundry room, all those metal machines, but it came out louder than I'd intended. Dungan and the techs stared at me, though I noticed Jax stepped closer, closing ranks. I cleared my throat and clarified. "We'll keep working that one. Already have some traction."

It was a lie, but I wasn't interested in seeing the OCU take a murder case that they didn't care about. Whoever Jane was, she had a roommate or a lover, a family or maybe even a kid like Ronald depending on her, someone who deserved closure. And the dead woman herself deserved to be more than a bargaining chip in a plea deal designed to get some mobster to roll on another.

"Good for you." Dungan shrugged, as if he were fine either way, then resumed his sprawling lean against one of the other washing machines. I figured I'd throw him a bone to cheer him up.

"There's a security camera on the alley outside," I said.

The candy in his mouth broke with a crunch. "No there ain't."

"We almost missed it, too. Can't see it from the ground."

Jax crossed his arms. "Are you going to get the footage from the building owner?"

"Yeah," said Dungan. "You want a peek at it?"

"We do," said Jax.

"I can make that happen," he said. "But you know . . . Body in an alley. In this neighborhood, at this time of day? I'd almost think they were trying to get you two on a case that'd fly under the radar."

I scratched my jaw, while Jax examined the heel of one shoe. There wasn't much point in denying it.

Dungan nodded.

"And if that's the case, this is the wrong place for the two of you to be standing. Because this?" He tilted his head, tipping his hat's brim toward the bloodied laundry lid. "This is gonna get some attention." He showed his teeth again. "So how'd you like to get involved in something a little more interesting that's still got a low profile?"

I exchanged glances with Ajax. It made sense to at least hear Dungan out.

"Alright," he said, rolling onto the balls of his feet. "We'd better get the two of you out of here before any press shows up. Follow me, gentlemen."

Dungan led us down the stairs, running his mouth the whole time. Mostly with stories of the old days, when we were younger, dumber, and had an exaggerated sense of our ability to heal wounds.

"When me and Carter was on Vice," he said to Jax, "we used to deal with all kinds. Pimps, candies, dealers, johns and janes. Spent a lot of time undercover making buys for all sorts of services." He slapped my shoulder with a touch more force than needed. "Your partner here had this uncanny ability to never actually get a candy to go anywhere with him."

"That's true," I admitted. Partly it'd been because I found it unpleasant, like we were picking on the wrong person. But also, I was genuinely bad at it. Picking up candies takes a certain gift of gab. You have to make them feel comfortable. My social strengths lie in getting under people's skin, irritating them enough that they forget themselves and say something they shouldn't. "I suppose we all have our own talents."

We emerged onto the street, blinking in the breaking light of the post-noon dawn. The name Titanshade was deceiving. Since the Mount sat on the northeast side of the city, it provided almost no shade at all to the low-seated sun. Winter daylight was fleeting, but unrelenting while it lasted.

"So who played the candies, then?" said Ajax. "Was that you?"

"Me?" Dungan waved him off. "Nah. I was too good looking. Nobody believed I needed to pay for it."

He grinned, and I rolled my eyes.

"But this guy," he jerked a thumb my direction. "He couldn't even get a candy to even talk to him, right? But he could buy dope all day long. *Everyone* wanted to take his money."

Ajax rolled his head, laughing from his throat while his imposing mouthful of teeth glinted in the short-lived daylight. "Now that I believe."

We reached Dungan's vehicle. It was another Hasam Motors model, though nicer and roomier than ours. One more OCU perk, I supposed. He opened the passenger door and pulled out an accordion file, the kind my old man used to keep recipes in. Dungan's had a photo stapled to each pocket. Mug shots, mostly of shiny-plated Mollenkampis in suits, with the occasional human or Gillmyn thrown in for good measure.

"These," he said, "are the major players in the local Harlq Syndicate. And these," he pulled a second accordion file from the car, "are the CaCuri twins and their assorted hangers-on."

The CaCuris were from the salt plains, dark hair and eyes, freckles over their cheeks and noses. I mostly knew them by reputation. Thomas was a shark, a well-dressed slab of muscle with no instinct other than violence. I wasn't as familiar with his sister Catherine, though I understood she was cut from the same cloth. They were major players in the neighborhood, and they'd both been depicted in Jane's alleyway mural.

"I've built up relationships with most of these characters, one way or another." He held an accordion file in each hand, raising and lowering them as if he were the very scales of justice. "And watched them escalate with each conflict."

"We get the idea," I said. "You said this Anders guy had it out for St. Beisht."

"I said he was on Anders's shit list. But I think someone beat him to it." Dungan raised the CaCuri file while lowering his voice. "Bad blood's been simmering between those two organizations for months. Way longer than Thomas can normally keep his act together without beating someone into a coma."

He set the files on the roof of his car, like a city attorney presenting at a trial. "I think the CaCuris lured St. Beisht onto their territory, then chopped him up in that laundry room to send a message." He rippled the tabs on the Harlq file, pausing at a thumbnail photo of a stocky, smooth-headed Gillmyn and a lanky Mollenkampi, presumably the deceased St. Beisht and a bodyguard. Dungan flicked the photo as he hunched his shoulders and glanced around, giving a sense of shared scheming. He was laying it on thick—baiting the hook for whatever he was about to sell us. "If the Harlqs and CaCuris go at each other for this, it could start a street war."

Jax lowered his head, almost muffling his speaking mouth behind his collar. "I've seen the Harlqs in action. They don't care about bystanders."

"Exactly. And after this?" Dungan pointed at the top floor of the building, where one of the Harlqs' key figures lay dismembered in a washer. "There's gonna be blood on the streets. Unless we do something about it first."

"Uh-huh." I tugged at my lip and stared at the building. Such a strange place to hide a body. It was a flashy crime, done with the intent to be found. "What do you want to do?"

"They're gonna go after each other," Dungan said. "There's no stopping that. But once they do, I can be in position to take down the CaCuris—hard. And maybe the Harlqs in the process." His eyes danced from Jax to me, his enthusiasm almost infectious. "The mistake they made, both the Harlqs and CaCuris, is relying too much on one source for almost all their funds."

"How's that work?"

Dungan rubbed the fleshy curve of his cheek. "White collar sleight-of-hand. Lots of cash accounts and complex math. You wouldn't follow it, Carter."

Jax widened his stance. "I would."

The cheek rubbing slowed. "Yeah, you might." Dungan

rolled his neck, but didn't provide any further details. "The point is that the Harlq's local financier is dead, and the CaCuris have a single weak point. Strike there and both organizations are gonna starve without laundered funds."

"So this single weak point," said Jax. "Do you have enough to bring him in?"

"Better." Dungan winked. "He's primed to roll on the CaCuris."

"You're going to need a plan." Jax's biting jaws clacked together, punctuating his skepticism.

I exhaled loudly. "He's already got one, kid."

Jax was sharp, but he didn't know Dungan like I did. For his part, Dungan jammed his hands in his pockets and smiled, a child caught nipping into the cookie jar.

"That's why he's telling us about it," I said. "Somehow, he thinks he can use us to flip his guy."

The older cop flashed his childlike grin, and the polyester fabric of his windbreaker whispered as he bounced from foot to foot.

"You got me, pal!" He leaned in. "Not everyone in this town hates you two. Turns out my potential CI is a big celebrity hound. A pep talk from the cops who rediscovered manna would be mighty convincing."

I winced, and turned my face to the Mount.

"Can't do it," I said.

Dungan's eyes widened, and he stopped his excited bouncing.

"What?" His lips pulled tight and his shoulders rose. He'd always had a temper. "Why the Hells not?"

Jax spread his arms, ready to step between us.

"Because this is the opposite of laying low," I said. "Half the brass wanted to fire us rather than get us in the limelight more often."

"That's bullshit," Dungan snarled.

"It's not." Jax's voice sounded a dual-toned soothing note, which Dungan didn't seem to register.

"You were right about us being on training wheels," I said. "If we do what you want, we're gonna get bounced right back to desk duty."

He considered it, frowning, then nodded sharply.

"You want to play it that way? We can do that."

"Dungan—"

"Nah." His frown had turned into a cruel scowl. "Don't worry about it. It's just something I've been working on for the last year. And a war between Harlqs and CaCuris shouldn't create more than a few dozen bodies. So who really cares, right?"

He stepped back, glancing at his watch as if he had other things to do.

"I'll get the paperwork going for St. Beisht, like I said." He spit out his candy, letting it skitter across the cobblestones. "And I'll take that girl from the alley, too. One more thing you don't gotta worry about. For old-times' sake."

My stomach clenched. Dungan had noted my earlier reaction to losing Jane's case and was now using it to twist my arm. Dungan had always been willing to do whatever it took to make people dance to his tune. Only this time he wasn't limiting it to drug dealers and street toughs.

"And what happens to the Jane Doe," I said, "while you're busy charming your pet mobster?"

He spread his hands. "Murders should get solved. But I've only got so much time."

"Are you kidding me?" I kept my voice low. Low as I could manage, anyway. Whoever killed Jane wasn't going to be a good citizen from then on—anyone who'd visit that much violence on a victim would do it again. If Dungan took Jane's case and let it sit fallow, then the next death would be on us. "What the Hells is the matter with you?"

"What's wrong with me?" He looked left and right, appealing to an invisible panel of judges. "I ask for a favor and you tell me to screw myself. And you want to know what's *my* problem?"

My throat constricted, a mix of disappointment and rage that I forced myself to swallow as I stepped forward, treading on some stray bit of trash and snapping it on the cobblestones. I twisted my foot, grinding whatever it was into the dirt beneath my sole. Getting into it with Dungan on my first day back wasn't smart. I took a breath and let it out slow, looking away from him.

All around us the neighborhood was decked out in signs of the season. The regular Titan's Day decorations of silver and blue bunting were supplemented by glitter-streaked posters, homemade things with glitter representing the iridescent shimmer of the manna as it rained down at the strike site. I noticed that none of these new representations had the rig workers' bloodied corpses or my severed fingers in the scene. But how much historical accuracy can you expect from holiday decorations?

I locked eyes with Jax. He gave me the smallest of shrugs. It was my play. And we lived in a city where rot and corruption always lay hidden behind the prettiest decorations.

Glaring at Dungan I said, "Fine. We'll do it."

My old friend's smile was forced. "See? We're all on the same team." He dropped the accordion files back into his car.

I stepped away. "Whatever. Keep your hands off our case and we'll fix your problem."

He shook his head like a disappointed parent. "Not just my problem," he said. "Everyone in this town is threatened by the CaCuris. They're priority for the entire OCU." Dungan shrugged, drawing a sigh from the fabric of his windbreaker. "That alley candy is all yours. Help me with this one guy, and it'll stay that way."

If it was a priority for the entire OCU, that explained Dungan's eagerness. I didn't know his standing in the department, but flipping this CI could be a career-maker. I grimaced at the blatant power play.

"I should've known you'd pull something like this."

"Don't blame me," he said. "I asked for a simple favor—"

Jax stepped between us, cutting off any further escalations.

"Are we done?" He looked at each of us in turn. "Because if so we'll head back to the Bunker." He gave me a slight push, enough to back me off a step.

For his part, Dungan appeared unconcerned. He unwrapped another hard candy. "I'll set up a little meeting for you and my guy. Tomorrow should work. I understand you don't have much of a caseload."

I snorted, not trusting myself to give him an answer. Across the street a camera crew had pulled up. The anchor exited the van, straightening her blazer and scouting the site. I turned my back, hoping we wouldn't be seen departing.

"Perfect." Dungan rubbed his hands. "Tomorrow we'll go meet the terrible twins' money man."

A JAX AND I WALKED IN silence, heads down, trying to keep a low profile as we made our way back to the Hasam. We slid into the car's familiar seats and I craned my neck, searching for an opening in traffic.

As I waited, Jax said, "Are we going to talk about your friend's request?"

"No." The wall of cars and trucks was unrelenting.

"Not at all? Not even a joke to minimize the weirdness of the situation?"

I hit the gas and the Hasam shot into traffic, greeted by a chorus of honks and shouts. I even earned an obscene gesture from a Therreau farmer whose beetle-driven cart careened to the side to avoid us.

"No," I said, and forced myself to loosen my clenched jaw.

We drove away from the dual crime scenes, letting the stop-and-start of traffic push the distaste of Dungan's extortion into the background. When Jax opened his mouth I hit the thick buttons of the radio presets, jabbing several until I found a track layered with enough squealing guitar and driving bass that it removed the possibility of conversation until we'd reached our destination.

The sprawling tower of concrete and steel at 421 Deland Avenue was officially named the Titanshade Police Department Central Building and Garage, but throughout the city it was known by a simpler name: the Bunker.

In conjunction with satellite precincts around the city, the Bunker housed the many divisions of the TPD as they fought a losing battle against the crime and corruption that accumulated like the snowdrifts beyond the city's perimeter. Tucked away among its mazes of corridors was also an assortment of holding cells, interview rooms, and medical examiner's facilities, in addition to the primary TPD garages. But those of us who worked the street suspected its real purpose was to give the administration nice views from corner offices.

We made our way to the third floor, which a simple placard declared to be the home of the Homicide Department. There, in the largest room on the floor, my colleagues' desks were arranged in a large rectangle, forming a loose open space with a blackboard at its head. This was the Bullpen, where detectives worked in ones and twos, doing the everyday tasks that kept the system running and might bring closure to mourning families. The kind of work that didn't make it onto TV shows.

When I entered there was no pause in the whir of rotary dials or scratch of pens on carbon paper; typewriters continued to clack and cops continued to bitch about their workload. But I knew they were aware of my presence. By both training and nature, cops take the measure of everyone who walks through the door, assessing threat and intentions. If you ever walk into a roomful of cops and don't get the once-over, then you know they're better at being subtle than you are at being observant.

Jax and I had a pair of desks that sat back-to-back, forming our own isolated cell in the greater wilderness of the Bullpen. I took my seat and slid the phone across the desk. On the way in we'd collected our messages from the wall-mounted mailboxes, and now I fanned them out on the desktop before me. Several were garbage, others simple return calls. Two had the same name at the bottom. *Gellica*. I pushed the bulk of the slips to the side, including the ones from her. They were the messages I had no intention of returning, or at least not until I could clear my head.

Then I started dialing.

There's something fundamentally satisfying about the mechanical click-click of the phone dial turning as you find the exact person you need to talk to. It's like you've entered in a secret code, and all the answers of the world are about to be revealed. A moment later my call went through, and the brusquely clipped voice of the supervising admin in the medical examiner's office announced herself and demanded to know what I wanted.

"Hey, Susan," I said, forcing a note of cheerfulness into my voice. "Is Doc Mumphrey in?" While she checked, I spread out one of the newspapers Jax had picked up earlier. She was back a moment later, to tell me he was.

"Great," I said. "Can you let him know he's got a Mollenkampi Jane Doe coming in? From an alley off Ringsridge Road."

While I waited on the answer Gellica's eyes still stared from the front page of the paper, her face half obscured by Ambassador Paulus's shoulder, daring me to return her phone call. I flipped to the sports page instead. My favorite carelbarra team had lost again. I crumpled the paper and chucked it in the trash.

Jax sat down across from me and laid out the three-ring binder that would eventually hold all our case information. The administration called these red-and-white folders Case Management Collections. Cops called them murder books.

"Okay," I told Susan. "Ask him to put a rush on that one and send me a note when he's done." I thanked her before hanging up.

Jax stared. "You always have someone else talk to doctors for you?"

"Doc Mumphrey doesn't do phones." I slid out of my jacket and draped it across the chair back. "Let's get through this paperwork so we can do something worthwhile."

Jax snapped the murder book shut, sending the paperwork on my desk fluttering away. Including the pink message slips that I'd neglected to discard. He stooped to collect the papers, and froze as he recognized the name on a slip.

"Are you kidding me?" He flipped through the messages. "You're talking with Gellica?"

There was anger in his voice, and it wasn't unjustified. Gellica's connection to Ambassador Paulus was undeniable, and the danger swirling around her wasn't easy to forget.

"It's not what you think," I said.

He raised one of the slips to eye level. "*I have your coat,*" he read. "*Call me or I burn it.*"

"Clearly I haven't been calling her back," I said. The last time I'd seen her, she'd been sneaking away from my apartment, and I'd given her my coat to keep warm. It had been an unexpected meeting, and one that hadn't played out like I'd have guessed. I sure as Hells wasn't comfortable discussing it with Jax.

I snatched the messages from him, intending to throw them away. But that would've given Ajax too much satisfaction. I made a show of shoving them into my shirt pocket instead.

"After everything that went down with her boss?" He shook his head. "I'm not saying I don't get the appeal. She's got a magic smile. But she's dangerous."

He didn't know the half of it. Gellica and I had more in common than I liked to admit. And it wasn't just her smile that was magic. She was nothing safe, nothing natural. And nothing short of extraordinary.

"I appreciate the concern," I said. "But don't worry. Everything's under control." I dropped my voice. "Besides, you and I still owe her a favor."

His jaws snapped shut, expression souring. "Did you forget what her boss did to Talena?"

I froze, and we both knew he'd crossed a line.

Talena Michaels was one of the few people in the world I truly cared about, and Ambassador Paulus set her up to take the fall on a murder charge. Another person used and discarded by the rich and powerful simply to make a bad PR situation go away. Titanshade's political machine was greased with the blood of innocents.

"I didn't forget," I said. "Never will." Gellica might report to Paulus, but she'd also helped clear Talena. "I don't need you to remind me."

Hands raised, Jax backed up and let out a gentle whistle. "I need more coffee."

As he walked away I grabbed the phone and dialed the Bunker's main switchboard. I asked to be connected to DO Guyer. As a divination officer, Guyer was one of the few people on the force who dealt with manna on a regular basis. I needed to know if the tingle and weird strength of the intoxicated woman was real, and she wouldn't spare my feelings. It rang through, but with no answer. I hung up with a frown. There was one other person who'd take what I'd encountered that day seriously.

I tugged one of the pink message slips from my pocket and flattened its crumpled edges. Gellica had her share of secrets, and experiences with manna that were far deeper and stranger than mine. I shoved the slip under my report pages as Jax returned with his coffee. He didn't take a seat like I expected. Instead he gathered up his suit coat and sighed.

"I suppose you want me to check NICI for similar mutilations?"

"Naturally," I said. "We both know she likes you better."

The National Index of Criminal Investigations was something I tried to avoid whenever possible. Sitting at a flickering terminal in the data lab, squinting at light green letters on a dark green background? It'd just be a matter of time before I put the whole thing out a window.

"I'll start the physical paperwork," I said as Jax headed to the fourth floor.

"That's fine," he called over his shoulder. "But you better have it done by the time I get back."

I waved him off, as if the very idea was insulting.

Homicide had a limited number of typewriters, so I wandered around until I found a spare. It was perched on a wobbly-legged metal cart whose wheels squealed a protest as I rolled it to my desk. Sitting down and feeding a form five pages thick—one original, two copies, and a black carbon sheet between each—I began to type up the field notes.

The one advantage of a month of desk duty was that I'd had time to relearn how to type with eight fingers. Still, it wasn't long before the boredom of pecking out the keys got to me. I found myself looking around, hoping for something less mind-numbing to engage with. The newspaper I'd discarded stuck out of the top of the trash can. It had landed with its crumpled front displaying the photo of Ambassador Paulus and the woman behind her.

Ajax was right in saying there was no separating Gellica

and Paulus. Each city-state in the Assembly of Free States had an ambassador from the central collective appointed to represent the interests of the other member city-states, an unelected albatross hanging around the neck of the local governing bodies. Largely despised, they were frequently deposed in the changing winds of political favor. Paulus, however, was a political institution as unwavering as the Mount itself. She was the perfect blend of calculating and callous, with the cash, political capital, and sorcerous talent to crush most opponents. Paulus was bureaucratic power incarnate, and Gellica was her right arm.

I turned my attention back to my paperwork, then nudged it aside to reveal the pink message slip one more time. I stared at the name and number. It took the memory of a tingle across my hand and the feel of walking through cobwebs before I finally folded the message slip in half and stuck it in my coat pocket.

By the time Jax returned with a stack of printed pages bearing the NICI seal, I was more than halfway through the paperwork. He seemed less than impressed.

"Couldn't find any similar mutilations." He dropped the stack of printouts on our shared desk space, displacing miscellaneous notes and scraps of paper as it landed. "I figured we could sort these missing persons together, but I guess I'll do it myself. Unless you need me to finish off the reports for you, too?"

"No, but if you wanted to get me a coffee, that'd be great."

Jax ignored me, taking a seat and beginning to separate the tractor-feed edging from the sides of the missing persons reports. I took the hint and focused on my typing.

We worked in silence for another hour or so before I couldn't take any more of the spirit-crushing boredom of paperwork. I rattled the cart to get Jax's attention. He ignored me at first, and it took another two attempts before he finally looked up, irritation clear in his eyes.

"I've been thinking about our Jane Doe," I said.

"Uh-huh."

"What do artists want?"

"So now she's an artist instead of a candy?"

"She might be a candy," I said. "There's no doubt she was an artist." I pulled out the last of the carbon forms from the typewriter. "She could be both. Anyway, what keeps an artist going? What do they want?"

Jax rolled his shoulders. "Money," he said. "Food. Shelter. Paintbrushes. Probably not in that order."

"And to get all that, she'd need what?"

"A day job."

"She just moved to town," I said. "Assume we're dealing with a dreamer here."

Jax drew a handkerchief from his coat and turned toward one of the leeward windows, cleaning his tusks as he looked across the city skyline to the hints of the ice plains beyond.

"She'd need an agent," he said. "A manager. Maybe a gallery owner?"

"We need an in with the art scene," I said. "How do we do that?"

Jax spread his hands. "How would I know?"

"You went to college," I said. "I figured you'd be into dressing in black and wearing berets."

"Okay." Jax tucked away his handkerchief. "First, I don't think artists actually wear berets. Secondly, I studied poli-sci and theology. I wasn't exactly hanging out in the art world."

"Your lack of culture never ceases to disappoint," I said.

"This from a guy who thinks belching out beer jingles is high art."

I slouched against the curved back of my chair, idly scanning the Bullpen while I let my mind wander. I thought about the strangely strong woman and her son, and how their small family was being torn apart by her battle against addiction. I thought about the morning's homicides, and Dungan's strange request. And I wondered why a dead gangster got four times the attention as a young woman killed in an alley.

I must have been staring, because Jax waved a hand in front of my eyes. "You okay?"

I pushed the completed paperwork to the side of the desk.

"I'm hungry," I said. "You want a snack?"

We headed to the hallway, where a pair of vending machines squatted on either side of a drinking fountain whose Out of Order sign was so old that the letters had faded almost to illegibility. I dropped in a quarter-tael coin and got a Black Gold bar. Jax opted for a tube of Lemonales, soft chewable candy that he could drop directly into his eating mouth.

"So do we have a plan for tomorrow," he said, "or are we still not talking about your pal Dungan?"

"Not sure he's my pal anymore," I said. "I'd never pull shit like that."

"You mean like breaking rules because he thinks he's serving a greater justice? Probably accompanied by an exaggerated sense of his own importance? You and he are *nothing* alike."

"I'd never let a case go untouched," I said.

"No," he grew serious. "You wouldn't do that. But you'd threaten it, if you thought it'd motivate somebody."

I nodded, talking through a mouthful of candy bar. "Maybe I oughta motivate you into a different line of questioning?"

Jax chuckled. "You've bent your share of rules since I've known you. And I haven't known you long."

I glared at him, and the soft flesh around his eyes wrinkled as he held in laughter. "I've got a list put together," he said. "If you ever want a nice, long read."

"I get it," I said. He started to respond but I cut him off. "No, I do. Dungan gets shit done and bad guys go away. I get the appeal. But you gotta balance it out with . . ." I bit into my candy bar. "With something."

The elevator at the far end of the hall slid open with a ding, and the familiar voice of our supervisor cut through the background buzz of the Bullpen.

"Carter! Ajax! My office."

Captain Bryyh stormed past us without breaking stride, and we were swept up in her wake. The captain had put in her years, making her eligible to take a pension and forget about the violence and deceit that defined the city. But here she was. For someone like her, there was always one more thing undone, one more gear in the machine that needed mending. For most of my career, I'd been one of those broken gears. Since I'd been tagged as the man who brought back manna, I wasn't sure if she viewed me as irretrievably broken or finally fixed.

We followed Bryyh as she pushed into her office. She wore her hair in long braids, and the beaded ends of each gray-streaked plait gathered into a ponytail that rattled as she turned to face us. She must have updated the blackboard recently, as chalk ghosted the fabric of her dark blue suit and the rich brown of her hands. Permanent frown lines etched the skin between her brows.

"What happened in that alley this morning?" she said by way of greeting.

I glanced at Jax. My partner looked as confused as I was.

Bryyh waited in silence, until I opened my mouth to speak. She immediately interrupted me. It was going to be *that* kind of conversation.

"Was there part of 'low profile' you didn't understand?" she said.

"There were two bodies," Jax said, words as precise as if he were on the witness stand. "Unknown if they're related. A Gillmyn named St. Beisht and a Mollenkampi Jane Doe. OCU took the Gillmyn, we've got the Jane Doe. Low profile. We're on it."

The poor kid thought he was saying the right thing. As Bryyh turned to him, the color drained from his face, making the brown tortoise shell coloration on his head plates and neck stand out more than usual.

"No, Detective Ajax, you are not 'on it.' You are the farthest thing from 'on it.' You're so far from it that I don't even know how to describe the distance between you and anything at all. This," she lifted the folder in one hand and rubbed her temple with the other, as if fending off an approaching migraine, "is an OCU requisition request for your Gillmyn. And this," she swapped the folder for another piece of paper, "is a request for comment from the *Union Record*. Asking if our hero detectives have any leads on the brutal gang murder. Low profile, gentlemen. You remember those words?"

Apparently we hadn't managed to escape the scene unnoticed after all.

"We were next door," I said. "We couldn't just ignore it."

"You mean you don't have the patience or self-control to call and get an okay from me before walking across the street."

"Since when do we need to get permission before responding to a page from Dispatch?"

Her eyes widened. "Since when do you respond to all your pages?"

I jammed my hands in my pockets and tilted my head. "If we called in, we'd have had this exact argument before you eventually told us to go look at it, only to get the scene pulled by OCU anyway. I thought you wouldn't want to be bothered with it."

"Oh, I know exactly what you were thinking."

"How would you even begin to—"

"Because I've known you since you drank out of a sippy cup!"

Bryyh held my gaze. For the first time, I noticed how tired she was. She'd looked like that at my mother's funeral, when she'd handed my old man the tightly folded twin flags of Titanshade and the AFS. I dropped my eyes first.

I stared at the floor, listening to her exhale through clenched teeth and step away from me, followed by the creak of her chair. By the time I raised my head she'd taken a seat and Jax stood cross-armed and unhappy. He didn't like this either, but at least he had the sense to hold his peace.

Bryyh flipped through a few pages on her desk. "You found a manna vial on the scene?"

I ran my tongue over my teeth and fought another spike of irritation. Our report was still sitting on my desk. She'd checked in with the tech crew. Curious about a random body, or checking on how we'd behaved in the field?

"We found a vial," I said. "Someone might have sold it as manna. We don't know yet."

"You'll have to file a CS report," said Bryyh. "Anything

that even looks like manna's being added to the controlled substance list. In the meantime, I can't stress enough that you need to stay out of the limelight." Another rattle of her braids. "You two . . . I can't keep the heat off you if you call attention down on yourselves."

I shifted my feet, and noticed Jax doing the same. The mayor and the AFS had spun the discovery of manna as stemming from a raid guided by city hall. It was a story that played loose with the facts, and that was why Bryyh insisted we stay out of the papers and off the news. Our mere existence was a liability to people of power and influence, and that meant that Bryyh had to fight tooth and nail to keep us from being thrown under the bus. I appreciated that. But I'd also reached that point in my life where I'd been a cop longer than I hadn't been, and six weeks cooped up in a hospital or behind a desk was a long time to be away from the only thing I knew how to do well.

"I don't know, Cap." I rotated my shoulder with a series of audible pops. "Trying to be invisible makes it kind of hard to do our jobs."

"Welcome to reality. Avoiding controversy is part of your job, now," she said, "same as getting dragged in front of a doctor on a weekly basis."

We didn't respond, and Bryyh narrowed her eyes.

"You *do* remember that you have your medical today?"

Jax nodded; I shrugged. The weekly exams were the smallest of headaches compared to a full month of paperwork.

"As for this Jane Doe . . ." Bryyh leaned forward, elbows braced wide on her tidy desktop. "If it's an OCU problem, don't let them dump it on us. If it's ours, don't let them take it." She stared past us, to the blackboard that perched at the head of the Bullpen, its layers of ghost letters holding the names of suspects and victims that had been erased and rewritten countless times. "I don't want OCU taking a civilian case and letting it fall through the cracks because it's not mob related. No family deserves that." She glanced at her watch. "I've got a meeting," she said. "You are not to take on any cases without my say-so. Understood?"

Neither Jax nor I said a word. Neither of us was happy

with Dungan's game, but neither of us was going to rat him out for it, either.

"I'll take that as a yes." Bryyh turned away and pulled open her filing cabinet. "When I say I've got a meeting, that means you leave."

We slunk back to our desks. Jax finished off the last of his Lemonales as I flipped the murder book open and closed.

"Well," I said. "Bryyh says not to let go of Jane."

"Great," he said, a wavering bass undertone making his sarcasm clear. "Maybe we can use that to justify this situation with Dungan if we ever get called out for it."

He stayed on his feet, clearly not eager to dive back into the stack of NICI's missing person reports. That suited me just fine.

It was time for our medical, anyway.

FLUORESCENT LIGHTS FLICKERED AND HUMMED in the fourth floor meeting room that was converted once a week for our medical check-ins. We were the first of the subjects to arrive, an unusual occurrence. I usually strode in late, with Jax ushering me ahead. Arriving early let us watch the room being set up.

Material and machines streamed in, carried or wheeled by a mix of nurses and soldiers dressed like nurses. The latter were a not-so-subtle reminder that the military was still in full control of the manna strike, as well as everything—and everyone—who'd come in contact with it.

An unexpected bonus of our early arrival was that the watered-down elevator music we were usually subjected to was also absent. Instead, the attendants had the radio tuned to WYOT, painting the room with a healthy dose of reverb-slathered guitars and thunderous drum riffs.

As the last chords faded the DJ broke in, his baritone crunching like a semitrailer crossing tightly packed snow. He told us we were halfway through a Super Rock Block before adding, *"And remember, babies . . . keep your eyes to the skies. There's more happening on the ice plains than they want you to know. Stay tuned and stay true, and Handsome Hanford will play it straight with you."* Hanford might spin the best tracks, but he also bought into the most ludicrous of conspiracy theories. Lately, his patter had devolved into paranoid melodrama involving espionage, mind control, and otherworldly Families visiting from beyond the stars, all covered up by mysterious and unnamed governmental agencies.

By contrast, I was sitting in the grip of a very real government agency and bored out of my head. After my stint in the hospital, I—along with everyone else who'd been at the manna strike before the military took control—had been enrolled in a preemptive monitoring program. The medical team came out every Trice to listen to our heartbeats, draw our blood, and make us piss in cups, all while assuring us it was in the name of the greater good.

The radio had switched to a public service announcement. A rendition of the AFS anthem swelled as Colonel Marbury, the head of the military encampment, assured us it wouldn't be long before the drilling freeze was lifted and we'd all share in the bounty of the strike. It was a PR campaign designed to distract the city from how much longer than expected it was taking for the strike to deliver commercially viable manna. The AFS was betting everything on the patience of the public, and those were long odds to play.

Before the strike, manna had only been found in the bellies of whales. It had fueled the first industrial revolution, but our ancestors had no more restraint than we did. Within a few generations whales were extinct and manna was a rare commodity. Until now. The discovery of an underground reservoir brought its own questions, primarily whether it was safe to use and how much was available to exploit. Not necessarily in that order.

The room setup was complete, but Hanford was back, responding to Marbury's appeal for patience. *". . . disrupted migrations, weird animal behavior at the strike site. What else aren't they telling us?"* A soldier-nurse silenced the radio, and a moment later the dull tones of elevator-quality smooth jazz filled the room as we waited for our fellow lab rats to arrive.

One by one, the dozen or so patrol cops who'd been first to respond to our distress signal at the manna strike filed in. Regular cops who'd become inadvertent test subjects. If we lived, and seemed mostly sane and healthy, the exploitation could proceed apace. But if anything seemed off about us—

anything at all—the people who controlled the nation's purse strings had every reason to want us hidden away.

One of the patrol sat next to Jax. A broad-chested Mollenkampi who greeted us with a nod and a gruff "Fellas."

"Hey, Andrews," said Jax. "You were going to see Busque in the hospital. How is she?"

A knot formed in my gut. Karma Busque was another of the lab rats, a patrol who'd begun to have especially vivid nightmares. She made the mistake of telling the docs, and now she was hospitalized, undergoing further observation "for her own safety."

"Yeah, they finally gave me permission to visit." Andrews emphasized his words with a low, disturbing hum. "They had her on so many pills she barely recognized me."

Busque's treatment was also a warning to the rest of us: Don't have bad dreams, don't have weird experiences. Anything or anyone that might cause issues with the adaption of the new manna would be paved over on the road to progress. And that included imaginary cobwebs and unnaturally strong junkies.

I shifted my legs, doing my best not to look at the array of medical equipment laid out on metal trays. Of us all, I had been the earliest and most intense test subject. It was very important that I not share any concerns or uncertainty while under examination.

Andrews had already moved on to another topic. "Hells, my brother-in-law moved in with us. Used to work a remote rig and never bothered to keep an apartment because his off-shift time was so low. These layoffs and drilling freezes . . ." He coughed a low, resonant note. "If we don't get control of the oil fields back, the whole town's gonna be out of work."

Another of the patrol, a human named Clarice, chimed in as she found her seat on the far side of Andrews. "Yeah, but when we do, though? It'll be sweet living after that."

That was a mixed bag of truth. The riggers might want to get back to work, but the companies were focused on deep-depth surveys, hoping they were sitting on the next manna reserve. After all, the oil wells had already been on the verge of running dry. Maybe manna really was the future of the industry.

The last test subject came through the door. A detective whose blond hair was pulled back into a ponytail that scraped the collar of her blue dress shirt, she said her hellos to the rest of the lab rats. Seeing her, my day got a little worse. Her name was Hemingway, and she'd been on my team once. She and her partner Myris had gone with Jax and me on the final raid on the Rediron drill site six weeks earlier. Of the four of us, Hemingway, Jax, and I had been wounded, lucky to get out alive. Detective Myris hadn't been lucky. She'd been torn apart by a mob of drug-addled roughnecks. Now, Hemingway was faced with two empty chairs, one by me and one across the room. She opted for the far seat, pointedly avoiding my eyes.

Ajax followed my gaze and hummed a note of consolation. Voice low, he said, "She doesn't blame you," which wasn't quite a lie. Hemingway understood the risks that came with carrying a badge. That didn't mean she didn't have emotions.

I considered going over to talk to her, but that was when our personal mad scientist emerged from behind the white cloth partition.

She was a Gillmyn, like the dismembered gangster found in the wash on Ringsridge Road, although unlike him she had a webbed fin bisecting her skull. The doctor was tall and lean, her skin a rich range of greens, while her primary distinctions from males of the species were longer fingers, narrower features, and bright yellow irises. There was no hint of breasts or curve to the hip. Gillmyn had no need for such mammalian traits. The handwritten name tag on her coat told me she was a sudden addition, and the flaring of the layered gills along her neck told me she was uncomfortable speaking to large groups.

"Good afternoon, officers," she said, her voice a breathy huff. "My name is Dr. Baelen, and I'll be working with you for the next several weeks."

She gave no explanation of what had happened to the doctor who'd overseen our exams for the last month. Just a simple assertion that she was in charge, and an expectation that we would accept it without question. The good doctor was accustomed to being obeyed.

Baelen paused, and a sound from the entry door caused

me to turn. DO Guyer had slipped into the back of the room. I hadn't laid eyes on the divination officer in weeks, since she'd been loaned out to Vice. Her normally meticulous hair was pulled into a tight bun and the circles that rimmed her eyes were as dark as the fabric draped over her shoulders. She didn't wear her sorcerer's cloak unless she was doing some kind of magical work, so I figured she'd come straight from a crime scene. She made her way to the remaining empty seat, beside me, as Baelen adjusted placement of the roll-out cart. I took advantage of the moment to lean over to the DO.

"Glad to see you," I said, and meant it. Guyer could be a smartass, but at least she could carry on a conversation.

She rubbed blood-shot eyes and grunted a reply.

Well, sometimes she could carry a conversation. I tried again, scratching my chin and trying to cover my interest. "If we get a break, you got time to take a look at a case-book with me?"

She responded with a weary shrug, but before I could press her further the medical master of ceremonies held up a webbed hand, demanding our attention.

"Most of the tests you've participated in have been relatively passive," said Baelen. "I'd like to change that. Please view this as an opportunity to contribute to the overall efficacy of this study."

The rest of us stared at her blankly. Baelen didn't bother to hide her eye-roll. Our new doctor didn't have much of a bedside manner.

I wondered what her Family specialties were; no one could be an expert in the physiology of all eight sentient species, and the differences between humans and Mollenkampi are trivial compared to the bison-sized Barekusu or tunnel-dwelling Haabe-Ieath. Most doctors tended to focus on the Families most common in their geographic location, leaving specialists to deal with the occasional outlier.

Whatever her expertise, Baelen now held our futures in the palm of her webbed hand. She scanned the room, settling on Guyer. "Officer?"

"Looks like I'm up." The divination officer moved to the center of the room. "Okay, you all know the routine here. I understand we've got something a little different today."

The TPD observers we'd had for the last month had been untalkative, mostly sulking at being expected to baby-sit a bunch of cops who'd happened to be in the right place at the wrong time. Guyer seemed to have been recruited into a more active role.

To her right, Baelen secured the wheels of a cloth-covered cart in the center of the room. I gripped the edge of my seat. One thing I've learned over the years: whether it's in the morgue or a courtroom, nothing good ever comes on a cloth-covered cart.

Baelen said, "Part of what we'll be doing is conducting a study of animal activity near the manna strike."

The same nonsense we'd heard on the radio from Handsome Hanford. That wasn't too much of a surprise; conspiracy theorists and government officials often have about the same grasp of reality.

Baelen pulled back the cloth to reveal a crime scene writ small. The bodies of two animals lay on the table. One was an ice hare, large rear feet pulled tight to its chest, caught in the moment of death as it sank its back claws into the creature that had killed it—a leamu. The latter's distinctive bulging eyes had glossed over, but even in death it was a formidable creature. Its long serpentine body half my height coiled across the table, its final prey in the leamu's single pair of muscular limbs.

Considering the presence of a divination officer, I could only wonder at what the Hells we were about to witness.

Baelen held her clipboard like a child clutching a favorite toy, hiding its face to her chest and checking it frequently.

"Ordinarily a divination officer connects with the echo of a recently departed. But here—"

"I'd only get some snarls and chattering," Guyer said, managing to pull a chuckle out of her audience.

"Yes, indeed," Baelen said. "So we will attempt something in a different direction."

She gestured to one of her assistants, and a soldier-nurse came over carrying a metal work light and extension cord. Clamping the lamp to the side of the table, he ran the cord to a wall outlet. A moment later the overhead lights cut out. When Baelen flicked on the lamp, the shadows of the animals projected on the near wall, black silhouettes etched on stark white paint. The dense body of the hare was a round blob, while the leamu's white and gray blend of scales and fur was reduced to a single, serpentine curl.

"If you'll all gather around. Closer, closer." As we complied, Baelen stepped back, until she stood outside the circle of light. "Please proceed, Officer."

From a hidden pocket in her cloak, Guyer drew a glass vial no larger than my thumb. Like the shards we'd found near Jane, the liquid it contained had an ephemeral sheen, the telltale shimmer of manna. The raw fuel of magic, manna was wonder and darkness conjoined, like a glistening film of oil concealing waters of unknown depth.

Andrews let out a trill of dismay. I shared his sentiment. This is what divination officers did, of course: use magic to communicate with the recently departed. But manna was so precious it was only rolled out for the most pressing of cases. To use it on a dead animal seemed almost sacrilegious. What could they possibly hope to learn? But both the doctor and sorcerer ignored the patrol officer's objection.

Removing the cap of the vial, Guyer pressed the tiny spray button, spritzing the animal bodies with the valuable liquid and allowing some overspray to mist the air on the side opposite the lamp. Then she did the same to her hands, applying the faintest possible coat to her flesh. The precious liquid glistened, and she muttered words of power, focusing her energy and binding the manna-touched objects. As she spoke, the runes on her cloak danced with sparks, lit with the power as she crafted the manna bond.

Guyer positioned herself behind the lamp, hands between it and the animal carcasses. For several long moments, we all stood in silence. On the other side of the pool of light I caught Hemingway staring at me. She looked away the second I made eye contact.

Taking a deep breath, Guyer said, "This isn't easy."

"Indeed." Baelen stretched the final syllable. "That's why you're here and not someone of lesser talents."

The corners of Guyer's lips curled upward. Either she liked the flattery or enjoyed the challenge. Maybe both.

Slowly, Guyer raised her hands, their shadows falling against the animal hides. Then higher, creeping upward, until her shadow hands touched the far wall, supplanting and blending with the carcass shadows. The shadows still edged upward, but were now no longer recognizable as hands. As they passed the shadows of the animal corpses, the absence of light seemed to trail in their wake, strands of darkness that quivered and tore, fighting to be free before collapsing, re-forming into the dark outlines of a hare and leamu. I thought of the shadow puppets I'd thrown on the wall of Talena's bedroom when she was still afraid of the dark. But these shapes were something more than crude imitations. They were perfectly realized beyond the skills of any performer, their forms carrying weight and their edges as distinct as crisply chiseled lines in stone.

Guyer stood behind the lamp, hands unmoving in its beam while their unnatural shadows took tentative steps, leamu on the right, the hare on the left, moving like the souls of the still and silent animals on the table. On the wall, the animals re-created their last living moments in two dimensions. The hare hopped forward while the leamu shifted up and down, grasping limbs pulled tight to its core as it studied the hare, its long body coiled below the snow, ready to propel it forward. No one in the room spoke. Even our breathing was hushed. It was eerie, watching the dark shapes, reading their movement and layering each beat with a life of its own.

When the predator sprang it was almost too fast to comprehend. I've heard stories of starving leamu attacking riggers or long-haul truckers who wandered onto the ice plains, but I'd never witnessed one in action. Even in stark, featureless black and white, it was astonishing. Its long body snapped true with a whip-crack speed, and it hurtled into the hare faster than my eye could follow.

But instead of the expected result, the ice hare flipped onto its back, rolling with the leamu's attack and diverting its course upward. The leamu overshot its intended victim, using its powerful limbs to turn and refocus rather than gripping its prey. It pushed itself off and landed on its target. Still on its back, the hare kicked and kicked with its powerful back legs, one paw hooking in the leamu's tiny eye horns, pulling the attacker's head back and exposing its throat and underbelly. The ice hare's claws raked along the leamu's vulnerable underside until it ripped open, kept kicking even as shadow viscera rained down the wall.

But the leamu had managed to grab the hare's neck, compressing and twisting. The predator's greater bulk gave added pressure, even as its grip slackened. Even in death, it managed to take one more life out of the world.

Beyond our circle, Baelen had crept back into the light. She ignored every moment of the struggle, her eyes fixed firmly on us. She wasn't testing the new manna, she was testing our reaction to the scenario. As if she wanted to see if we had a connection to either the leamu or the rabbit. I set my face, determined to give her nothing to work with.

Their story told, the shadows on the wall stilled. Guyer exhaled loudly, then allowed her hands to drop, merging the animated shadows into the natural darkness of the carcasses. One more deep breath and once again she cast only a normal shadow, two hands with ten shadow fingers. I kept my eight fingers of flesh and bones firmly in my pockets.

The lights came on and our examiner stared at her clipboard and muttered to herself. The sound of her pen as she made notes grew in volume, the swoop of each checkmark more prominent. I got the distinct impression we weren't up to Dr. Baelen's standards.

"That was adequate," she announced. "Take a short break and we'll regroup."

The collected lab rats began filing out. I stayed a moment longer, staring at the bodies on the table. The ice hare's eyes were closed, almost restful. As if it had found a victory in making its last moments ones of resistance. The leamu's eyes were wide and glassy, and held an expression that I couldn't help but identify as shock at the sudden reversal of the natural order.

There was movement to my left. Jax stood by, waiting, the cloth that had covered the animals in one hand. I took it and gently draped it back over them.

"Let's go find Guyer," I said. We needed to talk with our sorcerer-in-residence.

b

MOST OF THE OTHER LAB rats hung close to the vending machines, calling out friendly insults to Jax, and regular insults to myself. The two of us passed them by, strolling down the hall and peering in side rooms until we found DO Guyer. She was sitting in a small meeting room, fingers drumming the linoleum tabletop as she stared into space. She'd pulled the dark fabric of her cloak around her shoulders, wrapping herself in its near solid black, while iridescent symbols danced along the contours of her arms and shoulders, strange runes that disappeared when I focused directly on them. I wondered if those symbols would stick to my fingers if I touched them, and pull painfully taut when I tried to escape, a fly in a sorcerer's web?

I figured I'd be better off saying something charming, to break the ice. "You putting in some serious hours? You look terrible."

She gave me a befuddled smile. "Seriously?"

Jax slipped into one of the open seats and propped his chin on his hands. "I think he means that you look like someone who's so far gone past exhaustion that you've come back round the other side."

Her smile grew more steady, and I decided to push my luck.

"You know," I said, "we've got this Jane Doe case that could really use some of your expertise."

"Ask me later." Her eyes tracked the fall of my shoulders and she conceded slightly. "Look, I'll review the murder book, but you know I can't do any kind of divination without authorization."

I decided to drop the matter and ask about something where I knew we'd find common ground. Workload.

"You want to tell me what you're dealing with that's got you so worn down?"

Guyer hesitated, as if not certain she wanted to talk about it, but ultimately plunged ahead. "Black market manna. Snake oil, specifically."

That matched up with Bryyh's command that we fill out a controlled substance report for Jane's case. "Is that why Vice pulled you over to an ARC team?"

Another organizational change spurred by the manna strike, the Arcane Regulation and Containment teams had been cobbled together and assigned to help deal with the ongoing influx of sorcerers into Titanshade. All three of Homicide's divination officers had been temporarily transferred to Vice, helping deal with irate sorcerers.

"It is," she agreed. "But somewhere there's a factory or angel's roost where they're diluting manna. If that goes wrong, or if the wrong people get wind of it . . ." She spread her hands, indicating how things would go for the innocent people living in the surrounding buildings.

Jax flexed a mandible far enough to scratch his cheek. "Why are they taking the risk? Demand for black market manna is so high that whoever's got the material could sell it for tens of thousands of taels. Maybe hundreds of thousands."

Guyer managed a weary chuckle. "They could. Or they could cut it, dilute it . . . and sell it for millions."

"And that's snake oil," I said.

She pointed her index finger and forced a cheesy, game show host smile. "We've got a winner!" Her shoulders slumped after the exertion. "That's snake oil. It's usually cut into angel tears, which will make people see anything from visions of the Path to waking nightmares about the dead coming back to life. Worse, they think they're using magic, which means that they start thinking they can fly, or some other BS. You wouldn't believe what people think manna will let them do."

"They don't understand its rules," said Jax.

"Magic doesn't have rules," she said. "It has probabilities.

When you're using a lot of it, the more likely it is to have a predictable outcome. Back in the industrial revolution, when people were pouring gallons of manna into trucks, it was workaday stuff. But when the whales died out—"

"Hunted," said Jax. "They were hunted out of existence."

"Right," said Guyer, evidently not thinking the distinction was worth a response. "After that, people had to get by with much less manna. That requires more skill, and carries more risk."

"That it'll fail?" I asked.

"That it will veer off in an unexpected direction." Guyer glanced toward the examination room, where some soldier who'd drawn the short straw was carting away the hare and leamu.

I thought back to Sherri, the woman we'd tussled with earlier, her strange strength, the smell of roses and honey. I tried to keep Guyer talking, hoping to work my way around to the topics I needed to discuss. "The military's got the strike area secured like a national treasure. Any manna on the street's gotta be tied back to them."

She laughed in my face.

"I wish it were that easy! Hells, when they found you at the strike scene, you were practically floating in a puddle of the stuff. Think of all the medics and cops who were on that site before it was contained. Even if the military isn't swiping a drop—which I doubt—there's more than enough manna floating around to start pumping out snake oil."

It made sense. I'd heard the EMS crews and roughnecks who'd been on-site were being tested and monitored like we were, though on different days and in different facilities. Most of the rig workers exposed to the maddening gas hadn't fully recovered. At least not mentally.

Guyer swirled her mug, and stared into the resultant coffee vortex. "We've gotten pretty good cooperation from Colonel Marbury and her staff, all things considered. But if that changes, things could get bad real fast."

I thought on that for a moment, as Guyer pulled her cloak even tighter. "Manna means big money, and big money makes people act crazy. Like blowing manna on talking to dead animals."

"So does snake oil have any real magic?" I asked.

"No." She rubbed her eyes, blinking rapidly like someone forcing herself to wake up. "It's a minuscule amount of manna in a psychotropic drug. Users get high, they see things, they think they're sorcerers, they keep doing it until they overdose."

"There's no chance they'll actually make something happen? Or make themselves change?"

"Change?"

"Get strong," I said. "Just for instance."

Guyer rubbed her eyes. "Carter, do us both a favor and ask me what you want to know. Enough with the *for instances*, okay?"

"There was this woman," I said. "When we were door knocking. She was strong. Really strong. Right?" I pointed to Jax, hoping for backup, but he showed a sudden interest in a torn thumbnail. "She broke out of my hold like it was nothing."

"How'd you subdue her?" said Guyer.

Jax coughed. "I took her to the floor."

"So was she strong?" she said.

"Well . . ." He ran a hand along one mandible, looking embarrassed. "She did break Carter's hold, but she was obviously on something, and—" His gaze shifted to me. "It was your left-hand grip."

He didn't need to say that my mangled hand was weaker than it'd once been.

Guyer nodded. "Crazy beats strong every time."

It was a platitude taught in the academy, a warning to recruits to not tangle with addled minds. And it only made me more frustrated. I wanted to talk about the tingling, about the cobwebs, but Baelen was in the next room, and now Guyer was working for the doctor. She wouldn't sell me out, but she also might let something slip.

"I believe that she was strong, Carter. I do. But what you're describing is a brush with a junkie having an adrenaline rush, nothing magical."

"Even if she's on snake oil?"

"Even then," she said. "Manna's like thread. It doesn't do anything on its own, it's what binds objects together to make a whole, which can do the impossible. As long as that fabric is bound by a trained seamstress."

"Like you."

Guyer gave me a weary grin, then opened up the cloak to reach into the back pocket of her khakis, revealing the well-worn spot where her belt holster had thinned the fabric of her pants. Odd that she wasn't wearing a gun. She pulled out a business card, dropped it on the table and tapped it with an expensively manicured nail badly in need of a touch-up. After her name was the title, *AMd*.

"Those three letters cost me twelve years of training and enough student debt to last a lifetime." She straightened her finger, pushing the card in my direction. "So yeah, it takes someone like me to use manna professionally."

"Okay," I said, "that's *professionally*. What happens if someone untrained and hallucinating got ahold of manna?"

"Come on, Carter," she said. "There's a million variables to factor in before—"

"Humor me."

"Fine! If someone is hallucinating . . ." She exhaled loudly as she considered the question. "It's possible to tether two items without training, if there's enough manna or the motivation is strong enough. Back when you could get manna by the bucketful, it's what powered the first industrial revolution."

"But what if it's not items? What if it's something like shadows or an emotion or—"

"I'm getting there!" She frowned, and muttered, "Shortcuts!" before continuing. "It's *possible* to tether abstract concepts, but that's . . . look, even skilled, highly educated sorcerers struggle with that."

"It's what you do every day," I said. "What all the divination officers do."

"And you think that's easy?" She pointed toward the room where shadows had danced to her will. "It takes serious sideways thinking to make those bonds."

"Sideways thinking," I said. "Like the kind caused by hallucinogens? Maybe angel tears?"

Guyer blinked. She thought on it, gumming her lips.

"Maybe it'd veer off," I quoted her own words back to her, "in an unexpected direction?"

She leaned to the side, as though intrigued with the idea. When she did, her rune-marked cloak drooped over the back of her chair. I stared at it, wondering about the electric sensation that had danced over my hand and arm in the alley. If it wasn't in my head, could it be magic that I'd somehow sensed?

Shifting in my seat to cover my action, I edged my left hand forward. Bracing for a tingle, even a shock, I grazed the cloak and its manna-laced runes. But I felt nothing beyond the velvety softness of fine fabric.

"There's still a lot we don't know about manna." Guyer shoved her wallet back into her pocket, pulling the magical fabric out of my reach. "It's been rare and precious for so long that no one's been willing to experiment with it. And the new supply? Hells, half the world is terrified of it, and the other half wants to use it in everything from factories to toaster ovens."

Shuffling feet in the hallway told us that the rats were being called back to the lab.

Guyer ran a hand over her face, pulling her flesh tight, adding a white highlight along the curve of her lip. "I don't know how the new manna functions, because no one does. This new doctor of yours," she dropped her hand into her lap and glanced in Baelen's direction, "she's doing some pretty brave stuff, even if it is a waste of money."

I responded with a noncommittal grunt. The way Baelen had watched us was unsettling. Like an alien in one of Hanford's UFO stories, toying with Eyjan-bound beings for amusement or to satisfy some inscrutable design. Baelen might be interested in something, but it wasn't our health. And that made me wonder what she was really looking for.

The rest of the examination was the standard fluid samples and psych evaluations. After we were done, Jax and I drove the Hasam back to the Bunker's central garage. As we got out of the car a sudden banging came from the loading bay, where a trio of techs were wrestling a washing machine out of a crime scene van, each bump and clang accompanied by a string of obscenities. Cetus St. Beisht's metal shroud was headed for the evidence locker.

I rubbed my eyes. I needed to know whether I was imagining the tingling sensation and the surprising strength of the woman we'd encountered, and Guyer hadn't been able to help. When it came to people with the expertise and discretion I needed to talk about this with, I had a limited set of options and it was dwindling quickly.

"It's the end of the day," I said. "I'm beat. What do you say we regroup in the morning? Grab breakfast before we start."

"Sure," he said. "Usual place?"

"Yeah, fine." I held a breath. If anyone in the Bunker had earned my trust, it was Jax. I turned to my partner. "That woman on Ringsridge. You're sure you didn't feel her getting, I don't know," I waved my hands uselessly, "really strong?"

One of Ajax's mandibles quivered, and a sound came from deep in his speaking mouth, like a marble clattering through a box of nails. "She was high and worried about her kid. Of course she was strong."

"No, I mean like—"

"And then she pushed her way out of your left-hand grip. In the heat of the moment, I'm sure she seemed strong. I'm sure she *was* strong. But nothing beyond what you'd expect from someone with enough drugs in their system."

I eyed him, not sure how to answer that.

Jax gave me a sympathetic whistle and a pat on the shoulder. "See you tomorrow," he said, and walked toward the exit.

I turned away and rubbed my palms against my temples. When I raised my arms, I felt the crinkle of pink message slips against my chest. It was clear that I had one more call to make before I could head home.

7

SITUATED FASHIONABLY CLOSE TO THE Mount, Gellica's office in 1 Government Plaza was designed to make visitors feel small. It was spacious, for one thing, a conscious conceit in a city packed into such a tight footprint. It held a small couch, coffee table and chairs, and an ornate desk so large that it half-obscured the human woman who sat behind it, flipping through files and taking notes on a yellow legal pad.

When I entered, Gellica mumbled, "Help yourself to a drink," without looking away from her work. The room was hushed, and once her assistant departed the only sound was the scritch of fountain pen on paper.

I waved off the drink and claimed a seat on the couch. It was a significant step up from the threadbare sofa in my apartment. I idly traced the white-on-blue flower patterns, wondering how attached she was to the thing. Even if it didn't fit in my place, I figured it had to be worth at least half a month's rent at a pawn shop.

I cleared my throat to remind Gellica I was in the room. From her desk she said, "I'm not ignoring you."

"Yes, you are." I kept tracing the flowers. "Nice couch, by the way." It occurred to me that sooner or later the AFS would swap it out for a new one, and maybe I could talk Gellica into tipping me off when they did. A man with bills to pay should never be too proud to dumpster-dive.

"I'm not ignoring you," she said more firmly. "I'm simply finishing what I was working on so that I can give you my full attention."

"You're upset that I took so long to get back to you," I countered. "And now you're making a point."

"I am neither that petty, nor you so interesting, for that to be true."

I looked up from the stitched flowers. Her eyes were fixed on me, paperwork forgotten. Like the couch, her suit was expensive but not ostentatious. Quality fabric and professional tailoring made for sleek style in a light blue that complemented her chestnut brown complexion.

"Huh." I patted the pocket full of message slips. "All these calls must have been wrong numbers, then."

"I'll be with you shortly." She exhaled loudly. "And of course it's a nice couch. The whole point of an office like this is to impress visitors."

"Works on me," I said, and leaned into the cushions, which had a pleasant give. Gellica kept writing, pausing only to tuck an errant strand of hair behind her ear. While I waited for her to decide I'd been sufficiently chastised, I glanced around the office. She hadn't been lying—the entire room was decked out with signs of power and conspicuous wealth. Apart from Gellica's desk clutter, the place could have been lifted from the pages of a catalog. Tasteful knickknacks sat on expensive furniture, seashells carved into abstract sculptures, hand-blown glass vases that were half as sturdy and a hundred times pricier than similar items with a department store tag. All selected by a designer to convey importance.

Eventually she gathered the papers, rolling them tightly before sliding them into a plastic tube the size of my forearm. Sealing it with a twist, she stood and stepped to one of the many elaborate filigrees that decorated the walls. A gentle tug pulled the detail away, revealing a cutaway entry point into a hollow plastic pipe. She slipped the carrier into the void and pressed down on the surface, closing the seal. It went off with a *whoosh-thunk*, followed by a menacing hiss as air refilled the tube.

When she resumed her seat Gellica's attention was fully focused on me. "I'm glad you called."

I steeled myself for the conversation ahead. The problem with coming to Gellica wasn't that I disliked her, it was that I liked her too much. It was too easy to think of her as a friend, and forget the danger she posed. The only reminder I needed hung on her office walls. While most of the decorative art consisted of photos or paintings of historic treaty signings, there was a single, notable exception: a single portrait of a steel-eyed human woman with a dimpled chin and tightly cropped dark hair—the voice of the Assembly of Free States in Titanshade, Ambassador Paulus. She was one of the most dangerous people in Titanshade . . . and she was Gellica's boss, mother, and master.

Gellica pulled a small glass jar out of her top desk drawer. She opened it and dipped her finger inside, bringing out a pea-sized ball of ointment that she massaged into her hands. The room immediately took on the smell of sandalwood mixed with an earthy hint of proilers.

"Long day?" I said.

She tipped her head and rubbed the base of her hands together. "They're all long. But it's worth it. I love my job. Or," she amended, "at least I love the impact the job has." The cream gave a slight sheen to her skin, a gloss not unlike the polished wooden legs of her desk, each one carefully carved to appear as if they hid monstrous claws.

"The impact, huh?" I stood and took a stroll around the room, examining the small sculptures and mementos before gazing out the office window onto the flashing neon lights of the city at night. "Impact on what? Employment? Quality of life? The price of lobbyist kickbacks?"

"There's more to politics and administration than corruption and graft." She'd switched to her fingers, running her index finger and thumb of the opposite hand over each digit, squeezing and rotating as she went. "A little like there's more to policing than bribes and abuse of power."

"You should give a speech at the Bunker," I said. "They'd love you down there."

A harsh, humorless laugh. "I think Ambassador Paulus has more friends in service reds than you think."

"I don't know about friends," I said, "But I can believe she's got a lot of sons-of-bitches in her pocket."

"Hmm." She sounded both amused and put off by the thought.

"So why'd you want to see me?" I rapped the window with a fingernail, pretending to enjoy the view. The smell of sandalwood was thick in the air. "Why the flurry of phone calls?"

"Officially?" Her chair squeaked as she stood, a rare bit of equipment in the AFS machine that needed to be oiled. "Ambassador Paulus wants to extend an invitation to you. For the Responders' Remembrance ceremony."

"Last I heard it's a public event. I don't need an invitation." Part of the lead-up to Titan's Day, the annual Remembrance ceremony honored the police, firefighters, and EMTs who had died in the line of duty. A memorial to self-sacrifice.

"You do to be on the stage."

"And do what?"

On the window, Gellica's reflection stretched across dark outlines of apartment buildings. The wood and brass table lamp threw her silhouette against the wall behind her, a hulking shape that held its own secrets. It was a disquieting reminder of the transformative creature I'd seen once before, shifting and flowing between shadow and three-dimensional shape. But it was that strange, magical nature that made me risk coming to talk to her.

"Nothing much," she said. "Be visible during the ceremony. Remind people who you are."

I coughed out a laugh. "I'm okay with people forgetting."

"Stop catching criminals, and they will." She paused. "I'm not going to try and sell it to you, but I think it'd be a good thing to go to Remembrance."

I put my back to the city skyline. "Why?"

"Not for Paulus's reasons," she said. "She's maneuvering for the 24th Ward's special election, trying to keep the wheels from coming off the City Council."

I was vaguely aware of the special election, triggered by the recent death of an alderman. The winner would join the City Council at a crucial moment in the debate over armed AFS forces occupying the manna strike. According to the talking heads and pundits, the future of the city was at stake. I thought of political buttons on a backpack and slogans painted on alley walls. I thought of Jane's lifeless body and a gangster accountant, both abandoned on Ringsridge Road. Smack in the middle of the 24th Ward.

"They've got a formidable political machine down in the 24th," she said.

"The CaCuri twins." I thought of their images on Dungan's file tabs, and painted larger than life in Jane's mural.

"That's right." Gellica massaged her knuckles, cracking each one in turn. She was almost a literal political brawler. "But it's the rich guy, Louis Mah, who's leading the polls. We simply prefer a sane candidate take the alderman's seat." She grinned. "I feel *very* good about our chances."

"Who's Paulus's candidate?"

She stretched her legs and feigned indifference. "The AFS supports any duly elected official."

"But . . ."

"But Meredith Plunkett is certainly preferable to the other choices on the ballot."

I frowned. "Never heard of her."

"She's brilliant, with a long-range vision for the city. She'll make a great alderman."

"And she'll take orders, I'm sure." I raised a hand, cutting short Gellica's protest. "I'm not standing on a stage and leading cheers for anyone. Tell Paulus she can ask all she wants—it ain't gonna happen."

Gellica cupped her chin in one hand. "Okay. I told her you wouldn't do it."

I nodded, pleased with the small victory, but couldn't help from asking, "You said I shouldn't do it for Paulus's reasons. What other reason is there?"

She looked me in the eye. "Because you care about the names on that monument."

I frowned. She knew what to say, at least. Too bad it wasn't going to work.

"Not happening."

"Fine," she said. "I did my job. If you change your mind, let me know. Now . . . why are you really here?"

"Hey, you're the one who called me."

She stood, squaring her shoulders. "For weeks you're a pain in the ass to reach, and all of a sudden here you are. What do you want?"

I rubbed my jaw, and winced as the stumps of my fingers ground against chin stubble. Unnaturally cauterized stumps, painful reminders of events I tried daily to forget. Suddenly I wanted that drink.

"I needed someone—" I shifted my weight, a motion that rustled the message slips in my pocket. "I have questions about manna."

Three elegant strides brought her to within an arm's length, and when she spoke her voice was lowered to a hush.

"It's about time."

"I don't want to talk about the strike," I said.

"I do."

Her shadow loomed on the wall, intimidating, almost pulsing with the mysteries it concealed. My hand throbbed, and I pushed back memories of a desperate scramble, a fight with an oversized Mollenkampi and the snap of his jaws closing, the spiral of pain that danced up my arm, and the strange pull and tear as the last fabric of my fingers gave way. Memories of spray as a drill struck not oil, but manna—the most precious liquid in the world—spraying it in the air and letting it rain down, landing on me and soaking my clothes, drenching my skin, seeping into my makeshift bandages and that strangely soothing pain as it penetrated the wounded stumps of my fingers. Gellica's voice pulled me out of the reverie.

"We're both touched by magic." She reached for my shoulder. "It saved you. It's part of me."

"It didn't save me," I said. "I had a bandage and clotting compound on already." I hid my mangled hand in a pocket, but I didn't draw away from her touch. "And you're more than—" I cut myself off, remembering her secret visit to my apartment, the eerie magic as her shadow distorted and extended, turning into a living thing of darkness and power. A transformation far beyond even what I'd seen at the hands of DO Guyer that afternoon.

"You're more than Paulus's guinea pig."

Her hand fell away.

"I see." She walked back to the desk, pretending to review papers she'd already processed and sent on their way.

I should have simply left. But Gellica was the one person I could actually talk to about what I'd experienced without either being shunted off to the shrinks or treated like a specimen at a science fair. I followed her from the window.

"I didn't mean it like that."

"The technical term is takwin." She stayed a step ahead of me, striding from the desk to the couch. "If you can't remember that, maybe you could go with homunculus. Not accurate, but it's in the ballpark." She turned, blinking, eyes bright and voice artificially cheerful. "Or clone," she said. "Clone works, too."

Whatever Gellica's relationship to magic, it was an essential element of her existence. She'd been a clandestine creation, a fusion of human life and manna itself. Raised by Paulus as something between a daughter and a useful experiment, Gellica spent her life slipping between shadow and light, hoping that in the final tally she'd do more good than harm. It was a calling I understood all too well.

"I'm sorry," I said. "I shouldn't have called you a guinea pig."

"And?" She eyed me expectantly.

"And from now on I will only call you a . . ." The term escaped me, so I barreled ahead. "Magically-infused-clone-woman."

Gellica squinted at me, then snorted out a half-laugh, threw up her hands, and flopped onto the couch. "This isn't exactly how I thought this conversation was going to go." She gave me a fleeting grin.

Jax had been right about one thing: her smile really was magic.

"Unexpected is sort of the norm for us." I perched on the far end of the couch, facing her.

"To be honest, I didn't think you'd show up, even after you called," she said.

I shrugged. "You said you'd burn my coat."

Her smile reappeared.

"You can keep it," I said. "It was starting to shrink around the middle, anyway."

She eyed the hint of roundness that circled my midsection. "That happening with all your clothes?"

I rewarded her with an exaggerated frown, which only made her smile widen. In a city of millions, where corruption and murder were commonplace, there were a handful of people I could trust to be honest, to listen without judgment. But even them, the Jaxes and Bryyhs of the world, none of them had the twisted connection to manna that Gellica and I shared.

"Let's try again," she said, leaning forward. "What did you want to talk about?"

I took a deep breath, and the scent of sandalwood filled my lungs. Then I started talking.

I talked about Jane, left dead in an alley. I talked about the dead Harlq in the washer, about the tingle in my palm and the feeling of cobwebs wrapped around Ronald's mom. At some point she pressed a glass into my hand, and the sharp bite of alcohol on my tongue encouraged me to say more than I'd intended. But we had so many secrets binding us together, and it seemed like a little more couldn't hurt anything. I should've known better. "A little more" is what broke the tibron's shell.

When I was finally done, Gellica looked at me from the corner of her eye.

"The tingling you felt," she said. "That doesn't sound like manna."

We were still sitting on the couch, but now holding drinks.

"I know." I'd been coated by manna when I was caught in the strike, and it produced something more like a pinch than a tingle. "But then what was it? And why did the woman have threads or cobwebs around her?"

Gellica sipped her drink, her silence telling me what I feared was true: it was all in my head. I pressed the cold glass of my tumbler against my temple. But then she surprised me.

"I don't know what you experienced," she said. "But if you feel it again, I'd like you to tell me."

"You believe me?"

"It's not about belief," she said. "It's about possibility."

"I don't know what that means. You think it's *possible* that I'm making it up?"

"It means there's no evidence either way," she said. "But you've had more experience with the new manna source than anyone else. And the list of unknowns is extensive." She began to tick them off on her fingers. "Manna from the ground? We don't know what it is. That much manna in one place? We don't know how it will act. Is this the greatest find in history or the beginning of a toxic disaster? Still don't know!" She waved her hand toward the ceiling, demonstrating the mounting stack of uncertainties. "And me? I need it as much as anyone. I need manna to exist, and right now there's only one place—" She cut herself off, staring into her almost-empty glass. There was no need for her to name the source of manna she depended on. Ambassador Paulus, her eyes so like Gellica's, watched over us from the portrait on the wall.

"The girl in the alley," she said, changing the subject. "Does she have a name?"

"Everyone has a name," I said. "I just don't know hers yet."

"So what do you call her until you do?"

"Jane."

The corners of Gellica's lips curled. "Why?" She leaned closer. "Is that what you call all the dead girls?"

"Some," I said. "Jane Doe."

Her burgeoning smile fell away. "Ah," she said. "I suppose that makes sense."

I took another swig, letting the liquor bite my tongue. "I think she may have been into politics. At the ground level, anyway. She was an artist, drew some political stuff." I shook my head. "Seems like the push-back against the military camp is everywhere."

Gellica nodded. "People are scared and impatient, and they're lashing out at the AFS. That's why the special election matters so much." She was more at ease with politics than when she'd skirted the issues of her own manna-dependence. "The slow production from the strike and ongoing technical problems, there's already talk among other members of the AFS about nationalization."

I almost dropped my glass. "That's insane," I said. "Titanshade's supplied oil to the world for decades." It was true. There was no place on Eyjan more capable of extracting liquid from below ground. "If there's serious national-ization talk, there'd be riots in the streets."

"And if Titanshade becomes hostile to the rest of the AFS it's only going to make things worse. Which is why the alderman's seat can't go to someone who'll tip the balance in the wrong direction." She turned her glass from side to side, and I noticed the smudge of lipstick on the rim. Had she freshened her makeup before I arrived? "The special election is in two weeks, and it's an opportunity to help everyone. A rising tide lifts all boats."

I threw my head back and laughed.

"I've never heard a more Fracinican saying in my life." I leaned closer and stage whispered, "There're no boats in Titanshade." Fracinica was a coastal city, with balmy tem-peratures and the kind of corruption that only great power could bring to bloom.

"Fine," she said. "My time spent in the capital is show-ing. But that doesn't change the importance of the election. The winner will be the key swing vote on City Council. That's why Paulus and I—"

I cut her off with a groan. "You're bringing her back into this?"

"I'm only pointing out that she thinks the same as you about a lot of things. She's trying to make a difference for the city. What do you think I was working on when you came in?" A finger jab in the direction of her desk. "Mili-tary logistics, ambassadors to and from the other city-states, presentations to the AFS Council. Paulus is working on a scope far beyond the city limits."

"I don't doubt that she's got her thumb in a lot of pies." The portrait of Paulus stared down from the wall, her face so similar to the woman on the far side of the couch. Gell-ica was younger and wore her hair longer than her em-ployer, but now that I knew to look for it, there was no way to ignore the similarities between them. And as much as I was drawn to Gellica, that connection scared me. "Your boss would kill as many Jane Does as she needed, if it helped achieve her goals."

Gellica frowned, and the dimple in her chin deepened. I regretted running my mouth yet again.

"I don't remember you turning down my help," she said. "And when it all came to a head, you were on our side."

"No," I said. "Paulus's interests happened to align with the law. She'd have happily crushed my neck under her heel when she had the chance." Gellica's eyes flashed, but before she could speak, I leaned closer. "But she didn't, because you pulled me out of that room. You saved me and you saved someone I care about. I didn't forget that," I said. "When things went bad, you were on my side. Your boss never was."

"I don't know." She sighed, and, for a moment, the strain of her job was evident on her face. "Sometimes I wonder what we could accomplish if people would take all their scheming and dreaming and focus that energy into the here and now." She shifted in place, getting energized about the topic. Her hair tumbled as she tilted her head back, killing the last of her drink. "If they'd get their heads out of the mists and deal with real problems . . ."

I shrugged. "If politicians want to spend their days fighting each other, let them. Maybe it'll keep them from making life any worse for the rest of us."

"So optimistic!" She drummed a finger against her empty glass.

"I'm a glass half full kind of guy. Speaking of which . . ." I rattled the ice in my glass meaningfully.

Gellica either ignored me or missed the hint. "So what do you do next, to find who killed your Jane?"

"Talk to people in the art scene," I said. "Jane was an artist. Someone might know her."

Gellica's eyes widened and she leaned back, the fabric of her suit pulling tight to her leg. She placed a hand on her chest with an exaggerated gesture. "You may not be aware of this, Detective, but I'm something of a patron of the arts."

"You are?"

"Well, the ambassador is." She dropped her hand. "But everyone knows I tell her where to send the checks. Guess which one of us gets invited to more events?"

"What did you have in mind?"

"There's a happening at a gallery in Adams Square tomorrow night," she said. "I know the owner."

"Okay," I said. "What's happening?"

"A *happening*," she said, "is an event. One that pushes artistic and societal boundaries."

I didn't intentionally make a face, but judging from her laughter, I must have.

"There'll be free food," she said.

"Okay," I said, and even to my ear I sounded more chipper. "Give me the address."

"It's invite only," she said. "You'll need me if you want to go."

"Together?"

"Yes."

"Like a date?"

Her jaw dropped, and I couldn't quite tell if there was a smile behind it. She stood and took the empty glass out of my good hand.

"You'll need to be polite and behave yourself," she said. "So no, absolutely nothing like a date."

"Polite and well-behaved is my standard procedure for dates." I stood as well, a movement that brought us uncomfortably close.

Gellica presented me with an exaggerated frown. "Then your dates are pathetic."

Ushering me across the room and out of the office, she paused to say, "See you tomorrow night," before closing the door in my face.

Which was good, because I'd have hated for her to see me grin quite so broadly.

That night I grabbed an ice hare from the grocery along with a six pack of beer and box of noodles. When I walked through the door of my apartment I was greeted by a tan-and-white feline blur, as Rumple pounced on my leg, clawing at the fabric of my pants mercilessly before perching on the arm of my faded couch and commencing a long series of mews. Each was punctuated by flicks of his tail, as if to catch me up on his exciting day of watching the city through a window. With a final scritch behind his ear, I put an album on the record player, dropping the needle into the perfect groove, providing a soundtrack for my dinner and covering up the sound of my neighbors fighting.

As I made dinner the last glow of Gellica's alcohol faded to nothing. All the while I ran the events of the day back through my head. I thought of cleverer things I could have said to Gellica and I thought of the dismembered gangster in the washing machine. But most of all I thought about Jane Doe, lying alone in an alley. There was no end to the list of people who might take advantage of a newcomer, someone who hadn't yet learned to distrust even the kindest-seeming of offers.

I pulled out the chopping board and cut the vegetables first, scraping them into the saucepan along with a pat of butter, not too much heat, only enough to soften them and bring out the flavor. Beyond my apartment walls, the rumble of traffic continued, and the neighbors fought on.

Silently, I promised myself that I'd learn Jane Doe's name and the dark secrets that ruined her life, that brought her to that moment, in an alley where her head was caved in and her face mutilated.

With a turn of the wrist I sent the butter rolling along the bottom of the pan, keeping the temperature low enough that it wouldn't burn. I set aside the chef's knife and drew the longer, thin-bladed fillet knife from the wooden block by the sink. The board cleared, I laid out the hare and unwrapped the twine from the white fur that lined its rear feet. The rest of it had been skinned and the entrails removed, along with the head. But the rear feet were always left intact for the cook to remove. Titanshade was a city still ruled by old superstitions.

I trimmed the body, guiding the blade along the bone, slicing through tendons and stripping away flesh until I ran into a joint. I should have used the blade, separated the bones with a twist of my wrist. Instead I froze, wincing, teeth grinding as I imagined fingers being ripped asunder, and fought the image of a terrified creature, alone in a cage facing a predator. I gripped the handle of the knife tighter, meaning to press forward but encountering a wall of resistance, like an impenetrable shield. Finally I threw the whole thing in the pan, where it landed with a sizzle.

I cooked the hare, but couldn't bring myself to mix the

browned meat into the vegetables. After trying twice, I dumped it into the bowl on the ground, and Rumple padded over to enjoy a home-cooked meal. The neighbors' fight climaxed then silenced, and I ate my partial meal as the turntable arm caught on the inner track, pushing back and starting again, never quite able to reset itself.

THE NEXT MORNING I GOT to the diner early and picked a booth away from the rest of the customers, against a window that overlooked the stream of pedestrians on their way to work. I sat alone, doing physical therapy exercises with my left hand, gripping a half-tael coin at different angles, pressing it between thumb and remaining fingers and tapping it against my coffee cup. Jane's sketchbook lay open on the table. Its pages were thick, made for carrying watercolors or pastels, and each one held a cityscape or fantastically vibrant illustration. A portrait of a woman with jet-black hair and enticing smile was followed by a study of roughnecks lounging on a street corner, nursing hangovers and waiting for their ride back to an oil rig. I'd gotten halfway through both the book and my coffee when Jax arrived. The vinyl bench seat groaned in protest as he slid across from me and dropped the *Daily Saber* morning edition on the steel-banded linoleum tabletop.

Jax gave the menu a cursory glance as the waitress strolled over. Gretta's Home Cooking was a favorite spot of mine, with a waitress who addressed everyone as "Hon" and served generous portions, each crispy bite saturated in flavor and fat. It was a damn good breakfast, and there was almost nothing boring or healthy on the menu.

"Oatmeal," said Jax. "Thin. With cinnamon and a side of plantti fruit."

I shook my head in disapproval, then told the waitress how I took my hash and eggs. Before she left I added a to-go order of coffee and a half-dozen donuts.

Jax cocked his head. "You planning on having a snack in the middle of this meet and greet?"

"Nah," I said. "For after that. You'll see."

Jax loosened his tie and tucked a napkin into his shirt collar below his speaking mouth. "You have a good night?"

I had a brief moment of doubt, wondering whether he knew I'd been to see Gellica.

"Listened to the new Gravity Sister LP," I said. "Not their best work. Next topic."

He stared at me for a three-count, fingers crinkling the napkin's edge, and I thought he might push it. But in the end he only sighed.

"Fine. Let's talk about your pal Dungan, instead." Jax pushed the newspaper across the table. "He was right about the Gillmyn in the washing room."

The headline read: MONEY LAUNDERER FOUND IN THE WASH.

"This St. Beisht character was in pretty deep," said Jax.

I skipped the article and flipped through the rest of the paper. On page eight I found a one-sentence mention of an unidentified Mollenkampi woman found dead in an alleyway. It was in the Police Blotter, along with a summary of robberies and minor vandalism, tucked beneath an ad for a Titan's Day Blowout Sale on televisions and dishwashers.

My coin tapped a staccato rhythm against the warm ceramic of the coffee mug.

"Whoever chopped up the Harlq money man might have also killed our Jane Doe," said Jax.

"Like maybe she stumbled onto whoever stashed St. Beisht and got taken out rather than leave a potential witness?" I'd had the thought already. "Probably not. Jane's killing seemed panicked. The St. Beisht scene was a pro hit."

"But if they *are* linked . . ."

If they were, then Dungan might take Jane's case even if we helped him with his CI. I didn't answer, clinking the coin against my mug as I searched for anything else to think about. A television nestled high on a wall showed a morning news program, artificially perky anchors smiling their way through news summaries and sightings of local celebrities. The logo in the corner was bedecked with cartoon flowers and rays of sunshine, proclaiming, "It's a New Day, Titanshade!"

Which of course was bullshit. There was nothing new in the city. People still died and the only victims who got attention were the wealthy or tragically beautiful, and no amount of miracle liquid found in the ice plains was going to change that. The television cut to a man with perfect hair and no wrinkles announcing a shakeup in the 24th Ward special election. The one Gellica's boss was so focused on. The one Gellica implied was under control.

Over the anchor's shoulder appeared a photo of a badly burned man, identified as Louis Mah, one of the front runners for the vacant alderman's seat. The beating thrum of my pulse in my eardrums practically overran the announcer as he told how Mah had planned a public display of sorcery using ice field manna. He'd attempted to create an anima, a tricky conceit only the most accomplished of sorcerers even tried: an expression of the sorcerer's will in elemental form. It was the kind of arrogance that came with having too many yes-men. An incessant drumbeat underscored the newsman's false concern as they ran a brief clip of Mah's presentation going wrong, his charred face screaming. Mah had played with fire and it literally blew up in his face. The announcer said that at this point, the election seemed a lock for AFS loyalist Meredith Plunkett. Just like Gellica had anticipated.

The drumbeat grew louder.

If an AFS loyalist took the special election, would that push the feds toward nationalizing the manna field? And what would Paulus be willing to do to make that happen? When I'd confronted her a month ago, she'd pinned me to the floor with a creature of living air. Her face was casually indifferent as a giant invisible thing held me down, threads of living air twisting over my chest, past my arms, pressing against my lips as my heart pounded like a—

"Carter!"

I jerked my attention from the TV to find Jax staring at me. I stopped tapping the coin against my coffee cup and the drumbeat ceased abruptly.

My partner leaned forward. "You feeling okay?"

"Fine." I could feel other patrons peering at us. I searched for something to focus on as I regained control of my thoughts. The table's spice and sauce holder had a holiday insert, *Day's Dawning* in bold letters along with a list of dishes with joke names. I stared at it for a pair of deep breaths as I grounded myself. Then I set the coin on Jane's sketchbook, the interlocking loops of the AFS seal facing up.

"When we talked to that woman on Ringsridge yesterday," I said, "you really didn't see anything . . . off?"

"I saw several things that seemed off," he said. "I saw an addict trying to raise a kid, and that kid trying to manage his parent. And I saw my partner get lucky that for once there wasn't a photographer around when he got his rear end planted in a wall."

"So, you didn't feel anything in her vicinity, that was a—"

"We've been over this." He leaned forward, cutting me off before I could talk about the tingling. "She was on something. I believe that. But if she was moving extra fast or strong, I didn't notice."

"Yeah. Okay."

"If I did, I'd tell you."

"I know you would," I said. "You never miss an opportunity to tell me something."

He snorted, and dropped a vinegar packet into his coffee. A little splash of acid to bring out the extra bitterness.

"Anyway," I moved on to the next subject, "I've got a chance to talk to some artists. Gallery owners, that kind of thing. Might learn something about Jane."

"Good." Jax's brow crinkled. "How'd you turn it up?"

I spread my hands, false modesty that served only to buy a little time as I thought of some way to not tell him I was going with Gellica. I was saved when our plates arrived, along with top-offs on our coffee. I'd developed an aversion to anything with cinnamon in it after the Haberdine case, having had more than my share of unpleasantness with sweet-scented, madness-inducing Squib blood. So I was grateful the steam rising from my hash and eggs kept me from having to smell Jax's meal. It did not, however, protect me from the sight of him eating it.

Jax had ordered his oatmeal thin, which meant it was cooked on the runny side, an easier density for him to eat. He stared at a spot above my head, lifting his biting jaws high as he brought the spoonful of oatmeal to the opening in the middle of his neck, used for both speaking and eating.

Desperate to turn my attention elsewhere, my eyes fell on the booth across the aisle. It was occupied by two human men with the appearance of a couple well into the tail end of their relationship. One was horse-toothed and dressed like he enjoyed spending money, the other was clearly a gym rat, his shirt a size too small to better showcase the product of countless hours spent lifting heavy objects and setting them back down. They were arguing, the more muscular one gesturing at the television, where talking heads debated how the upcoming special election could affect the city's standing in the AFS, and our ability to utilize what they insisted on calling "next gen manna." As if a new catchphrase would do anything other than confuse things. A source of power was still a source of power, no matter what you called it.

I risked a glanced at my partner. He was between bites, so I faced him and returned to our conversation.

"So the Harlqs." I struggled with the pronunciation, but got an encouraging nod from Jax. "If they go after the killer, how do they know who to target? It could be any one of a dozen other organizations. Maybe even one of their own."

"Not one of their own." Jax waved his spoon in the air. "They're too disciplined. Any decisions of significance by the Harlqs are made by committee from another town, maybe even another city-state." He swallowed with a tinkle of the sharp, inward-curving teeth that lined his speaking mouth. "That's why I don't think it was this Harlq boss that Dungan mentioned—Anders. If it were an internal Harlq thing, the body wouldn't have been found. St. Beisht would've been killed in front of an audience and the body never recovered."

"An audience?"

"Of his peers." Jax lifted another spoonful of oatmeal, but didn't swallow. "They'd have stood and watched. Or been forced to join in." The spoon hovered in his grip, steaming, as if he'd forgotten about it. "As a lesson."

The waitress appeared at the end of the booth. "How is it, Hon? Good?"

I mumbled a thanks and Jax slid the oatmeal into his mouth.

As the waitress departed I leaned across the table. "Okay," I said. "What's your deal with these guys? Long as I've known you, you've clenched up as soon as anyone mentions the Harlqs."

"Doesn't matter." He took a sip of coffee as a bunch of teens who should have been in school sauntered past our window.

"Look." I dropped my voice. "Everyone's got their deep darks. I get that. I'm not asking for all the details, only what I need to know."

Ajax furrowed his brows and studied the streaks of oatmeal in his bowl as thoroughly as a divination officer studying the entrails of a murder victim. The couple across the aisle raised their voices. Whatever their conversation was about, it was starting to grow heated. I ignored them, focusing on my partner.

"Your life's your business," I said. "But if we're about to wade into something and you're gonna go sideways on me, I gotta know."

The couple's voices grew louder, snippets of insults, something about "keeping what's ours." Jax pulled the napkin from his collar and tossed it on the table.

"It's nothing you gotta worry about."

My pager buzzed, and I fished it out of my pocket. The morning news had moved on to the next story. Technical troubles at the manna strike meant that production was far below projections. More pressure on the city. If the new well didn't produce, then the shutdown of the other sites would have been for nothing. The number displayed on the pager was a Bunker extension. Dungan calling with our details. I signaled the waitress for the check.

As we waited, Jax shifted the conversation. "What about the CaCuris? I don't know much about them besides the name."

"They're Titanshaders," I said, "and operate by knowing their neighborhoods in and out."

"Know the city," he quoted my advice back to me, and I almost smiled.

"Yeah," I said. "Same concept, different goal. They run drugs, candies, gambling . . . Pretty much any racket you can name. But they keep their residents happy."

"How?"

"Stupid little things." I glanced at the trash-littered streets past the window. "Say someone wants a pothole fixed. They can complain for months, years even, to the city, and nothing happens. But go to the CaCuris . . ."

"Pothole gets fixed?"

"Gets fixed the *next day*. Doesn't cost the resident anything. Until," I said, "election time. Because when you go to the polls you—and your family—had better vote for politicians that the CaCuris are backing."

"Ballots are secret," said Jax.

"Yeah, well, bodies aren't supposed to show up in washing machines. But they do."

The waitress brought our check and I took it, waving off Jax's attempt to pitch in. I handed her a pair of eight-tael bills and told her to keep the change. Jax eyed me.

"Feeling generous?"

I was feeling depressed, and didn't see the need to spread that state around to the people who came into contact with me. At least, not the ones who didn't deserve it.

As she walked away the news show returned from commercial, announcing, "Now here's Brent with the weather!"

The phrase *"Lazy as a weatherman in Titanshade"* is an old cliché. In a town where the warmth of any given area is based more on its distance from the mountain at the crown of the city, and a swing of a few degrees is considered surprising, our meteorologists mostly say "same as yesterday," and cash a check. Everyone hates weathermen because we're all a little jealous of them.

I drained the last dregs of my coffee and we stood to go as Brent the weatherman began to deliver the forecast. By the time I'd set my mug down, two fur-suited figures carrying buckets burst in on Brent from off-screen. They doused the weatherman with what appeared to be a watered down syrup and multicolored confetti. A classic Imp's Run prank, part of the lead-up to Titan's Day. Brent sputtered and wiped sticky, glittering confetti from his eyes, doing his best to be a good sport while on camera.

Laughing, the anchors announced, "Look like the imps have struck early this year!"

The couple across from us burst into laughter. Whatever their dispute, someone else's misery brought them together. Maybe a war between the gangs would bring them both down. Or maybe it would unite them against a common foe.

On the television, the announcers concluded the program with a coordinated wave.

"Good Day's Dawning, Titanshade!"

I returned Dungan's page from a pay phone in the Borderlands and he gave me directions to a garishly ritzy neighborhood, where wealthy landowners could show off their income by living separate from the rest of us.

We arrived to find Dungan's Hasam parked on the side of the street, and we piled into his larger vehicle to talk. I claimed the front passenger seat, hefting Dungan's accordion files of crime families over my shoulder and into Ajax's lap in the rear.

"You two have a nice breakfast?" said Dungan. He puckered his lips as he chewed on what I assumed was another hard candy.

"Nice and healthy," I said. "What's your game plan?"

"My guy's up there." He indicated one of the mansions, a stupidly large house for a single family, let alone an individual. Real estate this close to the Mount was the ultimate in conspicuous consumption.

"Who's your CI, the mayor?" I loosened my tie. In this part of town the geo-vents released enough heat that we'd left our scarves and overcoats in our vehicle, and Jax had already slipped out of his suit coat.

Dungan shook his head. "It's No-Dick Donnie."

I let out a whistle of surprise.

Jax paused his admiration of Dungan's file organization. "I'm pretty sure I misheard that."

Dungan grinned. "You didn't."

"You really think you can flip him?" I asked Dungan. "The guy's entire business is founded on him being discreet."

Dungan's eyes lit up. "Which is why this's gotta stay below the radar. Nice and low-profile, like I promised." He held my gaze, an unspoken ask whether we could be trusted. A bit of arrogance, considering how he'd threatened to tank Jane's case if we didn't come along.

"Trust me," I said. "We don't put cases at risk."

His child's grin spread wider. "Knew I could count on you."

"That's great," Jax chimed in. "Now are you going to explain his name, or just leave me sitting back here to wonder about it?"

I craned my neck to face my partner. "Happened years ago, before you came to town. Donnie was a small-time crook who helped some city workers out of a flaming car wreck. When the redbacks arrived, they thought he was robbing the unconscious survivors. They worked him over pretty good."

"What, they didn't—" He made a slicing gesture toward his crotch.

"No," I said. "But they beat him bad enough to put him in the hospital. Then that went sideways, too."

Jax set the accordion file aside. "How bad sideways?"

"Complications from a catheter bad," said Dungan.

I shuddered. "He got a healthy court settlement from the city for the beating, and from the hospital for the emergency amputation."

"Still . . ." Jax indicated the tony neighborhood, with spacious plots and private parking spots. "Enough to live up here?"

"Enough to set up shop as a kind of dirt-ball venture capitalist," said Dungan. "He made his real money bankrolling organizations, laundering money, all the white-collar crap that funds the real thugs."

"And the City Attorney doesn't want the headache of

prosecuting him and making it seem like the city's settlement got used as seed money for a criminal enterprise."

"It don't matter how he got the name," he pointed at each of us in turn, "just don't use it around him. I've been working for months to get on his good side, so don't blow it by saying something stupid."

"Fine," I said. "So what are we supposed to call him?"

Dungan exhaled deeply, as if working up some inner courage. "He likes Donnie Starshine."

I was halfway through a laugh before I realized Dungan wasn't joking.

"He thinks that's an improvement?" Jax asked.

"He says it's because he parties till the sun comes up." Dungan spit through his open window. "Look, he wants to meet you. Just stand there and look famous, and you'll be fine. Long as you call him anything but No-Dick Donnie."

"That might be easier," I said, "if you'd stop saying it every time you mentioned him."

Dungan shrugged and opened his door. "Duly noted. Let's go."

The sound of the party was audible from the mansion's drive. There were echoes of laughter, music, and—incredibly—the occasional splash. Jax and I exchanged a look. *Did this guy have a pool?*

I rang the doorbell and waited. The front doors opened to reveal a man who stood a handspan taller than me, wearing a frown and a thin white tank top that put his muscular arms and their crisscrossed pattern of scars on prominent display. He might as well have had "bodyguard" tattooed across his forehead. But that would have been silly. Instead, the tattoo that arched over his forehead like a jail-yard rainbow read "*Ass-Kicker.*"

"Morning, Biggs," said Dungan. "These two are with me. Donnie's expecting us."

The man ignored Dungan, focusing instead on me and Jax, and his angry frown shifted into something more like amusement. But whatever his thoughts, he nodded and stepped aside. We walked ahead of him through the halls of the mansion, turning right or left according to surprisingly high-pitched orders from the big man behind us. In every passage and room the walls were lined with photos of a skinny young man posing with celebrities of all stripes and levels of fame. Donnie Starshine and his collection of heroes. I didn't need to turn around to know the bodyguard kept his eyes on us at all times.

We passed a wall of glass that faced the backyard, showcasing the upward slope of the hill and the centerpiece of the rear of the building: a swimming pool. It was the size of three or four parking spaces, and that made it a veritable luxury in a town where real estate was a precious commodity. Hells, I was a grown adult and I'd never been in a body of water deeper than a bathtub. A crowd of fifteen or twenty danced in and around the pool, writhing to a synth-rich track matched to heavily modulated Mollenkampi vocals. One woman in particular enjoyed the attention of the crowd. A fin-headed Gillmyn dressed in a cropped shirt and white shorts, she spun a slow circle on roller skates, pumping her fist in the air. The motions were more or less in time to the beat, but perfectly syncopated to the strobing house lights. Her other hand clutched a chain of prayer beads. With each fist pump she also flicked a thumbnail over a specific bead, as if she were flicking a light switch on and off. Or in her case, an entire houseful of light switches.

It wasn't the first time I'd seen the stupidly rich do something brilliantly wasteful, but before the manna strike the idea of such a display would have been scandalous, almost sacrilegious. Now it was only more proof that everyone in Titanshade believed themselves part of the bright and shiny future. An iridescent gilded age. But I didn't have time to ponder the economics of the pool party. Biggs directed us around a corner, moving away from the revelers and pausing at a pair of leather-upholstered doors, the seams of the material fastened with gold-plated rivets and door handles made out of refurbished pistol grips. The sound of voices raised in anger came from beyond the doors, muffled enough that we couldn't make out what was being yelled.

The bodyguard made a flicking motion. "Arms out."

We didn't move.

"You know we're cops, right?" Dungan was indignant, a little flush showing on his meaty cheeks.

"I know who you are." His voice was squeaky but confident. Past him the yelling continued. One voice deep, the other higher pitched.

"So you know we're carrying," I said. "Everything your boss says, he's saying to a group of cops. We're not wired, but I might as well be."

He gave me a once-over, weighing my words and deciding how much he wanted to push this particular set of houseguests. Beyond the doors, something slammed on a table. A book, perhaps, or a fist. Maybe even someone's head. Shouting followed. Biggs made up his mind with a roll of his eyes and a gesture to hurry along.

"Weapons," he said. "Show me."

I hesitated. The shouting beyond the door made me uneasy. Dungan elbowed past me and raised his windbreaker, displaying his service revolver nestled in its waistband holster. He muttered, "Do it," as he stepped to the side.

I gritted my teeth and followed suit, as did Jax. Biggs still patted us down, and Dungan and Jax told him where to find their backup weapons. I wasn't carrying one—I had a tendency to drop things as it was.

Apparently satisfied, Biggs stepped to the door and wrapped his hands around the pistol grip doorknobs as if he was about to draw two weapons out of the fabric of the door itself. He paused, the muffled shouting still coming from within.

"Carter." The bodyguard's high-pitched voice caught me by surprise. He stared at me intently. "If you meet him, don't call him No-Dick."

I nodded my thanks, though the usage struck me as odd. *If* I met him? But I didn't press the point, and the big man swung open the doors. The yelling ceased abruptly.

We walked into a living room, a sunken relaxation space that featured an immense television and a pull-down screen for viewing films. On the opposite wall was a small throne of stacked stereo components. Turntable, 8-track, reel-to-reel, receiver, and a massive equalizer, all flanked by a pyramid stack of over-priced speakers that were more about size than sound quality.

In the center of the sunken living space, a pair of well-dressed criminals waited for us. I recognized them from the photos in Dungan's accordion file.

We were standing before the CaCuri twins.

9

THE DOOR SHUT BEHIND US with a *click*. Biggs stood solid before it, arms folded, blocking our exit. To my right, Dungan was board-stiff, head pulled back turtle-like into his windbreaker. Whatever was going down, he hadn't planned it. A quick glance confirmed that there were no windows in the room. Perhaps to make for a more pure blackness when Donnie screened movies, or perhaps so that anything that occurred there would have no chance of being spotted by random passersby. Whatever the reason, the lone exit out was barred by double doors and the man with the Ass-Kicker tattoo. That meant our only way out was to go forward.

Slightly below us, in the middle of the fashionably sunken room, Catherine CaCuri sat in a plush chair, legs crossed at the ankles and eyes alive with a mixture of curiosity and malice. Thomas stood behind her, one hand resting on the chair back, the other fiddling with a watch chain that draped across the vest of his three-piece suit. They stared at us, united as one, as if they hadn't been at each other's throats a few moments earlier. Just like family.

The twins were in their late twenties, though they had the look of thugs who'd spent years honing their craft. They were overdressed for the neighborhood, and both had an air of casual malice, as if they'd have slit my throat to get a better seat on the bus. Thomas had embraced a retro fashion. His tall forehead was exposed, dark hair slicked back and held in place with a generous helping of gel. His suit was vintage cut, a dark wool that helped set off the sparkle of his rings, one or more on every finger. The kind of man who'd gotten his fashion sense from watching too many old gangster movies, never understanding that he was rooting for the wrong side.

Catherine, on the other hand, cut a contemporary figure. Her clothes were lighter weight, a beige-toned skirt and white blouse and vest. Her hair was the same lush black as her brother's, shoulder length and waved. She wore a quarter of the jewelry and carried twice the air of command as Thomas. She spoke first.

"Hello, Mr. Dungan. Would you like to introduce your friends?"

Dungan stuck his hands into his windbreaker pockets. "You know them from the papers."

"Oh yes," said Catherine. "The heroes of the ice plains." Lips pursed, as if she had more to say, but she held her tongue. When not speaking, her bottom lip had the same droop as her brother's. The twins' default expression was a perpetual pout.

I tipped my head. "Miss CaCuri."

"Call me Katie, please," she said. "It's such a pleasure to meet you both." She smiled mechanically and intertwined her fingers over a knee. "You can leave now, Mr. Dungan."

It was the second time she'd ignored Dungan's title of detective, and the first attempt to separate the three of us. The tension was spiking, but before it could ignite the doors opened and we had another visitor.

No-Dick Donnie strolled into the room barefoot and shit-faced. He wore white linen slacks and a light blue T-shirt that highlighted his rail-thin ribs, all topped by rainbow suspenders. His hair feathered out in cascading waves, sandy locks that swirled like wisps of snow backlit by the fading sun. The sorcerer on skates rolled in behind him, the squeak of her wheels barely audible on the carpet. Black and red ribbons threaded through piercings in her head fin, streaming in her wake as she zipped a loop on the raised circle that surrounded the sunken center of the room. The bodyguard pressed himself into the wall, allowing her to skate past unimpeded. She gave him a quick salute.

"Thanks, Biggs!" The words were a half shout, spoken

with the kind of unconscious volume that came from staying too long at a loud concert. The sorcerer braked behind our host, knee kicked out at a choreographed angle, head thrown back and a drunken grin on her face.

"Donnie Starshine!" she announced, a royal herald proclaiming the king's arrival.

Donnie ambled in our direction, his expression every bit as relaxed as the wide-grinning cartoon sun on his T-shirt, peeking out from behind the Mount and giving a thumbs-up. I cleared my throat, figuring it was worth trying to salvage something from this disaster.

"Hi, Donnie," I said. One sentence in and I'd managed to not refer to his missing junk. I hoped Dungan appreciated my restraint. "I'm—"

"I know who you are." His voice was soft and contemplative, seemingly oblivious to the possibility of violence erupting in his living room. He drew uncomfortably close, eyeing me and Jax like he'd discovered something rare. "Dungan said he could get you to come in, but I didn't believe him. Cops are all liars, right?" His smile uncurled for the first time since he'd strolled into the room. "No offense."

"Most people are full of it," I said. "Cops and crooks alike."

His face bloomed back to life, and he turned to Dungan. "Are you ready?"

"Ready for what?" Dungan's eyes danced around the room.

"I told you we'd talk if you brought your friends. You brought them, so we'll talk." He walked away, and paused at the door, beckoning to Dungan. "Coming?"

Dungan crossed his arms as he turned from Donnie to the twins, the flush of anger spreading upward from his collar. I imagined him doubling down, maybe even pulling Jane's case out of spite. If there was a chance to recover from this mess, we had to take it.

"Go ahead," I told him. "You might as well talk to him. We'll be fine."

Thomas grinned at my words and stuck one thumb in his waistcoat, idly pulling out his pocket watch with the other hand.

"Of course you'll be fine," said Donnie. "Micah will stay with you."

The Gillmyn sorcerer half rolled, half stomped across the carpet to give Donnie a hug, nuzzling the side of her head against his.

"Don't worry," she said. "If anyone acts up, I'll crush their skulls."

The doors shut behind Dungan, Donnie, and Biggs, muffling the sound of the pool party that continued unabated. It seemed the revelers didn't notice Donnie himself wasn't there. Or they didn't care.

Jax took a seat on the couch. I stayed on my feet, near my partner. Gold and brass-striped can lights shone overhead, their spotlights glinting off a chandelier's clear crystal teardrops, each one dangling down in perfect order, ephemeral and out of reach.

Thomas stared at me. His ears had more lumps than a pile of mashed potatoes, a result of countless strikes to the side of his head. The mark of someone who liked to use their fists even when the outcome wasn't certain.

"I met you before?" He had a deep voice, an impressive baritone that gave him a certain gravitas.

A shadow of irritation disturbed the calm lake that was Katie's face. "I doubt it, my dear. Detective Carter is a man who interacts with the most vulgar sort of people." She leaned forward and gave her knee a squeeze, a strangely patronizing movement, as if she were reading aloud to children. "But then someone has to keep us all safe at night. Isn't it so?"

As a Homicide detective, I'd crossed paths with plenty of underworld players. We mostly mopped up after low-level killings, while the OCU tried to pin the big players with racketeering charges, or the kind of intricate accounting errors that had brought down several untouchable giants of organized crime. Operators like the CaCuris stayed safe in their private clubhouses while the bleeding and dying happened on the streets. I'd spent most of my career cleaning up after puppeteers like them.

Katie peered at me over steepled fingers. "Let's talk about why you're here."

"Let's." I dropped my coat across the couch's back.

Micah pushed away from the liquor cabinet, now holding a fruity rum drink with a spiral straw and a small bowl of olives. She skated across the room and fell into an overstuffed chair, legs sprawled over a cushioned armrest as she kicked the wheels of her skates and stared at the ceiling. The prayer beads lay casually across her chest.

"You're here to listen to a proposition. That's all we ask." Katie's voice was modulated, with only the tiniest hint of excitement. A teacher telling students that the field trip is going to be fun, no matter how dull it seems.

I rolled up my sleeves and crossed my arms, shoulder holster on display.

"Are we here for that? Or because your crew's been leaving bodies around?"

"Don't know what you mean." Thomas sneered, and at that moment he seemed very much like a little boy who thought he was about to put one over on the adults.

"Cetus St. Beisht is dead," Jax said. "And we all know who'd like to see that happen."

Katie CaCuri's reaction was limited to a tightening of the lips. Her brother was much more vocal.

"Don't know about it." He stepped out from behind his sister's chair. "Don't want to know about it." Thomas positioned himself between us and his sister, feet hip-width apart, pulling back his jacket to rest his hands on either side of a garishly large belt buckle featuring twin grinning skulls, staring into each other's eyes against an oil rig backdrop. "So you and your throat talker can shut up about it."

There was a long, tense moment. Then Katie uncrossed her legs and extended one foot, stretching to tap the toe of her shoe against her brother's calf. Thomas frowned, but shuffled back to his place behind her chair, leash pulled in tight.

"There seems to be some confusion." Katie's voice was smooth, unfazed by the potential for violence. "I have no criminal record. I own and operate a social club."

Thomas rumbled, and Katie amended her statement with the slightest of smiles. "My brother and I own the club, that is." She gave a brief pause after giving Thomas his due. "And while he may have had some past issues with the law, his societal debt has been paid in full." Her hands moved to the armrests. "We take an interest in the community. Neighbors helping neighbors, the way it ought to be. Maybe if more people followed our lead there'd be less need for professionals such as yourselves."

"You might be right," I said, "if you gave a damn about the people in your neighborhood." I thought of the street dealer who Ronald, the local kid, claimed didn't work for the CaCuris. "Or is it even your neighborhood anymore? I hear you've got small-time dealers walking all over on Ringsridge these days."

Katie sat up straighter at the dig, a minor tell. Thomas's reaction was far more pronounced. The tendons of his neck strained at the starched collar of his gangster outfit, and his hand visibly shook as he pulled the pocket watch from its nest and wound the spring. I recognized the tactic, using a prop to focus and control his anger. The department shrinks had told me to try the same thing. Judging from the look on his face, it wasn't working. Thomas had a reputation for his temper, but to be set off like that from a single smartass comment meant it was far worse than I thought.

Ajax straightened the creases in his coat. "Care to hear my thoughts?"

"Don't care what you think, lockjaw." Thomas CaCuri's voice was guttural and slightly slurred. Not from drink or drugs, but simple rage. He drew the red pocket square from his coat, wrapping the pocket watch in its silken fabric before tucking it back into his waistcoat. He glared at us, grinning, head lowered, a bull preparing to charge. A chill settled over me. He wasn't using a prop to curb his anger; he was *focusing* it. I started to worry about our odds of walking out of there.

"Don't be rude, Thomas." Catherine was still seated. "And don't be overly specific. After all, we don't particularly care what either of these shit-heels thinks." She smiled, a little color behind her cheeks. "Not *just* the lockjaw."

The lights flickered on and off. The room fell silent as all eyes turned to Micah, still sprawled on the chair. Her thumb hovered over the prayer beads, her ribbon-decked head fin standing at attention. Both her nails and the tips of her fin spines were painted an amethyst purple.

"Forgot to mention," she said. "The hall with the photos? It's got a little spritzer in the ceiling, that put a fine mist of manna on your heads as you walked by. Linked your noggins to these." Micah poked the small bowl of olives that sat on her stomach. "So keep it civil or, you know, you'll get crushed and I won't get a martini." She raised her glass but missed the straw, twisting her lips to bring it to her mouth and slurp at the dregs of her drink.

Jax watched me, one mandible twitching. Was she bluffing? Maybe, maybe not. Either way, it wasn't worth the risk.

"Alright." I turned back to Katie. "We can all agree this is pointless."

"No, 'pointless' is the rest of your day," she said. "Taking payouts and protecting the filth who prey on the city. This conversation had a very real point to it."

"Did it?" I tilted my head, like a confused dog. "I hadn't noticed."

Her eyes bored into mine. "I got to see you in person and decide that I don't like you. And I'm not alone there, am I? You're hated by TPD, hated by the fools and cowards who cling to the AFS's apron strings. But because of dumb luck, you're a hero to the people, who associate your face with the manna strike. And those people are my voters. That's why I'm willing to set aside my feelings and make this offer." The muscles in her calves twitched as she shifted position. "I'll let you on the big stage. You can play the hero of the ice plains in front of a crowd. And all you have to do is say that the best choice for alderman is clear. It's CaCuri."

I tugged my lower lip, thinking things over. If Katie thought the idea of standing in front of a crowd was appealing in the least, then she didn't know half as much about me as she thought. It wasn't the offer that interested me—it was the trail of events that had led us there.

We were there because Dungan practically forced us, but he'd done that because he'd been leveraged by Donnie. And the appearance of the twins made it clear who'd spurred Donnie to make that request. Now we were listening to Katie's pitch to help them gain city-wide power and influence. Dungan had hinted that he wanted to play the gangs against each other, but was it possible the twins were playing him?

So yeah, I thought about her pitch. And I didn't like it.

"I'm a hard pass on that." I pointed at my partner. "Ajax?"

"Same here." He said it with a whistle of confidence.

Katie sneered. I stared her down and did my best not to sneer back.

I failed.

"Hypocrite." She leaned back, spreading her arms as if pronouncing judgment from on high. "You run your mouth about the city, but you don't give a damn about it." Her hands dropped to the armrests. "Do you realize what you're fighting? The special election is an opportunity to tip the balance of power and throw those newcomer bastards out on their land-grabbing asses. There's a flood of scavengers coming in to steal the wealth while the people of this town have been working for generations to keep the rest of the world flush with oil. Now that we found manna, the parasites are crawling out of the woodwork. You just haven't realized it yet."

"Believe me, I'm seeing no shortage of scavengers and parasites today."

She reclined her head against the dramatic swoop of the chair. "When you change your mind, you send us a message. Let us know that Titanshade should be proud." She beamed. "We'll know what you mean."

Jax and I stared at her in silence.

"It's been a pleasure to meet you, Detectives. I wonder if we'll speak again." She addressed her twin without breaking eye contact with me. "Let's go, Thomas."

He held out a hand and she took it, pulling herself upright. She had a hitch in her step, as if sporting an injury to her leg or foot.

"Thank you for coming," Micah called out. "There's someone outside the door to walk you out." She pointed to Jax and myself, and spoke in a quieter tone. "You two wait here. Give 'em time to leave."

I kept my eyes on the twins. "Be seeing you around."

I was answered by a silent snarl from Thomas, tucking the red pocket square back into place before the gaudy doors shut behind them.

"Well, that was something," Jax said. He stretched some of the tension out of his back, while Micah hummed a dissonant tune to herself.

"Should you let your boss know we're done?" I asked.

"He already knows. He's been listening in." She grinned and flipped one of the ribbons that hung from her head fin behind her ear. The flesh of her ear had a slight shimmer. If she'd had manna on her ear when she nuzzled the side of Donnie's head . . .

"He'll hear what we say, so don't get too flirty." She chuckled as she pulled the straw out of her empty drink. "But, you know, he's also trying to listen to your friend. So I'll let it loose. Besides," head tilted and arm cocked she ran a hand over her ear and mouth, undoing the invisible connection as if she were loosening the strings on a violin, "we don't want to use up the juice, now do we?"

A short while later the door opened and Donnie and Dungan returned, trailed by Biggs. Our fellow detective was red-cheeked and grinning like a wildcatter who just struck oil.

He came around the couch, and I slid to my left, blocking his path.

"We're good?" I said.

"Yeah." Dungan's pat on my arm turned into a slight shove as he pushed past me to the glass-faced liquor cabinet. "We're good."

I grabbed his shoulder, crinkling the fabric of his windbreaker as I turned him to face me.

"What're you up to?"

He leaned in, voice hovering above a whisper. "Donnie played it like the CaCuris made him ask me to bring you here. That gives us both cover for talking. It's coming together perfect."

I squinted at him. Did he really think that the stoned guy in rainbow suspenders was manipulating major players like the CaCuri twins?

He gripped my shoulder. "I'm on this," he said. "Just remember that all this stays between us." He'd already given me his rationalizations in the car. And the flush on his cheeks made it clear he was getting exactly what he wanted.

"Whatever," I said. "Stay out of my way with the Jane Doe and we're solid." I half turned, then paused. "And get that security footage to me in the next day."

"Sure, sure." He pushed past me, headed toward the wet bar on the far wall. "For the record," he said, "you know I wouldn't let a case get ignored."

"But you'd take it out from under us."

"Hells yes, I would." He helped himself to a glass of Donnie's liquor. "If that's what it took to get you to listen to reason? I'd do it in a heartbeat."

And that was the problem. Because no matter what he did with her case, someone would end up putting Jane on a back burner, a problem to be puzzled out when there was time between high-profile busts. Dungan might not bury Jane's case, but he wouldn't care about her as much as she deserved. As much as we all deserved.

I watched him for another beat, then noticed that Donnie had sidled up to Jax and started a conversation. I left Dungan to his cocktail as the financier of the criminal elite motioned me closer.

"We didn't get to talk," he said. "But it was nice to meet you. And believe me, a *lot* of people have plans for you." His grin was as big as his eyes were wide, and I couldn't tell if he was threatening us or not. Then he waved Micah over, and suddenly we were all shaking hands again. "In fact," said Donnie, "we wanted to talk to you as well."

"You couldn't just pick up the phone?" I asked. "Did you really need to drag us down in front of your friends?"

Donnie's brow furrowed. He looked in the direction of the door, and the pool of celebrants, then back at me. "Oh! You mean the twins?" His grin was as wide and calm as the ice plains. "I make lots of investments. Hard to keep track sometimes."

Micah nodded. "We're believers in spreading our bets."

It was a reasonable stance from investors in criminal enterprises.

She huffed out a chuckle. "The other day an old acquaintance contacted me, from out of the blue. Made an offer to sell us a personal product—" She cut herself off, eyelids drooping, though with enough clarity in her voice that I wondered if the inebriation had been an act. "Nothing illegal," she said. She bit her lip, clearly avoiding looking in Donnie's direction. "Purely cosmetic."

"I had an accident," Donnie said with a shrug. "People think it'd bother me. It doesn't."

"If you need that for satisfaction, then it shows a lack of imagination." Purring, Micah gave him a playful pinch on the ear.

He patted her hand, then turned to Dungan. "Have a seat and let's talk, Detective. Micah will see your friends out."

Micah, Jax, and I followed Biggs, leaving Dungan and Donnie alone in the isolation of the living room. As we reached the door, Micah gestured with her straw, and the bodyguard backed off a few paces. The sorcerer leaned toward us, the smell of rum and cola heavy on her breath.

"You oughta come back sometime when there's more people. You'd be surprised how much fun this place is."

"We're busy serving the public," I said. "Saving lives, locking up people like you."

She suppressed a laugh, and the tip of her tongue stuck out between her teeth, looking like Rumple when I surprised him mid-groom. "Oh, sugar, you have no idea! You're going to get so many requests for your time. You're the hot new thing."

Micah glided away across the carpet, wheels on her skates squeaking as she left us to stare at each other. We passed through the front doors, hands skimming the entry vent as we recited the traditional prayer of thanks. Even a place like Donnie's mansion was an oasis of warmth from the ice plains, a gift from the Titan who suffered far below.

10

FROM DONNIE'S WE DROVE FOR miles, doing lazy loops along the city's meandering streets. Ajax was behind the wheel, trying to follow my directions as he snaked us through traffic. He stared intently at the road and muttered to himself at intersections.

"Still learning the city map?" I said.

On Titanshade's fringes the streets were tidy grids and the buildings stood taller, able to sink footers into the ground without fear of disturbing the geo-vents. But closer to the Mount the neighborhoods grew organically, to match the natural layout of the vent openings. As a result, the streets of the inner city swerved and curved, narrowed and widened, carried traffic in broad loops or abrupt dead ends. It was notoriously confusing for anyone who didn't grow up on its streets.

He nodded his answer, keeping his concentration on the street. I grunted in approval.

"Know the city and you'll know the victim," I said. "Know the victim—"

"Know the killer," he finished for me, then took a deep breath. "Is this really what you want to talk about? After wasting a full day sitting in a gangster's living room so we can placate your pal Dungan?"

"Don't let that BS get you distracted," I said.

"From what? The *one* open case we've got right now? We'd normally have what, fifteen?" He clacked his biting jaws together. "Now stop talking. I want to see if this is Tengly Avenue up ahead."

He resumed scanning the road, hunting for the next street sign. A scooter shot past us, coming within a handsbreadth of my side mirror. I drummed my fingers on the dash and tried to dial in a radio station worth a damn as we moved farther from the Mount. Finally settling on a station with a commercial, I stared out the window. We passed a storefront with newly hung decorations. Silver and blue bunting in the shape of the ba, a sideways figure eight that symbolized the eternal winding path we all walked along. I decided to try another change of subject.

I jerked a thumb, indicating the bustle in the street. "Did you celebrate Titan's Day as a kid?"

Jax stared at the decorations and sighed. "No," he said. "It was on the calendar, but we didn't celebrate it."

That wasn't surprising. The celebration of the Titan's sacrifice for our city didn't spread far beyond Titanshade's borders.

"So this is your first Titan's Day?"

"You don't need to explain it," said Ajax, his words underscored by a series of annoyed clicks. "Maybe I don't quite get all the customs."

I grunted, taking advantage of the slowing traffic to get a better glimpse of the decorations along the street. Even out here, where drunks and candies manned the streets, the spirit of the season was on display. Or at least its trappings.

When we reached the intersection, he pointed in triumph at the white-on-green of the street sign. Tengly Avenue.

I grinned. "Keep it up and pretty soon you'll be a real cop." I indicated the street. "Keep going straight a little ways, till we get to Patterson Avenue." I looked back at the holiday activity on the storefronts and sidewalks. "It's a lot more commercial these days," I said. "The point of the thing is lost in all the decorations and sales."

"And what is that point?"

"Oh, are you saying I *do* need to explain the holiday?" He started to protest, and I talked over him. "Self-sacrifice, that's the point. The Titan gave the city heat, even though it meant an eternity of torture." I craned my head. A group of costumed revelers had turned the corner, leaping and leering, teasing passersby.

"Slow down." I covered a belch with my sleeve as I pointed. "I want a better view of the imps."

The costumes varied from reveler to reveler, but all of them represented the creatures said to torment the Titan far below ground. Some appeared lizard-skinned and reptilian, others were human caricatures. As traffic came to a halt, I pointed out a group of worm-bodied things, faces obscured by masks of blue nylon.

"Those are based on some demon from old Mollen-kampi folktales," I said.

Jax gave me a side-eye, one mandible twitching, its hooked end dragging along the length of a jutting tooth. "That much I knew already."

"I guess that figures," I said. "What're they called? The demons, I mean."

He told me. It was a word far beyond my ability to replicate, three syllables that sounded like wind howling through the eaves of an abandoned building.

But frightening costumes were in the minority. Most were played for laughs, hairy-suited figures with dangling false tongues and red spiraled horns ending in sharp, white-tipped points. Kids' stuff.

Still idling in traffic, Jax asked, "What are we looking for down here, anyway?"

I turned in my seat, still observing the costumed revelers. "They usually don't show up until closer to the actual day," I said. "But this year Imp's Run started early." The rediscovery of manna and the tension of the military presence had manifested itself in a burst of rebellion. Combine that with rising rents and growing unemployment, and maybe we all needed a little Hells-raising. Whatever the reason, this year the imps were on the street a full nine days before the holiday.

Jax sighed. "Or you could ignore my question." He tracked the troublemakers through the rearview. "So they do pranks?"

"Gambols," I said. "When they're in costume for Imp's Run, it's called a gambol."

Traffic flowed again, and we pulled away. It wasn't unusual to see humped, hairy backs disappearing into alleyways or even tall stilt walkers hurl balloons filled with water (or some other, less appealing liquid) across a busy street, dodging away before enraged pedestrians could catch up with them. Traditionally such stunts were treated with a slap on the wrist, so long as the prankster wore a decent imp suit and the prank wasn't particularly harmful. But this year tensions were high, and I suspected the holding cells back at the Bunker were destined to be brimming with hungover revelers in costume.

"Shouldn't let them get away with it," he said. "Like broken windows."

"Come again?"

"Say a couple apartments go vacant. Kids throw rocks, bust out a couple windows. No big deal, right?" He shook his head. "The windows don't get fixed, the kids don't get punished. So they break a few more. Someone else sees that, realizes the place is vacant and they tear out the wiring and plumbing for scrap metal. Squatters move in, maybe turn it into a chono den or angel's roost. And it started with broken windows."

I frowned. "It wasn't broken windows that got Jane killed."

The station I'd selected blared out yet another commercial, and Jax jabbed one of the preset buttons on the radio. "Your taste in music gets worse every day." He took his eyes off the road long enough to look me over. "Why are you so focused on this one case?"

"Because it's our first job back," I said. "Because Dungan might take it away, and no one will give a damn about finding who killed her." Ajax sped up to let a bakery truck slide in behind us, and I kept talking. "There's a million reasons to care. How can you not care that someone bashed in this girl's head and left her to die in the filth of an alley?" I noticed Jax's shoulders tighten, but he didn't interrupt me.

On the sidewalk, I spotted the person I'd been hoping to find. "Pull over," I said.

Jax swerved tight to the curb in a fire lane and threw the car into park. He leaned back and gave me his full attention.

"I never said I don't care." The menacing tusks of his biting jaw opened wider, adding an angry, bass undertone to his words. "I've buried relatives who looked like her. Who died like her. And if your pal Dungan is working on some plan to cut that cycle of violence at the source?" He spread his hands wide, bemused, as if I were a puzzle he couldn't get his head around. "Why the Hells would you not want to take it?"

"Whatever Dungan's up to, it isn't going to get justice for Jane," I said. "For this one, real, non-hypothetical person."

"And what about the others?" he said. "What about the next one and the one after that? You can't obsess over all of them, Carter."

"No," I said. "I can't. But maybe I can make a difference in one. So that's what I'm gonna do."

On the sidewalk our contact turned, stared at us, and propped a hand on one hip, brows furrowed. Talena Michaels never looked happy to see the man who'd helped raise her.

Dressed in layers, Talena showed a bit of holiday flair with blue-and-silver T-shirts under a pair of flannel button-ups, shirttails hanging over worn blue jeans. An ideal outfit for moving from one neighborhood's microclimate to another. She'd been talking to a trio of youths when we pulled up, all of them dressed as pragmatically as Talena. Most of them wore knit hats, though Talena was bare-headed, her hair pulled back against her neck. I expected the others to disappear as we approached, a typical response to two men dressed in the kind of low-end suits that a cop's salary could supply. Instead they eyed us with curiosity and waited on Talena's direction.

As we got closer she gave me a curt nod and smiled at Jax. I felt him stand a little taller.

"Ajax," she said in a loud, clear voice. "They still got you shackled to this dead weight?"

My partner rubbed the side of his neck and let out a resigned whistle. "TPD transfer requests are so slow these days." His eyes crinkled, amused at his own joke. "How are you?"

"Suspicious," she said. "What do you two want?"

I held out my peace offering: the coffee and crullers I'd gotten that morning from the diner. I handed them all over to Talena, along with the morgue photo. There was no point in hiding why I was there. I wanted to know if my Jane Doe was a candy, and Talena was a walking encyclopedia of faces and names on the street.

She dismissed the group with a clap of her hands and a reminder to "Check back in three hours. If I don't see you, we'll come looking." I watched her with surprise as the others marched off to interact with the candies lounging in doorways and flagging down cars. Talena had worked with other activists before, but this group was different. They were clearly taking orders. The idea of Talena ordering people around was difficult to process when I still remembered carrying her to bed in her Plucky Duck jammies after she'd failed to stay up late enough to watch the TV movie of the week.

Talena held the crullers and crime scene shot in one hand and the coffee in the other. Both wrists were bedecked with hand-woven bracelets of beads and yarn, gifts from the children of candies or homeless families she'd helped; Hells, some may even have been from candies who were children themselves. I spent my days chasing justice for the dead. Talena spent hers trying to help the living.

She brought the cup to her lips and frowned. "It's cold."

"You like iced coffee."

Talena brought the cup to her ear and sloshed the contents, as if listening for the clink of nonexistent cubes. "This isn't iced," she said. "It's just not hot."

I shrugged. "Ice would've melted by now. Then it'd have been not hot *and* watered down." There'd been a time when we might've ended up in a screaming match about forgotten ice. But it'd only been a month since she'd been hospitalized after ingesting poison intended for me, then arrested and falsely accused of murder. Maybe that had mellowed her. Maybe it made me appreciate her more. The reason didn't matter as much as the result—neither of us escalated the argument. She merely rolled her eyes and drank the lukewarm coffee as she studied Jane's mutilated face.

"Not a candy." Talena handed the photo back to me. "Or if she is, I haven't seen her."

I didn't put the photo away. "Not sure what makes someone do that kind of violence," I said.

"Hate's a pyramid," she said, as if I knew what that meant.

She noticed my confusion. "No one starts off doing something like that. It starts with something small. Little things teach people that being a little cruel is okay," she said. "And people who want to be cruel take that and run with it. Urging on others and telling them it's okay." Talena frowned, an expression of sadness more than anger. "It's like a single drop of hate can sour an ocean of kindness."

The street noise was increasing, probably some imps on a gambol, so I stepped closer. Behind Talena, the brick walls were dotted with gang tags and encoded messages. Some I understood, but most were meant for eyes much younger than mine. The gangs and crews that ruled the streets when I was a teenager were long forgotten now. But laid on top of the tags were signs even the most street-naive of readers could understand. *Strangers get out*, read a particularly direct version. A more poetic version proclaimed: *Let the Nation Thirst. Feed Titan First.* All variations of the theme we'd found at the murder scene. I slid Jane's photo back into my coat pocket, and rummaged around to see if I had a shot of the mural at the crime scene. I wanted to show that photo to her as well.

Talena sipped the coffee and grimaced. I'd gotten the sugars wrong, too. She popped the top off the cup and crammed half a donut into the light brown liquid. She kept talking as she ate. "Kids hear a friend call a woman a whore. Okay. Next time they say it to her face. Time after that?" She frowned. "It gets said with a slap. Then a fist. Then she's on a slab, and what did she expect? She's just a whore, right?"

Behind me, Jax said, "Broken windows."

Talena's eyes brightened. "Kind of like that, yeah." Then to me: "Next time make it hot or cold. This room temperature shit's barely drinkable."

There were shouts from down the street. I turned to my right. A group of imps sped through the crowd, jostling each other and the surrounding pedestrians as they slapped fliers on any available surface. Although costumed, I guessed they were young; they moved with the speed and frenetic energy I remembered having as a teenager.

The imps began chasing one another around a bicycle-driven food cart. The cart's vendor, an older man, attempted to shoo them away. One of the imps pushed the vendor. He staggered back, then another shoved him forward. The imps circled him, screaming insults and dancing at the edge of his reach as they jabbed him with their false horns and claws. The vendor staggered, falling against the cart. This was more than a standard gambol.

Jax started toward the group, but I moved in the opposite direction, back toward the Hasam.

Talena barked out a commanding "Hey!" but the situation was already escalating. Two of the youths put their shoulders into the food truck, toppling it over as another shoved the vendor to the ground. The older man hit the sidewalk hard, and when he tried to rise one of the imps followed through with a kick to the ribs.

Reaching into the Hasam I tripped the siren, and from the foot well the button cap flared once, painting me with red and making me look like an imp as well.

The kids turned and scattered. Ajax chased after them. "Dammit," I muttered. But I followed Ajax as he bounded toward the assailants.

The revelers turned the corner, running as fast as their over-weighted, long-haired costumes would allow. The foot traffic parted as they approached, many onlookers whistling in encouragement without knowing what they were cheering on. No one would slow down an imp in the middle of a gambol. That'd be against the holiday spirit.

My partner had slowed to a jog and stood glaring at the alley the kids must have disappeared down. There was no point in pursuing, and I called out for Jax to leave it be. They were long gone, and I already knew what would happen when we talked to the man whose street cart had been overturned.

I turned back to find Talena crouched by the vendor. She peered into his eyes and asked if he was okay.

"Yes," he said. He had a breathy Embarkam accent, heavy with aspirated h's and s's, distinctive to that city-state's territory. It was an accent that made the speaker sound like they were out of breath, while also giving you a whiff of what they ate for lunch. "But my cart . . ."

The food truck was in disarray, but not destroyed. The old-fashioned pedal-pulled street cart wobbled as we set it aright, but it held. Some of his fellow vendors came over to help, but others held back and watched us with hard eyes, as if they'd have preferred to see the imps finish off the old man.

I wondered if the vendor who'd been attacked had made enemies. Were the teens merely taking the Imp's Run gambols too far, or had he been targeted?

I snatched one of the fliers the imps had dropped to the ground. Torn and crumpled, it was still legible, a community announcement sheet advertising a rally for the special election and an upcoming street festival. Both of which were being hosted by the CaCuris. Amateurish design, but professionally printed. Seemed right on brand for the twins.

I held it in front of the vendor. "Were those imps talking about this?"

He squinted at the type. "No, no . . ." He patted a pocket, then rifled through the messenger bag slung across the back of his bike. He reached inside and pulled out a flier of his own. "Same as mine. Maybe I dropped it?"

A cursory glance told me it was indeed the same flier. Nodding, I said to Jax, "Those were CaCuri's punks."

The vendor's brow furrowed. "No, the flier is mine. Ca-Curi doesn't do things like this. She's helping people."

"Trust me," I said. "She's not."

He wiped a sleeve over a chin scraped bloody from the cobblestones. "Everything's stacked against us. The drilling companies, the AFS . . ." He stood up taller. "Katie CaCuri's the only person out there actually doing something for people like me."

"You're not from Titanshade," I said. "She's using you as a scapegoat."

The old man almost laughed. "Oh, she sent those thugs? You think she started that, too?" He jerked a thumb at the crowd, at the other vendors still shooting angry glances in our direction. "She only says what we're all thinking. I'm here now, and she's trying to keep other people from taking what's ours. Maybe not everyone likes us," his shoulders slumped, "but she's at least giving us a shot."

No surprise, really. I looked to the dark sky overhead,

then folded the flier into thirds and jammed it in my pocket. I nodded at the vendor. "Watch yourself out there."

The old man grabbed the handles of the food cart bicycle and began limping forward. He only got a step before Talena fell in beside him.

"Here, I'll give you a shove," she said. She glanced at us over her shoulder, waving a good-bye.

Ajax took a step in their direction, then turned back to me. "We got anything else for today?"

I tossed him the car keys. "Drop the Hasam at the Bunker," I said. "I'll bus it home and we'll regroup in the morning."

He turned and fell in step beside Talena, helping the old man gain momentum, chatting with the girl I'd helped raise, as they walked.

I eyed the skyline. The day had faded, and I needed to get home. I had to get dressed for my date.

11

I MET GELLICA AT A NOODLE stand near the corner of Franklin and Retroyer. I'd changed into a cleaner shirt and opted to make my tie fashionably absent. She wore a calf-length black dress, cropped at the shoulders, leaving her arms bare except for the bangles and bracelets riding just above her wrists. The halter neck cut tight to her throat but dipped low in the back. Its fabric was speckled with metallic thread, making it sparkle and shimmer with every sway of her hips.

She smiled when she saw me, and I bought us a couple orders of noodles with a side of salty bromi sauce and shelled hardfish. They came wrapped in wax paper and cardboard cones, along with small forks. Perfect for a meal on the go. We ate as we walked, picking our way through the streets. It wasn't a bad meal.

"Your hair's done up," I said in between bites, smooth talker that I am.

Gellica's eyes widened. "My, you *are* a detective." Her hair was indeed held up in loose curls, not as tightly done as a fashionista might wear, but definitely more formal than the relaxed style she'd worn before.

"I dress differently when going out." She patted her mouth with a napkin, sidestepping a street musician who wailed on a trumpet, underscoring our walk with a medium swing. "It's called playing to your audience."

I dropped a couple coins in the musician's hat. "So you dress to blend in?"

"Sometimes." We parted as a fin-headed Gillmyn in a

sharply tailored suit dashed between us, glancing at his watch as he ran. "Sometimes to stand out. Depends on my goal."

"How do you dress when you're seeing me?"

"I don't," she said, and color leapt to her cheeks. "I mean—" Her words tumbled out. "I mean I wear what seems natural." The air of diplomatic poise snapped back into place. "Comes with us knowing each other's secrets, I suppose. That's why I like you."

"Oh?" It seemed like the safest response.

"Well, partly why."

I may have flattered myself, but I thought her smile deepened.

"And you," she indicated my suit. "You're dressed as one of Titanshade's finest."

I straightened my jacket. I had considered changing it, but decided the one I'd been wearing was the less wrinkled option. "You saying I dress like a cop?"

She gave me a slow once-over.

"Carter, you look like a cop on his way to a costume party, dressed as another cop."

"Huh." I dug into my noodle container, searching for a last forkful of dinner. "I don't always dress like a cop."

"Yes, you do," she said. "Lucky for you, it's charming." She tossed her trash into a bin and her fork into the recycling. "Finish your meal. We're here."

I craned my head and spotted the sign overhead. The Lotus Petal wasn't a club I'd been to before. Not too surprising, as it'd been over a decade since I'd worn patrol scarlet and spent my days checking on bars. And even back then, The Lotus Petal was a little too high-end for regular police visits. The patrons here were more likely to cut with sarcasm and condescension than an honest blade. Not that I liked them any more or less for it. It was simply a different type of trouble waiting for us once we passed the threshold.

Of course, it appeared that it'd be some time before we crossed the threshold in question. A line of aspiring patrons stretched down the sidewalk, huddled together and whispering, waiting to be let into the place. Gellica grabbed my shoulder and towed me in her wake as we made our way

to the front of the line. She gave the doorman her name
and indicated I was her plus one. We were hustled in past
the glares of the line-bound masses and entered the world
of fashion art.

Once inside, I understood the line. The place wasn't a
stuffy gallery but a working bar and dinner space with a
low stage up front. The crowd wore uniform shades of
black or white, with one or two accent colors scattered on
their shoulders or hips. Many of the patrons were overdressed, a sure sign that they were slumming it. When
wealthy Titanshaders drift into lower-class neighborhoods,
they have a tendency to favor overly thick fabrics or sweaters and turtlenecks with a brand-new, off-the-shelf gloss
that causes regular residents to wince. It made Gellica's
choice of dress all the more interesting. Thick enough fabric to stay warm, but with enough skin exposed to show she
didn't think that going a few blocks leeward was the same
as camping on the ice plains.

We passed a table full of men in jumpers and bandan-
nas, all of them posturing for the sake of a nearby table of
women in turtlenecks and tight black stirrup pants. The
well-to-do patrons may have been embracing the lower-
rent neighborhood, but most still had designer labels on
their backsides. My well-worn suit suddenly seemed badly
out of place, and I considered telling people that I really
was on my way to a costume party dressed as a cop.

I scanned the room, focusing on the task at hand. Dinner
had been fun, but there might be someone here who could
help me track down Jane. "So do we mingle at the bar?"

"Don't be silly. We have a table reserved."

Gellica gestured to a man in a mock turtleneck, a lithe
Mollenkampi who came over and placed a hand on his
heart. Gellica spoke quickly and quietly, using phrases I
couldn't follow and adding in finger snaps as flourishes, the
same way Jax might punctuate his sentences with clicks of
teeth from his speaking mouth.

The man walked into the room, gesturing for us to
follow.

"You speak Kampi?" I asked Gellica, as she slipped
into the crowd ahead of me.

"Not well." She spoke over her shoulder as we wound

our way through round tables occupied by small clusters of patrons. "But a little goes a long way in my line of work."

"Diplomacy," I said. "Making people feel flattered."

"Showing I care," she said. "You might try it sometime." Grinning, she tilted her head to make eye contact, a movement that arched her back and emphasized the low cut of her dress's B-side. "Might be a nice counterpoint to your normal routine of acting like a prick until someone gets angry enough to say something stupid."

The host led us to an empty table and pulled out Gellica's chair before departing.

"Been flashing a badge for two decades," I said. "My technique seems to be working so far."

We sat down on chairs with thin leather pads on the back and seat that made them a hair short of uncomfortable.

"If it was working that well," she said, all bright teeth and shining eyes, "you'd have all your fingers."

I gave a slow whistle and a series of overlapping clicks, what I believed to be a suitable retort in Kampi. Gellica suppressed a laugh.

"If you meant to imply you're the head of maintenance services," she managed to keep a straight face, "then yes, your Kampi is excellent."

Feeling I wasn't going to win that argument, I turned my attention to the stage. A simple wooden table sat in a circle of light. It held a reel-to-reel tape machine, and a pair of headphones. No one seemed to be paying it any attention.

Gellica flagged a server, and a Mollenkampi woman arrived and introduced herself. Like the man who'd seated us she wore a black mock turtleneck. A wise concession, considering the location of Mollenkampi speaking mouths.

Gellica ordered a glass of house wine. I opted for tea, holding off on alcohol while I was working. The waitress turned to go but Gellica stopped her, adding an order for another glass, this one a specific vintage. The waitress gave a slight bow, and Gellica pointed to a corner booth. "Send it to that gentleman, with our compliments."

The waitress bowed again, deeper this time, and departed as the main lights dimmed.

"Who's that?" I asked.

"His name's Napier," she said. "And that's who we're here to see."

The man in the corner was entertaining a few patrons who drifted away shortly thereafter. I may not have known art, but I knew a boss when I saw one.

"He'll let us know when he's ready," she said. "But that's later."

"And now?"

"Now we enjoy the show," she said, lowering her voice as the room began to hush. "Watch carefully, Officer. There may be a quiz at the end of the night." She turned her attention to the stage, though for a long moment I couldn't take my eyes off her. Then I thought of Talena, arrested on a manufactured charge as she lay in her hospital bed. I took a sip of tea and reminded myself that it had all turned out okay, that in the end Gellica had been on our side. Movement onstage caught my eye.

A woman dressed in a severe black suit entered stage right, escorting a man in a wheelchair. The man was limp, his head slumped, his hands and feet strapped in place. He wore an off-white uniform, the kind that might be assigned to an inmate. The woman positioned him in the spotlight, next to the tape machine. Locking the wheels in place, she pulled his head back and fastened a strap across his forehead. The chair itself was oversized, an artistic interpretation of an interrogation chair, a prop from a spy movie. Picking up the headphones, she placed them on the man's ears. She loaded a spool onto the reel-to-reel and pressed Play. The man's eyes opened wide.

"My husband doesn't know this," he stage-whispered. "But I lost the engagement ring he gave me all those years ago. I dropped it down a sink while he was on deployment. I had a duplicate made, and he never noticed, so I guess I did the right thing."

He closed his eyes, still for a heartbeat, as if listening to the headphones, then said, "I cheat at cards." His voice was husky now, mimicking the wheezing voice of a much older man. "True to the Path, I cheat at every damn game I play." He laughed. "I never do it for money. It's the fun of the thing, I guess. I don't have to win the actual game, just not get caught and it's a guaranteed good time!" The statement ended with a delirious cackle.

Gellica leaned in, her shoulder against mine. She directed my gaze to the far corner where a simple, cloth-covered board stood, black curtains to either side and a hole the width of my shoulders in its front. Near the hole was a button.

"You stick your head in there," she whispered. "And press that button. It turns on the recorder, and you whisper your darkest secret. Edgar doesn't hear them in advance, simply relates them in the moment."

It was a neat trick, catching the tone and rhythm of different voices while also processing the words.

"I'd think he'd get distracted by the secrets," I said. "Some of these are funny."

"Some are scandalous," she said. "But he says that's the trick. He doesn't judge. Only captures the voice and repeats what he hears."

It was weird, but I had to admit it was interesting. "Why'd you bring me here?"

Her lips curved upward. I did like her smile.

"Apart from the obvious delight of seeing a detective listen to a room full of people's darkest secrets?" She shrugged, and I watched the rise and fall of her bare shoulder. "To meet Napier. After that you can talk to whoever you like."

The people at the tables around us had been engaged in their own whispered conversations, and I'd barely taken notice of them. But now a man approached from the table to our left. He was human, tall with dark brown skin and sharp features. The majority of his hair was cropped tight to the scalp, but the top unfurled into a perfectly mani-cured wave of dyed-blond curls, balancing the narrow beard that defined his jaw with an artist's precision. He wore a sports jacket over a light dress shirt, unbuttoned to mid-chest. A silk neckerchief lay in a careless knot around his throat, its ends draping over the chiseled lines of exposed pectoral muscles.

"Envoy," he said. "So good to see you." He stooped ever so slightly and rested a hand on Gellica's exposed back. His voice had a pulsing, side-to-side rhythm, like a snake charmer's flute.

Judging from the two women at the table he'd left, he clearly had some charms. Both stared daggers in our direction. More precisely, they stared at Gellica like they'd gladly have dragged her out to the ice plains and left her to freeze.

Gellica returned the man's smile, though I told myself it wasn't with the warmth she'd shown me. She gestured between us.

"Mitri, meet my friend Carter. Carter, Mitri Tenebrae."

We shook hands. It was close, but I think I won the battle of the increasingly tight grips.

The taller man pulled his chair from the previous table to ours. There wasn't so much as a whisper as it crossed the floor, or the slightest hint of asking permission to sit.

"I didn't expect to find you here tonight." He spoke to Gellica, of course. I might as well have been at the next table.

"It wouldn't do to let everyone know my social schedule. But I should have known you'd be here." To me, she added, "Mitri is quite the talented amateur sculptor. He's more at home here than I'll ever be." Gellica picked up her purse, a small black clutch with metallic thread that matched her dress. "I need to step away. If you'll excuse me, I'll be right back." We watched her leave, dismayed.

"So." Tenebrae's eyes raked over me. Or rather over my clothes and middle-aged physique fueled by coffee and takeout meals. "Are you part of the AFS transition team?"

"Not exactly," I said. "Apparently I'm with maintenance."

"Ah," he said, eyes already scanning the crowd for someone more influential than me. "I'm sure that's rewarding." He stood, leaving his empty wineglass on the table. "Great meeting you, really great."

And with that, he was gone. By the time he'd reached the next table, he'd glommed himself to another pair of patrons.

I sat alone for a few minutes, listening to the performer share the secrets of strangers and watching the crowd act out their own little dramas. There was a table full of wealthy women making gestures at the performer. I wondered if they were discussing purchasing some of his work, and then I wondered if that was even possible. Beyond them a younger couple were in the heat of an argument. Or rather the man was arguing, and forcing the woman with him to listen. I didn't like the body language on display.

A rustle of fabric told me that Gellica had returned to her seat.

"Having fun?" she asked.

I snorted. "You have lots of friends here?"

"I don't have lots of friends, period." I almost missed the way her lips tightened as she spoke.

"What about your swimwear model over there?" I pointed a thumb at Tenebrae.

Gellica laughed. "Please."

"He was clearly interested in you." I watched him. He was currently speaking to an older couple, apparently married, and they both seemed quite taken in by his charms.

"I don't think it's me he's interested in," she said.

I snorted, and she said, "Did you get a close look at that scarf?"

Glancing back at Tenebrae, I strained my eyes in the low light of the club. Black silk, with silver patterns . . . no, not patterns. Runes. My stomach clenched.

"He's a sorcerer," I said.

Gellica winked.

I coughed, eyeing the tall man more carefully. "Is it, you know, safe to be here?"

Her brows creased. "I don't know that any sorcerer is safe, necessarily."

"Yeah, but can't he tell about your," I hesitated, not wanting to use the word "condition." Instead I fell back on the pantomimed roar I'd used in her office. Only more subtle, suitable for a public conversation.

Apparently not subtle enough, because Gellica batted my hands down.

"What do you think, that we can scent each other out?"

I shrugged. I didn't know how it worked.

"If you met someone," she said. "A complete stranger. Would you know they were a cop without being told?"

"Probably, yeah."

She glared. "It's like scattering seeds on the ice plains with you." She lifted her wineglass and swirled the contents. "Even if you did, you wouldn't know what kind of cop, right?"

I wasn't going to argue the point.

"Mitri knows I've got the inside track on the manna reserves," she said. "But that's it. For that matter, everyone who knows what I do for a living knows I do something with manna. If he did get a sense of something, he'd probably assume it rubbed off on me from Paulus." I thought on that. If anyone could get manna from the strike, it was Gellica's boss. Was Paulus siphoning some for her own plans? If so, was it for more twisted experimentation? It was a thought I immediately regretted. Gellica might be a lot of things, but she wasn't a twisted experiment. If anything, she was a hostage to Paulus's schemes.

"Besides," she waved dismissively, "all Mitri wants is insider information on the manna strike and when it'll be available, same as everyone else. He's simply more motivated than most."

"Why's that?"

"He's with TCI."

My blank expression must have communicated my lack of understanding.

"Telescribe Communications," she said. "They use manna for secure long-distance connections. Contract out to governments, mostly."

"Big money."

"To say the least," she said. "Tenebrae's all over anyone he thinks can give him or his backers an inside connection."

"So you're trying to get rid of him?" I managed to keep the delight out of my voice.

"Well, I'm not in too much of a hurry." The corner of Gellica's lip curled as her gaze slid over my shoulder, in the other man's direction. "He may turn out to have some use. And he's pleasant to look at."

I took a swig of my tea, but before I could formulate a proper response the man in the corner booth had risen and gestured to us.

Gellica stood, collecting her drink and her purse.

"Come on," she said. "And try not to antagonize him too much."

We crossed the room and greeted this Napier we'd come

to meet. He was good-sized, with a heavy tightness to him that made it hard to tell if it was fat or muscle beneath his turtleneck, a match for the one the staff wore. He had carefully mussed hair, and carefully curated stubble on his cheeks. He and Gellica embraced in the distant manner of the extremely wealthy.

We slid into the booth, setting down our drinks.

"Thank you for speaking with us," she said.

"Dear heart," he said. "I never turn away a woman who brings me wine."

"It's your bar," she replied. "That means it's free booze and you pocket the profit. I'm paying you to drink."

"I suspect you want a bit more than a drink," he said before turning his attention to me. He placed his elbows on the table and steepled his fingers, looking me over like I was a tibron beetle at auction.

"Gellica," he said, with a bit of breathy excitement. "Is this who I think it is?"

Behind us, the artist continued to share the crowd's secrets. "It was my aunt. But I kept watching. I could have backed away and closed the door, but I stayed, eye pressed to the crack in the door as she went through my parents' dresser, drawer by drawer. Searching for something." He fell silent again.

"I'm looking for a girl," I said.

Napier interlocked his fingers and rested his chin on his hands, indicating his interest with raised eyebrows. I took it as a good sign.

"Mollenkampi," I said. "Young. Artist. A newcomer. Probably hoping to break onto the scene."

"A bit vague." The man puckered his lips, a playful denial. "Any more details than that?"

I reached into my coat pocket and retrieved Jane's photo. "She looks like this, now."

The playfulness vanished as Napier pulled back. His eyes flashed to Gellica's face. She wasn't smiling, either.

"You knew her." I said it with total certainty. Napier wouldn't have been much of a poker player.

"I met her." He stared at the photo, slowly reaching to touch it, as if it were a fragile flower. He stared for one heartbeat, then another.

"Poor child," he said finally. "I can't help you with this." He slid the photo back across the table, though I made no move to pick it up.

"What's her name?" I said.

He hesitated. "It was . . ." Chewing his lip, considering his words carefully before speaking to an unknown cop and a powerful political player. I didn't blame him. Not for that, at least. Finally he said, "There are so many aspiring creative souls who come to Titanshade."

"Bullshit." It was the kind of thing I'd say, but Gellica had beat me to it.

Napier blinked, taken aback, before breaking out the dimples again. "My dear, you know me."

"Yes." She folded her arms and pressed her back into the fabric of the booth seat. "I also know when I'm getting smoke blown up my backside. Titanshade has its charms, and it even has performers." She nodded to the man on-stage, keeping an audience in rapt attention with their own secrets. "But it's never," she said, "under any circumstances, been the place where artists go to break big."

Napier was silent, and I certainly wasn't going to interrupt.

"For that they go to Fracinica," she said. "Or Cloud-swar, or down past the Southern Crossing. Not up north to live beside the roughnecks and oil tycoons." She tucked an errant curl behind her ear, casually indifferent to Napier's indignation. "So a new face on the scene would catch your eye. Especially if that face was young and pretty."

I pushed the photo back over the table. "Look again," I said. "Look real hard."

Napier sighed. "I never said I didn't remember *her*, only that I don't know her name." He straightened the photo, as if it were displayed on his gallery wall. "She came round here. A young, pretty Mollenkampi showing off a portfolio of political satire. Good work, but not saleable in the current market. Completely ungrounded in reality, fascinated by the Titan First crowd and misty-eyed about the coming new age of manna."

"When was this?"

"Oh . . . Three, four nights ago?"

Only a couple of days before Jane had been killed.

I started to speak, but Napier continued.

"What I'm saying is that she was interesting," he said. "But not so interesting that I bothered to learn who she was or where she lived, or anything else you want to know."

"She never told you her name?" I said.

"I'm sure she did," he said, underscoring the words with a put-upon sigh. "But you have to understand, I meet hundreds of people at every opening. Despite what your distinguished friend may think." He batted his eyes in Gellica's direction. "There's no shortage of new faces, but there's a distinct shortage of healthy brain cells to remember them with." He punctuated the sentiment by downing the remnants of his wineglass.

I grunted. "Did she show any interest in particular artwork?"

Napier shrugged.

"What about artists?" asked Gellica. "Did she try to network?"

Napier hesitated, then nodded. "I did notice her talking to Lillian Moller." He leaned toward Gellica. "Are you familiar with her work? Mixed media, lots of garish colors that disorient the viewer. It appears simple at first, but it's actually—"

"Spell the name," I said. And he did, though only after another annoyed sigh. I asked for an address, but he balked.

"I have no idea. But!" He raised a palm, as if holding my next question at bay. "I'm sure I have one in my files. I'll have my assistant check and pass it on."

I nodded and tapped my notepad. "And where were you the night before last?"

The trick in dropping questions like that is to wait until they've already volunteered everything they're gonna volunteer. That lets you keep the disclosures separated from the panicked responses. But Napier didn't rise to it.

"Here, of course. Well into the night."

"And lots of people saw you?"

His lips curled. "It's my job to be seen. I'll send their names when I have Lillian's contact information."

It was the best we'd get from him. We said our thanks—or at least Gellica did—and left Napier to his wine. As we walked away, Gellica glanced over the assemblage of fashionably dressed art lovers.

"You want to talk to anyone else?"

Across the room Mitri Tenebrae's trim silhouette moved gracefully from one wealthy patron to another. As if drawn by my gaze, he turned and, when he recognized Gellica, raised a well-tailored arm.

"No," I said. "Let's get out of here."

We walked through the crowd, angling our shoulders to pass through the press of patronage. The crowd slowed our progress, and before long Tenebrae had caught up to us.

"Calling it a night, Envoy?"

His fingers rested between Gellica's shoulder blades, teeth gleaming in the club lights. I caught a strong whiff of flower petals. Tenebrae's cravat was not only embroidered with magical runes, it was perfumed. Not too shocking for a newcomer, who hadn't grown up with the sulfur smell of the Titan's agony creeping through the geo-vents.

"Afraid so," she answered, her voice just as charming as his.

"You're coming to my event, of course?" he said. "Just a discreet gathering of people who'd like to see the city and its resources used appropriately. Quaddro evening, at my apartment."

"I wouldn't miss it," she said. "If my schedule allows." It seemed like a dig at Tenebrae, or at least I decided to view it that way.

"Sounds great," I said, not willing to completely cede the conversation to the interloper. "Looking forward to it."

"Of course." Tenebrae blinked, looking as though he'd already forgotten who I was.

"Are you still planning to stay through Titan's Day?" she asked.

"Oh, yes," he said. "I want to be here for the special election, and I don't want to make several trips." His grin tightened, turning into something a little darker. "Travel is always tough on me."

"I understand," said Gellica. "I'll see you in two days, then."

"I look forward to it." His chiseled features lit up as he walked away, slipping back into the crowd.

"Travel's tough on him?" I said.

"He was in an accident when he was younger," she said. "Lots of reconstructive surgery."

"Huh." I craned my neck, catching another glimpse of Tenebrae's wide shoulders and trim waist. "They did a pretty good job of it." I thought of Donnie's sorcerer Micah, and the old friend who'd approached her. "Telescribe Communications, huh?" We were almost to the door, squeezing past the throng at the bar. "Is that—"

A face in the crowd caught my attention.

The young woman who'd been arguing with her companion stood to the side of the bar, eyes downcast, not far from the men's room. As if she'd been told to sit and stay until her date returned. I told myself it wasn't my business.

I was able to go another three paces before I touched Gellica's arm.

"Hang on," I said. "I'll be right back."

When I approached, the young woman looked up then immediately dropped her eyes.

"Hi," I said. "I got separated from my date. Do you know where the women's room is?"

"Over there." She glanced in that direction, raising and turning her head. Revealing a bruise the size and shape of a large olive under the bend of her right jaw. The kind of bruise left by a man's thumb.

I jumped back to eye contact, not letting her know I'd seen it. But I fished my badge out of my pocket and showed it to her, hidden from prying eyes by the flap of my jacket. Her eyes darted toward the men's room as if afraid her companion might suddenly reappear.

"Look," I said. "If there's anything else you want to tell me, go ahead. It doesn't need to be on the record."

She half smiled. "I don't know what that'd be." Shaking her head, blinking, looking anything but sincere.

"Alright," I said. "Here's my card." I flipped it over and scribbled the name of a patrol cop I knew. "If you'd rather talk to a woman, ask for Cardamom. She'd be interested in listening."

The card disappeared into the woman's purse, and she turned away from me, breathing fast. She didn't thank me, but she didn't throw it away either. It was probably the best

I could hope for. There's no place in this world for saviors, but—sometimes—people can save themselves.

I returned to Gellica, who greeted me with a raise of her brow. "What was that?"

"Nothing," I said.

"Didn't look like nothing."

I gestured to the door. "We should get you home."

"Yes," she said. "We should."

She took my hand and walked ahead, leading me to the way out.

We shared a taxi when we left, and the ride was quiet. When we pulled up to her home, I told the driver to wait while I walked Gellica to the door. When she reached the stoop she paused and turned to me. Waiting.

"Thanks," I said.

"It was fun," she said.

"Well." I took a breath. "Maybe we can do it again sometime?" I hadn't meant for it to come out like a question, and my voice cracked like a preteen. But I at least managed to smile. When something embarrassing happens, there's nothing for it but to keep blundering ahead. Which describes most of my life, if you get down to it.

"What are you doing now?" She leaned against the doorframe, fingers idling lightly across the knob.

I wanted to take that step, close the gap between us, and I knew she wanted me, too. I looked into her eyes and my heart picked up its pace. She tilted her head, emphasizing her sharp cheekbones and dimpled chin. Those features that were such a clear echo of Paulus.

Paulus, who'd almost destroyed and discarded Talena's life. Paulus, who'd forced my face into the carpet, the howling rage of her sorcery deafening as she prepared to crush the life out of me. I looked at Gellica and wanted to take that step, to close that gap, but my foot didn't move.

"I'm gonna talk to this Lillian Moller lady," I said. "See what she's got to say."

Gellica winced. "No, I meant—" She shook her head and smiled thinly at a joke only she could hear. "Forget it," she said, then opened her door. She hesitated on the threshold, not quite making eye contact as the alarm system's warning chime sounded its countdown. The metallic threads of her dress shimmered in the glow of the streetlights. "I had fun tonight."

"Me too," I said. "I meant it, about maybe doing it again. You know," I attempted a casual laugh, "sometime when I'm not worried about dead girls and justice."

Lips pursed, she said, "So not anytime soon."

I opened my mouth, but found I had nothing to say.

She slipped through the door. "Good night, Detective." The click of the latch punctuated her sentence, and I was left alone with my memories on her front stoop.

12

ANY SITUATION, NO MATTER HOW awkward or embarrassing, can immediately be made worse by a pep talk from a taxi driver.

"Hey, my friend," the driver looked at me in the rearview. "No luck back there, huh? Too bad, because, you know . . ." He shook one hand in the air, whipping it back and forth. A gesture that had absolutely no meaning to me, but seemed intended to bolster my good spirits. "That lady! Right?"

I didn't answer, and he tried again. "Maybe I should take you to good club, yeah? It's still early. Try again, you know? They say no man climbs the Mount on his first try. Fall down, get up and try again. What d'you say?"

We were headed back to my place, the air getting colder as we worked our way leeward, the shadowy shape of the Mount to our backs. I had no desire to go out and mingle with other people. I wanted to go home, listen to some music, scratch Rumple's ears, and fall asleep on the couch. Preferably with a beer in my hand.

But the way I'd ended the evening with Gellica meant that I'd be up for hours unless I did something to banish it from my mind. I pulled my jacket tighter and heard the crinkle of paper in the pocket. I thought of the massive mural Jane had been working on in the alley, and how it included political players from the 24th Ward. Players like the CaCuris. Napier had told us Jane had been fascinated with the Titan First crowd, and I wondered if there was anything to be found there. Advice I'd given Jax more than once floated back to my mind: *Know the victim, and you'll know the killer.* I glanced at my watch. It was still early, after all.

I unfolded the flier I'd taken from the imp-costumed teens and handed it to the cabbie.

The rally was well underway by the time I arrived, the hall full of lights and people, while outside a handful of wary patrol cops eyed the group of protesters on the far side of a barricade. I moved inside quickly, mindful of Bryyh's admonition to stay out of the limelight.

Inside, the stage was dominated by Catherine CaCuri and a pack of doe-eyed sycophants. Far more interesting to me was the makeup of the crowd. Judging from the moderately layered clothes, a good portion of them were probably paying their tithe to their neighborhood boss. What surprised me was the number of attendees who seemed out of place. Middle- and upper-class types mingled with the locals, and there was a smattering of roughnecks and folks who'd clearly gone straight to the rally after getting off work. The variety of clothing indicated that they weren't all 24th Ward people, and that CaCuri's message resonated farther than I'd suspected.

I pushed my way to the far end of the hall and found a spot close to the stage, under an overhanging sign that pointed the way to the men's rooms.

"Now this is an interesting development." The voice in my ear oozed with self-satisfaction. I turned, and found myself next to a lanky human and a Mollenkampi, both dressed in layers and wearing press badges. I recognized Taran Glouchester and his photographer, the SOBs from the *Union Record* who'd branded me a rogue cop, then hailed me as a hero once the prevailing winds had changed. Glouchester smirked and the photographer carried her camera with the same ease that a soldier holds a rifle.

"Are you here in an official capacity?" he asked. "Or are you just showing your support for the CaCuris in the special election?"

I didn't respond. Glouchester followed my gaze to the stage, where Katie CaCuri worked the crowd.

"Yeah, quite a show. Young Katie seems to be doing well, wouldn't you say?"

"No comment."

CaCuri wore more layers than she really needed for the neighborhood, and certainly more than she needed considering that she stood in the glare of the stage lights. But the fur trim set off her profile, and the thick coat over a light jacket made a statement about her connection to the working poor of all neighborhoods, to the cleaners and teachers and factory workers who kept the city alive. People who'd depended on the once-mighty oil fields, their production now halted; people who'd believed the discovery of manna would finally stop the city's tailspin, until the AFS seized control of the strike. Her brother Thomas was nowhere to be seen. He clung to the wings, hiding in the pools of darkness. Someone who did his best work in the shadows. Just like me.

"This kind of thing isn't your usual beat," I said to Glouchester, not looking away from the stage.

"We'll see." He scanned the crowd, absorbing details. "More interesting now that you're here. Let's memorialize it. Klare?"

The photographer twisted, angling her body to pop a photo of me. Her eyes crinkled, and she let out a high-pitched whistle as she raised the camera again. "One more for the morning edition!"

I turned my back but she pivoted, moving around to my other side to get the shot.

The flashes got the attention of the crowd, and people turned to look. That in turn drew more attention, more flashes, more photos of the manna strike cop at a political rally. I needed to fade away before I did something that finally gave Bryyh a coronary.

Onstage, Catherine CaCuri peered in my direction.

"Can we get some lights on the crowd, please?" No lights came up, and she repeated herself. "I mean it, put some lights on this crowd." She pointed at the sea of upturned faces. "This is Titanshade's true real heart and soul, right out here." She appealed to the very crowd she was praising, "Am I right?"

The crowd rumbled, and a series of spotlights came to

life. Shading my eyes, I could see that they were set fixtures that weren't on a swivel. Whatever she was up to had been preplanned.

She scanned the faces in the crowd. Her delight in the spotlight seemed genuine enough. I wondered how long she'd been craving the attention, pulling strings from the background and grinding her teeth as the puppets got the applause.

"Out in this crowd we have people from Old Orchard and Camden Terrace. People from the Estates and the Skytrails. We have—" She cut off, staring at me. Then she broke out in a wide grin. "We have a true hero here tonight. Friends, say hello to the man who helped ring in the new age of Titanshade. Say hello to the man who was there when the drills struck manna!"

The crowd cheered, and people in my vicinity edged away, letting the spotlight settle on me.

"Come up here, Detective!" Her amplified voice boomed out, "Come on!"

There was no way I was going up onstage, but I also didn't know what to do. I waved at everyone, immediately regretting the motion as the sight of my mangled fingers set them off again.

Crowds love two- and three-syllable cadences, and for a brief, vertiginous moment, the walls echoed with chants of *"Car-ter, Car-ter!"*

Katie's grin fell ever so slightly as the crowd chanted my name. She raised her hands, settling them down. Her words from our earlier meeting came back to me: *Our base loves you.*

"That's the kind of citizen Titanshade needs," she said. "Not demanding VIP treatment. A man who wants to get the job done, and doesn't need special recognition to do it." Ignoring the fact that special recognition was exactly what she was giving me, but the crowd went along with it.

Beside me Klare snapped more photos, the spotlight reflecting off her polished head plates as her partner grinned and watched from the crowd. I did my best to keep my features neutral, and listened to CaCuri whip the crowd into a frenzy.

"So how do we bring that attitude to the halls of power?"

Katie spoke with a finger raised, answering her own question. "By paying attention to the details. By insisting that your politicians, your leaders, your *public servants* prioritize Titanshade businesses and goods. Titanshade's citizens deserve to be treated as priority *number one*." The slightest twist of her hand, and the raised finger turned from questioning to insistent, a statement of priority. The crowd began to cheer.

Speaking louder she declared, "Titanshade . . ." Hand still raised, she pulled the finger back into a clenched fist, extended into the air. "Titan *First*!"

The applause and cheers morphed into wild support and adulation. She had them. I was forgotten, along with the milquetoast politicians at her side. Catherine CaCuri was a natural star, and she beamed as cheers echoed in the hall: *"Tri-ple C! Tri-ple C!"*

Katie stalked back and forth across the stage, one hand cradling the mic, the other outstretched to the crowd as she called out, "How many roughnecks in the audience tonight?"

There was a rousing cheer, which I knew was louder than the numbers might indicate. If my old man had been any indication, a typical oil field roughneck made about twice as much noise as a normal person. Three times, if they didn't wear their hearing protection often enough.

"And how many of you got laid off when the Squibs started buying up the oil wells?" Again there were yells, more subdued this time.

"You were all told that you'd get jobs on the wind farms, yeah?" She nodded, biting her lip. "I know that's what they told me. *'We'll take care of our roughnecks,'* they said. *'We won't forget who built this town,'* they said." Katie scowled, her eyes flashing. "And now that they found the manna, where are the jobs? Not on any wind farm, that's for damn sure."

True enough, the Squibs' foreign investment was on the back burner, now that the AFS had declared the fields a national security issue. It would be fought in court, but in the meantime, there was very little work to be had on the ice plains.

Her voice dripped with disappointment. "I'll tell you what," she said. "There was a time when Titanshaders were known as roughnecks," she said. "We were known as the toughest sons of bitches in the civilized world!" Cheers again. Everyone likes to romanticize their own history.

"So why are we rolling over now?" She paced the stage, a wild animal behind bars, with a glint in her eye that said that maybe it wasn't her who was in the cage. "Why are we letting the soft southerners tell us how to run our own house?" Katie pivoted, pointing into the audience. "If someone breaks into your home, to steal your property? What do you do?" She didn't give anyone time to shout a coherent answer. "I'll tell you what I'd do—I'd kick their ass and send them packing!"

The crowd surged, cheering. I had to admit, it sounded good. But the people stealing the manna strike were in the halls of government, on City Council and the AFS, not the streets of Titanshade. I tried to tune out the rhetoric and focus on the reason I'd come: looking at the crowd through Jane's eyes. I searched for whatever it was she'd been fascinated by, the thing that had driven her to draw these people on buildings and in notebooks.

"If they won't do it for us," Katie pointed over her shoulder, back toward the Mount and the wealthy city center, "then we'll have to do it for ourselves!"

Cheers again, raised fists mimicking her earlier gesture. I wondered what drew Jane's eye to the CaCuris and their followers. Was it fear, hatred, or an artist's desire for empathy? I also wondered how the crowd would have reacted to her, a newcomer, attending a rally like this one.

"They're coming in from Fracinica." Katie gave the AFS capital a sneering sibilance. "They're coming in from Norgaerev." Even the longtime ally of Titanshade sounded sinister on Katie's lips. "They're coming in from everywhere, like a lottery winner's new best friends. And why did they come? To take *your* jobs. To take *your* homes. To take *your* share of the manna."

Boos and hissing from the crowd. I pictured them confronting Jane after hearing Katie's speech, imagined the insults and objects they'd hurl at her. Or would they refrain, holding their real anger for the politicians responsible for freezing the oil drilling, and the resultant lack of steady paychecks?

"The Squibs. The Fracinicans." Katie listed her chosen scapegoats with loathing and disdain. "The Therreau. The newcomer leeches and manna-swipes. When you see them in the street, in your stores, when you see them in the bars and in food pantries, you tell them . . ." She raised her voice to a scream, "You tell them Titanshade is for Titanshaders!"

Fist raised, a symbol of defiance, the long tail of her coat whipped around her and the crowd ate up every minute of it.

She stormed off the stage, past the flustered politicians, and into the role of professional fearmonger.

To my right, Glouchester grinned at his photographer. "Did you get a shot of Mister Popular in the spotlight?"

I winced, imagining what Captain Bryyh would say about my night out. The photographer nodded, and gave me a friendly nudge with her elbow—a polite gesture from an opponent who knew she had me beat.

Glouchester patted his belly and cackled. "Too bad Thomas hasn't beaten anyone to death in public for a while. That would make this little gathering more interesting."

The wording caught my attention. "Did you say in *public*?"

The reporter wiped a hand across his mouth, as though he'd just finished a burger on the run. "Oh, yeah. No one talks about it, but that's the only serious time he's done. He was ten, a nasty little shit even back then. Went everywhere with his twin sister and their older brother, Roger. Real tight family, loyal, best of friends, all the usual bullshit. Until one day Roger started picking on Thomas."

"He hadn't before then?" I asked. "Doesn't sound like most big brothers I've known."

"Maybe." Glouchester scowled. He didn't like to have his stories interrupted. "Maybe the brother was only big in age, not size. Could be that day Roger said exactly the wrong thing. Regardless, young Thomas didn't take well to it. He got his hands on his brother and started swinging." The newsman mimicked a slow-motion roundhouse punch. "And he didn't stop until dear old Roger was dead."

I whistled, low and appreciative, to encourage him to continue.

"It was such a vicious killing, the City Attorney tried Thomas as an adult," he said. "Only one thing saved him.

Ten-year-old Catherine stood in court, in front of all those adults, and testified that their beloved brother Roger had been out of control. She swore Thomas acted in self-defense, that he saved both their lives. She lied so well he got away with monitoring and probation. It's worked out for them since then, the brains and the monster on a leash." He gestured at the rally hall, the crowds who'd filled it. "Katie and Thomas united. And there ain't no living person coming between those two."

I chewed my lip, considering that story. Something didn't quite line up. Glouchester mistook my expression for shock.

"Didn't know about that, huh? Don't beat yourself up. The files are sealed and it was a long time ago. But hey, she probably saved her brother's life! A good deed, if you ignore the part about covering up her older brother's murder."

The crowd was dispersing, the occasional cheers of "triple-C" still being thrown about. Klare lifted her camera, snapping a few shots of the rapidly emptying hall and Titan First banners slumping toward the stage boards.

"Let's get backstage." Glouchester bounced on the balls of his feet, scrapping for another fight. "I got some questions to hit Katie with that'll get some great reaction shots. C'mon!" The two of them jogged away, leaving me in a rapidly dwindling sea of Titanshaders, each one eager to trade their fears for anger, and hang the result on the nearest scapegoat. But just because people are afraid of something, does that make it less real? The drilling freeze and manna seizure were concrete facts, and had pushed the city into a delicate, dangerous balance: unable to reap the benefits of the windfall, yet prevented from going back to life as normal. The manna strike had been a lifeline thrown to a city full of desperate people, and now it seemed like it was being pulled away just when it was within our reach.

I wandered out of the rally building and past the barricade, the police holding back protesters chanting angry slogans of love and acceptance. I scanned the faces, quickly turning my back when I saw a woman who might have been Talena near the front, leading the cheers and pumping her fist, a stark counterpoint to the figure Katie CaCuri had cut onstage. If it was Talena, I didn't want her to think I'd been there to support a mobster's political aspirations. I also needed time to process what I'd heard. I didn't like the CaCuris, and I certainly didn't trust them. They were preying on fear, but those fears stemmed from real issues. People were already suffering because of the drilling freeze, and even Gellica had admitted that there was talk in the AFS of nationalizing the manna strike. Was it better to have Paulus and the AFS running roughshod over the city, or a home-grown street thug in power?

I walked the streets as I thought, winding mountwise toward the warmer neighborhoods at the city's core. I considered heading home or to the Bunker, but the thought of either was unappealing after listening to the frenzied cheers of CaCuri's supporters. Especially after I'd found myself wondering if they were right. So I went with my always-present backup plan: I looked for someplace I could buy a drink.

13

WHEN AN ANIMAL IS WOUNDED and needs to regroup, it retreats to its den, a place where it feels safe licking its wounds and plotting revenge. Me? I go to a bar.

My favorite stop, Mickey the Finn's, was a bit of a hike, but I figured that anyplace that had beer and sandwiches would do in a pinch. So I slipped into a middle-of-the-road place on the south side of Planchette Avenue and took a seat at a wobbly two-seat table with a view of the door.

Perched on my chair, I laid out my notebook and flipped through the pages. It was an old habit driven half by hope that the answers would magically reveal themselves to me, and half from the knowledge that the truth was in there waiting for me to find it, buried under a half ton of lies, deceit, and distractions.

But in the pages of scribbles I found only the story of a forgotten woman in an alley, murdered and mutilated while no one could be bothered to remember her name. Maybe she knew an artist, maybe she was in an alley frequented by drug dealers. Or maybe she simply got caught up in the gang wars and political schisms that seemed to be tearing the city apart.

When the waiter appeared I gave my order and scanned the bar. The group across from me had cleared out, giving me a view of a corner table I'd overlooked when I entered. Detective Hemingway was there, beer in hand as she flipped through page after page of carbon copies. She already had smudged fingers and a dark mark on her nose where she'd absentmindedly scratched an itch. I had a minute to myself before my drink arrived, and if I didn't say anything, it was only a matter of time before she spotted me. So I headed over. It's always better to feel like a loser on your own schedule, rather than someone else's.

It's been pointed out more than once that I have a limited set of people skills. I can bore a killer into incriminating himself. I can cajole a blackmailer into revealing how they obtained the dirt on their victim. And I could irritate friends and family enough that they stop inviting me to parties. But I'm not so great at talking to people who are angry at me. And Hemingway? She was angry.

She was having a beer and sandwich with her new partner, a small-framed Mollenkampi named Andre. He was a nebbishy type, with bright red suspenders and a pair of armless glasses pinched on the bridge of his nose. I clapped him on the shoulder and led with my usual charm.

"Fuck off for a while, would ya, pal?"

Andre pulled himself up to his maximum height, mandibles spasming in anger. Hemingway put a hand on his arm.

"It's okay," she said.

I pulled out some cash and placed it on the table. "Get yourself and your partner another round. My treat."

He shot me a look full of nails and broken glass, but he went. Once I was alone with Hemingway, I started in on my pitch.

"I know exactly how you feel," I said. Her frown deepened, and it was downhill from there. She sat silently, eyes narrowed, sipping her beer as I gave reason after reason why I was sorry. But when I said I was hurt that she was angry with me—

"Oh, no." She put her drink down hard enough to slop some foam onto the table. "You don't get to do that. You don't get to play the victim."

"I'm not," I insisted. "I understand why . . ." I bit my lip. "You're right to hate me. Hells, sometimes I hate me."

"Uh-uh," she said, squaring her shoulders. "Let's get this straight. I don't hate you, I don't pity you, and I sure as Hells don't need to make you feel better about yourself."

I raised my hands. "Okay."

Hemingway's lips pulled back. "Myris is dead. She was a great cop, and my friend, and she's dead. And you know what?" She pointed at me. "If she were here, and you asked her to go back into that death trap again, she would. She'd do it every time, even knowing that she wouldn't walk out. Because that's what we do." She grabbed the sandwich in front of her, hard enough to squeeze pink dressing out its side and over her fingers. "We keep people alive. But that doesn't mean I gotta like it. And that doesn't mean I don't miss her. When I see you, I remember. And when I remember, it hurts. So pardon the Hells out of me if I don't want to hurt."

I was silent. One hand on the back of her partner's empty barstool, the other shoved uselessly into a pocket.

Hemingway tore off a bite and dropped the rest of her sandwich back on the plate. "Do you need me to go over that again?"

"No." I might have been a needy bastard, but Hemingway wasn't obliged to heal on my terms.

She wiped her hands and I stood there a moment longer, wanting to say something else and knowing I should simply shut my mouth and go. Which is when the crashing and shouting started.

Hemingway's head snapped up, scanning the room. I turned and looked out the front windows of the bar. There were shapes visible on the street, figures pushing and shoving, screams of anger and then screams of fear.

I broke into a run, throwing open the door with my shoulder and failing to thank the Titan for his warmth as I passed the vent. I hit the street and paused, assessing the scene. Two soldiers in uniform were ringed by a crowd, facing down four times their number. In the street was an overturned Therreau wagon, the tibron beetle that had pulled it sprawled on its side, powerful legs kicking the air, each capped with tarsal hooks that could easily disembowel an unobservant passerby. With pale faces and frightened eyes, a Therreau family struggled to get clear of the wreckage.

Hemingway was past me in a flash, wading into the chaos, pulling back gawkers and raising her voice to call for

order. She was a good cop. Better than me. I didn't intend
to let her down again.

I plunged into the crowd. The men around the soldiers
were swaying on their feet. Faces flushed, dopey grins on
two of them. Clearly drunk. The soldiers were likely on
leave, but their faces were drawn, serious. Not drunk, or at
least not enough to lose their faculties.

There was no obstacle in the road by the overturned
cart. There wasn't another vehicle in contact with it or
showing damage. What had it hit? I stepped in, dodging
the legs of the tibron beetle as it tried to right itself, and
guided one of the Therreau women away from the crash.
She hustled away with me, a child clinging to the fabric of
her long dress. The other woman still scrambled in the
shadow of the cart.

"Jameson!" she screamed.

The crowd roared as one of the drunks swung at a soldier. The soldier was smaller, but she was faster and better
trained than her attacker. The drunk was suddenly on his
ass, clutching his nose with a self-pitying moan.

"Jameson!" The woman's voice cracked as she scrambled along the cart, unable to get past the flailing legs of
the beetle as it attempted to regain its footing. Tibron beetles never cease moving, working their legs from the moment they crawl from their egg sacs to the day they die.
Their frenzy always made Therreau cart crashes dangerous. And this one's desperation to return to the road was
threatening to tear the cart to pieces.

I joined the woman, grabbed her by the shoulder. She
broke free, surprisingly strong, still screaming "Jameson!"
Then I saw who she was calling to.

Beneath the cart a middle-aged man was pinned to the
cobblestones. The buckboard of the cart lay across his upper legs, and each sway of the beetle's body turned the
cart's frame, grinding it into the ground and coming closer
to tearing the man open. The man's eyes were wide, and
bloody foam speckled his lips. Even if I could free him,
there was almost no chance he'd live.

Almost was better than nothing.

I slammed my shoulder into the heavy wood frame. The
cart barely budged. How drunk had those bastards been to

flip this thing? I tried again, this time with my head over
the edge. The woman had stopped screaming and joined
me in pushing at the wooden bulk. Another group of soldiers streamed out of the bar, joining their friends. Across
the street the other bars were emptying as well, drunk and
rowdy revelers taking sides in the fight, joining in or cheering on the chaos. Several were dressed as imps, embold-
ened by their anonymity. Hemingway appeared for a
moment, badge in hand, ordering people back. Then she
was gone, lost in the press of the crowd.

I left the Therreau woman's side, ignoring her screams
as she called me a coward, and ran toward the struggling
beetle. Rather than trying to heft an impossible weight, I
dodged between the beetle's madly swinging legs and
scrabbled for the leather straps that tied it to the cart.
Around me the screaming had grown louder. Sirens wailed
in the distance, headed my way but still too far. I pressed
closer to the beetle, safe from its legs in the space behind
its back. Up close I could see the many-colored flecks decorating the deep matte blue of its shell, and I could smell
the bug shit that had tumbled out of the waste sling in its
struggles.

I dug my fingers into the straps around the beetle's car-
apace. They were far too strong to tear, but they also hadn't
been designed to hold the weight of a suspended tibron
beetle. I focused on the weak spot: the stitching that held
the straps taut against the draglines. I fumbled into my
pocket, pulling out my pencil and jamming it between the
two pieces of leather. I pulled, adding my weight to the
dragline as I used the pencil as a lever against the almost-
broken stitching. The leather gave, but before it popped
free the pencil shattered in my hand before the job was
done. Desperate, I searched for a replacement, finding
what I needed on the ground—one wheel had shattered
when the cart toppled, sending debris across the street. I
bent, scooped up a slender piece of metal, and tried the
draglines again. This time the stitching ripped free and the
straps gave way.

I threw myself to the side, rolling onto my back, avoiding the beetle as its full weight hit the ground with a heavy
crack. The dragline I'd torn free flapped on the cobble-

stones, but the other held fast, and the beetle latched on to it with two legs, using it and the girth strap around its front to pull itself upright. Never ceasing its movement, the beetle surged forward, pulled to the right by the remaining dragline. My breathing space evaporated and I pressed tight against the cart, then climbed on top of it to avoid being crushed between the beetle and the heavy wooden frame.

The wagon didn't right itself, but it pivoted long enough for the woman and a pair of passersby to pull Jameson's shattered body out from underneath the sideboard. The beetle's clockwise path pulled the cart in a tight circle, turning on the flat of one wheel, screeching and keening as wood and metal scraped against the street.

Balancing on the buckboard, ignoring the blood on the seat, I stared out over the crowd. They didn't press close—even the most drunk and foolhardy fell back before the onslaught of several hundred pounds of wooden cart and angry beetle. All eyes were on me. I had the briefest of windows to stop this stupidity before it got any worse.

I raised my mangled hand high, letting everyone get a look at it. Letting everyone know it was that damn fool cop they'd seen on TV. It had the effect I'd hoped—everyone moved back, staying out of the big bug's way.

"That's right!" I yelled. "Calm down and back away." The sirens were closer now, the crimson shirts of the patrol coming to restore order. But other vehicles were already on scene. Men and women piled out of labeled vans in pairs. Some wore sweatshirts and held cameras, others had perfect hair and held microphones. News folk.

"Go home!" I told the crowd. "Anyone who stays and fights is going to jail."

I stayed on the cart, drawn round and round in tight circles, each orbit accompanied by the screech of metal and wood against stone. I stared down at the belligerents, and one by one they dropped their eyes. Hemingway and Andre stood side by side, facing the crowd, ready to protect each other's backs if things got ugly again. Andre had taken a solid blow to his face; his cheek was swollen and blood dribbled down his shirt.

I wondered if this was really what it took to keep people

from dividing into tribes and killing each other. A figurehead on a destroyed wagon, a night of violent rage.

My anger flared—if that was the secret to keeping the peace, that's what they were going to get.

"Get the Hells out of here and go on with your lives! Deal with the new world, because it's the only one you've got." I scanned the crowd from the back of the cart as I was dragged past their upturned faces like a bug on a turntable. Their expressions ranged from anger, to shock and resentment, to the thrill of an adrenaline rush. It brought home what I should have already realized: that even if a problem is real, even if the strike occupation was hurting the city and everyone in it, there was no excuse for making any group stand as scapegoats.

I stared into the cameras, knowing full well my face would be on the television, that the city would see me. That the fools in imp costumes and clenched fist logos would have to listen to my voice. That the CaCuris would hear what I had to say.

"Titanshade," I drawled, "you should be ashamed of yourself."

Police vehicles had finally arrived, and patrol cops streamed out. Someone yelled, "Redbacks!" and the crowd fell back. The crimson-clad patrol formed a cordon down the middle of the crowd, reaching the center and spanning out. They circled the wagon, giving me breathing room. I stepped down from the cart, escaping the glare of the news lights and finding refuge behind a wall of patrol cops.

I didn't know if I'd done the right thing, but I hoped that for once I'd made a difference.

14

IGNORED MY ALARM THE NEXT morning. And when my pager started buzzing, I ignored that as well. Partly because I was exhausted from a late night of paperwork and giving statements, partly because I knew that when I showed up at the Bunker I was in for a speech. Maybe more than one, depending on how many of Bryyh's superiors decided to come down to personally scold me for making a fool of myself in public.

But when I got there, the shit didn't come from the brass. It came from the other cops in the Bullpen.

Sitting in a place of pride on my desk was a toilet plunger, painted gold and decorated with glitter. A bow had been made out of the *Union Record* article that showed me at the CaCuri rally, and a card taped to the plunger's handle proclaimed me *Official Cart Inspector*. The press might have decided that declaring me a hero was the best way to sell papers, but my peers remained unconvinced.

"Great," I said into the roomful of smirks and chuckles. "Screw you all very much."

I set the plunger aside and took my seat across from Ajax as he swilled his morning caffeine.

"Eventful night?" he asked.

I started dialing a number on the desk phone. "Got a lead on Jane."

He perked up, and stopped riffling the stack of papers on his desk. But I put him off as my call went through.

Dungan picked up the other end of the line. When he recognized my voice, he broke into a howl of laughter.

"I thought you were supposed to be low profile," he managed to get out between guffaws. "You think TV coverage fits that description?"

"It'll be fine," I said, keeping an eye out for Bryyh's scowling face. "You get that footage from the alleyway security camera?"

Dungan cleared his throat and there was a rustling noise, as if he'd pulled the receiver in closer to the shoulder of his windbreaker.

"No-go on that," he said. "I talked to the super, but there's nothing useful I can pass on to you."

"What does that mean?" I said. "Let me see it and I'll decide if it's useful or not."

Dungan sighed. "Sorry, pal. The camera was hooked to a recorder set to loop. It'd already been taped over by the time I got to him."

I spoke through clenched teeth, doing my best to keep my volume under control. "This is bullshit! We met your damn CI like you asked."

"I know you did," he said. "Which is why I asked for the video. But there's nothing to give you." He sighed. "If I find something that'll help you out, I'll let you know."

Across from me, Ajax leaned forward, arms crossed on his desk, head shaking as he listened in.

I tried again. "Our deal was—"

"That you'd talk to my CI and I'd let you keep your Jane Doe," said Dungan. "You held up your end, and I'll hold up mine. So you can keep the JD, but the tape's something else entirely. Now listen, I gotta go. Next time I see you in Hammer Head's, I'll buy a round. Later, Carter."

The line cut off, leaving a ghostly static crackle whispering in my ear. I cradled the receiver and looked at my partner.

"You believe him?" he said. The resigned disappointment on Jax's face made Dungan's reversal even more painful.

"I don't know. It seems . . ." I leaned back, trying to ward off a tension headache by stretching the knotted muscles at the base of my neck.

"You said you had a lead on Jane." Jax changed the subject, giving me some mental breathing room. "Tell me about that."

So I filled him in on Napier and the mystery artist. When I finished the end of my story, he sat silently, absorbing everything I'd said, watching me with wide eyes.

"So . . ." He took a deep breath. "You went on a date with Gellica?"

"No," I said. "We went to an art show hearing. Happening. Whatever it's called."

"Because it sounds like a date."

"It wasn't a—"

"Did you have dinner, too?"

I rubbed my temples. "The point is that as soon as we have contact info on the artist, we talk to her. And in the meantime we check out Napier. Have any other would-be artists disappeared? Does he have a history of violence?" I raised my voice as my desk phone began to ring. "We finally have something to do, and that doesn't include worrying about who I spend my social time with." I snatched up the receiver and barked a hello.

When I heard the voice on the line, I checked my tone to be far more friendly. "Oh, good morning, Susan!"

It always paid to be polite to Doc Mumphrey's assistant. After a few words with Susan I hung up and turned my attention back to Jax. "Good news. We're going to the body stacks, kid."

Over time, any detective worth a damn builds a network of experts to turn to for help and advice. In my years on the force I'd come to rely on an extensive list of specialists and eccentrics. People like Big Mike, the pawn-shop owner on Gaius Street who could identify any kind of weapon or antique imaginable; or Lori Tompkins, who specialized in psychotic disorders and was willing to exchange consulting work for making her traffic violations evaporate. And then there was Doc Mumphrey, the senior staff pathologist for the Titanshade PD.

Mumphrey was an institution at the Bunker. Whether you needed to find out what route a body had taken before being stashed or just needed someone to sit in on a hand of poker, Mumphrey was your guy. He had an encyclopedia's worth of knowledge squeezed into his head, and he loved gnawing on new puzzles.

We found him in the ME's offices, in a back examination room, conducting an autopsy on an elderly human. With a red-handed wave he shooed us into the small office in back. I glanced at Jax, and found him standing stock-still and wide-eyed. Detectives are frequently confronted with death, but we rarely see medical pathologists at work. And while seeing a corpse is one thing, watching someone root around inside of it is another. So it was a relief to retreat to Mumphrey's office; the examination room was all stainless steel and bone saws, but back in the doc's little spot of sanity it was earth tones and books. Of course it still stank like formaldehyde. That was one smell you didn't escape quite so easily.

This was Jax's first visit to this part of the Bunker. He'd been on desk duty as long as I had, and our earlier work hadn't brought us into direct contact with the ME's office. He peered at the samples and historic medical instruments that Mumphrey collected as decorations. With strange shapes and obscure uses, the tools ranged from cringe-inducing to downright malevolent. The collection may have been part of the reason why most detectives preferred to read the medical examiner's reports rather than pay a personal visit to the body stacks.

After a moment, Mumphrey joined us in the office. He was wearing a paper apron made of the same waxed material as the booties we wore at gory crime scenes. He unclipped the apron and dropped it into the medical waste bin by the door; even in Titanshade you can't recycle everything. Then he gave us a wide grin.

"I don't believe I've had the pleasure of making this young man's acquaintance." Doc Mumphrey's baritone rumbled like a bowling ball toward a 7–10 split, deep and resonant but with a congested tone and swallowed vowels.

I was careful to accentuate my words as I made introductions.

"Doc Mumphrey, please meet my partner, Detective Ajax."

Mumphrey extended a hand that had been in a corpse moments before. "Pleasure to meet you, Detective."

Ajax gripped Doc's hand with only the slightest hesitation, admirable considering how recently he'd seen that hand inside a corpse.

"Likewise. I understand that Carter thinks you might have something to tell us about our Jane Doe?"

Mumphrey's smile faltered. "I'm sorry. I didn't quite catch that." He tilted his gray-ringed head toward me. "Could you . . . ?"

I slid out my notebook and flipped to an empty page. "He said we want to talk about the Jane Doe that rolled in yesterday, Doc." To Ajax, I added, "You don't have any lips for him to read. Give him the murder book."

Jax hesitated. "What do you mean?"

"He's deaf," I said.

"Mostly deaf," corrected Mumphrey. "Hearing aids help, but I don't like to wear them in the examination rooms since I can't adjust them because, well . . ." He wriggled the fingers of one hand, summoning the image of body-fluid-covered gloves. "Anyway, I get by, but I may miss a word or two."

"Right," I said. "Jax, give him the package so he can do his thing."

We'd stopped by the evidence room and tech lab, picking up the suspected murder weapon and crime scene photos. Mumphrey could've requested them himself before the autopsy, but we sped the process from a matter of days to a few hours by walking them down ourselves.

Ajax passed over the file. Doc went straight to the possible murder weapon. The evidence bag was mostly paper, to allow the blood to dry and prevent mold growth, with a plastic window to allow inspection without contact. Mumphrey pulled the bag taut, smoothing its wrinkles as he peered at the thin cylinder with a small spike at one end and a paddle at the other.

"My, my. Look at that."

His eyes danced, taking in the materials, condition, everything. I wiggled my fingers on the edge of his vision to get his attention.

"Safe to say it's what caused the neck wound?" I asked.

I watched his eyes to see if he followed me. If needed, I could supplement my words with the odd bit of sign language. I wasn't anywhere close to fluent, but I'd picked up a few signs from Mumphrey over the years. Things like *Explain,* and *Why?* and *Vodka or gin?* The bare essentials for police work.

"I'd assume so," he said. "It certainly matches the size and shape of the puncture. You found this where?"

I fanned the crime scene photos across his desk, pointing out the one that showed the gore-covered weapon on the ground.

"I'm thinking the killer tossed it to the side," I said, though I might as well have saved my breath. Mumphrey was engrossed in the photos, and wasn't aware I was speaking. Jax's eyes were on me and I gave him a shrug—we'd have to wait for the doc to be ready to talk on his own time.

"Hmm." He flipped back to the photos. "The blunt trauma was severe, and not caused by a direct blow from a fist, but you probably surmised as much. No sign of sexual assault, and I've sent the prints off, so you should be hearing back in a day or two. The more interesting wounds were to the face. Specifically the left mandible and both sets of jaws."

"Did you—" I paused, wiggling my fingers again to get his attention. "Doc, did you say *both* sets of jaws?"

He gave a curt nod. "Yes. The left palp mandible had been removed, along with the lower front left cuspid from the biting jaw and a pair of cuspids from her esophageal dentition." Mumphrey never missed a chance to use eight syllables when two would do.

"Wait a minute," I said, processing the description. "Teeth were missing from her speaking mouth?"

"That's right," he said.

"So someone reached into her speaking mouth and pulled out teeth?"

To my left, Ajax held one hand to his speaking mouth, as if imagining the pain involved, and his biting jaw was slack with shock. I turned back to Mumphrey.

"How is that even possible?"

"Well, with this." He broke the seal on the evidence bag and dropped the metal implement into one palm, comparing it to the photos. "Even when fully dilated, the Mollenkampi speaking mouth is only the size of a half-tael coin.

There was minimal damage to the outside of the speaking mouth. It would have been very difficult to see in the alley light," he added, as if to make us feel better. "This dental spatula," he indicated the metal tool, "opened up enough of a wound to give access to the victim's speaking mouth. We probably should place it against the corpse, to be—"

"Hold up," I interrupted him. "Did you say dental spatula?"

Mumphrey nodded. "Dentists and technicians use them to clean off plaque." He blinked. "You have been to a dentist, correct?"

I shifted in my chair. "Yeah, but I don't pay attention to the scrapers they're using." In truth, I usually squeezed my eyes shut and wished the whole thing was over. I pointed at Ajax. "He didn't know what it was, either."

My partner raised his hands defensively. "My dentist uses tools that are . . . more aggressive." He tapped a tusk with one mandible.

I attempted to refocus Doc Mumphrey. "Okay, the murder weapon was used to pull out her teeth."

"Oh, no," he said. "It wasn't the puncture wound that killed her. She was killed by the head trauma."

"Does that mean the killer came back to finish her off and rip out her teeth?"

"That's right." Mumphrey pulled an evidence label from his desk. He signed the label, then used it to reseal the possible murder weapon.

"But the way the body was searched, the killer was looking for something," said Jax. "Or killers?"

I nodded. "Someone might have come along and taken her teeth later."

Mumphrey interjected. "Not much later. The teeth were removed immediately after death. Possibly before, but I expect I'd have found more signs of struggle if that were the case."

At least Jane hadn't had to live through that torture. Though the mention of struggle jarred a memory.

"Doc," I said. "The techs said it looked like there was debris under her nails. Anything to go on there?"

"No," said Mumphrey. "Nothing useful under her nails, but there was residue in the throat puncture wound. Human, brown skin tone. Judging from the location I'd say it tore off when they pulled out her teeth, though I can't guarantee it."

"You think it left a mark?"

"Certainly. Not requiring stitches, but it'll take some time to heal. Your killer likely has one torn-up hand." He perked up. "Oh! I do have the autopsy photo. I assume you'd like a copy?" He stepped out to the examination rooms, presumably headed toward the more administrative offices of the medical examiner. When he returned, he carried a glossy head shot of Jane's cleaned body. It was slightly better to see her like that. She was still pale and motionless on the slab, but it was at least more dignified than the crime scene photos we'd been carrying around. "Sorry I couldn't be more help," he said.

Now that the autopsy was over, she'd be put into the system. If we didn't learn her name and contact her family, she'd be processed and disposed of without formality or respect.

I turned to Ajax. "Is there any reason you can think of—"

"To collect teeth?" he said. "Absolutely not."

I stared up at the pocked surface of Mumphrey's ceiling. How was I going to tell Bryyh that we had a homicidal dentist on the loose? I could already imagine the headlines.

"As long as we're here, Doc, do you got time for a few other questions?" When Mumphrey didn't object I went on.

"You should have the body of Cetus St. Beisht in the queue," I said. "Gillmyn. The body'll be in your waiting parlor shortly, if it's not there already."

"Already done." Mumphrey folded his hands and sat beaming behind his desk. "It was a priority rush."

"Pushed him to the top of the line," I said. "Ahead of everyone else."

Mumphrey's smile faded. "The same way I moved your Jane Doe. Only I put up with a distinct lack of paperwork on your end."

There was a bad taste in my mouth. It still staggered me how much justice depended on the dead having the right friends. "Otherwise Jane would have sat untouched."

Mumphrey sat perfectly still.

"I must be misunderstanding," he said. "You couldn't possibly be implying that I'd ignore a patient."

I inhaled deeply, regretting my words.

"Because," he continued, the nasal tones in his voice becoming more pronounced as his temper flared. "I'd have to point out—*again*—that I pulled your Jane Doe from the queue ahead of dozens of other homicide victims."

"Yes," I said.

"And each one of those victims has a family, and every one of them deserves closure."

"Yes," I said again.

"So you certainly aren't implying that I don't care about my patients." He breathed out through his nostrils, a snort of indignation.

"I didn't mean it like that," I said. "I only—" I ran a weary hand over my face. "I didn't mean anything, Doc. I'm sorry, okay?"

He chewed the whiskers on his lower lip, which at least meant he was done yelling at me.

"What did you learn from St. Beisht's body?" I asked.

Mumphrey harrumphed. "From that mess? Hardly worth my time."

"It's worth mine, Doc. Did you get anything at all?"

"Well . . ." He looked at the ceiling with half-closed eyes, as if mentally reexamining the victim. "The body'd been moved, that's for sure." He trailed off, probably mentally cutting into the corpse again.

Beside me, Jax's head popped up, and he looked at me. He started to ask a question, then caught himself and began writing in his notepad.

I got Mumphrey's attention with a finger wave. "OCU thinks the murder happened in the laundry room," I said. "And the body dumped straight into the washer."

Mumphrey ruffled his shirtfront, the way a diner might sweep away crumbs after a meal. "Hardly."

Ajax held his pad in Mumphrey's line of sight. *The stain,* he'd written. *On the floor.*

"Oh, I don't doubt that the poor fellow was on the floor at one point," Doc said. "I've seen the crime scene photos, and the blood sample collected matches the victim's." He steepled his fingers, probably relishing the role of wise old dispenser of knowledge. "But the body as found didn't have near enough blood in it, even accounting for what was lost in the wash and on that floor. No, I suspect that the victim was killed and dismembered elsewhere before being brought to the laundry facility." He peered at Ajax and myself. "Unless you found more fluids somewhere in the vicinity?"

We hadn't, and apparently neither had the techs. Mumphrey nodded, as if his expectations were confirmed.

"A bit lucky on it," he said. "If the person who discovered the body had found it later, or had left the machine running while they called it in . . ." He shrugged. "Well, I'd have had a much harder go of knowing for sure."

"Pretty specific act," said Ajax. "And a strange place to stick the body."

I squinted, trying to recall the layout of the building. It's not like the washing machine was a good hiding spot. If the killer didn't care about the body being found, why not simply dump it in an alley, or trash can, or almost anywhere other than an apartment building laundry room?

"What about time of death?" I asked Mumphrey.

"I'd put it around half a day before the body was found," he said. "Can't swear to it, though. By the time I got the remains, they'd already been tainted."

"Tainted?"

Mumphrey winced. "That wasn't the best choice of words."

"Doc . . ." I leaned forward. There was nowhere I was going to let him slide.

He fidgeted with his pen, clicking it open and closed. "The techs." He cleared his throat. "I'm not sure what happened there. The OCU techs are normally top rate. Professional and careful."

"But not this time," I prodded.

He tossed the pen onto the desk. "No. There were enough mistakes and errors that it could throw the whole process into doubt. No single thing was blatant, but everything as a whole?" He shook his head. "Any good lawyer could find enough mistakes there to scrap every bit of evidence. We're not going to get a conviction using anything gathered from that crime scene."

"Was this on purpose?" I leaned forward in my chair, feeling like the ground threatened to open up beneath me, as Dungan's behavior and withholding the videotape took on new meaning.

"I certainly wouldn't imagine it was," he said, then hesitated. "I can't swear to it either way. Sometimes you get two different teams of techs. Might have been the result of a pissing contest. Or each team thought the other had the requisite checks in place." He rubbed his hands together, as if he were scrubbing down for surgery. "Either way, it's a messy affair."

A mess that seemed coordinated. Jax stared at me, unasked questions evident in his eyes.

"Thanks, Doc," I said as I stood. "You've given us a lot to go on."

Doc Mumphrey stood. "My office is always open," he said. "And let me know the next time you can make poker night. I always enjoy separating you from your paycheck."

We moved toward the door of his office. "Carter, a word before you go?" Mumphrey glanced at Ajax's back.

I let Jax pull ahead of me while I leaned in to hear what the Doc had to say.

"How're you holding up?" He peered into my eyes. "Are you good on painkillers?"

Mumphrey had given me meds back when I still suffered leg pain—now a thing of the past.

"I'm great, Doc," I said. "Pain's all gone. But thank you."

He smiled and patted my shoulder.

"One question though," I said. "The other day I had some tingling here." I raised my left hand, displaying the stumps of my two missing fingers. "I've had some sensations before, but this was different."

"Different how?"

I glanced back at Jax. He was giving us some space to talk, but I still lowered my voice.

"I don't know," I said, trying not to get my hopes up. Both Guyer and Gellica had said the explanation wasn't magical, so maybe it was physical. And that meant maybe it wasn't all in my head. "Like it came from *inside* my hand, not from the damage. That make sense?"

Doc pursed his lips. I could tell the answer was *No*. I walked away before he had a chance to say the words, moving to catch up with Jax as I wondered what the Hells was wrong with me.

15

A S JAX AND I BEGAN the march back to Homicide, I decided to tackle the most pressing issue at hand.

"Wanna grab a bite?" I asked.

"You're hungry?" Jax stared at me. "Your buddy Mumphrey just dropped a bombshell on us and you want to get food." He made a chittering noise, agitation clear in his narrowed eyes. "We went through this same let's-not-talk-about-it routine after Dungan first leaned on us. We're not doing that again." He pulled out his handkerchief and swiped at a tusk. "Also, you should've told me Mumphrey's deaf."

"He's good to call if you need a sign language interpreter," I said. "But don't play poker with him. He's never rattled by the trash talk."

"Nice to know," Jax said. "What we need to discuss is what he said about the techs at the St. Beisht crime scene. Because to me, that sounds like they're covering for someone. Add that to Dungan shutting down our access to the video surveillance . . ." He spread his arms, his implication clear as we reached the third floor.

"Oh, I know. Believe me, I know. But we're gonna get that video, and we're gonna find out what's going on with Dungan." We paused by the wall-mounted mailboxes at the periphery of the Bullpen. "This isn't the kind of thing we can let slide unchallenged."

I peered into my mailbox, hoping to find a message from Napier about the artist's contact info. Instead there was a hand-written note on plain paper, the message in Captain

Bryyh's crisp and easily decipherable handwriting. *See me. Now.*

I showed it to Jax.

"We'll talk later," I said. "Gotta go get my daily dose of chastisement."

When I reached Bryyh's office I found Guyer sitting in the chair across from the captain, one sandal half off, kicking a foot as she laughed.

"Don't get me started!" she said. "Have you watched *Eileen Quinby, DO*? They throw manna around like it's confetti. I have three different forms to fill out before any usage gets approved, and even then I have to account for every drop. Half the time I testify in court I have to explain to the jury that magic isn't found on every corner."

I rapped on the doorframe. "You mean the cop shows on TV aren't accurate?" I raised my brows. "I think my innocence may be shattered forever."

Bryyh waved me inside, saying to Guyer, "Excuse me while I talk to our local celebrity."

I winced, and Guyer stood. "No problem," she said. "I need to follow up on a few things while I'm here. I'll be on the floor if you need me."

Bryyh nodded, though she was already eyeing me and chewing her lip. "Close the door on your way out."

I slipped into the seat Guyer had vacated, mentally prepping myself for the speech I expected to receive.

When the door shut, Bryyh clasped her hands and took a breath. The smile she'd worn when talking with Guyer had faded completely. Once again I was struck by the droop in her cheeks and bloodshot whites of her eyes.

"First of all," she said, clearing her throat. "I want to tell you that you did the right thing in the moment."

My stomach tightened. Compliments weren't Bryyh's strong suit.

"What I don't get," she continued, a little heat entering her voice, "is why you felt the need to make a speech afterward."

I had no intention of talking about the CaCuris, but I didn't need to worry: Bryyh had no interest in hearing my comments anyway.

"Frankly," she said, "the riot was the only thing that

kept your appearance at a political rally from being bigger news."

"I was at the rally to observe. CaCuri made a thing of it."

"Which is exactly why I told you to not attract attention." She spread her hands across the desk, palms down, as if she were trying to hold it to the ground. "Imp's tits, Carter! I don't worry about you having opinions, you're allowed to think your own thoughts. What I worry about is other people latching on to you." She grimaced. "It'll pass. This kind of thing always does. But until then, you need to keep your head down. It doesn't help anyone if you drag department resources into your orbit."

"I don't have an orbit," I said.

"Everyone does," she snapped. "The question is whether the hassle of dealing with it outweighs your contribution to the force."

I slumped backward, rocking my chair onto its back legs. "How many of the drunks are being charged?"

"Two."

I raised my brows, but she waved off my concerns.

"Hells, Carter, we're not going to pretend it never happened. But there's a bigger picture to consider. The officers on scene were a little more concerned about getting the crowd dispersed before they had a full riot on their hands."

She was right. If the situation had escalated, there'd only have been more violence, more victims in the hospital. And it's not like I'd arrested anyone, or interviewed the witnesses. I'd been bundled up and hauled out of there as fast as possible. In the same way that a paramedic has to stabilize a victim before bringing them into the hospital, the redbacks present had opted to get me out of the crowd's eye before processing the situation.

"In the same way," she said, "I need you to get off the brass's radar." She slipped a departmental form out from under a paperweight. It was an assignment sheet, like I'd been given when moved to desk duty after the manna strike. "I'm putting you on NICI data entry for two weeks."

"What?" I stood, shocked and angry. "You're punishing me for doing the right thing?"

"No one's punishing you. I'm worried that you're overly focused on your single case." She tapped a finger on the assignment sheet and exhaled loudly. "And I need you out of my hair while I clean up after your performance."

"Performance? I was at the scene of—"

"You stood in front of a half-dozen news crews and told the city to be ashamed of themselves."

She had a point. And I couldn't tell her the message was for the CaCuris unless I ratted out Dungan and whatever he was working on. Though I also didn't know if Dungan was worth protecting anymore. Basically, it had all gone to Hells like everything in Titanshade did, sooner or later.

Bryyh was still talking.

"Where do you think I spent my morning? I've been in front of the brass for hours, explaining that you just happened to be in the wrong place at the wrong time."

"So putting me on NICI isn't your idea?"

She ignored the question. "This isn't a full-time switch. I only need you to lie low for a few days. You're still free to work your Jane Doe case, make phone calls, whatever. As long as you do it where no one sees you. Don't show up on the news or irritate other departments or whatever it is that you do most days." She paused, and stared at me. "This is what I convinced them would work. This *needs* to work. Can you handle that?"

I fumed. I didn't want to sit at a computer terminal, blindly pecking at a rubber chiclet keyboard. I wanted to be left alone to do my job.

"Carter?"

I released my legs, letting the chair drop forward. "Yeah, I can handle that." I took the assignment sheet, doing my best to not snatch it out of her hand. "Am I excused?"

Bryyh's forehead creased. "You know how many open requests I have from officers looking to transfer to Homicide?"

I didn't answer.

"Twenty-eight." She held my gaze. "There are patrol cops who've been pushing a cruiser for more than a decade, waiting for their chance to move to a new assignment. There's no rule that says I can't transfer who I want in and out of my department. I've gone to the mat for you more than once. Don't make me regret it."

I left her office, assignment sheet clenched in my fist. Jax was at our tandem desks, standing as he ended a phone call. He squinted as I paced, resisting the impulse to punt my trash basket across the room.

"How 'bout I grab a couple sodas," he said. "Then you can tell me how screwed you are."

He headed toward the hallway vending machines, and I tried to settle myself with a few controlled breaths. Across the Bullpen I spotted Guyer, studying the big board with Hemingway and Andre.

I made my way over and hovered until they acknowledged my presence. Andre didn't seem happy to see me, but he wasn't openly hostile, and Hemingway even favored me with a polite nod. Her normal ponytail was absent, blond hair loose at her shoulders, not quite hiding the bruises she'd picked up while holding back the crowd the previous night. Andre, too, was sporting a bandage along his cheek. Neither of them had been featured in the coverage of the near-riot. It was the kind of thing that contributed to the hostile gazes I normally received from my peers.

The press loved to talk about the daring raid that helped return manna to the world. They didn't like to talk about the death toll. Myris and dozens of rig workers had lost their lives, men and women who hadn't done anything to deserve their fates. Maybe the press didn't talk up Hemingway because her partner's death made her less heroic in their eyes. Maybe it was the same reason the newspapers referred to her as a "female detective." Or maybe it was a cost-saving measure—all that extra ink from the word "female" probably made her more expensive to write about.

"Can I borrow you for a minute?" I asked Guyer. "I want to show you something."

She made her excuses to Hemingway and followed me to my desk, where the golden plunger still occupied a prominent position.

"You must be so proud," she cooed. It was worth it to see a bit of humor in her face.

"You said you'd look at this." I chucked the plunger beneath the desk and opened up the Jane Doe murder book. When I got to the photos, Guyer dropped her smile and leaned closer.

"Shit." She flipped through the photos. "It'd take a lot of force to take off a chunk of her jaw." She looked at the murder book's cover. "Jane Doe on Ringsridge Road? I got cc'd on the lab work for this one."

"And?" I hadn't seen the results yet. Another joy of governmental bureaucracy.

She nodded. "The liquid on the shards of glass came back manna-positive, mixed with angel tears. Whoever it belonged to had actual snake oil."

"Could this damage be magic?" I managed to keep my voice even. Whatever I was dealing with, it apparently wasn't triggered by touching manna. Was it all in my head after all? I had a brief, nervous moment as I worried that Baelen might get wind of my inquiries and pull me in for observation.

"Don't know." She squinted at the photos that showed the damage to Jane's face. "The teeth, they could be used for a divination or communication spell. But this?" She indicated Jane's missing palp mandible. "Mandibles aren't used for speech. So whoever took it didn't know Mollenkampi very well. Or they weren't thinking clearly."

"Wait a minute," I said. "You said divination or communication. What kind of communication?"

"The top secret kind. It's one of the biggest uses for manna in the military, diplomacy, high finance. That kind of thing."

I thought of Tenebrae, Gellica's handsome friend at the art gallery. She'd said he was involved in long-distance communications. He'd also sat next to me at the table, and I knew he didn't have so much as a scratch on his manicured hands, let alone the kind of gouge Mumphrey had told us would mark Jane's killer.

Guyer slurped her coffee, then continued. "Let's say I create a bond between two trusted people, and when they speak it's like they're whispering into each other's ear. Instantaneously," she shrugged, "or close enough to it. The point is that it's totally secure. No one can eavesdrop on a manna connection."

I chewed my lip. Donnie had eavesdropped on our meet and greet with the CaCuris, thanks to his friendly sorcerer Micah. What kind of background did she have?

Guyer and I stared at the photos for a few seconds. "These ARC teams," I said. "How do I get one on this?"

She sucked in a breath through her teeth. "I'll help you

put in a request. But frankly? We're spread too thin right now. Unless we have one-hundred-percent certainty, you'll be at the bottom of the list. But if you see anything else let me know. If it is magical, you don't want to mess with it on your own."

Ajax ambled up to the desk, holding a pair of sodas. "I didn't grab one for you," he said to Guyer.

"I'm fine." The DO held her coffee high and took a deep whiff of its aroma. "Nothing's more magic than java." She patted Jane's murder book. "Good luck with this one, boys." Then she merged back into the crowd of officers milling through the Bullpen.

Jax handed me a soda and popped the tab of the other, tugging on the front rim where the metal was engineered to be weaker, allowing the round can lid to taper to a point.

"You want to look into your art dealer today?"

"Napier?" I said. "That's what I *should* be doing." I waved the assignment sheet in the air. "I've got a NICI orientation class this afternoon."

Jax examined the paperwork and whistled. "Well, on the bright side you'll . . ." He tipped his head one way, then another, searching for a silver lining. "Nah, you're gonna hate it."

"Thanks, kid." I tucked the paperwork into my top drawer. "Tell you what, how about I give you a ride to Napier's gallery, and you can try and shake the info about the artist loose."

"The one Napier saw Jane talking to?"

"That's the one. I'll circle back here and report for my orientation with NICI, and we'll compare notes tomorrow."

I hoped he'd say yes. Anything to feel like I wasn't being pushed off the one case I was permitted to work.

"Works for me," he said, and we headed out. I managed to not even look in Bryyh's direction as we left.

We walked to the garage in silence, sipping our beverages and stewing in our own thoughts. When we got to the Hasam, Jax glanced around to make sure no one was within earshot and sat on the hood. "Let's talk."

"You'll get to talk to the gallery owner," I said. "Once you get off the hood."

"Not until we talk about the OCU techs tainting the St. Beisht evidence."

He knew exactly what it meant. But he also knew Dungan was my friend, so he wasn't going to be the one to say it. Fair enough.

"Maybe Dungan was lying about how and where St. Beisht was killed," I said. "Or maybe he was just wrong. I don't know." My soda was almost gone, and I listened to the remaining liquid slosh as I waved my hand. "Either way, we can't confront him until we've got more information."

"Why not?" Jax crushed his can and tossed it into a nearby trash container. "Because it'd be awkward for you?"

"Because he can lie his way out of it," I said.

"Says a lot that you think he'll lie."

I pressed the cold metal of the soda can against my temple.

"I think everyone lies," I said. "Some people do it on purpose, some because they've lied to themselves so long they can't keep the truth straight anymore." I killed my drink, shaking the last sugary drops onto my tongue. "If you want to chase this down, we're gonna have to investigate the St. Beisht killing."

He snorted. "We *were* first Homicide on scene."

"I'm not finished." I took a breath. "Looking into St. Beisht means talking to anyone who might've wanted him dead. I know you don't want to talk about your hometown, but—"

"Again with this?"

"St. Beisht was a Harlq. If we're gonna do anything with that case, we need to talk to them. And we can't go through OCU to do it." I let what that meant sink in. "Are you willing to make that call?"

He wiped one hand across his biting mouth and stared at a point over my head. "If I have to. But *only* if I have to." He shifted his eyes to meet mine. "The real question is, are you willing to deal with Dungan if it turns out he's covering the crime?"

"What do you think?" I tossed my can toward the bin as

well. It bounced off the side and struck the ground with a
clatter. Jax stood and plucked my can off the grease-
stained concrete.

"You want to get out of here?" he said.

"Yeah," I said. "I'll drop you off so you can pay a visit
to that gallery owner. Maybe he's got a beret you can borrow."

Jax cleared his throat. "I'm not saying Dungan's dirty."
He took two paces toward the car. "Just so you know.
That's not what I'm saying."

"I know you're not, kid."

"He's got his own agenda, but that's not the same thing."
He did his best to meet my eyes, to broadcast his sincerity
right after he picked up my trash. "He can have his own
agenda. That's fine."

Jax barely turned, and tossed my can in a smooth arc. It
landed in the bin, striking his with a clink. A pair of shiny
tin cans for the trash heap, like so many shiny tin badges
that had gone there before.

He slid into the passenger seat and buckled himself in.
"It might still be good to work with him on this one."

"We'll see," I said, and started the engine. "We'll see."

16

THE REST OF MY DAY was spent in the data lab. My instructor was a muscle-bound Gillmyn named Trevor who seemed to hold two great passions in life: computer code and physical fitness. He explained the proper way to load and unload NICI's storage devices, then regaled me with tales about his favorite flavors of protein shakes as I shuffled reels of magnetic tape the size of my chest from a spindle-covered cart onto metal data machines that were taller and broader than me. NICI had been created about a decade earlier, a system to braid together the police databases of the various AFS city-states. Each of those deceptively heavy tape reels was a weekly shipment from another city-state, with a list of their case updates. Titanshade sent out weekly copies in exchange. And that's where I came in.

My two-week assignment was to type in the many sins of the city. Or at least the ones that had been reported. Trevor showed me how it worked; the pertinent details of a case were entered into a generic NICI form using specific keywords, and that was followed by a long and painful proofing process, for which we logged in to an emulator that showed us what our entries would look like to an officer from Fracinica or Gibston, or any of a number of AFS city-states. No one used NICI to look up local cases, since any local system would be more up-to-date and more convenient. Still, NICI was a way for the myriad enforcement agencies to at least share a portion of their information, such as when Jax had searched the system for attacks similar to Jane's, or for missing persons who matched her description.

At the end of the day, Trevor congratulated me on my efforts, and told me that for our next session, I'd earned the privilege of progressing to data entry. Feeling like I'd spent a day breaking electronic rocks in a prison yard, I stumbled home and spent my Friday night with a TV dinner and the new vinyl from a garage band out of Norgaerev called Imps of the Perverse.

Halfway through the album I heard an off-beat thumping, and assumed my neighbors were pounding on the wall. I cranked up the volume. When the thumping persisted, I realized it was someone knocking on my door. I padded over and peered through the peephole. Jax and Talena stood in the hallway. I froze. I didn't want to talk to them, didn't want to hear from anyone who'd shower me with pity. I considered simply standing silently until they left. Talena threw her head back and flashed an obscene gesture.

"We can see your shadow under the door," she said. Beside her, Jax held a bag of takeout big enough for three.

I slipped open my locks and let them in.

Talena and Jax spread the takeout across the coffee table while I wandered into the kitchen and tried to remember how to interact with houseguests.

"You want something to drink?" I opened the fridge. "I got water, and half a soda, and milk." I pulled that last from its shelf, sniffed the container, and tossed it in the trash. "No milk."

"We brought our own," Jax called from the couch, shaking a to-go cup.

I reemerged with the half soda and joined them in the part of my apartment I called a living room. "So what do you want?"

"You're welcome," said Talena.

"For what?"

"I don't know, for showing up with real food? For not letting you spend a night alone sulking about your training date with NICI?" Jax took a bite of his veggie wrap. "You need to interact with people who aren't on the force. It keeps you grounded."

I waved away the sentiment. "I see plenty of people. I don't have trouble keeping up with them."

Talena was wearing her standard issue jeans and layered shirts, but Jax had traded his suit and tie for a long sleeve shirt with a moderate weave. He'd dressed up for the visit, and I found it hard to believe that was for me. I narrowed my eyes as he and Talena sat on the couch, a hair too close for my comfort.

Rumple strolled into the room, drawn by the smell of food and familiar voices. He leapt onto the couch and gave Talena's hand a nuzzle before walking over her legs to reach Jax.

"Hey old man, good to see you, too." Talena stroked Rumple's back. Rumple had belonged to Talena's mom, and when we'd lost Jenny to cancer, I'd somehow inherited her cat. When I was in the hospital after the manna strike, Talena had stepped up to take care of him. I appreciated the gesture, especially seeing as how so many of Talena's headaches were a direct result of knowing me. But then again, she wasn't the kind of person to take out her frustrations on an animal. People, on the other hand . . .

Jax redirected Rumple's raised tail away from his chin. "So you know Talena's looking at getting permanent space?"

I turned to her. "You're buying an apartment?"

"A permanent *work* space," she said. "Somewhere for volunteers to gather and people who want help can find what they need."

"As long as what they need includes a speech about the Path?" I asked. Talena's desire to help was sincere, but was intertwined with her belief that religion was the best, most lasting way to assist those in need.

She let the dig slide off her back, which surprised me. I was surprised again by how much she'd mellowed since her brush with poisoning. "If they want, but more like how to file a complaint about utility services, or how to register to vote. There's more people coming into the city every day, and it's not getting any easier for them to start a life here."

"Because of the CaCuris?"

"They didn't create the anger," she said. "But they're exploiting it. You can't throw gas on an already burning building and claim you're not an arsonist."

"Not sure that distinction matters to the Therreau family in the hospital," I said, and took a swig of my soda.

Talena sat up a little straighter. "By the way . . . Standing up to the crowd and calling out their bullshit? You did the right thing."

"People keep telling me that. Be nice if doing the right thing wasn't hazardous to my career."

Jax's laughter was resonant and rolling. "Carter, everything you do is hazardous to your career!"

Talena smiled. "No, I mean it! Things are tense out there. At this point, even tiny acts stand out and make a difference."

Humming through his biting mouth, Jax nodded. "*A single star shines all the brighter in the blackest of nights.*"

The unchecked optimism almost made me choke on my soda. "There're no stars in Titanshade." I wiped a hand across my chin. "And the only lights in town advertise what's for sale."

Ignoring me, Talena looked at Jax through narrowed eyes. "Was that from a poem?"

Jax's eyes crinkled, and he couldn't hide his delight that she'd caught one of his references. "From Robeson's final collection. I have a first edition."

She laughed. "You are *such* a nerd."

His eyes smoothed, and he shifted in his seat, but she grinned wider and leaned in his direction. "I didn't say it was a bad thing."

I looked at Talena, thinking of all the ways she offered assistance and friendship to the most vulnerable, no matter how many times that kindness was rejected. For a moment, I wondered if I was wrong about the stars in Titanshade.

The conversation drifted, and at some point I simply relaxed and watched the two of them talk. It was surprisingly pleasant.

Talena gestured with her hands as she spoke. She wore a bracelet in the shape of a ba, the figure eight that symbolized our eternal trek on the Path, and with each emphatic statement it caught and reflected the light from the lamp and television. Talena's faith had arisen with no urging from me. I'd never given myself to much belief in anything I couldn't grab and throttle with my own hands.

"Oh!" Jax struggled to reach his back pocket without dumping Rumple, who was perched on his lap. "You never asked how the visit to The Lotus Petal went."

"Well?"

"Pretty much how you'd expect. Napier fobbed me off on an assistant, who was happy to gossip once her boss was out of the room. Most of what she said confirms what he told you—tons of fresh faces in the gallery, new artists hoping to make a name. Hard to remember details of any one person."

"Great," I muttered.

"But—" He finally managed to reach into his pocket, despite Rumple doing his best impression of a blanket. "Thought you'd want to see this." He flipped open his notepad and tossed it in my direction.

I caught it and rotated it upright. There, in Ajax's neat handwriting, was Lillian Moller's name and address. The artist Napier had seen Jane talking to. I broke into a grin, delighted to finally have something we could work with, rather than more rumor and innuendo.

"Finally!" I swung the notepad overhead like a trophy. "First thing tomorrow we're gonna pay this lady a visit."

"Not quite first thing. You've got class with NICI tomorrow." Jax's eyes crinkled, betraying his amusement.

Talena's attention had wandered, apparently settling on the Jane Doe murder book that leaned against the side of the couch. She lifted it, and out spilled the collection of photos and documents that painted a view of a young woman's death. Talena slid the crime scene photos to one side, lips curling into a frown as she saw Jane's corpse, lit by flashbulbs and surrounded by bright red crime scene markers. The next photo was of the setting. Talena lifted that photo and stared.

"I've seen these before," she said. "It's good. The mural, I mean."

I nodded. I'd intended to ask her about Jane's art before we'd been interrupted by the attack on the street vendor. "She can really draw."

"No," Talena said. "I mean—yeah. But what's powerful is the message."

"Message?" I sat straighter.

"She's talking about the occupation of the city, and denying people the ability to feed themselves."

Jax peered over her shoulder. "This is about the military camp?"

"The occupation," Talena repeated. "This," she tapped the broad-jawed woman at the side, "is Colonel Marbury, from the AFS occupation force, and this," she moved a finger to indicate a family of Mollenkampi, "is clearly the Mount."

I raised an eyebrow. "Run that last one by me again."

"Look how they're posed, in that roughly two-peaked triangle. You think that's by accident?" I'd looked at the wall and seen skillful renderings of recognizable faces, but as Talena expounded on the intricacies of the mural, it became clear that every choice Jane made had a purpose, every pose and shade told a hidden story. Up until that moment, it had never occurred to me that art could lie.

"The message," said Talena, "is that denying someone the ability to use their resources is unethical."

"Like sending someone home when they're trying to solve a murder?" I said.

Talena smirked. "Sure. But here," she indicated the shadows in the background, "this is everyone else who could use that food, those resources."

"The bigger picture," Jax said quietly. He set Rumple aside, then walked into the kitchen to help himself to a water.

Talena favored him with a smile, one that carried a distinct warmth. "It's a shitty thing to use resources without regard for the wider world." She looked back in my direction. "Kind of like plunging ahead with no regard for how your actions will affect others."

"So who's right?" I asked. "Who does Jane think should eat, the people who own the food or the strangers in the shadows?"

"Both," she said. "Everyone should get to eat."

Irritated, I shook the photo in the air. "But you said—"

"I said there's a *message*, Carter. I didn't say there was an answer."

Jax slid back onto the couch beside Talena before allowing Rumple to reclaim his perch. "You learn something?"

"Yeah." I tossed the photo back on the table. "I don't like art."

Public drawings of people who represented other things was a nice concept, but it didn't get me any closer to finding who'd killed Jane. And a message without meaning didn't tell me a damn thing.

"Well, I'm glad that's settled," said Talena. "We should go. I didn't want to come at all, but your partner made me."

I looked at Jax, who only shrugged. "I thought you might need a couple friendly faces. And I *knew* you'd need something decent to eat."

They stood to go. Rumple showed his displeasure by stalking into the corner to groom himself.

"Thanks for coming by." For once, I didn't qualify the statement.

"Well," said Jax, "stop showing up on the front pages and we won't have to."

"So tomorrow," I said. "Are you gonna—"

Jax cut me off. "I'll run a background on Napier, make sure we're not missing anything. We'll meet up after your date with NICI and go see Moller together."

I nodded, grateful. I said good-bye and closed the door. The apartment seemed much bigger and less welcoming without them.

17

SPENT MY MORNING WITH ANOTHER long session in the computer lab, learning to hate NICI and her bizarre set of formatting demands. My respect for Jax crept a little higher as I wondered how he was able to make his brain work in a way that let him navigate the almost incomprehensible command lines and emerge with information about cases from across the Assembly of Free States. One by one I entered individual case information, having to enter each line perfectly so it'd show up in searches down the line. Then it was all captured on those machines that looked like oversized reel-to-reel tape recorders. Copies of the latest tapes were sent to all the AFS city-state police departments each week, and we received a similar tape from them. All in the name of efficient searching. It was tedious, mind numbing work, and by the time Jax showed up at the end of the day I practically ran for the door.

"Turn anything up on the gallery owner?" I asked as we approached the Hasam. I held up my hand, though my partner didn't turn over the keys.

"Tons," he said. "But nothing violent. Drug possession, some tax issues." He slid into the driver's seat. I grunted and took shotgun. "I wrote it up. Details are in the book."

I glanced in the back seat and saw the Jane Doe murder book and sketchbook lying beside his overcoat.

"Not bad," I said.

Jax turned over the engine, and the 8-track in the dash came to life. Layered vocals and a synthesized brass section blared from the Hasam, threatening to blow the speakers.

I yanked the tape out of the dash player and stared at it. A Dinah McIntire album. I tossed it in the back with the murder book.

"Seriously, you're going to give me a bad reputation driving around with you. Do you know how to get to this artist's place?"

He nodded, and pulled into traffic, almost immediately coming to a stop behind an ice truck about to make a delivery. Its hazard lights flickered as the boom crane used for hoisting ice blocks to rooftop water towers rattled to life, the crane motor spewing exhaust. Jax urged on the Hasam, and we escaped the cloud of obnoxious black smoke. I segued into a new topic.

"Tell me about this you and Talena thing," I said.

"What thing?"

"You know what thing." I crossed my arms. "You showed up at my apartment looking like a teenager on his first date."

"You think that's my idea of a date? Bringing a depressive cop fast food?" He let out a harmonized snort of derision. "I told her you were having a rough time, and we should drop in and check on you."

"How did you even know where to find her?"

"Seriously? Finding people is my job." He leaned back and looked at me through narrowed eyes. "Did you not realize I'm a detective?"

I grunted as suspiciously as I could, and kept my peace until we reached the address Jax had gotten for the artist.

Moller lived on the fifth floor of a worn brownstone in a low-rent part of town. We knocked on the door of the apartment twice, loud enough to piss off the neighbors, though none of them bothered to open their doors to find out if someone needed help. It took another minute of continuous knocking before the door jerked open and we got our first look at the occupant. A thirty-something human woman with jet black hair, falling unfashionably long and straight over her shoulders. She wore a light gray leather jacket over a pair of layered T-shirts, each pocked with strategically placed holes to give the impression of distress without having to actually expose skin to the chill air. The shirts were topped by a wool scarf and the jacket paired with black denim jeans and a belt lined with an alternating string of rifle casings and doll arms. Her boots looked to be steel-toed, but I likely wouldn't find out unless she decided to kick me. Judging from her expression, that wasn't out of the question.

I flashed my badge. "Lillian Moller?"

She didn't answer. That in itself told me several things. First, she either was or knew Lillian Moller. Second, she didn't like the police. Lastly, she didn't have so much to hide that she closed the door and went running for a phone book to find a lawyer. That meant she might work with us, as long as we handled her right.

Jax's voice was deferential as he made introductions. "I'm Detective Ajax, this is Detective Carter. We'd like to speak to you for a few minutes. Would it be possible to come in?"

"No."

"I understand if you're uncomfortable, but this will only take a moment."

"Moment's over," she said, and began to close the door.

Jax shifted gears, immediately changing his tone. "We can do this downtown, if we need to."

She smirked, as if she liked the challenge. There was something in that smile that was familiar, but I couldn't place it.

"Tell you what," she said. "Show me a warrant or break out the handcuffs. 'Cause you're not getting in without one or the other."

Jax had tried the all-business cop persona. Ordinarily not a bad strategy, but not the right choice for someone who carries all their mental armor facing authority. I tried a different route.

"It's about a girl."

She paused, waiting for me to say more. That door wasn't closed all the way, not yet.

I condensed Jane's description as best I could, figuring we wouldn't get another chance. "Young," I said. "Mollenkampi." Moller stared, unmoved. "She worked with pastels and chalk graffiti."

"Oh." The woman's lips turned up. "Her I remember." Her ghost-thin smile evaporated. "She in trouble?"

"So you knew her?"

"Not well." The door opened a little more, as she rested a shoulder against the frame. "She was here for a night."

The Jane's file and sketchbook was under my arm. I rummaged around and pulled out the morgue photo. "This her?"

Moller blinked. "Oh, Hells. I—" She let out a long sigh. "Shit. Alright, come inside." She turned abruptly and walked into her apartment, leaving Jax and me to close the door behind us.

In contrast to the rest of the neighborhood, Moller lived in a surprisingly tidy studio apartment, with the kind of quality furnishings that cost real money. Whatever she'd been doing in the art world, it was paying off.

She led us into the living area, and stood behind a wing-back chair, elbows propped on the headrest, using the furniture like a shield. Jax took a seat on the faux-fur couch, while I stood nearby, my head on a swivel as I took in the setting. The walls were covered with artwork in a range of styles, mostly modern things with slashes of color, inter-mingled with portraits of generals and queens remade with select body parts replaced by supermarket items.

"What do you want to know?" Moller had stopped sneering, but she still wasn't happy to have us there. I'd been treated worse.

"We'll start simple," I said. "What's her name?"

"Don't know." Quieter now, almost hushed.

That didn't do my temper any favors.

"Think," I said. "She must have told you."

"I just don't. I—"

"She's got a name." My words gained volume. "How can you take someone home, spend the night with them—"

"A single night." Her back straightened.

"—and not ever get around to asking their name?"

"I probably did." Her jacket buckles rattled as she stood so tall she practically strutted in place. "But that doesn't mean I remember. She wanted to go home with me." Moller forced an exaggerated leer. "You may not get that kind of attention, but I sure as Hells do."

Maybe I should have known better than to expect this woman to remember Jane. People everywhere found ways to insulate themselves with indifference.

"Fine. Okay." I waved it off. "We're not saying you know what happened to her. Just tell us what you do know so we can contact her family."

Moller pursed her lips and took a breath before speaking. "She was new to town."

"That's right," I said.

"It wasn't a question, dumbass. I'm telling you what I know about her." Moller pulled a package of belca root from her jacket pocket. She shoved a grub-like root into her cheek and bit down, muttering to herself: "Imp's blade."

I kept silent. Belca root gave users a gentle buzz. As someone who fueled my days with coffee I was in no position to judge, but the fact that she'd fallen back on it meant the conversation may have been more upsetting than she let on. I noted the lack of purple stains on her lips; that meant Moller could afford the quality stuff.

"People come to this town for a reason," she explained. "And they're not always eager to be reunited with their family. Something to consider as you stumble around on whatever crusade you're on."

I dipped my head. Point taken.

"Still," I said. "She ought to be put to rest with some dignity."

Moller stared at me long enough that I wondered what she was searching for. Finally she looked away.

"We talked," she said. "But it wasn't anything you'd find useful."

"Try us," I said.

"We got back here late," said Moller. "I don't remember what time."

"This was after you met at the gallery?" I asked.

"Yeah."

"What did you talk about while you were there?"

"Nothing that mattered." Moller picked at a hangnail. "She told me she liked my work. I told her I liked her body."

"And then?" I prodded.

"She blushed. It was cute." A smile crept back onto Moller's lips, and the sense that I'd seen her before returned. "I did the social rounds with the buyers, and she was still there at the end of the night. After that, talking wasn't exactly the goal."

"Pastels and chalk," said Jax.

Moller started, as if she'd forgotten my partner was in the room. We both looked at him.

"You remembered her when we said she worked in pastels and chalk." He tapped his notepad. "If you didn't talk, how did you know that?"

She frowned, slightly abashed. "Yeah. Look, I'm not saying we didn't talk at all, just that I don't remember much of it."

"That's okay," Jax said, and motioned for her to continue.

"She had photos of her work." Still hesitant, Moller turned her head and I saw her in profile. I realized why she looked familiar.

I reached for Jane's sketchbook and fumbled it open. Flipping through the pages, I found the drawing of the beautiful woman with hair the color of a moonless night. The corner of the page proclaimed the title: *Allura Shade*. I handed the book to our host, who cradled it in her hands as she studied the image.

Jane had focused on bringing out the beauty of her subject's eyes, the curve of her lips. The woman in the portrait held none of the cynicism and doubt that Moller wore as tightly as her leather jacket, but there was no doubt it was the same person.

"Whoever killed her is counting on nobody caring enough to remember her," I said. "Whatever you know, it might help."

Lillian stared at the drawing. She took a breath and frowned, not quite fast enough to cover the quiver of her lip.

"Fine." Moller came out from behind the chair, closing the sketchbook and shoving it into my arms as she crossed the room, making her way to a desk that sat low to the ground, a workspace appointed with typewriter, calculator, and small filing cabinet. She fished around in a cardboard inbox with decorative cutouts ringing the sides, one for each of the eight Families of the Path. A moment later she pulled out a trio of photos.

"She gave me these. Not sure what she wanted me to do

exactly, but . . ." Moller squinted at them, then nodded to herself, as though she'd taken a mental photo, before handing them over.

I examined each one before passing them to Ajax. Even my unsophisticated eye could recognize real talent. Jane had been drawing politicians, movie stars, and the manna strike on walls and sidewalks. Plenty of street artists did similar work, the kind of things that might attract passersby with a few taels to drop in their hats. But Jane's work went beyond quick caricatures and rapid portraits to pawn off on tourists. There was something there even beyond Talena's explanation of the symbolism. The portraits bit into the soul of the subject, or rather, the soul that Jane hoped they had.

"She said she wanted to see the world. Wanted to try manna." Moller's scowl softened, perhaps the hint of a pleasant memory peeking from behind her world-weary persona. "She said something about using manna in her chalks, like it would turn them into animations, or some damn thing."

"Did she try it?" My question chased the softness away, and we were back to full scowl and double the attitude.

"She did." Moller punctuated her sentence with the crackle of leather as she removed her jacket and dropped it in the seat of the chair. "She'd bought some manna. Or thought she had." The artist returned to her defensive spot behind the wingback chair, fingers weaving through the tassels at the edge of her scarf.

"Don't suppose you know who sold it to her."

"You think I missed her name but caught her dealer's?" She snorted, letting a strand of hair fall across one eye.

"Okay," said Jax. "Do you—"

"There was one thing." Lips pursed, eyes unfocused, as though she were fighting for a memory. "She bought some other stuff, supposed to be stronger. And no," she shot me a look, "I don't know who sold her that, either. Said it was some punk with a fish eye."

"A fish eye? Like it was injured, or bulged? That could mean anything."

"Whatever—it's what she said. The point is that she swore that she tried it and it made her artwork move."

"Did she have any with her the night she stayed with you? Or show you the moving art?"

"No. She had two vials. Used one, then was working on throwing up a new piece in an alley when some pretty southern boy came up and asked if she was selling manna. He was tweaked out, but she said he acted like he expected someone to be there. He flashed a wad of cash and she ended up selling him the stuff she'd picked up for ten times what she'd paid."

"Why'd she tell you this?"

"Because it's a funny story," she said. "Rich guy who looks like he walked off the cover of StyleMag ends up buying from this girl who's so new to town she's still excited to see Therreau beetle wagons in the street?" She rocked back on her heels, pulling the wingback chair onto its rear legs along with her. "What's not to love? It was how—" She bit her lip. "How she could afford to go to the gallery. How she met me."

"You never heard from her again?"

"No. Didn't expect to. It wasn't that kind of night."

I tapped the sketchbook's cover. "Maybe not for you."

Moller's lips tightened, betraying her emotions.

"She did ask if I knew any galleries with open submissions," she said. "It was a little awkward, but I get that kind of thing sometimes."

"What did you say?"

She leaned on the chair a little more, causing it to creak under her weight. "I told her I'd be in touch."

"But you didn't know how to contact her." I said it softly, without the heat of an accusation. I didn't need to.

Lillian released the chair. It fell back into place with a thump.

"No," she said, much quieter than before. "I lied to her."

We stood in silence, none of us quite sure what to say.

Finally, Jax stood and let out a gentle cough. "If you think of anything else . . ." He handed her his card.

She looked at it, considering, before dropping it into the inbox, where she'd kept the photos from the dead girl.

"So, maybe—" She struggled to form a sentence as we walked to her door. "Maybe when you find her name, you could call me."

"Maybe," I said, and passed my hand through the entry vent. "We'll be in touch."

She held my eye, not giving an inch.

"Day's Dawning, Miss Moller."

When we reached the street Jax let out a low, discordant whistle.

"What?" I demanded.

"It's sad," he said.

"Yeah, it's sad." I turned my head and spit, clearing my mouth and mind. "The whole damn thing's sad." I practiced the controlled breaths the department shrinks swore by, and stared at the window of Moller's apartment.

In a world of uncertainties, Jane had been drawn to this woman. Maybe they would've been perfect for each other. Maybe Jane was the person who could have persuaded Lillian Moller to shed some of the many layers of armor the city had forced her to wear in order to survive. Or maybe Lillian Moller was too self-absorbed to notice, and had simply racked up one more fleeting encounter. I didn't know the answer. All I could think of was Gellica's face the last time I'd seen her, and how I'd screwed up my own chance at a connection as she closed her door.

"Hey kid," I said. "I got an errand to run. Would it be all right with you if—"

"Yeah," he said. "I'll take the car back."

I tossed him the keys, and Jax caught them with a smooth, swift flash of his arm. I watched him walk away. Then I fished in my pocket for loose change. I had my own calls to make.

18

ONE OF THE PERKS OF being a detective was access to a vehicle. The taxi system in Titanshade was passable at best, and a lice-filled deathtrap the majority of the time. I'd heard that the water taxis in Fracinica navigated tourists through the canals with bouquets of flowers and the occasional serenade. In a Titanshade taxi, you crossed your fingers that the smell of urine wasn't going to be accompanied by the real thing. But life was short and you work with the hand you're dealt. And as I'd just been reminded, you have to make connections while you can. So I hopped a Ghaba taxi from Lillian Moller's neighborhood.

When I'd called Gellica's answering service I'd been told she wasn't in. I asked to be transferred to her assistant. From him I found out that Gellica was at a fundraiser. It stretched my social skills, but eventually I got the address out of him.

Arriving at the downtown address Gellica's assistant had provided, I found it to be a tony apartment building. The lobby of the Armistice was easy enough to get into, but a trio of tuxedoed gatekeepers stood at the entrance of the unit I needed to enter, armed with a roster of invited guests.

I showed my badge to the most haggard looking of the three, and let him draw his own conclusions.

"Oh!" he said. "Captain Quinlin is inside already. Go on in."

Sometimes things are shockingly easy if you keep your

mouth shut and ride the wave of other people's assumptions.

Once inside I kept to the fringes of the crowd, doing my best to avoid eye contact as I scanned the attendees. I'd have liked to blend in, but there was no way that was going to happen. The invitees were decked out in the height of conservative fashion. All the clothes were thin, demonstrating wealth, but not scandalously transparent. The neighborhood was warm enough that I kept my overcoat draped over my arm, and I smoothed the rumpled fabric of my suit coat in an attempt to appear professional.

I knew Gellica was there, and the tuxedoed lackey at the door had mentioned Captain Quinlin, the head of the OCU and Dungan's boss. That meant this was likely a political function. As I moved through the crowd of attendees there were more faces I recognized, mostly from the boring bits on the news before the sports came on. It was clear this group was more high profile than I wanted to deal with.

After a quick turn around the front area of the apartment, I still hadn't found Gellica. So I relocated, settling on a spot against the wall beside a marble statue of a rearing bull. The statue was larger than my torso and mounted on a chest-high pillar, so that its broad horns and hooves towered above me. On the plus side it kept me somewhat hidden while allowing me to eyeball the comers and goers.

There was one person in particular who seemed to be the star of the show. A human woman in her mid-thirties, she still had the energy of youth tempered by the control of experience. It took me a moment to place her face, especially since I hadn't known her name until Gellica mentioned it the other night. I'd stumbled into a fundraiser for Meredith Plunkett, the pro-AFS candidate for the 24th Ward's upcoming special election.

Plunkett passed through the crowd, drumming up support and shaking hands. Not that she had to work particularly hard. These were her people after all. Or more accurately, she was theirs. The well-dressed crowd around me were the people working in opposition to the CaCuris, a battle that would come to a head in six days, on the Titan's Day special election.

I'd witnessed the CaCuri machine in action at their rally, and the fallout their brand of fear had at the attack on the Therreau. There were far fewer people at this gathering, but probably twice the net worth. There was also less anger, less fear. The players in this room lived in a state of self-satisfied luxury. Titanshade was a town where the rich enjoyed lifestyles obtained through a hard-nosed work ethic and backbreaking labor. Just not their own.

There was another familiar face in the crowd. Detective Angus, the Bullpen's most prominent social climber, clearly couldn't pass up this opportunity. His head plates were polished to a shine and his suit looked sharp, even if the fabric was a little thick for the crowd. He was laughing and shaking hands with a rotund, generously mustached human. Angus had the kind of social grace that made my skin crawl, and I had absolutely no intention of letting him regale the Bullpen with stories of me making a fool of myself.

To avoid being seen I stepped around the intricately carved sculpture, keeping an eye on Angus through the marble bull's rear legs, where it became very clear that the sculptor had wanted no question as to the animal's masculinity. Distracted by that artistic detail, I almost ran into someone hiding on the opposite side of the bull's shadow.

"Watch your step." The woman's voice was firm but not unkind. "We can't both hide back here."

The victim of my near-collision was plain-faced and unadorned and all the more striking for it. Half a head shorter than me, she was another face I knew, though it took a moment for me to place it. From the front page of the paper, the photo with Gellica in the background, the one I'd kept coming back to. The woman had been in that photo, standing next to Paulus. I'd almost run over Colonel Marbury, the head of the AFS military force "protecting" the manna strike.

Clearly a career officer, Marbury was well into middle age, but even standing still she evidenced a channeled energy that gave her the air of a younger woman. I suspected that she'd plateaued at colonel because she preferred to be involved in the doing, rather than the deciding. The kind of person who'd push you aside from your task and do it better, simply because it pained her to witness inefficiency.

She was also eying me with dawning recognition.

"You're the cop from the manna strike . . . Parker, right?" She held out her hand. I took it without bothering to correct her. "I understand you stood with some of my troops last night."

"More like we all stood with some people who needed help."

"It shouldn't have happened at all." Her voice drew tighter. "We're not here to invade the city, despite what your local press has to say about it."

"When you're in the thick of it, you don't get the luxury of not being involved," I said. "Opting to do nothing in the face of violence is a dramatic choice."

She nodded. Probably the most effusive praise I'd get from her.

"There's a price we pay to keep the peace." She drew in a sharp breath. "I suppose that's why I attend things like this. The political machines reach right out and grab us. I'm afraid I have no end of unpleasant lunches and meetings in my future." Marbury glanced at the bull sculpture and the decorative glass candle holders that illuminated our hiding spot. The corner of her mouth crept upward. "I think we're both a little out of our element here, aren't we?"

"I guess so. I'm not planning on staying long."

"Me either," she said. "Speaking of which, have you seen our host lately? I need to check in before it gets too late." Her gaze drifted past my shoulder, scanning the crowd. It wasn't an idle motion, or a social climber's constant surveillance for more important conversational partners, as when Tenebrae had scanned the crowd at The Lotus. Like me, Marbury was looking for someone specific. And I had no intention of admitting I didn't know the host of this little gathering.

A caterer walked past, and it seemed like a good chance to step away. I mumbled a good-bye to the colonel and grabbed two glasses of champagne off the server's tray. I walked through the crowd glasses held high, body half turned as if I were delivering a drink to a friend, trusting in my speed and sense of purpose to dissuade anyone from speaking with me.

I made it through the entire room, but still didn't find

Gellica. If I hadn't gotten confirmation she was there, I'd have fled for the streets. Instead, I took a deep breath and considered my options. I'd reached a hallway leading farther into the apartment, flanked by two plants, each taller and healthier than me. I dumped the champagne into one of the planters, then handed the glasses to another caterer with a collection tray. In the middle of the crowd Angus peered in my direction. I retreated down the only unimpeded path: the darkened hallway.

Away from the wealthy attendees, I had a moment to appreciate the luxury of the apartment. Plush carpet was matched by high-end detailing like scalloped light fixtures and the tighter-weave carpeting that ran over one wall as an accent. The wall carpet was broken up by an occasional triangle-shaped slice of mirror, arranged to give the impression that the glass had been scattered across the wall.

I considered moving back into the main room but paused when a woman's familiar laugh echoed from somewhere down the hall. Could it be Gellica? I tried the handle of one door and it opened into darkness. The air was thick with the smell of damp soil. A window let in enough light for me to hit the wall switch, and I found myself in a nondescript study holding an office chair and a desk, littered with wire armatures and blocks of plastic-wrapped clay, no doubt the source of the smell. Kidney-shaped scrapers and lengths of wire capped by wooden handles lay to the side, near canvas bundles that hinted at containing tools. In my line of work, they'd be more likely used as murder weapons than to create beauty. I thought of the bull sculpture. Was this another artist's home? If so, I'd greatly misjudged the income potential of the working artist.

I took a step toward the canvas rolls but stopped when the laughter sounded again. Gellica's voice carried to me from somewhere nearby. I eased the door closed and went on farther down the hall, my steps hushed by the carpet underfoot, the sound of the crowd hushed by the carpet on the walls.

The next door's handle didn't turn, as if it had been locked by the last occupant. But that person had been lazy; the door hadn't fully latched. I hesitated. There were no voices from within, no real reason to enter. I was uncomfortable entering, but the possibility of catching my breath for a few minutes before plunging into the crowd again was more than I could resist. With a slight push the door swung open.

In this room the curtains were drawn shut, leaving it in blackness. I stepped inside and swung the door shut behind me, being careful to silently close and latch it against unexpected intrusion.

I ran the backs of my fingers up the wall on either side of the door, pausing when I stumbled into a strand of cobwebs. I exhaled slowly, telling myself that I was overthinking, and pulled my hand back slowly, disengaging from the sensation of silky webbing. A moment later I struck a light switch. With a snap, the lights came on and I found myself in a luxurious bedroom. There was a neatly made bed, a pair of dressers, what looked to be a closet, and a small rolltop desk with padlock. But the focus of the room was a massive steamer trunk that stood in one corner.

Set on end, it was taller than me and wide enough that I'd struggle to wrap my arms around a single side. Redundant locks lined the opening, several of them clearly added to the original design. Whoever owned it had either very large valuables or their share of secrets. And I've never been able to resist poking at a secret.

I crossed the room and caught another whiff of damp soil. Similar to clay, but with an undercurrent of something else. There was a luggage tag on one of the trunk's sturdy handles. I flipped it over, revealing a typed address in Fracinica followed by the owner's name: *M. Tenebrae.*

I examined the room with new eyes. Gellica had told me that Tenebrae was a sculptor, and he'd invited her to some kind of party when we'd run into him at the Lotus. This was his "small event," a gathering of the city's most wealthy and influential in a luxury apartment that I couldn't afford for a single night. More importantly, Gellica had accepted his invitation. I'd shown up to find her while she was at Tenebrae's party.

At that moment I heard Gellica's musical laugh again, along with what sounded like a man's voice. Stepping toward the sound, I moved to my right. On the dark wood of the side table sat a metal box, a lock on the box itself, and a secondary padlock holding it to the table. More secrets, more boxes. Whatever the truth, I wasn't going to be breaking it open that night. The man's voice spoke again, and I turned my attention to the desktop. A gold necklace inset with a red stone draped across a stack of correspondence, letters addressed to Tenebrae. I stooped closer, and brought my ear toward the necklace. Was it a radio receiver? As soon as I crossed over to the desk I pulled back, feeling as if I'd walked into another spiderweb, this one stretched in the air between the desk and the door. Something skittered across my skin—no, *under* my skin, and I swung my hands, moving like I'd woken to find a spider perched on my pillow.

Two steps away from the desk, my cheeks burned with embarrassment as I caught my breath. I rubbed my finger and thumb together, wincing at the echo of the cobweb sensation. Tenebrae was a sorcerer. Was the thing magic, and I was somehow feeling it? But then why hadn't I felt it around Gellica, or when I touched Guyer's cloak? I raised my hand, and tentatively moved toward the desk once more. Hand out, I waved it through the air over the desk.

Nothing.

That lack of anything was more painful than the initial feeling of cobwebs. I didn't want to feel any of these sensations, but the possibility of it being completely in my head was even worse. Trying to re-create the sensation, I bent my head over the desk once more. Still nothing. I ignored the cramping in my stomach and hovered over the necklace. No cobwebs, no voices, no weirdness at all.

I swallowed. None of it made sense. I felt like a fool, attaching deeper meaning to a tingle with absolutely no proof, standing alone in a stranger's bedroom arguing with myself. I was embarrassed and shivering, and I wanted to walk away, turn my attention to real, physical things I could put my hands on.

I slipped out of the room, footsteps once again hushed on the carpet. At the end of the hall I stared across the crowd. In a city where clothing indicated so much about the wearer's status the fabrics of suits and dresses meant as much as the expertly cut gems on the necks and fingers of the attendees. An entire economy was on pause while drilling was suspended, manna quarantined, oil running out, the potential wind farm deal scuttled indefinitely. But these people were more concerned about the tax implications than furloughed workers unable to make rent. Unlike the CaCuris, they didn't feed on hate . . . just greed. My stomach rumbled and clenched again. It seemed like the sight of them was making me sick.

I turned away. This time I turned to the left, pushing past the dark-clothed caterers and moving toward the kitchen, lit by light fixtures shaped like sea life and lined with glimmering faux-manna trim. The smell of food was strong, and I was surprised to feel hunger pangs. I tried to remember when I'd eaten last, and that was when I entered the kitchen.

Bigger than my entire apartment, it held a dazzling array of dishes and platters. An island with a sink and supplemental burners was covered with finger foods waiting to be distributed, while a surly human man in an apron and yellow rubber gloves processed the dirty dishes coming back from the front.

I caught a snippet of conversation: ". . . a new Rubrik K7 Turbo back home. When you're in Fracinica we should take it to the test track."

At the far end of the kitchen, Gellica leaned against a counter, sharing a conversation with Tenebrae. The blond man's arm was bent at his side, holding a drink. His smile was wider than hers, and she was half turned, leaning into his space.

I came to a sudden halt and stared at her like a fool gaping at a circus performer. She noticed me and stopped talking, which confused Tenebrae, who looked past me into the hall beyond, as if there surely had to be something more interesting than me to catch Gellica's eye.

She said, "Carter?" As if she needed confirmation.

I swallowed. "Envoy Gellica. I need a few minutes of your time. Police business."

Tenebrae wore a well-tailored two-piece suit. I wasn't an expert, but I was fairly certain the pin on his rune-covered tie cost more than a year's rent on my apartment.

Gellica turned to Tenebrae and put a hand on his arm.

"You remember Detective Carter from the other night at The Lotus Petal?"

The tall man's eyes widened and his smile beamed at me. He reached out a hand, and I took it without meaning to.

"So sorry we didn't have time to speak at that event." His grip was warm, firm and even. I wondered if he'd taken lessons to get it that way.

"Pretty sure we said it all." I let his hand drop. It appeared recently manicured, without so much as a cuticle damaged or out of place. A perfect match for the rest of him.

My words barely fazed him. He took it in stride and actually chuckled, as if we were old friends having a laugh. "Well, if I'd known you were *that* Carter I'd have had more to say."

His eyes twinkled, and for a moment it seemed like the most logical thing in the world that he only ignored nobodies.

I focused on Gellica. "Good to see you." I felt my cheeks redden. What the Hells was wrong with me?

She disengaged herself from Tenebrae, who scooped a metal chain and pendant from the kitchen counter and headed to the main gathering. Gellica followed me a few steps away, to the far end of the kitchen, near heavily manicured plants flanking a window that overlooked the Mount. The rent here must have been mind-boggling.

"Imp's blade, Carter. Why didn't you return my calls?" Her hands were clasped in front of her. "I saw you on the news after that Therreau cart thing. I was worried." She narrowed her eyes. "You look awful."

My mouth was dry, and her voice sounded muffled, as if there was something in my ear.

"I had to come here for work," I lied. "Wanted to say hi when I saw you." My lips kept moving, as if there were more words to be said. The flaws in my story apparent even as the words tumbled past my lips.

She started to speak, and I interrupted her. Her expression moved from concern to irritation.

"Gotta get going," I said. "Good luck with . . ." I glanced toward the party, where Tenebrae had taken his movie-star smile back to the crowd. "With your friend. Or whatever." The man's face was as miraculously free of wrinkles as his suit.

"Carter . . ." Irritation moving to anger.

"Good luck," I said again and walked away, half hoping she'd call out for me to stop, and half determined that I wouldn't show her how much it confused and hurt me to see her there, in that world of corruption and power brokers.

Back in the press of the well-heeled crowd, I forced my way past politicians and sycophants, the cream of high society who bought and sold neighborhoods as if they were toys to be used and discarded. The CaCuris were sharks preying on the working class, but these people were commercial fishing boats. And Tenebrae was as bad as any of them.

At the thought of the gathering's host, I saw the man himself. He was next to Colonel Marbury, smiling as he talked about something that allowed him to bat his eyes, flex his muscles, and add in the occasional flirtatious touch. The colonel, who'd seemed so skeptical of the gathering, was more than a little encouraging of the attention. I remembered her scanning the crowd, searching for a face. There was no doubt in my mind who she'd been hoping to see.

I turned away and searched for the door, head spinning, clammy sweat starting to drip down my back and from my brow. Every step I took moved me farther away from Gellica, the woman I'd rushed across town to find. The apartment was big enough that I'd managed to get disoriented. I found the statue of a rearing bull where I'd spoken with Marbury earlier and stepped beside it, catching my breath and getting my bearings as I searched for the exit.

A woman a head shorter than me blocked my path. With tightly cropped hair styled into curls and a gray silk blouse that exposed tattoos creeping down her biceps, I didn't need to examine the cheekbones or dimpled chin to recognize her. It was the same face that presided over Gellica's office from the oil painting on the wall. Ambassador Paulus.

Even as she boxed me into the space by the statue she barely spared me a glance, sipping her drink and looking back out over the party.

"Detective," she said. "What a delightful surprise."

I froze, pulling my arms in tight to my midsection and doing my best to control my breathing.

Paulus looked so like Gellica, only older, and drained of passion and concern. How far had the acorn fallen from the tree? I wanted to trust Gellica, and she wanted us to have a connection. But was that enough, even in the most tenuous of relationships?

"I had a message for the envoy. But I'm leaving. Now." The metal clamp continued to squeeze my cheekbones and eye sockets, and the distant whisper-filled buzzing grew louder, the sound of an angry colony of bees emerging from the bottom of a long-dead well. It was time for me to get the Hells out of there.

Paulus smirked. "Oh, did our hero get his heart broken? Maybe you'll still find it in yourself to save us all from peace and prosperity?" She lifted the miniature sword from her tapered glass, brandished it playfully in the air, its blade heavy with a trio of stuffed olives.

"It's especially tragic," she said, "considering it was Gellica who came to your rescue the last time we talked. Maybe she won't care enough to bother next time." She finally turned her gaze on me directly. "Just like your Captain Bryyh, who I hear is greatly in disfavor at the Bunker these days. Every time she defends your public appearances she burns a little more of her influence. Must drive you mad . . ." She slid her thumb across the flat of the tiny blade, pushing the olives toward its tip. "Gellica. Captain Bryyh. All the people who shield you from the consequences of your actions. Dropping away, one . . . by. . . . one." The olives plopped back into her martini, spilling expensive liquor and accenting each word.

Like the rest of the crowd, Paulus was focused on her personal gain at the expense of everyone else. But while they might be dealing in the manna futures market, Paulus had the opportunity to bend the flow of manna to her will. Whatever laws she had to break to lay hands on the new manna, she likely was already exploiting it. It was no wonder Tenebrae was trying to curry favor with her. And that Gellica wanted to escape from under her thumb.

"Yeah. I suppose you'd know what being alone feels like. You had to make your only friend in a lab." I leaned closer. "And how'd that work out for you?"

A form slithered across her shoulders. I wouldn't have

seen it except for the ripple of silk on her blouse. It was almost invisible, a shift of the air like heat rising off the hood of a car. My right foot slid backward, an involuntary reaction to the memory of the fiendish thing Paulus commanded, and the memory of claustrophobia, of fear, when it had pinned me to the carpet in Gellica's living room. The buzzing in my ears continued to grow, now almost sounding like distant voices raised in song, a kind of radio station that wouldn't quite emerge from the static.

"So many things are beyond you," she said. "Why do you persist in getting in my way?" The tone was disdainful, but there was a glint of something else in her eye—pleasure. She enjoyed making direct threats, probably in a way she could never do in a political setting. For all her wealth and power, Paulus was no better than the street thugs I dragged into the Bunker on a daily basis.

I gathered my courage.

"Haven't you read the papers?" I managed. "It's my job to take out the trash."

The candles in their holders flickered then gutted out, their life snuffed by the air, or wind, or whatever the thing was that Paulus controlled. I had to get away. I pushed past her, pressing my hand against her arm. Her tattoos recoiled, but as with Guyer's cloak, I felt nothing. No tingle, no sense of connection. Whatever suspicions I'd had about sensing manna, now I knew they were delusions. In addition to everything else, I had to contend with the idea that I might be going mad.

She let me pass, enjoying her drink as she watched me stumble for the door.

Gellica came across the room, moving too quickly for me to track. She'd saved me from Paulus once before, and I wondered if she'd do the same now, or if I was too much of a liability. A wave of nausea-tinged hunger hit me, and the room seemed to retreat down a narrow corridor. The sound of muffled singing grew louder, and my nostrils burned like I'd taken a deep whiff of the sulfur-infused air in a geo-vent. For all of it, I couldn't help but pause to see if Gellica was going to stand by Paulus or to slip a hand onto Tenebrae's finely sculpted arms.

Gellica gripped Paulus's tattooed bicep and whispered

sharp words in her employer's ear. I turned and shoved my way through the crowd, batting at invisible cobwebs as I pushed past Tenebrae and Marbury and other less familiar faces. Another shiver wracked my body. I didn't care anymore if they stared, if I looked deranged. All I really hoped to do was make it to the door before being sick. I pressed forward, venting my anger and frustration as I batted at the threads clinging to my hands and face. The shrill sound of feedback filled my ears followed by a sudden crack of an explosion as a concussive force impacted my back.

Behind me, Tenebrae spoke in the loud forced-calm of someone seeking to avoid panic. "Not to worry! Simply an overheated glass candle holder. My apologies, everyone!"

The alarmed crowd milled about, ignoring me in the confusion. The air was warmer near the door, and my nausea drained away, though I was still weak-legged. I took a deep, ragged breath, and with it came a flood of regret. I'd come hoping to reconcile with Gellica, and I'd walked out with the composure of a drunk stumbling from an all-hours bar. But disgrace wasn't the only thing I'd incurred at the fundraiser.

I turned to stare back into the room. Standing by the sculpted bull, Tenebrae held a hand tight to his chest, as if he'd been wounded by some kind of debris. The glass candle holders that Paulus's creature had been skulking around were indeed shattered, her anger probably the thing that had triggered their "explosion." Gellica didn't notice me at all, intent on examining her clutch purse, which looked like it had been torn open in the confusion. Paulus herself ignored the press of concerned partygoers, one hand pressed to her cheek, blood oozing past her fingers like bright red tears. Despite the crowd between us, we locked eyes, and my stomach clenched once more. The ambassador glared at me, furious and vengeful as all the imps in the Hells.

19

THAT MORNING THE BUNKER'S DATA lab was empty except for myself and Trevor, and I blamed my discomfort on the company and my surroundings in equal measure. The data lab was designed by data experts who had apparently never seen a human in person. Judging by the dim lighting and constant need to crouch, I doubted if they were even Mollenkampi or Squib. It seemed more likely they were from one of the non-bipedal Families, maybe a muitisegmented Haabe-Ieath who'd gone their entire life without understanding sunlight or how a decent chair was supposed to work.

And that chair was where I'd be spending my workday. I'd moved past lugging data tapes around and on to actual data entry. Trevor insisted on explaining the programming behind NICI, expounding on the joys of Formula Transmission, Expression, And Notation. "It's all about FORTEAN, bud!" he'd shout, and run a palm over his smooth green head.

The big Gillmyn had muscles on muscles, but his nearsightedness meant that he frequently leaned his bulk over my shoulder, squinting through soda-bottle glasses to identify each error I created while entering the cases. Which was often. The lab's flickering fluorescent tubes made the NICI terminal screen's dark green letters blend in even more with the light green background. About the size of a paperback novel, the screen was marred by a ceaselessly rolling horizontal line that broke my concentration every time I thought I was about to understand something.

Halfway through the morning, even Trevor's enthusiasm seemed to be running thin.

"Okay, bud," he said with an annoyed burble. "I need to stretch my legs. You flip through these cases," he dropped a heavy cardboard box at my feet, "and think about how you'll classify them, but *don't* actually do any data entry, okay? We'll regroup for another session and talk our way through it."

"Alright," I said. "Have a good walk."

"Roger that. You be ready for a quiz when T-Bone gets back!"

He slapped the top of the doorframe on his way out of the lab, breaking into a light jog while he was still in the hallway. His departure provided me with two things: a few minutes to myself, and a deep conviction that I would rather take a bullet than refer to him as "T-Bone."

I lifted a file from the front of the box he'd left in my care. It was the first of several auto theft cases. There was quite a backlog to enter, as violent crimes were NICI's priority. The National Index of Criminal Investigations was an attempt to put a stop to the bad old days when criminals could leave a trail of bodies in one city-state, then pick up and start fresh in another.

The idea of starting fresh had more than a little appeal at the moment. I had not only managed to fail to connect with Gellica, I'd blown up whatever remained of the relationship just as surely as Paulus's strange air creature had burst the candle holders to explode at Tenebrae's fundraiser. The corporate sorcerer had covered with an obvious lie, blaming the event on an overheated candle. Had he simply been trying to calm the crowd, or was he hiding something deeper? The thought brought me around to my own secret. I knew I couldn't continue to ignore the cobwebs. I'd encountered them multiple times, and the sooner I addressed them, the better.

I pushed the car thefts to the back of the box, hoping to find a case to enter that wouldn't put me to sleep, as I ran over the possible explanations I'd identified.

One: I was crazy.

Two: I was experiencing some kind of intermittent phys-

ical sensation, probably related to the violent removal of
my fingers.

Three: I was somehow interacting with magic.

I didn't want the answer to be option one, and Doc
Mumphrey had cast doubt on option two. But if I considered option three, that I was interacting with magic, then I
had some serious logic issues to deal with. Why was it
sometimes more intense than others? Why did it bring cold
darkness, and a roaring in my ears? And most of all, why
didn't it happen around objects I knew were magical, such
as Guyer's cloak, Paulus's tattoos, or even Gellica in her
entirety?

The next batch of files rustled under my fingers. I pulled
one out and glanced over the details. A summary of mug-
gings in the Old Orchard neighborhood—they went to the
back of the box as well.

No, if I truly was interacting with magic, then it only
made sense for the cobwebs and tingling to be present
whenever I was around manna. The fact that it wasn't indicated there had to be a simpler, more mundane answer,
like Jax's theory about the adrenaline-fueled strength of a
drug addict.

I leaned back, temporarily abandoning the box of files
and the whole concept of data entry.

If it wasn't magic, what did that leave as far as options?
A long talk with the department shrinks? Hardly. At best
I'd be taken off of Homicide, and relegated to a lifetime in
the data lab with Trevor. And if there was a physical cause
I'd likely end up under Dr. Baelen's loving care, waiting to
be probed and dissected like Cetus St. Beisht, the dismembered mobster at the heart of Dungan's investigation.

I paused. Dungan had said that St. Beisht had given
them the slip, and they knew he was dead after they'd
found his car.

Flipping the box around, I returned to the car thefts.
There were even more than I'd first thought. Luckily, the
one I wanted would be recent. If they'd found St. Beisht's
car, then there was a chance it had been reported missing.

A few minutes and a half-dozen papercuts later, I'd
found what I was looking for. A write-up on a stolen vehicle, the owner listed as Cetus St. Beisht. And it had a case

number override code, folding it into an open OCU investigation.

I considered this. Individual open cases could be masked from interdepartmental searches; this was needed to keep sensitive details restricted and confidential. So Dungan could block me—or anyone in the TPD—from digging into his case. But he might not have anticipated an overeager OCU data clerk. If details had been entered on the basic case, NICI might give me a way in.

I entered the emulator mode, making it appear to NICI that I was an investigator searching from Norgaerev. It was how Trevor had taught me to verify the cases I'd entered. But now I was using it to see if Dungan had let his guard down. I waited as NICI pondered my request, each scroll of the green horizontal line twisting my gut a little more. Finally it came up: an open case on a male Gillmyn, found dismembered four days ago. For more information contact Detective Dungan. But it also had a few more details: The nature of the crime was described, as well as the types of physical evidence, including the body, a washing machine . . . and a surveillance tape.

That son of a bitch! I leaned back, hands balled into fists. I'd had suspicions before, but this was incontrovertible. I logged out of the emulator and jotted a note to Trevor, telling him I'd be out that afternoon. I wasn't sure why Dungan had lied, or what else he'd covered up, but there was no way in all the Hells that I'd spend the rest of the day behind a terminal.

Jax responded to my page, and we met up a block from the Bunker, down the street from the food trucks shilling their fried delicacies to cops and civilians who craved a hot meal. Ajax had already gotten food, and we stood near the Hasam, as I agitatedly paced back and forth while waves of pedestrians rolled past us.

"We gotta see that video," I said.

Jax spread his hands, one empty, the other holding a sandwich. He'd already listened to a string of obscenities and vitriol I directed at the non-present Dungan, and even his patience was wearing thin. "I agree. You want to sneak into the OCU office and swipe it? Because I don't think that's going to end well for either of us."

I paced a tight circle, trying to walk off some of my frustration, when a trio of teens pushed between us, decked out in leather and chains. Their costumes and strut were an advertisement, displaying their anger like a warning, doing their best to not be hassled by someone else. After all, warnings only dissuade if they're visible. As I watched them walk away I felt a memory jog loose.

"Do you remember," I said, "how well the security camera was hidden. Tucked away behind the streetlight?"

Jax bit into his sandwich and gave it a dubious look. "I do. What about it?"

"Anyone who hides a camera like that is hoping to *record* activity, not prevent it."

"I think that's what I said at the time." Jax poked around in the to-go bag. "Did we not get any extra hot and sour sauce?"

"Tell me something," I said. "Do you think anyone who wants a secret recording that badly would give up their only copy of the video?"

Jax paused, then rubbed a thumb along one mandible, considering. I flashed him a grin.

"Whaddya say we pay a visit to the super at 5150 Ringsridge Road?"

He nodded, and I opened the passenger door.

"Good. Let's keep this between us right now. After the video and what Mumphrey said . . ." I trailed off, letting my words drown in the buzz of traffic and the conversations of strangers as the flow of pedestrians marched by. There really wasn't anything to add.

20

THE LOBBY OF 5150 LISTED the building superinten-
dent's name as Walter Williamson. I ran a finger down
the building directory. No Williamson on display. As I
looked a second time, a tenant passed us on the way to
check his mail. I badged him and asked where the super's
apartment was.

"Oh." Behind a pair of fashionable glasses, his eyes
darted from Jax's face to my badge and back. Mandibles
working, the tenant said, "You want Harold. 1C."

I glanced at the directory. 1C was H. Frazier. The fact
that he lived on the first floor was a sign he had a sweet-
heart deal with the landlord. In most of the city the lower
levels were more desirable, as the warm air from the thermal vents didn't rise as well to higher levels without expensive fan assists.

"But he's not home." The guy shifted in his oversized
sweater as he collected his daily ration of bills and ad fliers
from the mailbox. "I passed him earlier, on the way up to
Miss Esterhaus's unit. 4G."

A few flights of stairs later, we knocked on apartment
4G. The door opened a crack, and an older human woman
eyed us through the links of the door chain. "Yeah?"

It was Jax's turn to show his badge, and it gained us
slightly more grudging cooperation than shown by the tenant in the entry.

"We're looking for Harold Frazier," I said.

"Hang on." The woman closed the door, then opened it

fully, calling out, "Harold, there's police here for you!" To us, she added, "He's in the kitchen."

Harold was, indeed, in the kitchen. Specifically, he was under the kitchen sink, a pair of brown slacks and a curved belly sticking out from under a faded blue-and-white-striped shirt.

"Titanshade PD, Mister Frazier," I announced. "We need a minute of your time."

"I'm in the middle of somethin'," he said. "Come back in an hour." The drainpipe under the sink was open, and Frazier fought to feed a slender metal wire into its depths. I'd once seen my own super do something similar in order to break up a clog in my bathroom sink.

"It's about the camera in the alley," I said.

Frazier twisted, revealing the edge of his head, one eye visible between corroded metal pipes as he looked me over. "What about it?"

"We believe it may have captured something connected to the death in the alley."

He snorted. "You don't know what you're talking about. It was the laundry room. The other cop at least knew where the body was."

Jane's death hadn't even registered for this man. "The last cop," I said. "You remember a name?"

"Dun-something. Dunwich, maybe?"

Close enough. I exchanged a look with Jax. *What did this guy capture that Dungan didn't want us to see?*

"The camera's hidden," I said. "Why's that?"

"It's there to catch the sneakers," he said. "Comin' in and out by the fire escape."

"Sneakers?"

"Subletters!" he roared, underscoring the word with a metallic whack on the pipes. "Renting out cots to people who ain't on the lease, not paying the additional rent. They know they can't come and go through the front door, so they sneak in and out by the fire escape. Filthy animals."

"They got rights, too!" Miss Esterhaus's voice crackled from the kitchen doorway.

"Yeah, yeah, they got rights," Frazier responded while the metal clanking continued. "They got rights to use more water than the rest of us, to need more maintenance than the rest of us. They oughta be paying more rent than the rest of us, too!"

"Alright," I said, interrupting him before he could slip into a full tirade. "So you installed a camera where it wouldn't be seen. What were you going to do with the video?"

"Imp's tits," muttered Frazier. "This snake won't go anywhere." He pulled the flexible metal cable out of the drain, getting viscous black gunk on the inside of Esterhaus's cabinet.

"You're gonna clean all that up, Harold!" She still perched in the doorway.

"The video?" I reminded him of the topic at hand.

"It's for the lawyer. The landlord's got a lawyer working on evicting the deadbeats."

"And you'd never give away your only copy," I said. "Not when you're trying to get rid of your sneakers."

"Course not," he snapped, snaking the cable back into the drain. "Lawyer's got a copy of everything. That's the whole point, ain't it?"

"We're gonna need you to contact your attorney," I said. "Let 'em know to give us a copy of that tape."

"I'm occupied," Frazier said, and rapped the pipes again. "And I already gave you a copy."

"No, you gave a copy to the officer investigating your dead body in the wash," I said. "We're investigating the dead body in the alley. You don't want to cooperate? That's fine. But our next step is to turn the investigation onto maintenance people who keep having bodies appear around them."

The sound of struggle from under the sink ceased.

"Fine," said Frazier. "I'll call him after I'm done here."

"There's a phone right here." I pointed at a light green wall-mounted unit with a heavily tangled cord. "I'm sure Miss Esterhaus would be okay with you using it."

"As long as it's not long distance," she called from the doorway. "The prices they charge are unbelievable!"

"Can't stop when I'm half done," Frazier muttered. "Gotta find this clog and put it all back together."

Jax moved across the tiny kitchen, closer to the super. "The drain connects to the next-door unit."

"Course it does. So?"

"So if the snake's feeding too far, it's probably because the junction is a T, rather than a Y." Jax drew the capital letters in the air as Frazier stared at him from under the sink. "With a T junction, you're pushing through into the unit next door and spinning the snake around their sink." He clacked his jaws at the mess inside the cabinet. "Probably oughta clean up their place, as well."

Frazier glared at the pipes as if they'd personally insulted him.

"I'd guess someone repaired it a while back," said Jax, "but they used the wrong junction." He didn't bother to point out that the most likely *someone* was currently lying under the sink. "You can cut out the junction and replace it, or try using a heavier bit on the snake to help it drop down instead of pushing through."

I looked at him with eyebrows raised.

"My parents owned a rental," he said. "I picked up a few things."

Two steps took me to the phone. I untangled the cord and handed the receiver to Frazier. "My partner just saved you a couple hours' work. You can say thanks by calling that lawyer."

After a trip to the landlord's lawyer and an interminable wait in the lobby while they made a copy of the tape, we were back at the Bunker, having requisitioned a video machine from the tech room. We rolled the AV cart inside one of the meeting rooms, thinking that a bit of privacy might be required. We'd damn near had to take out a mortgage to get the video player. The technology was amazing, but the TPD administration watched their use like hawks.

The top of the player opened up, and we inserted the copy of Frazier's tape from last Friday evening. Then we took our seats and hit Play.

The video had no sound, and captured images in short bursts when its sensor detected movement. It had a good view of the hinged fire escape stairs, and being behind the streetlight meant that the view was well lit and clear. Frazier had placed his camera well for his purposes, but not for ours—the street level alleyway wasn't visible.

For the first couple hours, there wasn't much to see, other than the occasional coming and going of tenants, the "sneakers" that Frazier had been so determined to gain his fair rent from. At the three-hour mark, there was movement at the bottom edge of the screen. I leaned forward, waiting. Then a young Mollenkampi woman with vibrant red and orange head plates climbed into the view. Jane, alive and full of energy.

She was practically bouncing as she paced back and forth on a platform of some kind.

Jax leaned forward. "Is she standing on something?"

"The dumpster," I whispered. "She's pushed the dumpster back to the wall."

He clicked a note of agreement as Jane pulled out a wide piece of chalk and began laying out her mural design, nodding her head to the sound of some internal rhythm. Her vitality came through even in grainy still images on a security camera.

Jax stirred. "Why wouldn't Dungan want us to see this?"

I didn't answer, unable to take my eyes off Jane, knowing that she was doomed, and there was nothing I could do about it.

We watched her work for hours, in snapshots one second apart. We could only get a glimpse of the mural, but I knew how far she'd gotten on it, the delicate lines and colors on the wall of the crime scene. I wondered if she had more plans for it, or if it was only a test piece for a larger project, a rough draft waiting for inspiration to strike. I rubbed my hands, wincing as my palm ground against the stubs of my missing fingers. Jane stepped back, teetering precariously on the end of the dumpster and surveying her work.

"Who are you?" I whispered, chewing my lip. "Who would hurt you like that?"

Her head turned, and Jane stared into the camera, eyes narrowing. The next second she held up a hand, shielding her eyes from the streetlight as she peered out at us. Then she was grinning wide and flashing an obscene sign. She'd spotted the camera and laughed at it.

Then she was back to work, no cares at all for who was recording her. I smiled, cheering her on. *Damn right, Jane*.

After another half hour or so, she turned as if talking to someone in the alley, then jumped down, and out of sight. A painful period of inactivity followed. As hard as I tried, I couldn't prevent my mind from imagining the violent scene occurring unrecorded in the alley below.

Jax pushed back into his seat, causing metal chair legs to squeak in protest as they dragged across vinyl flooring. "Maybe Dungan was right," he said. "There's nothing useful on there."

"Wait." I leaned forward, squinting at the screen. "What's that?" In the dark shadows of the fire escape a figure had appeared, lurking and watching. Though mostly obscured, I could make out the figure of a man in a nice shirt and slacks, fabric too thin to be one of Frazier's sneakers. The outline of mandibles made it clear it was a Mollenkampi watching whatever was playing out in the alley.

"Looks familiar, but I don't know who that is. Do you?" I asked. Ajax shook his head.

The figure on the fire escape recoiled and pulled even deeper into the shadows. I guessed that Jane's death had turned to a mutilation.

Another long sequence of still shots, long enough for the watcher to remain, unobserved, as Jane's killer abandoned her body. Then the figure on the fire escape came forward, stepping onto the counter-weighted stairs, descending step by step, his every feature captured by Frazier's camera.

I turned to Ajax. He shrugged. Whoever it was, my partner didn't recognize him any more than I did.

But we had a witness, and we had an image. Better yet, it wasn't an unrecognizable blur. The mysterious watcher was an adult male Mollenkampi. He was gangly, taller than most, with dark brown, almost black head plate speckled with bright blue speckles.

"He look familiar to you?" I asked. "I kind of think I've seen him before."

"Not really," said Jax. "But that expression tells me something about his character."

Nodding, I looked back at the figure, lingering at the bottom of the screen as he pushed the dumpster back into place. With the casual way he'd waited for Jane's killer to finish before waltzing past her still-warm body, it was a good bet that he wasn't a stranger to violence. Or the criminal justice system.

I rubbed my hands together in mock excitement.

"Let's break out the mug shots."

It was another few hours of combing through photos before we found a match. On an open book, surrounded by half-empty carry-out containers, we found a match for the face we'd freeze-framed on the TV.

The man on the fire escape was a thug named Anson. He'd come to the city five years earlier, and had known connections to the CaCuri organization. We sat at our cluttered meeting room table and attempted to force the various pieces of the puzzle to fit.

"He's tied to the CaCuris." I pointed at the figure on the screen. "But Dungan said he thought the Harlq boss Anders was behind our dismembered friend in the wash." I swung my finger toward my partner. "And *you* think it looks nothing like a Harlq killing."

"Exactly," said Jax. "And the pathologist reported St. Beisht had been killed elsewhere. Which means Anson chose to put the corpse someplace it'd be found."

"Found but scrubbed in bleach." I scratched the salt and pepper stubble coming in on my neck. "This Anson guy wanted the world to know St. Beisht was dead, but still give himself some cover."

"The way he hung out on the fire escape," said Jax. "I don't think he was planning on running into the scene with Jane. That indicates the killings aren't related."

I grunted an agreement, still trying to remember where I recognized Anson's face from. "And we didn't pick him up entering the building, so he likely came in the front door." The mention of the alley triggered a memory of Dungan thumbing through his accordion files, showing us the faces and snapshots of gangsters.

"St. Beisht's bodyguard," I said. "That's where I've seen this guy before."

Jax hummed, uncertain.

"What would happen," I said, "to a mobster bodyguard whose charge gets knocked off?"

My partner rolled his shoulders. "Nothing good."

"So Anson needs to disappear," I said.

"But first he wants his bosses to know that St. Beisht is dead?" Jax sighed, a musical tinkle through dagger-like teeth. "That doesn't make sense."

"Does it need to make sense?" I asked. "We find him and get the details of Jane Doe's murder. I don't care why he was there."

"So where is he, and how do we make him talk? I don't think either of us wants Dungan to know we're onto this."

"No." I leaned forward, peering at the video machine. "Whatever he's up to, it's only going to complicate things for us."

I hit Rewind, and watched time spool backward, watched Jane come back into view, smile and insult the camera, and begin stripping her artwork off of the alley wall. One by one the portraits disappeared, until she worked on the image of a pair of twins. I hit Pause, freezing the moment in time.

"This Anson character has a record," I said. "Let's find out if his parole officer knows how to find him."

"Okay."

"He's a witness to Jane's murder. And he's likely the guy who stashed St. Beisht in the laundry."

He watched me, fingers drumming on the chipped surface of the conference room table, waiting to see where I was headed.

I nodded slowly, easing into the ask. "I know you don't like talking about the Harlqs . . ."

Jax didn't raise his head. "It's where the case led." He sighed, a whistling mournful tune that I couldn't bring myself to interrupt. Then he stood and headed for the door, never once meeting my eye. "I'll make some calls. No guarantees."

"Without Dungan knowing?"

His eyes widened. "That'd be tricky. OCU will have surveillance on the Harlqs day and night."

"It'd save us a lot of headaches," I said. "We don't need Dungan running this up the chain of command."

He made an irritated, trilling noise with both mouths. "I'll try."

"Okay, but—"

"I'll make the calls, Carter." He said it louder, with no room for argument. His eyes moved back to the TV, where we'd watched Jane's last moments, and he breathed out some of the tension. "If I can make it happen, it'll happen."

"Alright," I said. "That's all I can ask."

But I wasn't sure it was all we'd need. Not if we were going to fight through the levels of bureaucracy and corruption that infested Titanshade from the temperate warmth of the city's core to the snow-dusted Borderlands at the ice plains' edge. From Bryyh's well-intentioned reassignment to Dungan's questionable motives, I figured it was only a matter of time before we burned every bridge we'd ever crossed.

21

THE NEXT DAY, JAX AND I drove to Coffin Corners to find ourselves a Harlq.

We rumbled along in silence, neither of us wanting to talk about what we were getting ourselves into or the possible motives behind Dungan's game. Jax was behind the wheel. We'd spent most of the morning making calls from various pay phones. I'd been trying to track down Anson's parole officer, while Jax had been negotiating a meeting with the local Harlq leader. It was important to find a location Dungan and his OCU buddies weren't likely to have wired. There was still the chance we'd be seen, but there was absolutely no reason to have the conversation preserved on audiotape.

Coffin Corners was a fashionable neighborhood, named after the odd architecture of the building that dominated its busy five-points intersection. In truth, the building was simply a tapered hexagon, and likely wouldn't have been perceived as coffin-shaped anywhere with a less grim view of the world. Then again, we cremated our dead or left them on the north face of the Mount to be picked apart by Sky Shepherds, so maybe Titanshaders simply didn't know what a coffin was supposed to look like.

Jax pulled up near a no-parking sign and killed the engine. "This is the place. Our contact should be inside." He set the roof cap siren on the dash to avoid a ticket, and opened his door.

"Hold on," I said. "First we gotta have the talk."

He leaned back, letting the door almost shut. "I had *the*

talk when I was younger. And, frankly, I don't think you even know where Mollenkampi babies come from."

"You didn't want to get involved with the Harlqs," I said. "And I know that's it's been tough for you to set up this interview."

"Uh-huh."

"And I know I said you didn't have to tell me why, as long as it didn't impact an investigation."

He tipped his head to one side. "Yeah . . . I don't think that's actually what you said."

"But here we are." I crossed my arms. "And now I need to know."

"It's just that you make yourself sound a lot more sympathetic than the way I remember that conversation going."

"Kid," I said, louder than I needed to. "You gotta tell me." I held his gaze, waiting him out. After a moment he sighed, adjusted the rearview mirror to keep a visual on the restaurant, and started talking.

"I told you the Harlq Syndicate struggles in smaller towns?"

I nodded. I remembered our breakfast at Gretta's just fine.

"It's because the outsiders stand out more. Small towns sometimes take care of these things themselves." He rubbed his eyes, as if banishing visions of old memories.

"Meaning what? Vigilantes?" I hoped I sounded sympathetic as he continued.

"The Harlq bosses in Kohinoor were killed by shopkeepers and crossing guards who got their courage up with whiskey." Jax sighed. "And you know what? I didn't like it, but I could've slept at night," he stared at the mirror, watching the restaurant past a never-ending parade of shoppers and street hustlers, "if it had stopped there."

"It never does."

"I suppose they felt like heroes. Like they were on the side of justice. When they ran out of gangsters, they took out people who helped the Harlqs. Then people who they thought *would've* helped the Harlqs eventually. By the end, it was just people settling old grudges."

"You had to stop them," I said.

He nodded.

"So it worked," I said. "The Harlqs were out of town. The vigilantes were stopped. Happy ending?"

I asked it out of a sense of obligation. Because of course I knew the answer. The only happy endings are in storybooks.

"We arrested the ringleaders, the ones most out of control. Things calmed down," he said, "and we all patted ourselves on the back. I put in for Detective, on the heels of helping to clean up the mess."

The first time I'd met Ajax he'd told me he'd made detective only a couple weeks earlier.

"You left town right after that," I said. "Came to Titanshade. Why?"

"You ever read a paragraph in a poorly written textbook? You get through the whole thing and realize you didn't process any of it." He glanced at me. "Look who I'm asking." Jax chuckled, but it was an empty sound, and he let his mandibles droop. "I should've known what was coming." He gripped the steering wheel, arms braced as if heading for impact. "Remember when I said that Harlq recruits are shipped off to other cities, a combination of foot soldiers and hostages?"

"Yeah."

"Families started getting packets in the mail." He drew a ragged, jangling breath. "Photos of their kids and cousins, who'd gone off to join the Harlq organization. Executed in front of their peers."

He turned in his seat and looked me in the eye.

"Now you know why I don't like the Harlqs."

He didn't slam the door as he got out of the car, but he didn't close it gently, either.

The Crown Block was a nice sit-down restaurant. The kind of place with a friendly host and hostess to show you to your seat. And when we told them we were meeting friends, they simply smiled and took our word for it. We were only a few tables in before we were intercepted by a young Gillmyn who I assumed was Jax's contact.

On the short side for his Family, the Gillmyn wore

flared tan slacks and a blue satin shirt with looping red-and-orange patterns embroidered on either breast.

"Come with me," he said. "We're already running late." He immediately walked toward the back of the restaurant, and we fell in alongside him. We tromped through the main eating area, past all the normal-looking families and couples enjoying lunch. He acknowledged my presence, but spoke to my partner. "You're Ajax, right?" he asked.

Jax nodded.

"Man, it's really great to meet you. I'm Weston, but everybody calls me West. I'm from Norgaerev, and I can't tell you how much—"

"I know," Jax cut him off. "You told me earlier, on the phone."

"Yeah, okay." He grinned, almost toppling a service tray as a server emerged from the kitchen. "I'm really indebted to Miss Ruena. She's how I got this position with Echo Unchained."

"Echo Unchained?" I said. Neither Jax nor West responded to my question.

"She's been a huge influence on me, you know? She's like the lead in this book she gave me, *The Ringmaster's Secret*. She's just got so many layers going on."

"Betrayal," Jax said. "It's called *The Ringmaster's Secret Betrayal*."

"Right! You totally get it. Anyway," the kid barely took a breath between sentences, "she's been huge for me, and I'm happy to help out any way I can." He led us toward a pair of Mollenkampi flanking an open archway leading to a private dining area. We maintained our pace, but now flipped out our badges. I tucked mine into my breast pocket. The two thugs exchanged a glance and shifted their feet, ready for a confrontation.

West raised his hands. "It's cool, guys. They're with me!"

Jax stepped past him and addressed the guards. "We're expected."

One of them leaned into the room and, eyes still on us, called out something in Kampi. I didn't hear the response, but the muscle men faded back, and we entered the darkened room.

The private space was sized for large family gatherings

or corporate lunches. This day only a single table was occupied. A Mollenkampi man sat before a lavish meal spread out on a red-and-white checkered tablecloth. He was flanked by another pair of guards, a Mollenkampi and a Gillmyn who looked older than the pair at the door. West circled the edge of the room to stand next to them. The man at the table was who we'd come to see—Anders, the Harlq boss who Dungan claimed wanted St. Beisht dead.

Anders had watery eyes that passed over us briefly before he muttered, "Let them be," to his companions. Then, louder, to us: "What can I do for you, gentlemen?"

The Harlq boss wore a casual shirt, unbuttoned to midchest, and a dark blue sport coat with thick shoulder pads and buttons the same bright gold as the band of his wristwatch, which itself was decorated with precious stones. His biting mouth clenched slowly as he waited for our response, and there was the glint of gem studs set in his jagged teeth as well. Not a man afraid of appearing overly showy.

"Just a few questions," I said as Jax and I took seats at the table, angling ourselves so that both the bodyguards behind Anders and at the door were in sight. "Does the name Anson mean anything to you?"

Considering Jax's feelings about the Harlqs, I figured it'd be best if I did the talking. Anders seemed to have other plans.

He answered my question with a curt, "No," while staring at Ajax, as if deciding what to do with him.

I tried again. "He never did any work for you?"

Anders kept his eyes on Jax. "You gonna say something, or does your keeper do the talking for you?" He indicated me with a jab of his fork.

I pulled out Anson's mug shot and placed it in the middle of the table. "This may jog your memory."

He shook his head, still talking to Jax. "You don't got your family temper, do you, kid?"

Ajax didn't answer, and Anders spoke to the Gillmyn who stood two paces away.

"Lou, this is Two-Tongue Ruena's nephew. You know her?"

The guard shook his head, still silent but peering at Jax with curiosity. For my part, I stared straight ahead, doing my best to not let surprise show in my face or body language.

"Eh, you know *of* her, I bet." Anders looked back at Jax. "But what I'm wondering is if she knows you're here. I'm also wondering if she knows you used her name to get in to see me."

Near Anders's guards, West uncrossed his arms, head swiveling as he looked from his boss to Jax, who finally broke his silence.

"Doesn't matter how we got in. We're here now."

"Heh." Anders returned to his meal, shoveling meat and sticky rice in his formidable jaws, mashing it into a ball against the grinding plates on the roof of his biting mouth.

"Maybe here's someone you'll recognize." I slid the morgue photo of Cetus St. Beisht across the table. It came to rest next to Anders's plate of meat and rice in red sauce.

The Harlq boss worked his mandibles, daintily plucking chewed food from between his biting jaws and depositing it into the secondary mouth in his throat. He swallowed before answering. "Yeah. He was in one piece when I knew him, though."

I left the photo where it sat. "Do you know anyone who would want him dead?"

"Showing me snuff photos ain't the way to get me to talk." He placed another forkful into his biting mouth, chewing as his speaking mouth rattled on. "Not that I'm eager to cooperate with your investigation or—" he waved a steak knife in the air, "whatever you're doing. You wired up, by the way?" He leaned toward us, calling out as if to an audience. "Hello-o-o, cops!"

"Tell me about your relationship with him." I sat with legs crossed, chair tipped back to keep the Harlq's flunkies in sight.

"Interesting that you're not the usual cops harassing us." He leaned to one side, addressing the Gillmyn who'd shared his table, waving his fork at us as he called out, "You ever see these two before? I never did."

The Gillmyn was once again slow to respond, the kind of guy who required intense mental effort to speak. "Not in person."

"Not in person?" Anders swallowed again, giving me

another view of the chewed meal as it passed to his throat. He tilted his head, as if considering that comment.

"Cetus St. Beisht." I pointed at the photo. "And his failure of a bodyguard. How exactly did you know them?"

Anders lifted the napkin to his tusks and began wiping them down. He was well into middle age, as evidenced by the fading color of his head plates, and he carried himself with the constrained movements of someone who woke each morning with aches and pains. It was a process I knew firsthand.

"The manna strike cops!" he said. "That's where I know you from. You're on the television shows."

"And in the papers," I said.

Jax snorted. "I'm guessing he's not much of a reader."

Anders stared at Jax, then raised the tapered lip of his wineglass and took a long swallow. "Cetus, he was a sports fan. Nice guy. Used to get me tickets to carelbarra matches."

"You a c-ball fan?"

"Yeah." Anders snapped his fingers in the direction of the shadows. "Hey, Westie, ask one of the boys to get me another glass of this."

The Gillmyn left without a word, and I tracked his path to the door. It was possible that Anders never had a second glass of wine with lunch. It was possible that his request was a sign to do some violence to us as we left. Life was full of possibilities. That's what made it interesting.

"And what did you do to earn these c-ball tickets?" I asked. "Or was that just out of the kindness of the dearly departed?"

"Introductions," he said. "I know people, and Cetus wanted to meet the people I know." He leaned back and rested his hand on the swell of his belly. "I'm a people person."

"I'm sure St. Beisht's death will inconvenience you," I said. "Slow down the number of box seats you get. Or," I leaned back, feeling the give in the seat, "maybe it's caused more problems."

Anders snickered.

"Like money," I said. "Getting it moved from one location to the other. That's important for you Harlq boys, right? Need to keep cash flowing to the people farther up the food chain."

Anders watched me as he impaled a bite of food with a mandible. He took his sweet time swallowing, then swiped a napkin across his tusks.

"Cetus was a nice guy who liked to go to games from time to time," he said. "But not only did I not have anything to do with him ending up dead, there's no chance I would."

"Why's that?"

His eyes crinkled, and there was laughter in his voice as he answered. "Are you kidding me?" He looked at his muscle men, appealing to them to share in the joke. "The cops who were there at the strike, and they don't even know how big a deal it is."

"So explain it to me." I put my arms on the table. "It'll be like a public service."

Anders seemed to consider that. "It's like a legitimate money mill." He plucked another glob of chewed food from his biting jaws and shoveled it into his eating mouth with a mandible. "I keep telling the cops in this town, I work for a nonprofit." He waved a hand absently over his shoulder. "Give him a card."

The big, tight-lipped Gillmyn stepped closer, hand in his jacket. My heart picked up its pace, and Jax's posture tightened, ready to strike out. But the muscle only drew a pair of business cards, and handed them to us. Gold foil announced Anders's name and title as advising board member of Echo Unchained.

"We're working to bring fair treatment for those in the Harlq Syndicate who've been forced to work outside the laws." Anders trilled the words slightly, displaying a bit of pride. "Some of the leadership in the Syndicate were . . ." He brought a hand to his throat to cover a belch. "They were a little on the gray side of the moral compass."

The understatement might have been comical in another context. "Why here?"

He raised his hands, silverware pointed at the ceiling in exaggerated frustration. "The amount of money the manna strike will bring in is gonna change the world, let alone the city. In all of Eyjan, the best place for an organization to transform itself is right here, right now. Anyone who wants to start over from scratch," he pointed his knife at the ground, "this is the place to be."

Anders nodded, as if satisfied he'd made his point. He shifted in his seat, and the open front of his shirt moved far enough to expose a pair of round scars that looked like old bullet wounds.

"You keep calling St. Beisht a money launderer," he said.

I crossed my arms. "I never said that." But I knew Dungan had, and so had the papers—I'd seen the headline.

"That's nice. Anyways, St. Beisht wasn't a laundry man, he was a CFO. Without him, we're at a disadvantage."

"The Syndicate always plans for contingencies."

"See, your failure to listen is why we have communication issues," he said. "I'm not with the Harlq Syndicate." He pointed at the card. "Echo Unchained. Right there in front of you."

He took another bite. "But I'll tell you something. There is a Harlq Syndicate. And they won't forget that a good man got diced up by some inbred locals." He shook his head. "I understand you got a job to do, but you really oughta focus on whoever wanted him dead, you know?"

"Your bosses want results," I said. "And there's people like the CaCuris nipping at your heels. You afraid you're going to end up in a washing machine yourself?"

Anders tossed the napkin onto the table. "I work for a nonprofit! I don't got those kind of bosses. And as for Thomas CaCuri," to either side, the guards twitched, as if someone had whispered the boogeyman's name, "the guy's a menace. You'd do well to get him off the street before he hurts more people."

Interesting.

"More people?" I said. "What's that mean?"

His eyes dropped to the mug shot. "What d'ya think happened to Cetus's bodyguard?"

"Anson cleared out of town," I said.

Anders snorted. "Bullshit. He's scared shitless, because the guy he was protecting died on his watch. But he's still around. Ask Thomas CaCuri if you wanna know more. I hear Anson's his house guest these days. Beyond that I don't know—but I will say this," he leaned forward, gesturing with his knife, "you boys in red don't get around to taking care of CaCuri, someone else is gonna have to do it for you. Someone with the balls to do it right."

The man might have called himself a legitimate businessman, but in the course of one conversation he'd gone from never having heard of Anson to being able to tell us where to find him. It was time to change tactics. I reached into my jacket and retrieved a photo of Jane. Printed from the surveillance video, when she was alive and smiling at the camera. It was a step up from the morgue shots we'd had before. I held it at arm's length, keeping my eyes on Anders.

No strong reaction.

"I dunno. But you guys are Homicide. So she's a killer or a corpse, right?" He scratched the surface of one tooth with a mandible, bringing out the shine of its decorative jade stud. "So which is it?"

"She's dead," I said. "Near your pal St. Beisht."

"You got photos of all the dead people today, don't you?" His eyes crinkled, laughing at his own joke. "Hey, was she cut up like Cetus was? That'll save you some time on his funeral, right? That's what you people do here. Cut up the bodies and take 'em on the rock for the vultures to eat?"

Jax's voice trilled beside me, a piping birdsong of trills and clicks. I caught a couple words, something about loyalty and tradition. Whatever he said, Anders froze. He stared at Jax, fury lighting his eyes.

"You got in here on your aunt's name," he said. "Because I respect her. And her name's what's gonna let you walk out of here. After that, it's all used up. Remember that."

The missing Gillmyn returned with the next glass of wine. The only sound in the room was the scrape of his leather soles on the floor. Anders leaned forward and picked up his utensils. Without looking up from his plate, he said, "The redbacks are leaving now."

The guards moved in. I risked a glance at my partner. Jax had a death grip on the notebook. There were a few different ways this could play out and only one of them involved everyone walking out on their own two feet. I raised my hands slightly. Enough to indicate compliance, not enough to indicate surrender.

"We're going," I said.

I stood, slowly, and a moment later Jax followed suit.

We were almost to the Hasam when Weston caught up with us.

"Guys! Hey!" He slipped through the crowd with more grace than he'd shown in the restaurant.

I slowed, but Jax wasn't interested in hearing what the young gangster had to say.

"C'mon, guys! Hold up!" West put on a burst of speed and reached the Hasam as Jax unlocked the door. "You can't leave me to hang like that, okay?"

Ajax turned, squaring his shoulders and looking like he might tackle the wide-eyed Gillmyn. "You want to not be in danger? Then stop hanging around killers."

"But I thought—"

"That you knew me? Not even close. Now get away from my car."

West stepped back, mouth open, buccal cavity flaring. Jax got behind the wheel, then leaned over and unlocked the passenger door. He turned the ignition and we pulled away before West had processed things enough to respond. The young Gillmyn stepped into the road, waving his fist and shouting, "Any one of us is worth ten of you!"

We left the agitated figure in the distance, and I let Ajax drive in peace. I wanted to process everything we'd learned. There was something in particular that bothered me. There were only two times Anders had really gotten rattled, when Jax spoke to him in Kampi, and when I mentioned the CaCuris. But even then, it had felt off somehow.

"He didn't care about Katie," I said.

Jax ignored me, and I finished my thought in silence. Anders and his crew had their eye on the wrong CaCuri. Thomas could end the lives of a few of them, but Katie might actually change the landscape of the city. And Anders's comments about taking a wing of the Harlq Syndicate legit was chilling, but not nearly as disturbing as the notion that he didn't want St. Beisht dead. Mostly because of what that meant a legitimized Harlq political group might mean for the city, but also because of what it told us about Dungan. Did he know more than he was letting on, or had he read Anders completely wrong? Police work depends on different officers sharing information, and when that communication breaks down, the bad guys slip through the cracks. Everything we learned was only muddying the water further, and our faith in our support network was growing increasingly thin.

Beside me, Jax drove in silence. Whatever thoughts he had on the matter, he was keeping them close to his vest. Outside our car, we passed tailors and noodle shops, apartment buildings and candy-haunted alleyways.

"What did you say to Anders back there?"

"He was trying to get a rise out of us," said Jax. "I told him what he could do with his provocation."

That sounded like a lie, and it didn't match up with the few words I'd made out.

"Sounded a bit more specific than that," I said, but when he didn't respond, I decided not to push it. After all, I'd recently been told my Kampi wasn't as good as I thought it was.

The cars lining the street were parked at odd angles, the result of people doing their best to fit into whatever space was available, desperate to escape the endless cycle of circling the block and hoping someone else would be pulling away.

"I can tell you'd like to put Anders on a slab," I said.

Ajax's eyes didn't leave the road.

"I want him, too," I said. My head hurt, and I pressed on my temples, trying to squeeze away the pain. "But we don't handle organized crime work. We don't got the tools or the support to put in the hours it takes."

I wasn't sure what was more disturbing, the Harlqs attempting to go legit or the fact that the manna strike provided both them and the CaCuris an opportunity to do so.

"I know," he said. "I'm not about to do anything stupid."

"What you told me about the kids from Kohinoor, it was awful." I didn't add that he'd left out a crucial part of the story, the name he'd dropped to get us into the meeting with Anders. Jax looked almost ready to speak, if I could only let him know it was okay to do so.

"Bunch of bastards," I said.

"There was one bastard in particular," his eyes stayed on the road as he spoke, "a Harlq sub-boss in Norgaerev, who was originally from Kohinoor. One of our own. Growing up, I called her Auntie Roo." Jax paused. "I didn't leave my hometown. I was run out because I was too close to the woman who butchered our children."

Ajax steered with one hand and spun the radio dial with the other. He paused briefly on WYOT, just long enough to catch the crescendo of drum and bass.

To our left a cargo truck overflowing with scrap metal tumbled past. The clanging of discarded pipes and sheet metal created enough noise to drown out the sound of my pager, pulsing and ringing, demanding my attention as the song on the radio ended and the DJ began his patter.

This is Handsome Hanford, guiding your way through the longest nights, on into the morning light. Coming up we've got a new track from Ride the Universe. Ride with me, Titanshade!

Ajax moved to change it once again, but I stopped him. I needed to answer the pager, but not yet. Some days, a favorite DJ can make even the worst nightmare seem like it will pass before long. So I rode with Hanford, closed my eyes and leaned my forehead against the cool glass of the passenger window. The lights of Titanshade flickered past, each set of bright neon letters announcing a different vice for sale.

22

WE DROVE FOR SOME TIME before I had it in me to
check my pager. I fished it out and found a number I
didn't recognize. We pulled over at the next pay phone. I
wiped the receiver on my suit coat before putting it to my
ear and making the call. I reached Anson's parole officer,
a scratchy-voiced woman who didn't much care for a couple Homicide detectives poking into the life of one of her
charges, but eventually coughed up his address. I hung up
and reported this to Ajax, who simply looked at his watch.

"We've got our medical this afternoon."

I threw my head back. "It can't have been a week already."

Jax crossed his arms.

"It won't take that long to rattle this guy and find out
what he saw. Even if he doesn't roll on what he saw, we can
get into his head and see where he runs to."

He didn't answer, but kept his eyes on mine.

"Do you really feel like getting stuck with needles today," I said. "Or maybe watch more shadow fights between
ice plains critters?"

He clacked his jaws and looked away, and I knew I had
him.

"Fine," he said. "Where does this Anson guy live?"

Bryndel Grove sat on the mountside edge of the Borderlands, smack in the middle of the CaCuris' seat of power,

the 24th Ward. Like the rest of the city, it had no groves of any kind, bryndel trees or otherwise. But it was relatively clean, and temperate enough that I didn't need an overcoat for the short walk from our car to the apartment complex that Anson called home.

The public often thinks of paroled prisoners as being set free. The truth is that a parolee is still serving the rest of their sentence, only they're doing it outside a prison's walls. Just like guards can search a jail cell with no preamble, in the course of an investigation we could enter and search any parolee's apartment at will. No need for a warrant or probable cause—the fact that Anson was still part of the system was all the justification we needed.

As we approached I noted the streets were well-maintained, with prominent Titan's Day decorations and assorted youths idling on the corners. Young teens or even children, they were the kind of lookouts common in gang-controlled neighborhoods, and I expected to see them on the CaCuris' home turf. Less expected was the scarlet patrol car, parked down the street from an unmarked Hasam that indicated fellow detectives were on the scene. We hadn't even entered and my stomach was already tightening.

Anson's apartment was on the first floor, a relatively spacious flat well outside the price range of a factory worker, the occupation given to us by his parole officer. A lone patrol cop stood sentry at the door, controlling the flow of traffic. He acknowledged our badges with a nod and allowed us entry.

Across the threshold we found Andre, Hemingway's new partner, jotting notes as he did a slow turn in the main living area. His eyes narrowed when he spotted me, though he relaxed slightly at the sight of Jax. Andre let out a low whistle that my partner returned, and that seemed to confirm the personal dynamics of the room. Hemingway stood near the far wall, studying the movie posters tacked to the wall, mostly old heist films that ended with car chases and shoot-outs. Beyond Hemingway was the bathroom, and I froze as I caught sight of the shower. Blood-streaked glass walls obscured the details of the crumpled body within, but I could make out the dark blue-black of the head plates.

"Anson," I said.

Hemingway turned and looked me over as if tallying up the good and bad, before apparently deciding that I at least broke even.

"Appears to be his name." She chewed her gum with purpose, as if she had a quota of pieces to get through in a day. "You know him?"

"Not personally."

She hooked one thumb in a belt loop. "Then why are you here?"

A few steps away, Jax pointed at the shower stall. "Most people shower at night or first thing in the morning. You know which it was?"

"Not a hundred percent." Hemingway peered into the bathroom. "No steam on the mirror or shower door, so it's been at least a little while. But there's water still beaded on the body, so I'm guessing it happened this morning."

"Shit." I turned away. That lined up with our call to Anson's PO. "Who reported it?"

"Anonymous tip," said Andre, a trill of suspicion underscoring his words. "You didn't answer my partner's question. What are you doing here?"

"Witness interview," said Jax. "Or was going to be, anyway."

A bustle of activity caused us all to turn toward the door.

"Tech team got here fast," said Anders.

The crew began to set up a perimeter, and one mustached man approached, hands raised as if he might drop them on our shoulders and guide us to a new path. "Step away from the bathroom, please."

It wasn't a crew I was familiar with, though I recognized them from somewhere. I blinked, trying to put context to the man's face, his thickly bristled mustache. *The St. Beisht crime scene.*

Doc Mumphrey's complaints about the OCU techs came flooding back. I had no intention of seeing another crime scene rendered useless.

I ignored the tech and stepped into the bathroom, peering at Anson's body. He'd had his head bashed into the shower wall. It'd taken great strength to pull that off. Great strength and the ability to enter the apartment unheard.

Or someone who'd already been there when Anson entered the shower.

"Sir, I do need you to step out of the bathroom. Detective?"

The tech's voice was drowned out by other, louder voices raised in anger. I turned and found Dungan standing in the living area of the apartment, apparently responding to some comment from Hemingway.

With a whisper of polyester windbreaker, Dungan pulled his driving cap lower as he stared her down. "Tell whoever you want, blondie." His gap-toothed smile spread a little wider. "Fact is that this crime scene is related to an active OCU investigation. So you can stand around with your thumbs up your asses for the next couple hours until the paperwork comes through, or you can screw off right now. I don't really care one way or the other."

I crossed the room, sending the tech team scurrying out of my way.

"What did you know about this?" My voice raised louder than I'd intended.

Dungan blinked, his grin morphing into a scowl. But he didn't answer, so I leaned in closer, spitting each word into his face.

"No video, huh?"

"I said there was nothing you could use. This bastard," he indicated Anson, "was at the very least a witness to the St. Beisht killing. Maybe the one who hid the body. He might have blown open the whole thing. *If* I'd had time to crack him."

"And he saw what happened to Jane."

"Maybe," he said. "Or maybe he was perched on the fire escape waiting for a ride. We'll never know, now that you got him killed off."

"What are you talking about?" I said the words, even though I knew exactly where he was going with all of this.

"Why do you think I kept the video close to my vest, anyway?"

"I needed to know what he saw!"

"So you stirred up the pot about the twins who have their fingers in every bureaucracy in the city?" A flush spread up Dungan's neck, blooming from his collar to his ears and splotchy cheeks. He looked ready to spit out his candy. "Carter, you dumb bastard. You think it's been easy keeping everything about St. Beisht secret?" He pulled off his driver's cap and ran a hand through sweat-matted curls as he leaned in, whispering, "I even have my techs holding details back from the ME's office."

"You think Mumphrey is working for the—"

His jaw dropped. "No, dammit! I think some petty bureaucrat who has access to the ME office's files is willing to pay back the CaCuris for getting them their job. The twins are more subtle than you're giving them credit for," he said. "Or at least Katie is. She's working her fingers into the very mortar lines of the city's foundation. A street thug's dangerous, civil servants are deadly."

I opened my mouth to reply, but a hand on my arm stopped me.

"Carter," said Jax. "You're the one who told me the CaCuris have tendrils all throughout the city government."

I pointed back to the bathroom, where Anson lay dead, one mandible almost detached from the force of the blows. "Why weren't you watching him?"

"Because I don't have unlimited staff and funds," he said. "I've got eyes on the CaCuris, I've got eyes on the Harlqs. I'm eating up money and resources on this damn case hoping to break something and you go and—" He swiped a hand over his eyes, leaving white trails across beet-red skin as he fumed. "We're in the middle of gang wars, a military occupation, political upheaval, the biggest economic revolution the world has ever seen . . . and all you want is to find out who killed a girl in an alley?"

I stepped in closer, words snarling. "Every death matters."

But it was more than that. It was every assault and bashed-in car window. Every kid with a black eye and strap marks across their back. Every woman denigrated and man demoralized. Each Gillmyn or human or Mollenkampi denied an opportunity because of who they were, or who they loved, or how they pronounced their words. They all mattered, every single damn one of them. But at that moment there was only one I'd been entrusted to find justice for, a Jane Doe found in an alley. And I'd rather have been shredded by the imps than let her be forgotten.

I wanted to make Dungan understand that, and maybe I would have found a way, but we were interrupted by the sudden sound of cheering from the street. I walked to the door followed by Dungan and my fellow Homicide detectives.

Down the block a crowd was gathering, centered on a squat building with blacked-out windows and a sign that declared it was the Paradise Parlor. I knew the name. Despite sounding like a low-end strip club, the Parlor was the central hub of the CaCuris' organization. It was a private club, a place for the twins and their high-rolling friends to meet, scheme, and assuage each other's consciences. Or at least what passed for consciences. Among what passed for friends.

On the front stoop of Paradise, Katie CaCuri stood above the crowd, grim-faced and wrapped in fur. Behind her, Thomas brooded silently, his hollow, sunken eyes roaming the assembled citizenry. With his dark suit, drawn face, and ostentatious jewelry, Thomas looked like an over-accessorized undertaker. He wasn't in his element in front of a crowd. Not like his sister.

Katie was well into her performance as we drew close enough to hear what she was saying. "Withholding manna is like dangling a sandwich before a starving man. This city," she swung a hand, "*our* city, finally has a chance to get back on its feet. And what does the AFS do?" She paused. "It puts its heel on our throats and keeps us down. It's time to take back what's ours, take back our rights. And take our damn manna!"

At the fringes of the crowd, the younger CaCuri thugs we'd seen on the corners pulled a steady stream of people from nearby stores and sidewalks, directing them to join the impromptu rally. They'd even drafted some bystanders who seemed to have overindulged in the city's vices, including one large human who stared into the sky, muttering to himself and tugging on his generous beard.

"Katie's appeal isn't exactly organic," said Jax.

"Doesn't need to be," said Dungan. He pointed at the twins as a pair. "The two of them go good together, like in the old-time religions, before the Path. Gods of good, gods of evil. The people in these streets love Katie and fear Thomas."

Jax watched the crowd. "They could always leave."

There was a hint of remorse in his voice. Maybe he was thinking about what had driven him out of his own hometown.

"Costs money to move," I said. "People struggling to pay their electric bill don't have much in the way of surplus cash. And if they moved into a neighborhood controlled by the Harlqs, or the Hollow, or the Royal Smiths, would that be any better?"

On the stoop Katie still worked her crowd. "The special election changes everything! Two more days and we'll be up all night, celebrating with a festival, then going straight to the polls Titan's Day morning. We're going to make history, and we're going to take back our city!"

Performance complete, Katie waded into the crowd, shaking hands and making promises. Farther down the street the crowd parted, revealing a familiar figure peering around, as if lost. A tall man with dyed-blond hair and chiseled good looks. I felt my lip curl as I recognized Mitri Tenebrae, incongruously perfect and tidy as always, even in the raucous crowd.

Jax noticed my reaction. "Who's that?" Tenebrae moved through the crowd, drawing closer to the twins and their entourage.

"An asshole," I said. "Who shouldn't be in this neighborhood."

I chewed my lip. Tenebrae could be the connection between the twins and Gellica, and through her—Paulus. He was how Gellica knew Louis Mah was going to be injured ahead of time. Tenebrae was the linchpin. All I needed to confirm it was to see them welcome him warmly. I did my best to remain anonymous in the crowd as the wealthy sorcerer reached the twins.

Tenebrae waved his arm, beckoning Katie and her brother closer. *This is it.* They listened to whatever Tenebrae was saying, then Katie shook her head. Insistent, Tenebrae stepped forward and grabbed her arm. Thomas's rings flashed as he pivoted at the waist, putting the full power of his core into the backhand strike. The *chukk* of knuckles and rings connecting with Tenebrae's cheekbone was cringe-inducing, even at a distance. The rich man collapsed just as quickly as my theories.

Thomas and Katie walked away, while two of the Ca-Curis' goons moved in on the prone executive. I groaned and ran in their direction, Jax a step behind me. I didn't like Tenebrae, but I couldn't watch them beat the idiot to death.

As we crossed the street Tenebrae rolled onto his stomach. The CaCuri muscle each grabbed an arm and began dragging him away. He broke free of one and kicked, striking one of the men at the ankle then pivoting to face the second.

I liked the way he handled himself. *If I end up being friends with this guy, I'm gonna be pissed.*

The twins were being hustled into the Paradise Parlor, but Thomas was dragging his feet, staring at the departing Tenebrae like he was willing to try his fists against an angry sorcerer. I reached the fray, but before I could do anything beyond announce my presence, the thickly bearded human crashed into me, embracing me with powerful, cobweb-shrouded arms.

"I'm gonna fly," he said, foul breath hot on my cheeks. "Fast as the wind."

I grabbed his overcoat, turning my hips and intending to use his momentum to throw him past me. But the glue-like cobwebs caught in my fists, immediately plunging me into the cold and pressure I'd come to fear. The man went limp and I supported his weight without thinking, even as the tension built behind my eyes. More CaCuri guards moved in, pausing only when they saw Jax with his badge out, identifying himself loudly and clearly. "Police! Stand aside!"

Cobwebs and skittering spiders danced up my arm as the wild-eyed man regained his footing and pushed away from me, confusion and terror distorting his face as he fled into the crowd. For a mad, confusing moment, I had the wild impulse to give chase, to grab and clutch and take more of whatever the cobwebs held. I don't know if I would have given in to the urge, because the twins were on us a moment later.

Thomas came in like a freight train, brow furrowed and wearing a snarl that stretched from ear to swollen ear. He plowed into the crowd, planting a massive shoulder into

Tenebrae's chest. The leaner man dropped, striking the cobblestone street, bounced, then scrambled to his feet and fled. Still hungry for a victim, Thomas turned his attention to me.

Katie grabbed his arm, but her bigger twin pushed through her as if she were made of mist. He was a shark locked onto his prey, and his eyes carried no emotion, only the sheer joy of destruction. Katie pushed herself back in front of Thomas, face spasming as her bad hip took her weight. She gripped his bicep with both arms and lifted her feet, throwing her full weight into her ploy to stop him. Catherine CaCuri risked herself, preventing her brother from attacking the manna strike detective and sabotaging her campaign.

Red-faced, she said something to Thomas that reined him in. Her brother temporarily under control, Katie immediately turned the crowd's attention to me.

I stood with hands on knees, struggling to catch my breath. The cold enveloping me was enough to tighten my chest, and the distant singing roar in my ears made it difficult to focus. And Katie was in my face, making it impossible to reason.

"Look at you, crawling back in here after your stunt on TV. You're a hypocrite," she said. "You drone on about the city, but you don't give a damn about it. I'm not the villain here!" The buzzing and whispering swelled in my ears, overlapping and adding a hiss to her words.

The other officers from the crime scene had followed us into the fray, and now formed a protective ring around us. The patrol cops, Hemingway and Andre, even Dungan. When your family is threatened, you step up. No matter what.

For a tense moment we all stared at each other. Then Katie called out to her bodyguards, directing them back to the Paradise Parlor. She left a hand on Thomas's arm, keeping her brother on a short leash even as she held my eye. "I've got your number, Carter."

As they departed, the tension seeped out of the crowd.

"Could book them on assault," Jax muttered, low enough to keep the bystanders from overhearing. "Thomas, anyway. Dozens of people saw him hit your friend."

"Not my friend," I said, fighting the chill and wishing I had my overcoat. "And they all saw what he did to the guards, too."

"Won't stick either way." Dungan grinned, the sudden burst of white teeth and wide gaps making him look like a living piano. He pointed at the dozens of onlookers. "CaCuri money buys everything around here. Especially eyewitnesses."

I watched the CaCuri twins entering the Paradise Parlor. "Everyone screws up at some point."

"The other gangs have their fingers in the pie, too, but they're not playing the long game the way these two are. Katie's got her thumb on the scales of justice. And I'm telling you," he swung his hand toward me and Jax, "both of you. She's just getting started." He stepped away, no longer standing with us now that the immediate threat had passed. He pointed a thumb at Hemingway and Andre. "Tell your friends to expect requisition paperwork. I'm gonna do my best to recover from this massive shit-storm you've created."

Dungan stormed off, and Jax and I stood alone.

My partner turned to me. "So where does this leave us?"

"Leaves me freezing. I need my coat." I started walking. "We've got other leads. Napier, Lillian Moller . . ."

Jax easily kept pace. "You really think Moller hunted her down to this neighborhood and killed her?"

"No," I said. "Which is why I'm back to the St. Beisht killing."

"And Anson."

"But not Anson himself," I said. "Whoever he watched kill Jane. Someone he didn't challenge or run away from." I winced, as the cold clamped down on my chest even tighter.

"Someone he expected to see there? An accomplice." Jax was thinking through the steps, coming to the same conclusion I'd already reached.

We passed locals engaged in the bustle of festival preparation. They seemed excited about the looming holiday and CaCuri's speech, even with the tension at the end. It felt wrong, like welcoming a malignant tumor into the family.

"An accomplice," I agreed. "Or a boss. Who'd be on the lookout for any signs that Anson had been compromised."

"Anson's PO," said Jax. "With his address she must've known he was lying about his job."

We reached Anson's apartment building and slowed our pace. He seemed to consider it, then shrugged. "Lots of parolees lie about employment."

"Most of them don't end up beaten to death when a couple cops are headed their way. And in the shower?" I huffed hot breath onto my hands, but couldn't shake the numbing chill. "Whoever did it, either Anson let them inside or they had the key to the apartment."

Jax peered at me, mandibles flexing. "Are you feeling okay? I know humans get cold easy, but this seems a little extreme."

"Not really." I cleared my throat. The buzzing was still strong in my ears. I squared my shoulders and faced him head-on. "It happened again. Cobwebs, cold, the whole thing."

"When, right now?" He looked closer. "Do you need to go to the hospital?"

"It started when I ran into the big guy with the beard." I closed my eyes, hoping that the world would be brighter when I opened them again. "It's gotta be some connection to the manna strike."

He rubbed the back of his neck. "Does it?"

"Hells, yes! It just makes sense!"

"All these places where you ran into cobwebs," he said. "I was there for most of them, but I didn't feel any of that."

"So?"

"So I was at the strike, too." He paused, hoping I'd make the connection on my own. I didn't give him the satisfaction. "If that's what's causing your reactions, then why aren't I having the same thing?" He stood straighter. "The Hasam's close. We should get you to a doctor."

"I was soaked in the stuff," I said.

"And I was there when we pulled you back to the site and loaded you onto an ambulance." He shook his head. "Carter, we need something more specific than that."

"You don't believe me." The light dimmed a little more.

"I didn't say that." He swiveled slightly. "You talk to eyewitnesses all the time. How often do their statements match exactly? Just because their recollection or interpretation is off, it doesn't mean you don't believe them, right?"

"I'm telling you, this is real."

"Okay," he said. "I believe that. So let's figure out what to do about it."

"I've tried." I started walking toward the Hasam, and the warmth of the overcoat and scarf.

He let out a harmonized roar of frustration. "You think I like seeing you suffer? Besides," his voice softened, "what if it's contagious?"

I managed a grin. "So take my mind off it and tell me if you can figure a way that someone could get access to Anson's apartment."

Jax wagged his head, but did me the favor. "You said it'd be someone with a key . . ." He stared at Anson's building, then at the other buildings on the block with their almost identical detailing and paint jobs. "I think I can guess who the biggest landlords in the 24th Ward are."

"What do you bet that the ownership of that building traces back to the CaCuris one way or another?" I kicked a discarded bottle from the sidewalk into the gutter. "With the amount of force that planted Anson's face into his shower wall?" I grimaced. "Thomas CaCuri killed him. And that means Thomas probably killed Jane. For any reason. She was there at the wrong time, drawing the wrong gangsters on an alley wall." I thought it through. It felt right. But why had he taken her jaw?

Jax stooped to grab the bottle I'd kicked, then turned to find a nearby dumpster. I curled my lips, feeling a mix of admiration and despair. My partner was one of the noble few who didn't just push problems down the road. And that was the kind of guy who inevitably got stabbed in the back, sooner or later.

When his walk toward the dumpster became a sprint, I was confused. Until I saw the body sprawled in the alley.

I ran forward, thinking it was Tenebrae, that now we'd be cleaning up after the murder of a wealthy political player right under our noses. But the heavily bandaged man propped against the alley wall wasn't the pretty-boy sorcerer. And he was still alive, if only barely. Jax stood on the other side of him, checking the alley for any immediate threat.

"Call for help!" I barked, but Jax was already racing back to the Hasam.

I pulled out my handkerchief and balled it up to put pressure on the wounds, though I knew it was a lost cause. Though he was decked out in bandages, the most dramatic of his wounds were fresh. One side of the man's skull had been staved in, and each shallow breath rattled in his chest. But what stopped my heart were the wounds to his face. Images of Jane's mutilated jaws crowded my mind, layering over the poor bastard who lay dead in yet another alley. His front teeth and a large portion of his jawbone had been ripped out, torn lips hanging limply on either side of his jaw.

Reaching toward him with the handkerchief, I immediately felt the sticky cling of cobwebs. I froze, afraid to move. The thought of more cold and darkness left me trembling. The man coughed, a weak, wet noise as it struggled past his ruined mouth, and that snapped me out of it. No matter how he'd gotten to that point, he deserved whatever comfort I could offer.

I pushed through the webs, pretending I couldn't feel them tugging at my flesh, like peeling off a day-old bandage. He gripped my wrist as I attempted to slow the bleeding, squeezing my mangled left hand tighter to his wounds as the bundled handkerchief bloomed red, then saturated, allowing bright drops to scatter onto the cobblestones. I nodded encouragement and whispered in his ear. "Hold on, buddy. Hold on." As though I could will him to stay alive, to tell us what he'd seen, who'd done this to him, to Jane.

Pressed close to him, I noticed that he had one arm in a sling. Then I noticed movement across his face. A series of bumps ringed the wounds on his jaw, and with each dying shudder, they grew. Within seconds, they swirled down his neck, under the skin but still continuing to expand. By the time they reached his shoulders they were fist-size spheres, sliding under the skin of his arms and collecting in his hands. The hands themselves swelled and burst, overcooked sausages on a too-hot grill. They healed immediately and swelled again, splitting and mending in turns as they expanded into grotesque caricatures.

I tore my gaze from his hands to find the man's eyes locked on mine. One iris was brown, the other a filmy pale blue, as if a fish scale obscured it from the world. Uncertain what to do, I simply stared back, unable to even offer a last bit of comfort to a dying man. As the crowd noise increased, he opened his mouth, trying to speak, but the only thing that emerged was a stream of even more blood, gushing across his chin and over his chest. His tongue had been removed as well.

Then he gave a long, shuddering breath, and grew still. His hands were still swollen, but no more shapes rippled underneath his skin. I stared at the poor bastard, wondering what the Hells I'd just seen. I paused, looking into his discolored eye, and a memory flared. *A man with one dead eye.*

I pulled out my notebook, putting down every detail of this newest murder scene I could remember, ignoring the desperate, shivering cold that ran through my arms and legs. I kept writing, trying to find the details that escaped me, even though I knew there was no way Thomas had killed this man. I paused only to wipe my hands with the blood-soaked handkerchief, clearing away the cobwebs and telling myself I'd be fine. I stood, as lightheaded as if I'd just climbed to a great height, hot and sweaty. I realized that the pressure had eased and I took deep, instinctive gulps of air. I was still struggling to get my bearings as the sirens approached.

23

I DIDN'T GO HOME THAT NIGHT. Other officers may have been on scene but I was the only one who'd been in physical contact with the man in the alley during his transformation. And that meant everyone involved with the newly formed Arcane Regulation and Containment units wanted a piece of my time. As the night wore on, I slipped Jax my apartment key and asked him to feed Rumple while I spent one long, fruitless hour after another in various interviews and debriefs. I managed to stay awake and mostly coherent as I repeated again and again what I'd seen. But I kept what I'd *felt* to myself. That was something I couldn't trust to just anyone. If alarms were raised and Dr. Baelen got her webbed hands on me, I'd never find justice for Jane or the new victim. But I also knew I needed help. During breaks I called Gellica incessantly, growing more anxious with each unanswered ring. I was desperate for someone to believe me and terrified of what might happen if they did.

By the time the day shift was trickling in to the Bullpen I was red-eyed and exhausted. I wanted to get some sleep. I wanted to not think about the media or manna or invisible threads and what it meant for me. I wanted to do my job. But even that option was about to be taken away.

I got the news in Bryyh's office, standing next to the beige metal file cabinets topped with pictures of her grandkids. Bryyh was pacing from her desk to the cabinet, busying herself with paperwork and sparing me the least amount of attention possible as I crumpled the paper she'd just handed me, an OCU requisition paper claiming the Jane Doe and Anson cases. They were now officially combined under the umbrella of Dungan's St. Beisht investigation. I took a breath then smoothed the paper against the cool metal of the filing cabinet. Sometimes we have to fight our impulse to tear to pieces the things we might need later.

"Are you sure there's nothing you can do?"

Bryyh retrieved a file and slammed the cabinet drawer shut, narrowly missing taking a chunk out of my remaining fingers in the process. "There isn't."

She stalked back to her desk and took a seat. "And you know what? I think this may be for the best. You need a little time to clear your head. Maybe we rushed you back to active duty too fast." The beads in her braids clinked as she pulled her chair closer to the desk. "You know what happens when your plate gets too full."

"Too full?" I said. "We had one case. And it got taken away."

"Hemingway and Andre were first arrivals on the Anson murder scene." Bryyh's voice softened. "I notice they aren't in here fighting for the right to chase his killer."

"Hemingway and Andre have other cases," I said. "I don't." I didn't say that I needed to find something to think about other than strange magical phenomena. I tried another angle. "You were the one who told me to fight to keep Jane."

She frowned, but it wasn't without sympathy.

"Well, that's not an option now. Unless you think you can call up the OCU and make this go away."

We both knew I couldn't. Dungan wasn't going to back down after he'd marked his territory, and the OCU was well within their rights to snatch the case away.

"Listen," I said. "The OCU detective who requisitioned the cases—Dungan—he's pulling something."

"He's pulling your cases," she said. "And you don't like it." But she set down her pen and gave me her full attention.

"He doesn't give a damn about Jane and the new victim," I said. "He's got some ego-driven idea about playing the Harlqs and CaCuris against each other, and he's snatching up these homicides to get me and Jax out of his hair." Even if Dungan succeeded in whatever he was doing, he might or might not get around to charging someone with Jane's murder. "He's pulled the case to spite me, and those killings are gonna sit neglected while he chases his whales."

She took a deep breath and held it, cheeks puffed out as she stared at me. When she released it, her shoulders slumped.

"Sorry," she said. "There's nothing to be done. If we could make—"

"Come on!" I whacked the side of the file cabinet, causing the pictures of her family to totter.

"OCU are detectives, too," she said, "and they're fully qualified to pursue a murder investigation. As I was *saying* . . ." She chomped down on the word, as if crushing a candy between her teeth. "If we could make an argument that we've got a unique ability to work the case, we could try to pull it back." She picked up her pen. "Think on that, and let me know when you have something that doesn't waste my time."

Bryyh returned to her work, but was kind enough to let me stew for a few seconds in the relative privacy of her office.

I was still staring at the pictures of her family when someone knocked on Bryyh's door. She bellowed a gruff, "Come in!" and Guyer leaned into the room.

"Looks like it's my turn to talk to you," she said. "You ready for more?"

I wasn't, not even close. But Guyer was at least a friendly face.

"Why not," I said, and we went back to the interview room.

Guyer wore brown dress pants and a crisp cream-colored blouse. Dark circles no longer rimmed her eyes, and she actually had a light smile as we talked.

"You get some rest?" I asked.

"I had a day off," she said. "You should try it." The table between us was clear of distractions, the slightly pitted vinyl surface reflecting the overhead fluorescent light in a muted brown. "I understand there was a sorcerer on site?"

I nodded. "Mitri Tenebrae. He had some kind of fight with the CaCuris and got out of there before he got his ass kicked. I'm all in favor of you rattling his cage, but I don't think he had anything to do with the body."

"No?"

"The damage to the victim's face matches my Jane Doe." I winced. "The Jane Doe on Ringsridge Road. There was flesh from the killer's hand in Jane's wounds, and Tenebrae doesn't have any corresponding damage." I'd seen him up close, and both of his hands were sculpted perfection, just like the rest of him.

Guyer made a note of that, but it wasn't anything I hadn't already told the other ARC officers.

"Any word on the victim's ID?" I asked.

"Nope. Empty pockets, no wallet, and we sure as Hells aren't getting any fingerprints off him. We'll get it one way or another, though. Now," she set down her pen and rested her hands on the table, "let's go through what happened in the alley one more time."

In the previous ARC questionings that night I'd been hesitant to talk. I'd tried playing dumb, I'd tried indicating that someone else must have had to do something. Ever since the first twinge from the shards of snake oil at Jane's murder, I'd been more worried about what the brass and the shrinks would say than what I needed to do in order to get to the bottom of things.

But the situation was at a tipping point. And I realized that I had a way to prove I had a unique connection to the alleyway killings. If I did that, then maybe Bryyh could fight to keep the cases out of the grip of the OCU. I drew a deep breath and counted to three.

"I can do better than that," I said. "I can show you."

Guyer was silent, but she raised an eyebrow. I barreled ahead.

"Do you have your cloak? Or something else manna-linked." I squeezed my hands into fists. "You got anything like that on you?"

She nodded.

"What is it?" I asked. When she hesitated again, I added, "Trust me."

Guyer sighed and tapped the brooch pin on her jacket. "It's tied to a collapsible baton on my belt. A bit of self-defense magic I learned back in school."

"Can I see the baton?" I said.

She unlatched it from her belt and set it down on the tabletop.

I put my hand over it and felt nothing. No tingle, no itch, not a single strand of cobweb. I shifted in my seat and tried my left hand, paying special attention to the stubs of my fingers. Nothing.

Still, I focused, trying to convince it to grow, to bloom like I'd done to the poor son of a bitch in the alley. I stared and urged it on, and the sweep of the second hand around the clock told me nothing was happening.

Guyer cleared her throat.

My cheeks warmed. "You sure it's still magicked? It's been a long time since you were in school."

"It wasn't that long." A bit of ice crept into her voice. "And I never used it, so it's still good."

"I don't know," I said. "I'm not getting anything. Are you sure—"

"Shortcuts," she swore. Then she grabbed the baton and tossed it across the room. While it was still in the air, she plucked the pin from her lapel, gripping the thin metal tight between thumb and forefinger. The baton jerked to a sudden stop, hovering in the air. It danced around the room, responding to the motions of the pin, amplifying them. If she'd been surrounded by attackers, she could have clubbed each one with only the simplest movements of her hand. It was as clear and simple a demonstration of magic as I'd ever seen.

And there wasn't a single thread or cobweb to be found. "Satisfied?"

I studied my hands, knuckles white as I gripped the edge of the table.

"Because," she continued, "I just signed up for an hour's worth of paperwork to reimburse me for the manna to re-treat the baton."

"I get it," I said.

"Yeah? I'm not sure you do. The reason I'll get reimbursed is that I'm authorized for manna use in this case. That's only happening because something clearly magical happened with that corpse you found, and the ARC teams needs to know what it was."

I didn't respond, determined to let her run her course.

"That poor bastard in the alley had something unnatural happen to him. Our best theory is that his body was being taken by manna rot."

I looked up. "Say more."

"Manna burns itself up as it's used. If it runs out while the magical bond is still in place, the tethered materials will be consumed. If the victim had some kind of magical bond, and it wasn't severed properly . . ." She deflated slightly. "Well, you saw what happened."

I thought of the half-magical Gellica. No wonder she was so dependent on Paulus and her supply of manna. Without thinking, I rubbed my left hand. Guyer's eyes widened.

"Oh, Hells." She covered her mouth. "If you're asking about what happened to you, I don't know. No one's ever been exposed to raw manna the way you were." She looked at me, brows furrowed. "You must have been told all this before, right?"

I nodded. But I couldn't ask about Gellica's status without betraying her confidence. Did she have a half-life? Did she need to keep consuming manna to stay alive? If so, what did the manna strike mean for her?

"Look." Guyer tried to offer words of comfort. "Back in the first industrial revolution, the old manna cars ran like champs. Hells, they ran all the time. People just put them into park, locked the doors, and topped off the manna tank. The engine would keep going forever as long as the central motor at the car plant stayed in operation. There's no reason to think you might . . . you know."

I shook my head. "I'm saying I could feel a web of—"

"I don't care what you felt," she said, her note of sympathy evaporating. "I don't care about your hunches or guesses. We're trying to find out what happened. You know how this works, right?" She paused long enough for me to bow my head in acknowledgment. "So do us both a favor and stop yapping about imaginary itchy cobwebs, and focus on the facts."

There was pressure around my temples, a headache settling in for a long stay.

"If I knew why it happened, I'd tell you. I tried to show you, but . . ." I gestured at the baton helplessly.

"Okay," she said. "Whatever you were trying to pull didn't work. Happens to all the best smartasses from time to time." She raised the brooch and the baton hovered over the table. She narrowed her eyes and murmured, and the baton fell from the air, landing in her waiting palm.

"Now," she said, "let's start back at the beginning. You and Detective Ajax were on the street . . ."

I fought the impulse to shove the condescending words down her throat. I knew what I'd seen—what I'd *done*—in that alley. It had to be tied to magic, but it didn't seem to have any consistency. I started to tick off the places and times I'd encountered the tingles, starting with—

"Carter!"

Guyer glared at me. "Stop daydreaming. The faster we finish here, the faster you can get on with figuring out who's out there cutting the jaws off people."

"Someone might," I said. "It won't be me."

She pursed her lips like a disappointed teacher. "Carter, I know you care more than anyone, even if this guy turns out to be a dealer or a thug."

I slung an arm across the back of my chair. "Not my case."

Guyer tossed her head, confused. "But you were first on scene. It's clearly a homicide, even if the ME doesn't have a ruling yet."

"OCU," I said. "Requisition paperwork already came in."

"They're taking your case?"

"They're taking *all* my cases." One arm still hooked on my chair back, I leaned closer. "And how much time do you think they'll spend on a few dead newcomers in alleyways?"

She sat back, apparently pondering this development. "Has Bryyh—" She looked in the direction of the captain's office, then stood and paced around the table. "No, don't tell me. Because no one's told me about any transfers. So as far as I know, you're still lead on this case." Guyer patted her pile of paperwork. "And I've got the forms to prove it."

I stared at her, and after a heartbeat or two I was able to piece together a semi-coherent thought. "And so . . ."

"So I'm officially inviting you to come along."

I stood. Anywhere was better than sitting in that meeting room another minute.

"To do what?"

"What I'm paid to do," she said. "I'm going to go interview the victim."

24

GUYER AND I WALKED SIDE-BY-SIDE down the halls of the Bunker, making our way to the Medical Examiner's offices. It was still early, the mist-swirled darkness of morning turning the hallway windows into dark mirrors.

At that hour Doc Mumphrey wasn't in. We were greeted by another pathologist, a stocky, slightly bowlegged Mollenkampi named Dilla who peered through a pair of recently repaired glasses as Guyer filled out the paperwork for our nameless victim.

"I wondered when one of you folks was going to come take a look at that fella." Dilla turned without giving us a chance to respond, grabbing an empty gurney as she escorted us into the body stacks.

Space is always at a premium in Titanshade, and considering the number of people who suffer investigation-worthy deaths, the ME's office didn't have much choice but to find a compact storage solution. The body stacks were past the offices and examination rooms, an immense room that was nothing more than a walkway and stack after stack of floor-to-ceiling shelves. Each shelf touched the next, and only the first had space for the gurney. The end of each shelf had a hand crank, and when Dilla turned the first, the entire shelf slid to the side, gliding along recessed tracks in the floor and ceiling, until it occupied the open space. Then she moved to the next shelf in line and repeated the process, until a lane was opened up in the middle of the stacks.

Dilla wheeled the gurney down the newly opened aisle

and pulled an expanding metal stick from its side. Consulting the checkout card, she positioned the gurney and began pumping a foot pedal, activating a hydraulic press that raised the gurney to slightly beyond head height, lining it up with a refrigerated cubby. She used the telescoping metal pole to hook the end of the metal body tray within the cubby and slid the entire tray and body out onto the gurney. The pathologist released the hydraulics and rolled our John Doe out of the stacks and into the examination room.

She unzipped the body bag but didn't open it. "I need to observe," she said to Guyer. "I'll be in the next room, so don't close the door."

Guyer walked a slow lap around the table and pulled back the sides of the body bag. Then, under the fluorescent lights, I got the first good look at him since the alley. I'd remembered his dead eye correctly, and the fact that he had one arm in a sling. Some of the deep facial bruising also appeared partially healed, though it was difficult to tell amid all the additional damage and resultant gore. Still, the guy had gotten his ass kicked something fierce not too long before he was killed. Guyer fidgeted with the bandaging on the side of his head, pulling it away and revealing that one ear was twisted off. The poor bastard was a mess.

But all the old wounds were mundane things that someone might suffer, and they paled in comparison to the damage to his face and hands. The latter had swollen so large that a single fist was larger than his entire head. The skin was horribly scarred and torn, and it was hard to believe that the missing teeth and tongue might not have been the worst pain he was in as he died.

"I did this to him." The words were out of my mouth before I realized I was speaking.

Guyer was stooped over John Doe, examining the damage to his mouth and jaw. She glanced up, holding my gaze for the briefest of moments, before turning back to the victim's body.

"No, you didn't. And the fact that you couldn't move this," she patted the baton on her hip, "is proof of that."

I didn't argue, just turned and walked to the door. Dilla sat in the other room, radio playing as she tackled a crossword. I stood in the doorway and caught my breath. A somber-voiced news anchor announced that a Barekusu caravan had been spotted heading in the direction of Titanshade.

The oldest of the Eight Families, the Barekusu had welcomed each of the other sibling Families as they awoke, teaching them the ways of the Path and how to live in Eyjan safely. Humanity had been the last Family to appear, a boisterous younger sibling that the others tolerated. Maybe we were expected. Eight is a sacred number in the Path, after all.

I hovered in the door a few seconds too long, causing Dilla to look up from her pencil-smudged newsprint and clack her jaws.

"Unless you can think of a seven-letter word for someone who interrupts me when I'm busy, I'm not interested."

"Sorry." I held up my hands. "Needed to catch my breath, is all." I turned back to face Guyer and the body.

"Hey!" Her voice stopped me. "You want to, you can wait out here. No rule that says detectives gotta see that stuff firsthand."

True. But then, most detectives didn't have a matter of hours before they were removed from the case. I nodded my thanks, and crossed back into the examination room.

Guyer stood beside the body, rolling her shoulders like a prizefighter. "You ready?"

I gave a thumbs-up. "What do you need me to do?"

"Stay out of the way and take notes." Guyer reached into her cloak. She pulled out a vial of manna, identical to the one she'd used at the medical check-in to animate the shadows of the ice plains animals. I knew it was different, though—at the end of every shift, DOs had to turn over their manna for weighing and calibration to ensure not a single drop had been used without authorization. One more practice that might become antiquated if the manna strike proved to be as deep and fruitful as the public hoped.

Guyer hooked a thumb in the dead man's jaw and pulled down, exposing the ragged stub of his tongue. She sprayed a fine mist of manna on the damaged flesh, as well as the missing tooth sockets and exposed jawbone. She peered at his face, creasing her lips into a slight frown. Then, seemingly satisfied, she released the victim and took one long step backward. She spritzed her own tongue, teeth, and jaw. Her thumb had a streak of congealed blood from the inside of the victim's mouth, and she wiped it along the length of her own jaw, on the side that reflected his wound. Returning the vial to its inner pocket, she began to mutter, the words indistinct at first, then becoming clearer.

"Wanderer of the Path," she said, "share a traveler's tale with me. Tell of your last thoughts, sights, and experiences. Tell the story of the injustice done to you." The runes on her cloak, normally indistinct, began to glow with an eerie radiance as she tied the bond between herself and the corpse. Their iridescent shimmer intensified, becoming apparent even in the flickering, deathly yellow of the examination room's lights.

Guyer lengthened her breath, and with each inhale and exhale her mouth worked erratically, as if she were having a spasm localized to the lower half of her face. Her eyes began to roll back and then, just as it had started, she appeared normal once more.

I relaxed my grip on my notepad and glanced at the clock. It had only been a few seconds. Guyer blinked and narrowed her eyes as she studied the corpse on the gurney. She muttered again, running her hands through a series of positions with the formality of a martial artist stepping through forms. Suddenly she halted and began pacing around the body, muttering to herself and adjusting her cloak.

I hazarded a question. "What's wrong?"

"Someone else is talking to the victim's echo." She scratched her nose, then crouched, viewing the body from a different angle.

I crossed my arms. "You mean whoever killed him is trying to work divination magic."

"Most likely."

"Wait a minute . . ." I rocked back and forth, thinking through the motivation. "If the killer needed to talk to this guy, why would they kill him in the first place?"

Guyer examined the man's previous wounds, the bruises, broken arm, and missing ear. "Sorcery's expensive, but kidnapping is complicated, and definitely riskier than running around with a few body parts. I mean, you have to be okay with killing whoever it is you want to talk to, but that bit doesn't seem to be a problem for your guy."

"No," I said. "It doesn't." I hesitated. "Can you get around whatever it is they're doing?"

"Of course I can. It's just . . ." She rolled her wrist. "It's tricky."

"Tricky how?"

"What I'm doing is like trying to talk to someone at a party, when they're already in a conversation with someone else."

I grunted, thinking of getting Gellica's attention while Tenebrae was committed to charming her.

"Plus," she said, "rigor mortis sets in a little earlier in the jaw."

"Oh."

"Happily, we have an advantage. Your killer has bits and pieces of this guy. But we've got the rest of the body!"

I shivered. "Yeah, happy."

She brought out the vial and pulled back the corpse's clothes, this time letting a fine mist fall over his entire torso.

"You're approved for this much use?" I said.

"Are you kidding? Look at his hands." She grimaced. "Whatever happened to this guy, we need to know about it."

I got another chill. I knew what had happened to him. *Carter* had happened.

"Now." She tucked away the vial. "Let's try this again. You'll need to ask the questions."

"What?"

"I'll be occupied." Guyer dragged a finger down the length of the dead man's torso, collecting a thin film of manna. She used the same finger to circle her face, tracing her jaw, forehead, and temple, as well as the sides of her throat. When she started her chant once more, she spoke faster and louder, moving crisply through the hand positions. I didn't know how much of it mattered and how much was to help her focus, so I kept my mouth shut and waited.

When the body sat up with a jerk, I almost dropped my notepad. The dead man stared blindly ahead, his face going through the motions of speech, but with no tongue, a partial jaw, and no air in his lungs, there was no sound beyond the slosh of his torn flesh dragging across itself. I didn't let myself think what would have happened to the body if he'd been in full rigor during the ritual. I wondered if that had even occurred to Guyer. In a way, both she and Baelen were like Handsome Hanford's absurd conspiracies about otherworldly visitors—they all toyed with abductees for their own bizarre purposes. Behind me the door snapped shut; Dilla had abandoned any pretense of involvement.

A moment later Guyer began speaking, lower and raspy. On the gurney, the dead man, tongueless, breathless, mouthed the words as Guyer gave them voice.

"*She's . . . hitting me . . .*"

I remembered that I was supposed to be asking questions. "Who?" I said. "Who is?"

"*New boss . . . hitting all of us. So strong . . .*"

Katie CaCuri was in charge. Thomas was strong.

"*She's . . . HITTING ME!*" The victim's torso jerked, and his wounded arm slipped from its sling. Flopping at an unnatural angle, it had clearly been broken and badly tended to, as a ridge of bone pressed out of the forearm, ready to pop through the skin. I looked away and managed to ask my next question.

"In the alley," I said. "Who is in the alley with you?"

"*The alley,*" Guyer spoke, her voice rattling. "*There was someone . . . someone who knew . . .*"

The man tilted his head, as if listening to a different voice. His shredded lips twitched, and Guyer spoke again.

"*No . . . Sssseed tearssss . . . all gone.*"

Seed tears? What did that mean? I risked a glance at Guyer. Her eyes were white, rolled back into her head, and she swayed back and forth, her face contorted to be a match for his, giving him a voice even as his killer fought to wrest control away. Seeing the powerful magical connection, I couldn't help myself—I stepped closer, and put my hand between her and the victim's body. I felt nothing but empty air, no tingle, no threads. More evidence that I didn't know what the Hells was going on.

"No more sssssna . . ."

"No more what?" I said. "What is it?"

"So ssstrong. Please, make. . . make her sstop!"

The dead man's torso slammed back onto the steel support tray. Guyer staggered forward, steadying herself against the edge of the dead man's gurney. I tucked an arm under her shoulder, supporting her as much as I could. We were silent, staring at the corpse and listening to one another breathe.

When we gathered ourselves, we left Dilla to replace the body and headed back to the Bullpen. We didn't speak as we walked. Both of us were exhausted, and I was processing what we'd learned from the victim. He'd talked about a new boss, maybe a gang leader taking out her anger on him? And seed tears, what did that mean? The obvious connection would be to angel tears, but . . .

"Watch out." Guyer's muttered warning brought me out of my reverie.

Dr. Baelen stormed down the hall, clipboard clutched to her chest. Her face erupted with disapproval when her gaze lit on me, head fin rising to attention as her eyes widened and buccal openings flared to display the pink-tinged gills beneath.

"You're late for the medical," she snapped, grabbing for my arm. I batted her hand away, but the delicate claws skated over my hand, raising hair-thin scratches.

I stepped away, swearing. "What are you doing?"

Baelen backed up and reapproached, as if she were starting the conversation over in her head. Her immaculately starched shirt was misbuttoned, leaving it skewed and awkward.

"You had an outside experience with unknown magic," she said. "Possibly next gen manna tainted with psychotropics. We need to check your measurements against your chart—"

"Detective Carter had nothing to do with the events of last night." Guyer's tone was firm. "I've already conducted a thorough—"

"You've conducted?" Baelen threw her hands in the air. "What possible qualifications do you possess to conduct anything?"

Guyer's face darkened, and I slid back another step. It never pays to get in an angry sorcerer's line of fire.

Baelen, however, didn't seem to notice. Her voice gained momentum with each sentence. "Can't you see?" She looked from me to Guyer. "This is a possibility to establish a real connection between altered next gen manna and a site survivor. Are you blind to what this means?"

Finally, someone believed me, and it was the one person who had the power to hold me for indefinite observation. I could be locked down as thoroughly as the oil wells, if Baelen convinced her superiors it was in the national interest.

"There is a room full of participants in this building, ready for their exam, and the two of you are sabotaging it." Baelen crossed her arms and huffed loudly. "I insist that Carter come for immediate testing."

"How long will that take?" I said.

"As long as it takes!" Baelen's eyes were still wide, her gills still on display.

Guyer whistled through her teeth.

"Okay, how about this. To do additional testing on our friend here, you'll need to go through the TPD liaison to your program. And currently," she tapped her chest, "that's me." The sorcerer moved a step closer to the agitated researcher. "And in my official role, I've duly considered your request, and my response is," her voice rose to a shout, "fuck off!"

"Is there an issue here?" Bryyh had emerged from the Bullpen, whether due to the shouting or simply coincidentally.

Baelen spun on her heel and raised a finger, but Guyer cut her off.

"Nothing concerning. I need Detective Carter's presence for a little longer to conduct an ARC inquiry."

Bryyh looked at Baelen, one eyebrow slightly raised.

The Gillmyn quivered with rage. "The medical check-in is today, and all participants need to be on time and present!"

"No," Bryyh said. "They need to attend when they're available." She turned her attention to me. "You and your partner have anything booked for Friday?"

I shook my head.

"Good," said Bryyh. "Report for your check-in first thing Friday morning. Issue settled."

Baelen rose onto the toes of her shoes, as if about to launch into another speech, then thought better of it. She squeezed her mouth shut, nodded, then departed.

Bryyh threw a skeptical look at Guyer and me. "Where were the two of you coming back from?" She held up a hand. "Never mind. Guyer, I need to borrow you for a few minutes. Come up to 5D with me."

The captain departed, but I turned to Guyer. "Listen, the dead guy said *seed tears*. Like angel tears, right?"

"We'll go over it later," she said. "I've got more work to do."

"So what if it's the snake oil that triggers—"

"Later!" She jogged after Bryyh, and I stood in the hallway, alone with my theories and the memories of a dead man talking.

Sitting at my desk, rolling a half-tael coin across my palm, I watched Jax walk toward me through the Bullpen with wrinkled clothes and slumped shoulders.

"What did you say to Baelen?" he asked as he dropped into the chair across from me. "She stormed into the exam room squeezing that clipboard so tight I thought it'd break in half."

"She thinks I'm keeping secrets."

"About the cobwebs?" He leaned into the desk and lowered his voice. "We started talking about this before we found the body. You have to talk to someone. What about Guyer? She'll listen."

"I tried. Didn't work out so well."

"Try again!" He double-clacked his formidable jaws in a show of frustration.

I pressed a hand to my heart. "I promise. But for now, listen to what I just learned." I gave him a quick rundown of the confrontation, what the dead man had revealed, and why I thought he had some link to the CaCuris. Jax seemed unimpressed.

"The victim got worked over by someone strong, and an unnamed 'she' hit him? That could mean anything. Besides, we both saw the twins walking into the Paradise before we found him. There's no way they took his jaw. Especially if whoever did that was able to interfere with Guyer's work."

I ran both hands through my hair, massaging my scalp. "It still seems connected . . ."

"Well, regardless, we've got a two-day reprieve on the medical." He yawned and stood, rising up onto his toes as he stretched. "I got almost no sleep and it looks like you got less. If we try to function now, we're going to make mistakes." He stepped away. "I'm going to recharge, and we can come at it fresh tomorrow."

"Yeah, that sounds good. I'm right behind you, just need to talk to Guyer."

"Carter . . ."

"Hey," I dropped my voice, "I made you a promise."

He wagged his head. "Fine, but don't wait around here for an hour."

In fact, it was several hours before Guyer returned to the Bullpen. Hours to mentally replay the victim's words and my own failure to manipulate the magic that threaded Guyer's baton. Why, now that I finally decided to prove what was happening, was it all falling apart? I sat at my desk and drew lazy figure eights on the newspaper, hoping for inspiration.

The newspapers had extensive coverage of the pair of murders and impromptu CaCuri rally in the 24th Ward. *The Titanshade Union Record* featured unflattering photos of the CaCuris. Thomas's was a mug shot. Catherine was shown with a slack face, the easy look of disdain she wore when not smiling for a crowd. The headline of *The Daily Saber* had a photo of Catherine standing in front of her supporters. The caption read: *Loud, Proud . . . Destined for Greatness?*

Tossing the papers to the side, I kneaded the cramped

muscles at the base of my neck, digging the eraser into each knot in search of relief. I was exhausted, and every time I thought I was beginning to grasp what was happening, it slipped away, like trying to carry a snowball to the city's center. And to make things worse, I couldn't shake the image of the dying man in the alley. I kept seeing his arms morphing and changing even as he struggled to survive, staring at me with his good eye.

I blinked. The single dead eye. Jane had told Moller that she'd bought true manna from a dealer with a "fish eye." As I put the pieces together and realized what two murders in alleys might have in common, Guyer cut across the Bullpen, probably heading home, or back down to her temporary assignment in Vice. I dropped the pencil and intercepted her.

"Snake oil!" I said. "The victim will have it in his system."

She stared at me.

"When you were here for the last medical," I continued, "you told me that it's impossible to know what effect angel tears would have when it was mixed with manna."

Guyer frowned. "In theory."

"Close enough," I said. "Snake oil is the answer."

She squinted one eye, as if fighting off a headache. "What's the question?"

"Why I couldn't do anything with your baton," I said, managing to keep the exasperation out of my voice. "We need to get some snake oil, and then I can show you."

She shifted the portfolio to her other arm. "I can't do that."

"Sure you can," I said. "You just need to—"

"I mean I *won't* do that." She stared me down. "I'm not going to jump through any more hoops. I don't know what happened to that poor bastard in the alley, but you didn't do it to him."

I stared, wordless.

"You're not a sorcerer," she snapped. "You don't have some kind of connection with the universe, and you can't control manna." She closed her eyes and forced her face to calm. When she reopened them, her voice was softer. "Whatever happened to that guy, Carter, it's not your fault.

Stop blaming yourself for everything that goes wrong in this town."

Guyer walked away, headed toward the elevators, leaving me with a single person who might listen to my theory. I knew that what I'd seen had been real, and I needed to talk to someone who had experience with manna beyond standard sorcery.

I needed to talk to Gellica, now more than ever.

25

THE LOBBY OF 1 GOVERNMENT Plaza was in fine form, with a well-dressed crowd swigging free drinks while holding small plates of even smaller finger foods. A string quartet lent an air of class to the affair, and the people making small talk looked almost as wealthy as the crowd at Tenebrae's fundraiser. The AFS couldn't officially support a candidate in a local election, so there were no posters or collection cards for Meredith Plunkett, but the purpose of the event was obvious.

Unlike the last such party I'd attended, I was able to find Gellica almost immediately. She was talking to a small group of people, holding their attention as casually as she held her wineglass. I approached the group and stood beside her, causing the polite chatter to fall off immediately.

"Yes?" she said. Not a drop of irritation showed in her voice. She was good at her job.

"A word, Envoy? Police business."

She bowed out of her conversation with more casual grace than I could muster in a lifetime. We made our way behind a serving station where we could get a semblance of privacy, and she faced me with a frown.

"Here for another awkward confrontation?"

If I wanted to earn her time, I'd have to start by owning my track record of screw-ups.

"No." I ran a hand across my brow, knocking a few more hairs loose from their fragile roots. I felt old and uncomfortable, and I wondered what the Hells I was doing there, and if this was a good idea after all. "There's something we need to talk about. Privately."

She glanced toward the lobby filled with the wealthy influential. "I don't have time for this."

"You'll want to hear what I've got to say." I stepped to my left, sliding back into her line of sight. "Trust me."

Gellica glared at me. "Trusting you is a bad habit." She circled around, putting her back to the crowd. "What's so important?"

Over her shoulder the room was a blend of executives and lawyers, judges and bankers making small talk, even Mitri Tenebrae, as well-polished and perfect as ever. Though it amused me to know the sorcerer was probably wearing a thick layer of makeup, since there wasn't so much as a bruise where CaCuri had struck him. With him and the others there, this was no place to talk about sensitive topics. I had to get her out of there, and I could think of only one thing she might want.

"You wanted to talk about that trait we have in common."

She hesitated, and I pressed harder.

"Now I've got something major to share."

Her frown deepened. I started to think she was about to have me thrown out of the building before she finally said, "Follow me."

Gellica's office was tidy as ever. Impressive, considering it seemed like she spent more time there than her home. Thoughts of her home conjured images of my hesitation at her doorstep, and I pushed them away as I reached for the light switch. Gellica batted my hand away from the wall switch and strode into the dark, turning on the desk light instead.

"I don't want anyone seeing my light on and stopping in to say hello." She leaned against the desk, her eyes more guarded than the Bunker's holding cells. "I can give you five minutes," she flicked her wrist, checking the time on an elegant gold watch, "starting now."

"Thank you," I said, not quite sure how to proceed, and wondering if I should be there at all. What if I had the same effect on her that I'd had on the man in the alley? If I was right about the cause, we were safe, but if not . . .

When my pause grew uncomfortable, Gellica crossed her arms. "What's this about? I can't imagine you're here to apologize for causing a scene and storming out of Mitri's party."

"No," I said. "I mean, I should apologize, but—"

"So, no meaning yes?" She pulled herself up to her full height, holding the wineglass she'd carried up from the party. "I'm a little unclear on your usage."

I paused to collect myself and glanced around the office. Somehow the place had grown intimidating since the last time I'd visited. The portrait of Ambassador Paulus glared over my shoulder, the dark pools of her eyes boring into my back as I made my case to Gellica. It occurred to me how easy it would be to string mics throughout an office. Under the coffee table and inside the lamp, anywhere that would defy simple observation. How many deals had been made in that office? How many lives ruined and pleas ignored?

Gritting my teeth, I helped myself to a seat on the couch, perched on the boundary of the lamp's pool of illumination, bridging the shadow and the light. It wasn't until I set my fingers on the blue and white flower pattern of the fabric that I began to calm.

"Good to see my favorite couch." I did my best to fake a laugh.

She didn't bother to reciprocate.

"Well, when I don't want you coming around anymore, you can have it."

I didn't know how to respond to that, and she didn't give me a chance to gather my thoughts.

"Do you have something to say? I need to get back to the party."

I took a deep breath and pulled an evidence bag from inside my coat. The broken glass shards we'd gathered from the alley pressed against the envelope as I broke the seal. It was out of protocol, but it was also the best chance to learn what happened to Jane. And what might be happening to me.

I shook loose one of the shards, careful not to touch it.

Gellica leaned forward, eyes fixed on the faint iridescent shimmer. I had her attention now.

She stretched out a hand, then hesitated. "Is that . . . ?"

"Not quite," I said. "It's snake oil. Manna mixed with angel tears. That's a street drug that users put in their eyes—"

She stopped me. "I know what angel tears is."

"Okay." I cleared my throat. "Point is, this is mixed with manna. It's a tiny amount, but I was wondering if you can bind it to something?"

"I'm not a sorcerer," she said. "Which you already know."

"Are you telling me that in all your training, Paulus never made you learn any magic?"

She curled a lip. "I never got farther than an introductory binding and bonds class. I can't do anything useful, especially not with diluted manna."

"It doesn't have to be useful," I said. "Maybe it's better if it's not."

She set her wineglass on the coffee table and glanced around. "It'll have to be something light, if it's as diluted as you're saying." A few strides took her to a shelf with long-stemmed flowers in a delicately etched vase. Gellica pinched the stem, the bloom of the tallest flower falling into her palm. Returning to the coffee table, she pressed the bloom into the glass shards, letting the flower's petal soak up most of the iridescent liquid. Muttering commands and weaving her fingers, Gellica focused on the two items. The moment stretched, and the minute hand of the desk clock ticked once, twice.

"Does this count against my five minutes?" I asked.

Her frown deepened. "Shut up." It was several more minutes before she sat back, beads of perspiration dotting her brow. "Done."

I shifted uncomfortably. She'd done it, and now the question of my sanity sat in the empty air between the shard and the flower. If there was nothing there but the same lack of sensation I'd experienced with Guyer, I'd have to face the fact that it really was all in my head, no matter what I'd seen or thought I'd felt. I reached out, dragging my hand across the coffee table. Soft cobwebs tugged at my fingers. I sighed, relieved and terrified. Now I faced the next question: could I show it to someone else?

"It's a one-to-one bond," she said. "And it won't work if the flower and shard are more than a hand's-width apart. Basic, but with the dilution and how rusty I am . . . Frankly, I'm pleased I was able to do that much."

With a deliberate motion, I nudged the shard toward Gellica. Next to it, the flower pushed forward the same distance. Perhaps even slightly less.

Gellica cleared her throat. "That's as much as I can do with what you gave me to work with." She sounded self-conscious.

"Bear with me," I said.

Concentrating on the threads, I willed them to grow, to be bigger, stronger.

Nothing.

I rolled my neck and grimaced. "Hold on," I told her.

Redoubling my focus, I stared at the shard, only looking up when Gellica said, "I don't know what you're hoping will happen, but I have a roomful of people I'm supposed to be entertaining."

I frowned, muttering to the invisible thread I believed stretched between shard and flower. "Come on, you little bastards."

Shoving my hand between the two objects, the stub of my missing fingers caught on a thread, and I focused on the unnatural tug against phantom digits. Trying to remember the sensations I'd encountered before, I counted to ten and breathed out slowly. The exhalation was accompanied by a painful drag, as if there were a creature sucking at my mangled hand. I choked back a shout, but with a rush the cobwebs grew thicker, the air heavier, and the cold crept in with spider legs. But it was a light chill compared to the overwhelming, bitter frost of what I'd experienced in Bryndel Grove.

I tugged my jacket tighter around my shoulders and smiled. "Watch this."

I tapped the shard, and it bumped forward with no corresponding movement of the flower. I tried again—nothing.

"Dammit," I muttered. "Maybe it's out of manna?" My stomach rumbled, even though I'd grabbed a quick meal on the way over.

"Even then, it would still be linked. But there may be an

issue with the binding." Gellica tugged a curl on her hairline back into place. "I told you I'm no sorcerer."

If it was still linked, I hoped I could reexamine the threads. I placed my left hand between the two objects, and found the thinnest, weakest shadow of a web. I selected a single thread and wrapped it in my left fist, imagining that I was weaving the other threads around it, first with my three fingers, then including my missing digits in my mental image. The pressure in my sinuses and ears drained away, and I sucked in a sudden breath. Gellica was looking at her watch.

I pushed the shard again, no harder than before, but this time the flower shot forward, sliding over the top of the table and striking Gellica's wineglass with enough force to tip it off balance.

She grabbed the glass before it toppled, saving the carpet from a stain even as she stared at me.

"What the . . ." She stared at the glass. "It multiplied. It scaled up on its own!"

"I guess," I said. "I told it to, and it responded."

"What do you mean, you *told* it to?"

"I'm not entirely sure." I wiped a hand across my forehead. "I kind of encouraged it to boost?"

"That's not how magic works."

I raised an eyebrow. The flower in the middle of the table proved her wrong. It was wilted, like it had aged a week in that single jump forward.

"No." Gellica blinked several times, as if trying to hit some kind of internal reset. "Carter, I don't mean that what you're saying is difficult. It's flat out impossible."

"So how did it happen?"

"I don't know," she said. "I'm not a sorcerer. But I know that's not supposed to happen." Gellica chewed on her lower lip, brows furrowed.

"For what it's worth . . ." I ran my hand between the shard and the flower, searching for any trace of cobwebs. "I don't think they're connected anymore."

"How do you know?"

"I'd feel it, I guess?" I sat on the edge of the couch, elbows on knees, hands clasped in front of me. "So that's what I wanted to talk to you about. Now . . . what do we do about this?"

"Okay," said Gellica. "Okay. That was unexpected. And exciting." She stared at the wineglass in her hand, that had almost been knocked over by a delicate flower. She drained its contents in a single slug, then looked at me. "Start from the beginning."

"So when you ran into this the first time, you came straight here and talked to me?"

"Right. You said it wasn't how manna felt."

"That's because it doesn't. And you weren't doing," she stared at the shards and withered flower petals, "*that* as a demonstration."

"I thought sorcerers could sense magic. You skip that class, too?" We'd gone over every detail, and a deep exhaustion had settled over me.

She gave a weak laugh. "Everyone can hear music," she said. "What you're talking about is like seeing the notes in the air." She scratched her leg and looked around the office. Her eyes widened. "These strings you felt. Are there any in here?"

"You mean around us now?" I asked. "No. And they're more like cobwebs than strings."

"And around me?" Insistent, her voice rising as her throat constricted. "Nothing?" I could see her consider the odds that whatever I was doing could affect her as well.

I shook my head, speaking slowly and with certainty. "No. I wouldn't have come near you if I did."

Her shoulders relaxed. "Thank you." She didn't need to elaborate.

"But," she said. "If you don't feel it around me . . ." She stared at the shards again. "The drug." She rubbed her dimpled chin, sounding more confident as she went. "It must be something to do with the combination of angel tears and manna."

I flopped back against the couch cushions, unable to hide a smile. Gellica had come to the same conclusion I had. Not only did that mean I wasn't crazy, but it also explained why the effect didn't take place consistently. If the cobwebs were only present around snake oil, it made sense that I couldn't affect Guyer's bonded brooch pin and baton, or why Guyer's cloak and Paulus's tattoos hadn't sent tingles racing down my arm. It also explained why I couldn't sense any cobwebs around Gellica. They all used undiluted manna, free from contamination.

"A single drop of manna," I said, "and a single drop of angel tears. That's all it takes to transform magic into something we can feel and interact with." In the same way one person, one single act, could change a situation.

"No," said Gellica, snapping my train of thought. "Not *we*. You." She pointed at the shards. "I can't do this. As far as I know, no one else can, either. And we don't know anything about why you have this connection, or how we can test it."

"Who said anything about testing it?"

"I did." She sat back, tugging on her upper lip. "Because whatever this is, it deserves study. We need to get snake oil. Is that something you can, you know . . ."

I stared at her.

"Just because I'm a cop doesn't mean I have unlimited access to illicit activity," I said. "And the connections I do have are with people smart enough to never sell drugs to a cop."

She sat back, pondering this information.

"What about Paulus?" I asked. "She's experimented before, pushed boundaries, ignored proscriptions."

Gellica raised an eyebrow. We both knew that Paulus's experimentation was how Gellica had been created. I hurried to clarify.

"She's rich, influential, and not afraid to flex her muscles," I said. "If anyone would have snake oil lying around—"

Gellica interrupted me. "Let's say she does. I don't know about it, and you're not detecting it. So what's that tell you? She's not using it."

"She's not using it *herself*."

Gellica let out a growling sigh. "Fine. But that's the same thing as far as we're concerned."

It wasn't, not in the least. But it was as far as I'd get on that topic with her that night, so I let it drop. Besides, I was just relieved to have someone believe me. I sat back in the couch and let myself relax.

"This is exactly what I tried to tell the DO, but she wouldn't listen, no matter—"

"Wait." She broke in with hands raised. "Carter, this isn't something you can talk about."

"Not with just *anyone*. But I'm trying to figure out what in Hells is happening. If there's someone who can fix it—"

"Nobody!" she said. "No one can know about this. If people knew you can do that—" She shook her head. "We'd end up in adjoining observation cells."

We both looked at the coffee table. The flower bloom crumpled inward, shriveling and growing thin, its petals losing color and puckering like a decaying orange rind. We watched it become increasingly gossamer, until it was barely there at all.

"That's what'll happen to me," she said, her voice soft.

"What?"

"If I don't have access to manna. I'll get manna rot and fall away to nothing."

"Not everything magical rots."

"As long as the sorcerer who made the connections severs them," she said. "Or if the connection isn't used. Or if, or if . . ." She trailed off with a roll of her wrist, indicating that the list went on and on. "But I'm half magic, remember? I need regular manna treatments to stay alive. It's a trade-off—Paulus got her clone, and I got a lifetime of magical addiction."

Gellica pressed a knuckle against the flower bloom and it collapsed. A withered husk that could float away on the faintest breeze.

I ran a finger along my collar, giving myself a little more breathing room. "I'm sorry."

"I respect the ambassador," she said. "But I don't enjoy being chained to her supply of manna. Whenever I've thought about leaving, starting out on my own . . ." She flexed her hands, and I could practically see her fighting the urge to ball them into fists. "Well, you can imagine why I find the issue of manna supply of personal interest."

"If my life depended on it, I probably would as well."

She cocked her head toward the decaying mound that had been the flower. "Are you so sure it doesn't?"

I started to spit out a smartass comment, only to feel my grin slip away. Would I end up a withered husk, eaten away from the inside by magic?

"Don't worry too much," she said. "We don't know how this works, but we can find out."

I felt a warm rush of gratitude. Gellica might have needed someone to share her secrets, but I needed her just as much. I dealt with that kind of revelation like I always did: I changed the subject.

"Listen," I said, "I want to say I'm sorry about the other night."

"You already did."

"Not about crashing that fundraiser. About ending the night so soon."

"No need to apologize." She straightened. "You want to keep things professional. That's fine."

I cleared my throat. "No."

Gellica snorted. "No meaning *no* or no meaning *yes*?"

"No meaning I don't know."

"Well, I notice that you feel comfortable coming in and running your mouth. And I'm guessing that that's the hallmark of most of your relationships."

"Is this a relationship?"

"I don't know what it is. I wanted it to—" Gellica grimaced, and for a moment I was afraid she was going to be sick. "I wanted it to be *something*." She crossed the room, and grabbed a decanter, the brown liquid inside swirling with her anger. "But you weren't interested. You made it clear."

"I'm not very clear about anything in my life."

She turned, empty glass in one hand, half-full decanter in the other. "Are you going to find who killed your Jane Doe?"

I turned away. "Don't know."

"When will you stop?"

I shrugged. Scratched my ear. Shrugged again.

"You won't," she said, and poured herself a drink. "Pretty clear how you feel about that. Pretty clear how you feel about me. And about my . . ."

"You mean your—"

She cut me off, raising the decanter like a weapon.

"If you say 'rawr,' Carter, I swear on the Path that I will club you to death where you stand."

I didn't say anything, and let my pantomimed claw drop to my side.

"Look," I said. "I'm exhausted, and I need some food. I know you've gotta get back to your crowd."

"Oh no, this is more interesting than the stuffed shirts downstairs."

That gave me a small bolt of energy. "I'm glad I could interest you in something."

She took a long drink, wiped a drip of liquor from her lips with the back of her hand, the hand that still held the decanter. "You think I like being a freak?"

"No," I said, then clarified. "No meaning you're not a freak. You're just you." I slid forward, bouncing my weight on the end of the couch cushion. "I mean, takwin stuff is weird. But I've got my own bag of weird I bring to the table." I clasped my hands, left hidden inside right. "It's the trust issues."

"Trust issues?" Gellica refilled her glass and set the decanter down with a clatter. At least I wouldn't be clubbed to death. "What kind of trust issues do I have?"

"Not you," I said. "Me. About you."

"Okay." She joined me on the couch, glass nestled in her lap. "What kind of trust issues do you," she nodded in my direction, "have with me?" She settled back into the cushions.

"Well," I said. "I mean, Paulus created you."

"Yes." Her voice was hard. Suspicious.

"For a reason," I said. "She doesn't do much of anything without a plan."

"Yes." Still tense. I was on thin ice.

I rubbed my eyes.

"Okay," I said. "Paulus can control weather, she can control motion. So . . ." I chewed my lower lip, briefly, before continuing. "Can she control you?"

Gellica was slow to respond. "Wow. You *do* have trust issues."

"You work in a morally ambiguous organization, for a shit-heel of a person who is also your clone mother. And she's a sorcerer. Is it really outrageous for me to wonder how independent you are?"

"I was plenty independent when I dragged you away from Paulus and saved your life."

"Yeah," I said, remembering the attack a month ago, when I'd experienced firsthand Paulus's control over her wind creature. "You probably pissed off your mom on that one."

"I prefer 'boss,' thank you." She scowled at the floor. "And yes, she was angry. But I'd do it again. You know why?"

I didn't answer.

"Because it was the right thing to do." Her jaw clenched and she stood, pacing away from me, back to the safety of the other side of the desk. She stood behind her chair, where she drained her glass and began shifting it from hand to hand. "I'm my own person. If anyone should understand that, it's you."

"Why?" I said. "Because I got manna on my fingers? Because the doctors prodded me and think I'm a freak?"

"No, dammit! Because I told you who I am, and I—" She turned away. "I thought you accepted it." She slammed the glass down and stood there, chest heaving, one hand resting on the desk, the other clenched into a fist. "I trusted you with a secret that could destroy me, and no matter how thick-headed and stubborn you are," she let out a controlled breath, "I know that you've got a right and wrong in that head, and it guides you true. Even if I don't always agree. But here's the thing," she stood a little taller, "no one else knows what I am. I can't tell anyone else. You have friends who know what you went through. You have departmental psychiatrists and coworkers. My whole life, I've only had Paulus. And then you."

I saw her now. Maybe for the first time. She'd been so alone for so long. She wasn't interested in me. She wanted an honest relationship with someone. Anyone. I was just the guy who filled the suit.

I ran ruined fingers over my knee and wondered how long I'd have lasted if I'd grown up like Gellica. A lifetime locked away and told to lie to the world about who I was? Hells, I'd probably never have made it past my teenage years.

Relaxing my hands, I let out a long sigh and said, "I lost Jane."

"What?"

"You asked me when I'd stop trying to find Jane's killer. I screwed up, should have kept things closer to the vest, and got the case taken away from us. So . . ." I shrugged, a feigned indifference as I let the word trail off.

She nodded her understanding, staring at the withered remnant of our flower.

"We all make mistakes," she said. "I misread Mitri Tenebrae."

"Oh?" I strove for indifference again.

"I thought he was a friendly face, a social butterfly at worst. But freaks like us, we walk our paths alone." Her lips curled, then dropped. The humorless smile of someone laughing at their own foolishness. "He's more desperate for a manna connection than we thought. He's willing to put people in danger for it."

"He threatened you?" I sat up.

"I can more than take care of myself."

It was hard to argue the point, considering she'd saved my life at least once. But I recognized an evasion when I heard one. "That's not an answer."

"The explosion at his fundraiser—the one he blamed on overheated candles?"

"I know," I said. "It was Paulus's creature."

"No," she said. "It was the necklace he'd given me. It burst, like it was a poorly crafted spell."

That didn't sit right with me. "Tenebrae's a communications expert."

"Right, so maybe he used something unusual, something unstable to make the binding." She looked at the shard.

"Snake oil. That would explain why I felt cobwebs around his apartment."

"He's in charge of TCI's secure communications for the military encampment," she said. "He's dropping hints that if he doesn't get a personal manna connection, he knows enough to make things complicated for TCI, the AFS, and more." Gellica sloshed the remnants of her drink. "Depending on what he knows, it could put people's lives in danger, cost jobs—Hells, he could even start a war."

"He can't think he'll get away with it."

"He's a rich sorcerer. He's gotten away with everything his entire life. Why would he think any differently now?"

Coming from someone whose mother was a rich sorcerer, that was saying something.

"Besides," she continued, "it doesn't matter if he gets caught. Once the information is out, the damage is done." She rubbed her eyes, pressing hard enough to leave temporary white marks on her cheekbones.

"What are you going to do about it?"

"I've hired some people to follow him, track his movements. If he's collecting information and we can prove it, we'll turn him over to the military."

"And if you can't prove it?"

She rolled her head back to look at the gilded ceiling. "I do what Paulus tells me to do. And I'm not going to tell you what that entails. But I'm not some kind of secret assassin, if that's what you're asking. Paulus has plenty of other ways to incapacitate enemies, even one as powerful as Tenebrae."

It was a reminder that Gellica had the kind of political power that could change lives. She'd helped Talena, and maybe we could use it to help someone else.

"I have an idea," I said. "Hear me out on this, okay?"

Gellica didn't answer, and I went on.

"You admitted there're people in the Bunker on Paulus's payroll."

She looked at me with a raised eyebrow. "I'm not so drunk that I'd respond to that."

"You want to make an impact," I said. "How about you flex Paulus's political muscle and get me back on the Jane Doe case."

"Carter . . ."

"I'll do something for you in return," I said.

"What could you possibly do that we'd—"

"The Responders' Remembrance," I said. "If you get me reassigned to the cases I want, I'll stand onstage and be a supportive face for Paulus."

She blinked. "You do the Remembrance and I'll see what I can do."

It was the best option I had. "Deal."

We stared at each other, and it seemed like we'd said everything that had to be said. She stood, and I followed suit. I looked at the clock on her desk.

"I think I made you miss your party."

She considered that.

"It was still worth it to see your parlor trick." She smiled. "And Carter, if you find out more about this ability, you'll tell me, won't you?"

A muscle in my jaw twinged, and I thought back to my distrust, my fear of her connection to Paulus and the powers that be. Then I put all that aside.

"Sure," I said. "Any excuse to see that couch."

26

TRUE TO MY WORD, THE next day was the Responders' Remembrance, and I was there onstage in my dress reds, standing alongside the brass who oversaw the city's police, firefighters, and emergency services. It was early evening and the sky was pitch black, the shimmering moon obscured by clouds. All around us the stage was bedecked with Titan's Day decorations, silver and blue the traditional colors of celebration and mourning, respectively. Scarlet streamers streaked through the decorations, representing the police, firefighters, and EMTs who'd lost their lives or been injured in the line of duty.

The mayor took his place at the stage front, standing tall and somber in a blue suit. Paulus was in the front row of the audience, a few seats away from Gellica, whose eyes stayed on me throughout the service. Jax stood to my left, a bit of sanity in a sea of surreal symbolism. I'd never felt more out of place, a cop who'd lost a couple fingers standing at attention to remember those who'd given so much more.

The mayor's speech washed over me and my mind drifted. At one point Jax's elbow dug into my side, and I realized everyone was looking at us and clapping. I didn't know what to do, so I smiled and nodded, simple motions that had no meaning on their own, and that let everyone read their own meaning into them.

Next, the newly engraved names were read from the memorial, a monolith of granite shaped like the Mount, with the silhouette of an arm hidden in its profile representing the Titan, who sacrificed himself so that we'd have warmth and life. Punished by his peers, cast underground and pinned below the Mount, he was condemned to eternal torture by the imps, his screams of agony fueling the geovents that gave us warmth. In Titanshade that's considered a good bedtime tale for kids.

The band struck up the anthem, and I found myself remembering the last time I'd seen my mother, before she went in to work and never came back. Long before she was a captain, Bryyh had been at my mom's funeral, another young cop telling me how brave my mom had been. Telling me that cops were heroes, and we were all a family, and a hundred other lies that I'll never stop believing.

The truth is, there are no heroes. Only occasional acts of foolishness from people who should know better.

After the ceremony the press and politicians moved to an area with better lighting for photo ops. What remained were sons and daughters, families and friends, spouses and partners. A crowd composed of those left behind. I slipped through the press of bodies, drawing closer to the stone, close enough to scan the names until I found my mother's. I stared at the engraved letters, tiny cuts chiseled into stone. It didn't even come close to capturing who she was and what she sacrificed for the city. I multiplied that difference by all the many names on the monument, and for the briefest moment I felt on the verge of some great truth. Then it was gone. Like all truths it was just mist in the morning, evaporating in the harsh reality of daylight.

A touch on my shoulder and Gellica was beside me, decked out in muted blue. Her eyes scanned my face, circling my features as if she could see something that others had missed.

"Sorry about your friend," she said, indicating the new names added this year. So many names between my mother and Myris, representing years, decades, and so many deaths.

"Me, too."

Beyond the memorial, under a light designed to shed favorable shadows for photo ops, the brass mixed and mingled. Paulus and the mayor, the chief of police and the fire chief. Angus was on the edges, hoping to get a little face time and expand his network. I turned my back on them and faced Gellica.

"And I'm sorry about the last time we talked. I didn't mean to dump all that on you."

Her lips raised in the smallest of smiles. "Yeah, you did."

"Maybe we can try again. Talking, I mean."

"I'd like that," she said.

Closer to us, and far from the photographers' scrum, Hemingway stood in dress reds. She stared at the newly added names on the memorial. Her eyes held no tears, only a fierce look of commitment. Behind her, Jax and Hemingway's new partner were talking quietly, giving her a little space. All around us were cops and medics, firefighters and their families. They were mourning, laughing, and remembering.

"Me too," I said. "But right now, I need to be with my family."

Hammer Head's was a traditional off-duty watering hole, and it was always busy. But on Responders' Remembrance we packed it to the rafters. From beat cops in scarlet shirts to the brass in dress maroon, there's a bond that ties us together. Brothers and sisters who might fight like rabid wolves when they're alone, but are quick to close ranks against any outside threat.

Of course, every family needs a black sheep. I walked in to a mixture of polite nods and indirect stares. I did my best to seem oblivious to all of it while I scanned the sea of faces. It was all cops and a smattering of family members. The fire department had their own gathering spot. The stresses they faced were similar, but not quite the same. When firefighters arrive at a disaster they're always the heroes. Nobody cheers when the cops show up.

I found Captain Bryyh standing next to Captain Quinlin by the dart boards. Bryyh was large, but next to her OCU counterpart she seemed downright insubstantial. I walked over to join them.

"There's no reason to continue this mess," Bryyh was saying. "Pissing on each other's territory doesn't do anyone any good."

"Except that it's already in motion." Quinlin swung his beer at the front door of Hammer Head's, and foam slopped over the side of his glass. "It'll continue one way or the other. Why not capitalize on it." Quinlin's shaved head was pocked with a scattering of moles that took regular nicks from the morning razor. He stopped talking as I approached.

Quinlin eyed me as if I'd stumbled into his home covered in tibron dung. In a way, I couldn't blame him. He'd made his reputation on absorbing smaller cases and using them to crack mobsters. Having the recent killings taken back out of his department's portfolio was bad precedent.

"Captains," I said, before turning to Quinlin specifically. "I was wondering if I can come to OCU and pick up the St. Beisht file directly. Save Dungan the hassle of packing it up."

Quinlin grumbled, a deep and intimidating sound. "I shoulda figured you'd pull something like this. You really are the next politician, aren't you?"

"What?" I'd been called a lot of things in my career, but politician was a new one.

Quinlin snorted. "You get cases moved from department to department, you're onstage with the mayor, you're front-page news, and you've been getting favorite status for as long as anyone can remember. Rules get bent for you, Carter, and everyone knows it."

I shook my head, forcing a half-smile to show I was in on the joke. I was nothing like Angus, or even Dungan—cops who lived and breathed the red tape and backslapping that was part of every public servant's life.

"I'll take that as a yes," I said. "And I'll be by tomorrow. Thanks for your cooperation."

For all of Quinlin's griping, Bryyh didn't seem disturbed. She was different at the bar. More relaxed than I was accustomed to seeing. It reminded me of when she used to visit me and my old man after my mom died. It was a side of her I sometimes forgot.

Quinlin's eyes flashed. He clearly would rather I wasn't there. Too damn bad.

"Imp's blade," muttered Bryyh. "Relax, Carter. Have a drink. Remember your friends."

It seemed everyone in the place was drinking a toast, whether with beer, whiskey, or soda. Everyone loved the departed. After all, the dead couldn't disappoint us. I stalked away and headed toward the bar.

Across the room Guyer was talking to a few guys from Vice. She wore dress reds like the majority of cops in the place, but I guessed she'd had hers tailored to fit a little better. When she dressed up, she liked to do it right.

She and the others laughed, and Guyer held her hands up, then headed to the bar, as if she'd lost a bet and was now on the hook for the next round. I intercepted her path.

"Got a minute?"

"Sure," she said. "I'm not on the clock."

I leaned closer. "It's about the interview we had yesterday. What I was trying to show you."

"Hey," Guyer squeezed my shoulder. "Don't worry. I took bad notes."

"What?"

"I simply noted that we discussed the victim's deformity. No point in recording the conversation about my school days and that baton trick, right?"

I blinked. She thought she was covering for my delusion.

"Don't mention it," she said. "You looked good up on the stage. Like a real pro." She leaned away from me, hopping up on the foot rail and waving an arm overhead. "Hey, Artie!" The bartender spotted her and moved in our direction. Guyer glanced over her shoulder at me. "C'mon and have a drink. I'm buying this round."

But the room was already spinning for me, and I stepped away. I wandered the bar, feeling like I was on the other side of the looking glass. I stood on the fringe of a circle, physically present but mentally calculating how many beers it would take to wash all this from my memory. I doubted I could count that high. No one spoke to me as I left, so I had no excuses to make as I slipped away, gliding through the crowd like a ghost heading home.

I didn't go straight home, of course. Since I was already in the neighborhood I stopped by the Bunker. My mailbox there held a pleasant surprise, the results on the search for the second alleyway body's identity. Apparently Paulus's political pull worked even faster than expected. I tucked it under my arm and headed to my apartment. Once there, I fed Rumple and kicked off my shoes, put on a record, and then flopped on my couch to see what I could learn about the man who'd died in my arms.

Turned out he'd been identified by his tattoos. That's never a conclusive identification—anyone can get a tattoo—but it was enough to make a high-probability ID. Our latest victim was Dale Turner, a former member of the Titan-shade Fire Department whose arrest records indicated a life that had spiraled downward in recent years. Turner had collected a few run-ins with the law as a kid but straightened himself out, at least long enough to pass a background check and serve on the TFD.

I flipped to his city personnel record. He'd been hurt in a fire, and took a disability retirement. The arrests started a few years after that, mostly for possession, then later for intent to distribute. It was a tragically common pattern, especially among first responders: an injured person moving from prescriptions to street drugs to help ease chronic pain.

Rumple leapt onto the couch, patrolling the cushions and purring as he selected which piece of paper to sit on. While he situated himself, I considered Turner's connection to the TFD. He wasn't active six weeks ago, but chances were good he still had friends in the department. Friends who might have been at the manna strike. And if one of them felt bad for a comrade in pain, or simply wanted to earn some extra cash, might they have bottled a bit of manna?

If so, Dale Turner might have been the source for the manna that fueled snake oil.

But would he have the connections to do anything with

it? Arrests for possession weren't the same thing as being able to set up processing or distribution operations. I paged back to the documents covering Turner's earliest brushes with the law. The details were sketchy, simply a list of dates and offenses, as well as the names of any other offenders arrested in the incident. But I found what I needed. Because back in his youth, Dale Turner had run with a group that included the man who now went by the name Donnie Starshine.

I set the paperwork down. We needed to find people who knew Turner, maybe even search his home. I needed to talk my way through things, and Rumple seemed uninterested. I paged Ajax, leaving my home number.

When he called back the booming sound of bar music was in the background. Hammer Head's was having a banner night, and my partner seemed to be planning on closing it out.

"Are you drunk?" I had to ask twice before he heard me over the noise of the crowd.

"No," he said. "Nope. Not at all . . ." A pause. "Maybe."

"Wish I was," I said, then gave him a quick lowdown on Dale Turner's criminal history. "What did we learn from Lillian Moller?"

"She likes redheads."

"What else?"

"Well," Jax considered, "somebody sold Jane snake oil."

I paced back and forth, holding the body of the phone as I spoke into the receiver. "And who do we know with ties to snake oil in that neighborhood?"

He paused. "Is this . . . Are you quizzing me?"

"No. It's the woman we—"

"Because I'm good at tests, but I need to prepare a little."

"No, dammit!" I shifted the receiver. "Think. When we found Jane we interviewed the neighbors."

"The woman!" he shouted. "With the kid."

"The kid who knew the dealer at the corner, the kid whose mother was using."

"I remember her," he said. "Susan."

"Sherri."

"Sherri, right." He sucked in a breath as though holding back a hiccup. "You're right."

"So tomorrow let's go talk to our friend Sherri and her son."

He gave an agreeable grunt, and I ended the call with second thoughts already brewing like storm clouds on the horizon. I wasn't comfortable thinking about my connection to the cobwebs and manna threads, let alone going back to a location where I'd first encountered them. But Jane's case was more important than my discomfort, and I could only hope that things would turn out okay.

27

I WOKE FRIDAY MORNING FEELING DELIGHTED that I could skip NICI training, though my elation drained away when I remembered why I was excused: everyone's least favorite doctor was going to get her chance to prod and examine us.

By the time I got to the Bunker and made my way to the examination station I figured I'd be one of the last through the door. But once again I was an early arrival. DO Guyer was right behind me.

"Why is it so bright in here?" she croaked. "And can someone get me a water?"

It seemed my colleagues were slightly the worse for wear from the evening at Hammer Head's. A good portion of my days had been spent hungover, but for once I was the one with an advantage of clarity.

Dr. Baelen walked briskly from station to station, pushing the attendants to move through the standard exams, so that she could get to the real stars of her show: me and Jax.

We only had a few minutes, so I leaned over to where Jax sat on his chair, back reclined, one arm draped over his eyes.

"How's it going, partner?"

He replied with a grunt, and an irritated wave of his fingers. I decided to take that as an invitation to continue.

"You remember our phone call last night?"

"Yes." His normally musical voice was a husky monotone.

"So we're still on for visiting the lady from Ringsridge Road. Make sure you're awake by then."

He answered with another grunt, and this time I let him rest. Baelen and her boys were headed over to begin draining our blood.

She started with an interview, asking us to rehash every detail of the encounter in the alley. I complied, covering for my exhausted partner. But I also noticed that Baelen was far more effusive in her responses and follow-up questions than at our previous exam. Some of that frantic excitement we'd seen the other day at the Bunker must have carried over. And that made me wonder if she'd be open to some questioning of my own.

I waited until she had a slight pause in her interrogation, before volunteering, "I think the guy may have said something about cobwebs. That mean anything to you?"

She jotted notes madly. "Cobwebs? Cobwebs, no . . . but I'll look into it."

"Yeah, I think he said he was tingling, like there was something all over him, clinging to his skin. Or under his skin, maybe?"

"Really?" She considered this. "Detective Ajax, do you remember the man's exact words?"

Oh, Hells . . . I didn't need to put Jax in the awkward position of defending my lie.

"So tell me, Doc," I said a little louder, "what are you trying to learn with all the poking and prodding?"

"I doubt you'd be interested in abstract concepts."

"It relaxes me," I said.

The doctor directed one of her assistants to begin drawing my blood.

"There is a theory," she said, "that the word *manna* is descended from the phrase *animus manda*, a Barekusean term used to describe a vital world force that connects all things. The words got shortened over time, resulting in 'manna.' It may have come from an older phrase in turn." She let out a burbling sigh. "The Barekusu are extraordinary linguists."

"But you're not concerned with language, are you?"

She looked from the syringe and into my eyes. "No."

"So why do you care about this?"

Baelen turned her attention back to the assistant. "Two more, Charles." As he moved to comply, she answered my question. "Because this is the first manna discovered outside of a whale."

"I kinda got that," I said. "Probably during the constant news coverage."

"Yes." Her voice was clipped, impatient. That was good— it meant that she wasn't considering what she was saying. "So if the whales produced manna naturally, as was long assumed, then how did it get deep below ground in a uncivilized, frozen wasteland?"

"You should talk to our tourist board," I said.

"And if it's not from whales, is this the same material at all? My belief is that it is, in fact, the same material, but that previously it emerged at depths in the ocean. The whales consumed it, or perhaps plankton consumed it and then the whales consumed them. Either way," she gripped her elbows as Charles swabbed and bandaged my arm, "it's possible that this manna is pure. A pristine connection to the threads that bind the world." She scanned the room full of unwilling test subjects. "Animus manda."

I thought it over. "Sounds to me like you have no idea what it is."

"I know exactly what it is," she said. "An opportunity."

"To do what? Why are we all here? Manna is the one thing that lets people cheat physics, so why try to force it into a categorized box?"

"Nothing defies physics," she said. "But there are admitted issues in reconciling the behavior of the very big, when we deal with distances light-years apart, with the very small, at subatomic levels. There is a theory that if we can understand how objects that have been manna-bound interact, we'll have the framework for a unifying set of rules that connects all of known space, from the infinitely vast to the infinitesimally small."

"You lost me," I said. "What I want to know is why are you doing this? For grant money? A tenured position?"

"I'm doing this to *win*, Detective." Her expression was as cold and piercing as any of her needles. "In twenty years

I want to look at the world and say that I shaped our understanding of it."

"And that's winning?"

"It's certainly not losing." She hugged her clipboard to her chest. "The sooner we know that this manna reservoir is safe, the sooner all your grime-covered rig workers can clamber back onto their jack pumps and drills, and resume dismantling the environment."

"All those rig workers are people, who have families. And the halt on drilling is destroying their lives."

Baelen frowned, and let out a disdainful huff that smelled of swamp gas and coffee. "Indeed. We can only hope that it's a situation that will be resolved posthaste. Now, I've been meaning to ask whether you've had any phantom limb sensations in your hand? There was something in your file about leg pain . . ."

"Yeah." I answered quickly. "Though everyone told me it was in my head." I didn't mention that Doc Mumphrey had given me a prescription to manage the pain, or how I'd finally laid it to rest.

She sniffed, her fin pulling tight to her scalp. "A common enough occurrence. Roll up your other sleeve."

Baelen prepared another round of blood draws. I closed my eyes and hoped to Hells that Guyer would keep my stories of cobwebs and magical tingling to herself.

28

AFTER WE WERE RELEASED FROM Dr. Baelen's clutches
we drove back to the neighborhood where we'd first met
Jane. I parked in a fire lane, popping one tire on the curb to
sneak between two other cars whose drivers had the same
idea. Jax exited the passenger door with a wobble, a pair of
sunglasses not designed for Mollenkampi ears in danger of
slipping off his face.

"You feeling okay?"

"I've been better," he said.

"Well, that's the price of a good time." We started across
the street, climbing the stairs to the sixth floor, where we'd
met the woman who'd shown such strange and unnatural
strength.

The building looked much the same as before, though
it had collected a few more holes in the walls, and at least
one torn-down handrail in the stairwell. One apartment
looked to have been abandoned, the door kicked off its
hinges and the opening covered with hastily hung plywood.
Sometimes it seemed like the whole city was going farther
to Hells with each passing day.

We arrived at our destination. I pounded on the door of
6F, but there was no answer. I knocked again, louder and
longer than before.

"I think you can stop." Jax pressed a hand to his temple
and kept his voice low. "No one's answering."

"She might be in there sleeping one off."

"Doesn't matter if she's in there or not," he said. "No
one's coming to the door."

I felt the slightest twinge of pity for him as I resumed knocking. The door remained shut, but another opened down the hall. A Mollenkampi woman poked her head out, mandibles flexing as she squinted at us.

"People are trying to sleep!" She clutched a nightgown around her shoulders, anger winning out over any fear of two strange men in the hallway.

Jax showed his badge and bent his head respectfully.

"Sorry to disturb you, ma'am. It's important we speak with the woman in that apartment. Do you know how we can reach her?"

The older neighbor waved him off. "Never spoke more than two words with her, and I've lived here about all my life."

The faded colors of her head plates made it clear that had been a long time indeed.

"What about her friends?" I said. "You know who she spends time with?"

"Don't know and not my business. All I know is that crazy Hellspawn can keep her distance from me!" She hmmphed and pulled her nightgown tighter.

"What do you mean? Is she acting erratic?"

"Erratic?" She snorted, a sound that echoed in her over-sized biting mouth. "I work third shift, and I sleep during the day, so I wouldn't *know*. But let me ask you this: Does this hallway look 'erratic' to you?"

Jax and I turned a circle, taking in the holes in the walls and damaged doors.

"Sherri did this?" It seemed hard to believe, even considering the encounter I'd had with her.

"More than that," she said. "Like I say, I wouldn't *know*. But I hear a couple young punks tried to shake her down the other day, right outside the building! That crazy woman beat the snot out of 'em, too."

"When you say—"

"I wouldn't know. But I hear it was broken arms and bloody faces. Even tore the ear off one."

I thought of Dale Turner's battered corpse in the body stacks, speaking through Guyer's voice, with half-healed injuries including a broken arm and missing ear. *What have I done?*

The woman sniffed the air. "Sherri can hop a one-way ticket to the Hells." She leaned closer, though she still spoke loud enough to be heard by anyone who might be passing by. "Her and that kid of hers both, far as I'm concerned."

I turned my back on her, towing Jax away by the elbow. "The kid," I muttered. "He said something about an arcade. You remember which one?"

He flipped through his notes, humming something to himself as he did. "I think . . ." he said.

"We find him, we can find his mom. We find her, we find her dealer."

"I know," Jax said.

"Then we'll get the dealer's connection to Turner, and then Jane." I could feel how close we were getting. But it was the night before Titan's Day, and celebrants would be in the streets. "We need to find the kid fast, Jax."

"Hold on . . ."

I thumbed the flaking paint of the door, sending flakes tumbling to the never-cleaned hallway floor. I'd walked through the cobwebs surrounding Ronald and his mother, telling myself I was imagining all of it. But her strength hadn't been imaginary, and the cobwebs that represented the strands of manna connection were every bit as real as the tingle in my hand when we found Jane.

I knew there was no way that Ronald's strung-out mother was a sorcerer. Had the angel tears really been enough to allow her to work magic? Or had I somehow accidentally triggered it?

"Got it." Ajax snapped his notebook shut. "Full Tilt arcade."

I gave the door one last touch. More paint fell, revealing the original crimson coat. Then we were on our way.

A quick call to information gave us an address on Foundry Avenue and a storefront whose garish neon sign proclaimed that we'd arrived at Full Tilt.

Inside, the arcade was lit only by high score screens and flickering graphics. The place was wall-to-wall games, a mix of pinball, mechanicals, and video games. The most popular attractions had teenager-sized spaces to either side of their cabinets so that the inevitable crowd of onlookers would have someplace to stand while chugging sodas and practicing swear words they didn't fully understand. We shoved our way through the aisles, surrendering to the ocean of buzzers and bells. Every step was accompanied by a peeling sound as long-neglected soda spills adhered themselves to the soles of our shoes, every breath by the bitter scent of patrons who'd opted for cheap perfume or cologne rather than a decent shower. The lights from the games pulsed and strobed, bathing us in alternating shades of magenta and teal, like the neon signs that guided drunks to barstools and flies to a buzzing, electrical death. The clientele was a mix of lanky teens and slump-shouldered adults, every one of whom stared daggers at us. Still, it was a nice change of pace from the bars and back alleys, in that no one was looking to make their name by beating down a couple of plainclothes cops.

We found Ronald playing something called Moon Diver, competing against an older boy, both of them huddled against the game, eyes narrowed in concentration. The older kid's pixel avatar expired with a squeak of protest. Seeing the graphics made me think that maybe NICI wasn't as flashy as the TPD brass wanted us to think she was.

Ronald raised his hands overhead, triumphant, but the older kid demanded a rematch. I glanced at Jax. The sounds and smells were hitting his hungover senses even harder than mine. I stepped up to the side of the game and tapped Ronald on the shoulder.

"We need to talk," I said.

"Naw, he's gotta play again," said the bigger kid.

"Huh," I said. The back of the cabinet was plain and utilitarian, holding only a screwed-on access hatch and a power cord that plugged into a central outlet. A simple sweep of my foot was all it took to put an end to the simulated space war.

"Technical issues," I said. "Go tug your joystick somewhere else."

"Screw you!" He threw his arms back, a gesture widely

favored by people who didn't actually want to fight, but wanted to look the part. I ignored him and turned to Ronald.

"Walk with us for a minute," I said. He waited long enough to show any onlookers that he didn't like the idea, then took the escape we provided. I led the way, Ronald at my heels and Jax behind, making sure the kid didn't stray. We paraded to the concession stand.

"You want a soda?" I asked. The stand had a hard plastic picnic table, suddenly made available as the group of teens occupying it faded away at our approach.

Ronald sat on the tabletop. "What do you want?"

I cleared my throat. "We want to talk about your mom."

His shoulders drew in and his eyes narrowed.

"We need to find her," I said. "Because she might be in danger." It wasn't a lie. Whoever had killed Jane and Dale Turner in public alleys didn't have any hesitation about resorting to more violence. If they were after snake oil, then Sherri was in danger.

The kid absently pulled out a pocket knife. That's never a good idea when talking to a pair of cops, and I had a flare of defensive reaction. But I exerted enough self-control, and Jax was likely standing there with his eyes closed, trying to shield himself off from the lights and sounds of the arcade, that neither of us did anything. Ronald began adding to the already significant amount of carving on the table's surface.

"Where does your mom hang out," I said, "when she's using?"

"I dunno." He kept his eyes on the knife's edge.

"We're not after your mom," said Ajax. "We want to lock up whoever's hurting people like her."

"The other day," I said. "Your mom seemed really strong. She ever act like that since?"

"No." The carving deepened, as he put the stress of his lie into the knife blade.

I leaned in closer. "Kid, listen to me. I promise she is *not* in trouble, okay?"

That earned a nod, so I continued.

"We want to find her," I said. "Because the person who's supplying her is dangerous. You understand?"

I pulled out an old mug shot of Turner, one that showed

his arrogant smirk rather than the scarred and mutilated man I'd found in the alley. I cleared my throat and started on the short speech to put Ronald at ease. "Do you think—"

"That's him," said Ronald.

I blinked. "Who? How do you know this guy?"

"Didn't you listen before?" Ronald shook his head, annoyed. "That's the guy who sold manna in the alley down the street. Before he moved to another spot." He creased his brows. "I already told you once."

I realized he had. Ronald had told us that someone he didn't know from the area was selling in the alley where Jane had been killed.

The kid looked at me, concerned. "You think he's gonna come after my mom?"

"No," I said. Firmly, letting him know I meant it. "He's dead." But whoever did that to him is dangerous, and we want to make sure your mom's safe."

The knife stopped. Ronald looked at me. "She can take care of herself."

I cleared my throat, and chose my words carefully. "I'm afraid she's gonna get a bad batch."

That got to him in a way more abstract dangers hadn't.

"She goes to a place on Welles Avenue, down by the athletic center."

"You know its address?"

"No."

"You ever been there?"

The kid's knife started moving again, carving away plastic and leaving his mental state imprinted on the bench surface with the elegant simplicity of straight gouges. "Yeah."

I didn't want to think about what it would be like, for a kid waiting on his mom to come out of a drug den. I didn't push him any harder than absolutely necessary.

He gave us a description of the building, told us his mom would be on the fifth floor, and to watch for the eye marking when we got there.

"Thanks, Ronald. Go on back to your friends."

The kid's lips pressed into a thin line. He stood, folded the knife, and walked away, shoulders slumped. I hoped that we'd be bringing his mom home to him that night.

29

IT DIDN'T TAKE MUCH DETECTIVE work to identify the building from Ronald's description. It was in the Borderlands, the outer ring of Titanshade, where the thermal vents were fewer, the buildings were taller, and the population denser. On the top floor, where the poorest of the poor huddled at night for warmth, we found the angel's roost. A hastily carved insignia of an eye on the doorframe was the ever-subtle sign angel tears could be found within.

We knocked, waited, and knocked again. The door opened a crack, and I opened it the rest of the way with a kick. I braced myself for the tingling sensation of cobwebs, and we walked into the angel's roost.

The front room held a scattering of furniture, most of it barely standing. The human man who'd opened the door had caught its edge in his face, and he rolled on the stained carpeting, while a Mollenkampi bundled in thick layers leaned against the far corner of the room, watching us slack-mandibled as he whistled an out-of-pitch tune.

"Special sauce is all gone," he said. "All we got is standard stuff."

Ajax and I spread apart, the distance allowing us to cover each other's back. I was three steps to the right when I noticed the absence of feathery cobwebs on my cheek, or buzzing tingle over my arm. A distinct lack of snake oil magic.

A couch was set up across from a television teetering on milk crates. The shredded fabric on the couch arms told me there was likely a cat somewhere in the apartment, and I fought the impulse to find it and take it to a rescue shelter.

The cushions were covered with dried stains, and made my own tattered couch look like the high-end furniture in Gellica's office. Sprawled on the couch, mostly covered by a blanket, was a human male, slack features and pallid color making it clear that we'd need a call to the coroner's office as well.

I put my knee on the back of the bearded man moaning about his jaw. Jax kept his back to the wall, weapon out and at the ready.

"Who else is here?"

"You're not s'posed to come in! Nobody comes or goes till Dale gets back. Boss's orders." His beard muffled his voice, but didn't hide the note of fear. Fear of someone other than me. I secured his hands and patted him down, fishing out the knife and vial in his pocket. I lifted it to eye level. It was milky-white, showing none of the manna-infused sheen of snake oil. I secured the Mollenkampi while Jax covered me, then we moved through the rest of the apartment.

The space was small enough that Jax was able to station himself at the end of the hall, observing the two restrained men while I cleared the rooms. The bathroom was filthy but unremarkable, while the first bedroom held only a linenless bed, collapsing nightstand, and a garbage bag full of dirty clothes and discarded fast food wrappers. The second bedroom had the same furniture, but it also held an occupant: an emaciated woman lay in the bed, wrapped in a stained sheet. Ronald's mother struggled to raise her head when I entered. Her once-lush brown curls had faded, and clumps of hair littered the threadbare pillowcase. I called out to Jax to update the ambulance run, then knelt beside her.

"Sherri?" I peered into her eyes, hoping to find a spark of recognition.

She gave me a wide grin.

"How'd you find me, cop?"

"Ronald," I said.

"My boy . . ." she mumbled through a smile. "All I ever wanted was to protect him. I was just never . . ." Her lips worked, as she searched for a word. "Wasn't strong enough. I wanted to be stronger."

Her voice was fading, and my mouth ran dry at the thought of watching another person die in my arms. I thought back to the first time we'd had a run-in, desperate to find common ground to play on.

"You almost fell on the steps outside your place," I said. "I caught you, remember that?"

"Sure," she said. "You kept me from falling."

I slipped on a mask of casual friendship and faked a laugh, trying to keep her talking, to stay with me in the moment. "You were out of your mind. You said you wanted to see the stars."

Her brows creased. "No stars in Titanshade."

"I know, but it's what you said." I made my voice as gentle as possible. "Ronald was there, too. You remember?"

"Ronnie." Her voice grew louder. "My baby was there." Her brow furrowed. "I just wanted to hug him, and I—I hurt him." Her lips pulled in and her shoulders shook. She was crying, though her body was too desiccated to spare tears.

"The drops made me strong, so I could . . ." She exhaled, her pungent breath so dense it was almost visible. "Protect him. But I got sick. And the only thing that made me better was more magic."

My heart beat faster as I put the pieces together. After I'd drained the strength from Jane's vial, I'd dumped it into the first cobwebs I'd come across—Sherri. I'd amped her up, she'd been burning through the manna in snake oil. She needed to get more, and I'd given her the unnatural strength she needed to take as much as she wanted. She'd cleaned out the roost, then beaten the hell out of Dale Turner and sent him out to get more.

"I gotta be strong for my baby." She struggled to stand, her sudden strength blossoming. I placed a hand on her shoulder, and the tingling danced up to my arm. Around us, the cobweb-filled air pulsed, delicate threads growing more tangible. The manna that fueled her magical strength was exhausted, but the threads between her desire and her strength still remained, maintaining a connection and devouring her. I reached for the invisible strands, trying to siphon their strength into her, trying to do something to make a difference for once in my miserable life. But it was too late.

Sherri's eyes rolled back and her back buckled. Her flesh puckered and shriveled, skin crumbling like a desiccated orange peel. Manna rot claimed her body and her life. Ronald's mother held my hand as she died, consumed by the magic of her love and the desperate measures she'd taken to find her own strength.

When I walked out of the bedroom, Jax held his suit coat crumpled in his arms. He had a phone to his ear, and was relaying details to be passed on to the incoming ambulance and coroner's van. Somewhat miraculously, utility services were still operational.

In the corner where Jax had him handcuffed, the Mollenkampi man chuckled and belched, sending rancid odors drifting from his eating mouth. His biting mouth was no better, where long strands of mucus dangled from protruding tusks. "She's just sleepin'. Boss always sleeps the sleep of the dead when she's high."

The boss.

My queasiness grew. How much harm had Sherri done after I amped her power?

I kept the man in my periphery as I approached Jax, though I didn't have the courage to look in his drug-addled eyes and confront the question of who was more complicit in Sherri's death—him or me.

Still on the phone, my partner turned to face me, and his jacket shifted in his arms. A single paw emerged, and a pair of feline eyes stared out at me. The apartment cat, frightened, confused, and—though she didn't know it yet— safe. Jax had been paying attention to the living, even as I left a trail of death in pursuit of justice. He was a single star, shining all the brighter for the surrounding darkness.

I needed to get out of there, only holding on because I couldn't abandon Jax. When heavy footsteps from the stairwell announced the arrival of paramedics, or patrol officers, or someone else to help manage the madness, I caught my partner's attention.

"I need some air. You got this?"

By the time he said yes, I was already at the door. I walked, barely paying attention to where I was, breathing in the sulfur stink of the entry geo-vent as I ran my fingers through its warmth, then the bracing chill of the Borderlands as I crossed the threshold. I stepped away from the building, keeping my distance from the clouds of exhaust from rumbling delivery trucks. I thought of Sherri withering like the flower on Gellica's table. Would any of that have happened if she hadn't met me? Would it have been kinder and more merciful if I'd let her tumble down the stairs, rather than catch her and draw her into this nightmare of manna and spiderwebs? Eyes clenched, I turned into the nearest alley, wanting a few moments' escape from the world's never-ending series of heartbreaks and disappointments.

I stumbled across the alley cobblestones, counting each exhale and fighting for control. It took a long ten count, but I got there. I opened my eyes. I was standing among scattered trash and debris, across from a dumpster flanked by puddles of mystery liquid. There were drag marks on either side of the dumpster's wheels, as if it had not only been pushed out to the street for collection, but also farther back into the alley. A pattern I'd seen once before. I took a long breath, ignoring the reek in the air, and looked up.

A massive mural stretched across the opposite wall of the alley. Its height would have required climbing on top of the dumpster, a clambering effort for an artist to create a display of pastel and chalk, in a style that matched the scrapbook I'd shown to Lillian Moller. But this design hadn't been in the book or in the photos Jane left with Lillian. It didn't show a politician or a figure from the city's past.

This mural featured a man with eight fingers leaning on the side of his cruiser, his Mollenkampi partner beside him. The heroes of the ice plains were framed by a rainbow spray of manna against a star-speckled sky that faded into the dirty brick of the building. It was an image only a southerner or roughneck would draw—city dwellers so rarely saw the stars.

The man in the mural watched over the alley with eyes that were kind and wise. He'd never have let a dead woman remain nameless, or been too afraid to speak honestly to someone who made his heart pound. The man in that mural was like a funhouse mirror, showing all the traits that I failed to display on my own.

Larger than life, the facts before me couldn't be ignored. Even as I was trying to find out who Jane really was, she'd believed in the man I never could be. My stomach rumbled and I doubled over, leaning against the urine-soaked dumpster and fighting to keep my breakfast of proilers and eggs in place.

Head swimming, I dropped lower to the ground, squatting on my haunches. To distract myself I focused on the mural, especially its field of stars. Was this what Sherri meant when she said she wanted to see the stars shine? No, that felt wrong. Just minutes ago Sherri had denied ever saying those words.

I racked my memory, trying to recall the exact moment I'd first encountered her, when she'd leaned into me, lacing the cobwebs around us, and telling me she wanted to go up . . . and see stars? No. *Starshine*.

I pushed away from the dumpster, eyes blinking as I stared at the silhouette of the Mount and the posh neighborhoods that grew at its foot. Those garbage-free streets where the wealthiest elements of society lived, along with the malignant tumor named Donnie Starshine.

30

I T TOOK SEVERAL HOURS TO process the scene at the angel's roost. The uniformed patrol cops hauled away the living and the crime scene techs processed the dead, giving Jax and me plenty of time to lean against one of the cleaner sections of wall and plan our next steps.

"What're you gonna do with the cat?" I asked. The bundle in Jax's coat still squirmed from time to time, but mostly seemed content to curl against his chest.

"I don't know," he looked at the filth-strewn carpet of the angel's roost, "but I can't leave her here. I was thinking . . ." He blinked. "What did you do to your pants?"

I followed his gaze to my feet, where I'd shoved my pant cuffs inside the frayed gray tops of my socks. "They don't teach you that trick at the academy?"

Brows furrowed, he shook his head.

"Then I suggest you pick up some flea spray on your way home. Or maybe something stronger." I jerked a thumb at the dilapidated couch. "I don't know what kind of critters like a bite out of Mollenkampi."

Jax considered that. "I'll need to spray this coat, at least. Speaking of which, hold her for me, would you?"

He transferred the bundled cat into my arms before tucking his pant legs as I'd suggested. As I held her, the cat peeked out at me, wide-eyed and confused, but trusting us to do the right thing.

I handed her back to Jax when he stood. "You ready to make the call?" I asked.

He sighed a discordant note and nodded. Then we dialed children's services, and arranged to have them present when Jax went to notify Ronald of his mother's death.

He waited at the door, as if I were going as well. But if Sherri had dropped Starshine's name when we first met her, it was clear there was some connection. And the fact that Jane had clearly been in the proximity of the angel's roost, combined with the fact that she'd told Lillian Moller she'd finally found manna—or what looked like manna to a dreamer—drew the threads even tighter. Throw the murder of Dale Turner into the mix, and it meant I owed a friendly visit to the man who had both the cash and connections to install the neighborhood dream factory where Sherri had died.

Even more importantly, if I wanted to learn about what the snake oil drug was doing to me without dragging my partner into it, then I needed to go alone.

So I made my excuses, and bore the disappointment in Ajax's eyes. Then I went back to Donnie Starshine's house in the Hills.

I arrived ready for a brawl, but when the door opened Biggs greeted me with a shrug and stepped aside. He led the way through the house, past the windows overlooking the party that seemed to always be going on around the pool, then back to the sunken living room, where we'd met the CaCuri twins less than two weeks prior. This time Donnie and Micah were its only occupants.

The pair sprawled on the couch in the sunken living room, the air thick with cobwebs that I did my best to ignore.

I painted on my friendliest face. "Hey, you two. How's things?"

"Oh, man . . . Just fine, officer, just fine." Donnie's smile was as beatific as before. Now, though, I wondered more at what darkness lay beneath it. "What can we do you for?"

Micah waved, cocktail glass in hand. "You wanna drink?"

"Couple questions, is all." I sat on a white leather armchair, the one Micah had occupied the last time I was there.

When she'd casually threatened to crush our skulls like so many stuffed olives. "Off the record, of course."

"Sure," said Donnie.

Biggs took his place at the door. His continued presence was a reminder that while they wore friendly faces, it didn't mean much. And if Gellica and I were right, the cobwebs I felt told me that they were using angel tears laced with manna.

"This is a nice place you got," I said. "Did I mention that before?" I wanted to ease them into the conversation.

"Thanks, man." Donnie tossed his head, carefully feathered hair swinging free. "That's kind of you to say."

"Well, I admire the way you keep yourself up above the fray," I said. "It keeps the heat off you, right?"

He let his wide grin answer for him.

I mirrored his smile and his posture as I said, "There is one thing I'd like to know."

"Like?"

"Like . . ." I leaned forward, one hand to the side of my mouth. "What the Hells do you have going on with the Harlqs and CaCuris?"

He chuckled. "Let's say you want to fix a carelbarra match," he said. "Something simple like not covering the spread. What d'ya do?" He looked toward the double doors, where his bodyguard sat in silence. "Biggs?"

The big man with the forehead tattoo considered. "Bribe players," he said in his squeaky voice. "A couple on each team."

Donnie threw his head back and laughed, a full-belly, knee-slapping guffaw. "No, no, no! Not if you want it to work."

I spoke up. "He's half right. Bribe a couple key players, but not the stars. The support players who make the stars look good. They keep the game close, and cost less money."

The criminal investor wagged a finger. "Not bad, but you're showing a blind spot." His quick pulses of laughter verged on giggles. "How many teams are on a carelbarra pitch?"

I pondered this obvious trick question as Donnie grinned on.

"Two . . ." The thick leather upholstery creaked beneath me. "No. Three!"

Donnie bobbed his head, encouraging me to continue. "Home, away, and . . . ?"

"The referees."

He chuckled. "Don't mess with the players at all, man. Too greedy and too high-profile. Go to the refs. They control the pace and penalties."

"So if the teams were gangs," I said. "The refs would be—"

"Cuff me, officer!" Micah snickered, and held out her wrists.

"That's it, baby! The trusty police force."

"So you bribed the refs." I hadn't pegged Dungan as dirty.

"I never said *bribe*." He slouched lower, allowing his head to rest against the soft back cushion of the couch as he stared at the ceiling. "You gotta have more smarts than that! What if you convince the refs that the players have been getting away with uncalled penalties and fouls all season? For that one game, the refs crack down, the players get angry with each other and take it out on each other. If the refs go too far, the crowd boos, and brings them back in line." He cracked his knuckles. "You do it right, there's nothing that can be pointed at as illegal. No bribes, no threats . . . but the result's the same." He sat back in the sofa, idly running a finger up and down Micah's arm. "And then you collect your winnings."

"There's no guarantee that'd work," I said. "In fact it probably wouldn't."

"Yeah, but there's, like, *way* less risk." He looked at a nearby side table, calling out, "Biggs, do we got any mints?" before turning his attention back to me. "And it's much less cash-intensive. So you can try it as many times as you need, till it works."

"Portfolio diversification," said Micah. "Spread your bets, and one or two wins will make up for the losses." She smacked her lips. "I want a mint too, Biggs!"

Donnie and Micah weren't typical gangsters. They were financiers, spreading their money across many bets. And the quickest way for them to identify a winner was to set them against one another, like a child trapping two beetles in a jar. I swallowed, remembering how the CaCuris had gotten furious when I'd asked about dealers on their turf—they'd allowed the snake oil operation to run on their territory as a favor to Donnie. The idea to pursue my support had been planted in the CaCuris' heads by Donnie and Micah, then they'd convinced Dungan to drag me to the meeting. Dungan thought he was playing the gangs against each other, and the twins thought they were positioning themselves for success, but at every turn we'd all been manipulated by Donnie Starshine.

There was no time to wallow in guilt. I rapped the arm of the chair, and put a note of wonder in my voice. "What I don't understand is how you got the manna."

"Whatd'ya mean?"

"Come off it," I said. "Someone was smart enough to get their hands on a batch of angel tears and instead of selling it right away, they experimented. Probably tried different batches, different percentages. What would it take to resist selling the manna on the black market? Serious self-control and long-term vision." I leaned back and draped an arm across the chair's back. "I gotta admit I'm impressed."

"I don't know what you're talking about," said Donnie. "But if I had to guess, I'd say that whoever is making this snake oil stuff you're talking about got the supplies from the initial strike. I mean, hey, they found you doing back-strokes in a lake of the stuff, remember?"

I shrugged, still playing up a casual indifference. "So next generation manna added to angel tears, just the slightest touch. It'd be enough to give the sheen without any effects."

"In theory." Donnie smiled. "But it would make a lot of sense, wouldn't it?"

"Sure," I said. "If you could find someone who had a connection to the first responders and guards at the manna strike. Maybe an ex-cop, maybe ex-medic." I expected Donnie's lips to pull downward, and his grinning, chuckling persona to drop away. But his relaxed grin only grew broader. "Could even be an old friend," I said. "Someone from childhood, trustworthy enough to sell snake oil."

"Snake oil's for narcs," Micah said, slurring her S's. "Not really your field, right?"

"Except people died," I said. "When people die, that makes it my business."

"Good thing I'm not involved then," Donnie said.

"Good thing," I agreed. "Because if you were, I'd come for you."

"I guess you would. And I guess we'd really find out who was smarter then, huh?" He practically beamed as he said it. Either his mask was still securely on, or he really did view the whole thing as a game.

I didn't say that I was disappointed, that I'd thought maybe he was different. Because of course he wasn't different. Nobody is.

"Well," said Micah. "I wouldn't touch the stuff myself."

I smirked. The cobwebs in the air told me that was a lie. "If you say so."

"My drug of choice goes in my mouth, not my eyes." Micah raised her drink in toast. "Plus, if you're right, then snake oil might be harmless for most people, but it'd be a bad, bad trip for someone like me." She shook her head vigorously and flexed her fin until one of the ribbons braided through it fell loose. She caught it playfully in her teeth, snorting with laughter as it gleamed with the silvery sheen of runes.

"So the manna you use," I said, keenly aware of the fibrous strands of invisible cobweb around me. "It's not snake oil?"

"Nope." She looped the ribbon around one finger and carefully rethreaded it through her fin piercing. "Not a drop of tears to be found."

If that was true, then why did I feel its presence?

"But it's new manna, isn't it? From the strike, I mean."

"Oh yeah," she said. "It's entirely next gen."

"Well," Donnie interjected, "hypothetically speaking, and all."

"Yeah, hypothetically." She trailed off as she drained her martini.

But if she didn't use snake oil and I could still sense the cobwebs of bonding, then . . . I slid back into my seat.

New manna versus old.

The times I'd felt the tingle or fought through cobwebs—Jane's vial in the alley, Sherri's sudden strength, and Turner's death. All of those had involved snake oil. But it wasn't the addition of angel tears that triggered my reaction. It was manna from the oil fields. Older magic, performed by traditional sorcerers like Paulus and Guyer using manna reserves harvested from whales, didn't have any resonance for me.

And if the manna was the key, then maybe Jane's killing didn't have anything to do with the drug trade after all.

Jaw clenched, I leaned forward.

"Micah," I said. "You told me you used to have a corporate gig. Where did you work?"

"Telescribe Communications," she said. "TCI. Big data. Big boredom, more like." She giggled. "Donnie is *so* much more fun." She rolled into Donnie's side, chuckling as he tickled her back.

I knew someone else who worked at Telescribe. A man who'd been gravely injured, and had extensive experience with bodily restoration.

"You said an old coworker contacted you about a fix for . . ." I nodded apologetically to Donnie. He only grinned and waved, watching the air behind his hand as if it were trailing colors or sparks.

"Yeah," she said. "Kind of a flake but he's easy on the eyes."

A handsome face at a fundraiser. Sculpted muscles and a jawline carved from granite. Skin so perfect he didn't sport a single wrinkle.

"What was his name?" I had to ask, to hear it said out loud, even though I knew the answer.

"Mitri Tenebrae," she said. "But the reconstruction work was just his way to get in the door. He really wanted to meet the CaCuris." She sighed contentedly. "Why, what about him?"

My chair groaned as I sat back, absorbing the impact of her words. Tenebrae had taken a full backhand from Thomas CaCuri's ring-covered fingers, but the sorcerer looked perfect at Gellica's soiree the next day. At the time

I'd admired his makeup job. But it had been much more than that.

We'd been searching for someone with the wounds on their hands because Mumphrey had found flesh on Jane's teeth. But what if her killer hadn't needed to bear those wounds? What if he'd repaired the damage using the same magical techniques he'd offered to Donnie? A sorcerer like that would be in dire need of manna, and would single-mindedly pursue anyone he thought could help him secure a source. Someone like Gellica.

I stood, all the pretense of friendliness gone from my voice. "I need to use your phone."

Biggs led me out of the audience room and to a side hallway with a small phone table. I picked it up and he stepped away. I forced myself to control my jittering fingers as I dialed Gellica's office once again. If she was with Tenebrae, she was in danger.

It rang through to her answering service, a bored-sounding assistant who seemed unimpressed by my insistence that Gellica call in to the Bunker for a protective escort. I hung up and stumbled away, thinking desperately, wondering what else I could do as I made my way out of the mansion.

I must have taken a wrong turn, because I emerged into the pool area. The backyard of the place had a bigger footprint than the apartment I grew up in, and attractive people in very little clothing strutted around in a half sober daze, wide grins and glassy eyes showing just how out of it they were. But the overwhelming sensation was of the webs, and the skittering, tingling sensation of tiny legs traveling up my arms, crisscrossing my body, my face, my mouth and eyes. The crowd writhed to the music. Celebrants at the back of the crowd had their heads thrown back, eye droppers in the air, tiny iridescent pearls of snake oil dripping into unblinking eyes.

I pulled back, but the webbing was so thick it almost pulled me in. The image of Dale Turner's rippling arms resurfaced, and I struggled to control myself, not to boost any of the webs, not to strengthen or weaken the fibers running from and through the glassy-eyed sycophants who sheltered in the wings of Donnie Starshine.

I sprinted away from Donnie's mansion, fumbling as I unlocked the door of the Hasam. I drove away, pawing at the radio and calling in to the Bunker. I put in a request for a warrant and a support team.

We were going to pay a visit to Mitri Tenebrae.

31

EVEN WITH THE BIGGEST PUSH I could manage, it still took a full day to get a warrant. Warrant writing is something of an art, and I was working on a tenuous-at-best connection between a pair of back alley murders and a powerful sorcerer aligned with the AFS military encampment. So I picked my audience carefully. Judge Robinette was a curmudgeonly son-of-a-bitch who delighted in any opportunity to annoy the establishment. I suspected he issued it because he simply couldn't pass up the chance to publicly embarrass the feds.

While I secured the warrant, my partner had broken the news about Sherri to Ronald. One of the worst jobs in law enforcement. He'd left the kid in the care of the children's services, and tried to leave the cat in the care of the kid, but that had gotten shot down by children's services, who were working to place Ronald in emergency foster care. So Jax now had a rescued cat in his apartment and was trying to distract himself with a stack of paperwork on the arrests at the angel's roost. When I crossed the Bullpen and waved the signed warrant, Jax abandoned his half-finished work with enthusiasm. Because some things can't wait.

Jax and I rolled in to the Armistice with a full complement of patrol cops and a single divination officer. DO Guyer was along for the ride because we weren't sure what we'd be getting into when we went looking through a sorcerer's travel bag. And also because she told me, "If you turn up one more manna-rotted body without me, I'll kick your ass."

I paused at the door and looked over our team. I kept my pep talk simple.

"Pretend there's a defense attorney watching your every move. Don't give them the chance to throw out evidence or restrict information. No mistakes, no missteps, nothing to clean up later. We do our job correctly, right here, right now. Understood?"

The building manager opened Tenebrae's apartment, saying, "Discretion and quiet in this matter would be greatly appreciated," as we pushed past him and into the residence. Jax and I moved with the patrol, while Guyer stood in the wide living area that had been packed full of Titanshade's wealthy elite a few days earlier. The patrol's call of "Clear!" rang out from the kitchen and bathroom.

I glanced over the shoulder of the patrol officer who opened the study. The weird animal sculptures still peered down at us and the smell of clay was the same as before, but the air felt closer, the tingling cobwebs thicker and more tangible. The patrol stepped aside and called, "Clear!" and I walked past her, to the set of tools wrapped in canvas. Knocking it open, an array of metal loops and scrapers spilled across the tabletop, along with a set of small-bladed metal implements, perfect for shaping details, that I now recognized as dental knives and spatulas.

From across the suite the call came from the second bedroom. "Locked!"

I called to Guyer. She was dressed far too sharp for the work about to be done. I wondered if she was hoping to get camera time, or if she had other plans after the raid.

"You want to magic that open?" I said.

She sighed and waved over the building manager. He unlocked the bedroom door.

"Manna's expensive," she reminded me. "No one locks doors with spells and incantations when a key will do the job just fine."

The bedroom door swung open and the manager stepped back. As before, the room was dominated by a travel chest so large that I could have stood inside with room to spare. It was closed, as was the smaller box on the side table.

"Nothing too extraordinary," said Guyer.

I eyed the latches running down the face of the steamer trunk. "We'll see about that."

On the other side of the bed, one of the patrol fiddled with the locked box atop the dresser, using a small pry bar on the lock. When it popped open, he immediately chocked out a "Dammit!" He threw his arm over his nose and mouth, letting the pry bar fall to the carpet with a muted thud. Inside the box was a collection of human and Mollenkampi jawbones. We'd found our missing body parts.

We circled round, the tech's camera popping and fizzing, recording the items for posterity and processing. The teeth, jaw, and mandible had tumbled out across the dresser top when the box opened. They looked as though they'd been exposed to a heat source, drying them out and preventing them from creating too much of a mess. The end result was a box of grisly, nightmare-inducing beef jerky. Guyer glared at the body parts, fingers intertwined in the hem of her cloak.

"Well?" I said.

"Definitely some kind of divination ritual." Guyer crouched, examining the bones at eye level. Even I could see that some of the runes traced on the bones had been corrected, like a kid struggling with their handwriting. "Piss-poor work," she said. "Looks like he had no experience with it."

"I thought he was a communications expert."

"Yeah, and you know how to make a long-distance call to someone on the coast," she said, "but that doesn't mean you can chat with your dead grandmother."

"Fine," I said. "But with what you see here, would he have been able to contact his victims?"

She mentally hemmed and hawed her way through the answer, before ending up on, "Can't guarantee it, but yeah. Probably." She rolled her shoulders. "I'd say the human remains look more promising than the Mollenkampi."

Jax scribbled something in his notepad. "What about you? Could you contact them?"

She frowned. "Doubtful. Your guy's already tried,

likely more than once." She eyed the remains once more. "It's what I ran into with your male victim, what's his name?"

"Turner," I said. "Dale Turner."

"Multiple attempts—It's like seeing the figure of someone wearing layers. Each layer added on makes the details less distinguishable."

I grunted and turned back to the grotesque display on the dresser.

"How much would this," I pointed at the pile of rune-scratched body parts, "whatever it is, cost?"

"For someone not used to divination? Pretty close to my annual salary," she said. "Which is why I think that whatever he tried with your Jane Doe didn't work." She indicated the Mollenkampi parts. "If it had, I doubt he'd have spent the time or manna on contacting the second victim."

"If he's so bad at divination," said Jax, "why would he try it at all?"

"Low profile," I said, replaying the conversation I'd had with Guyer in the body stacks. "Much simpler than holding a hostage. Assuming you're okay with killing them." I wished like Hells I'd heard back from Gellica by then.

The rest of our team was busying themselves by tearing apart the rest of the residence. One of them had been eye-balling the locked trunk while we talked.

"Am I clear to pop this thing open?" he asked.

I glanced over my shoulder. "Guyer?"

"Yeah, whatever," she said. Then her eyes widened. "No, wait!"

The patrol cop backed away, hand frozen in the air. Guyer crossed the room and stared at the steamer trunk. She grabbed the lamp off the bedside table and tilted the shade back, shining its light along the lid like a makeshift flashlight.

"There's something on here," she said.

"Magic?" I asked.

"No. I don't think so. Some kind of tripwire."

"Great," I said. "Okay, everyone out. Jax, call the bomb squad. Until we know what's in there, we don't do anything."

It was a half hour wait for the bomb squad to arrive, and

we had to evacuate the rooms on the rest of the floor and the floor below. Jax, Guyer, and I waited it out in the hall-way. So much for the manager's request for discretion.

"What I don't understand," said Jax, "is why the case would be booby-trapped, but not the room. What's more important to hide than evidence tying him to multiple ho-micides?"

The squad arrived and suited up in heavily padded blast-suits. They went over the trunk and all the surround-ing items. After a while the lead bomb tech came out and popped her helmet off. She had a round face, and the barely suppressed glee of an adrenaline junkie.

"Can't say for sure what it is," she said. "Can't open the case without disturbing the wire, can't move the case with-out snapping it."

I peered past her, into Tenebrae's room. "What happens if you cut it?"

"Don't know." She peeled a sweaty strand of hair from her forehead. "And you're not going to like the answer when you ask how we find out."

So the bomb squad went in to do their thing. They at-tached a remote snipper to the wire, then unraveled the control cord while backing up to a safe distance down the hall. The rest of us watched as, with a single nod of warn-ing, the bomb tech clipped the wire. From inside Tene-brae's room, a bell tolled, its sound deep and muffled. It came from inside the chest.

Once the squad was clear, we were left with the contents of the chest. The trunk doors folded outward, revealing a mirror-lined interior. With the doors open, it created a mirrored U-shape, like a portable changing room centered on the clay sculpture it contained. The sculpture was of Mitri Tenebrae, full scale and completely in the nude, an incredibly detailed work of art, except for a complete lack of hair. None of that was as disturbing as the fact that it seemed to be alive.

The steamer trunk contained an elaborate series of rods and supports, holding the sculpture suspended, like a human gyroscope, leaving it free to spin and move, which is exactly what it was doing. The clay Tenebrae twitched and moved like a living thing. The mouth even pursed and puckered from time to time, as if he were speaking, though it made no sound. It sometimes looked very, very worried.

"What is it?" I asked Guyer.

"Not sure." She reached into the trunk and located the small brass bell that had rung when it opened, like a convenience store with a bell above the door.

"Can you tell if it's magic?" said Jax.

"Like can I see the threads that connect the world?" she said. "The warp and weft that weaves us all into a universal constant?" She paused for a single, dramatic heartbeat. "Because no. I cannot. No one can."

I held my tongue. To me, the invisible sensation of cobwebs wrapped round the statue were clear as day. Reaching out, I touched one of the metal struts that supported the gyroscope, and gave the statue free range of motion. Immediately a tingling wall of spiderwebs wrapped themselves around me. Tenebrae had bound even the metal in some way.

Guyer continued. "What I can say, however, is that's pretty screwed-up shit. And if that's not magic, I don't know what it is."

"What about the bell?" Jax asked.

"Definitely magic." She moved closer to the trunk. "I don't know what it's linked to, but these," Guyer indicated the glyphs imprinted on the bell's sounding edge, "are for communication at a distance. And they are *very* well done. Not like the low-rent divination magic he attempted over there."

"So it's magic," said Jax. "What does it do?"

Guyer peered at it again. "Like I said, it's some kind of communication device. Nothing fancy. Maybe it rang another bell. Maybe it acts like a magical pager. I don't know for sure."

"And the statue is linked, too?" Jax said. "To Tenebrae?"

"Best guess," said Guyer.

"It moves when he does."

"Yeah, and it—" She pulled back. "Oh, you've got to be kidding me."

"What?" I asked.

"It's a simulacrum. A bigger one than I've ever seen, but that's what it is."

"A what?"

"A re-creation of the subject," she said. "Down to every detail. The fact that it's showing him move means that it's got a continuous link. Every cut and pimple he develops appears on the clay version."

We watched the statue move gracefully in place. It mimicked climbing movements, as if ascending a ladder. When the motions switched to going up stairs, it was a good guess that it was a fire escape. We watched him reach his destination, the simulacrum's leg swinging up, then over an obstacle.

"So it shows what he's doing?" I said. "What's the point of that?"

"If the sorcerer is skillful enough, and has enough manna, then he can make it run the other way, too." She studied the thing with narrowed eyes. "Add a wrinkle to the sculpture, the subject's skin puckers. Smooth it out on the sculpture . . ."

"The man looks younger," said Jax.

"That's the theory."

I imagined Tenebrae standing in front of his own sculpture, facing it as it mimicked him. Each of them reaching out a hand to the other, rubbing away the wrinkles and moles and imperfections in his skin. It felt dirty, almost unspeakably egotistical.

"So why hide it away?" I said. "It's embarrassing, but why kill for it?"

"Think how *big* it is." She circled the figure as it walked in place, suspended on its metal tracks. "And if he's been at this for years, then he's had to add manna to it to maintain the connection. Spritzed it down like watering a plant." Her voice fell to a whisper. "Sideroads, that's expensive."

"Tenebrae's rich," I pointed out.

"Not that rich."

Jax returned to riffling through drawers, looking for anything else that might be helpful. "That manna's gotta be coming from somewhere."

"From his company." I moved closer to the sculpture, peering into its hollow eyes. "He manages the manna reserves for some big company. Tele-something that I can never remember." I had a bad thought about those eyes. "Can he see us?"

"You mean Telescribe?" Guyer stared at the chest, considering this. "Huh. They've got to have more than enough manna."

Jax nodded. "And government contracts. They're probably cleared to assist in all kinds of classified sorcery. It'd be easy for manna to disappear."

Guyer pressed a finger to her chin. "You think he's embezzling manna. And then what, started to kill people to cover up white-collar crime?" She took a seat on the footstool by the dresser, long legs kicked out in front of her. "And no, Carter. He can't see or hear us. This kind of connection is surface level only."

A glance back at clay Tenebrae showed us he was standing in front of something, one arm raised as if holding up a lid, the other held out in front of himself, fingers close together, like a chef adding a pinch of spice to a dish.

"He could be bonding something," said Guyer.

"Any idea what?"

"None," she said. "I'd guess it's a vat of something, or a container with many small objects. I can't say for sure."

I stared at the perfect clay face of the simulacra, and thought of the cuts on Tenebrae's face after the explosion, the lack of bruises or swelling from Thomas's punch. Torn flesh from pulling teeth out of a dead woman's throat. What else could it heal?

"He's not killing to cover up embezzlement," I said. "He was in an accident, disfigured. What healed him wasn't medical, though, it was this thing. He sculpted a new face for himself." I turned from the simulacra to the others. "This is why he'll do anything. If he can't keep the flow of manna to this statue, he'll lose his perfect face. Hells, for all I know he'll die without it."

"Or from manna rot," said Guyer. That triggered thoughts

of Gellica and her eternal need for manna to exist. I wondered what someone like her, someone with a patron like Paulus, might do to stay alive.

I shook my head, banishing the thought.

"You're both missing the point," I said. "Changes to the sculpture show up on Tenebrae."

"I know," said Guyer. "I'm the one who told you, remember?"

Jax held my eye. "What about it?"

"So let's make some changes." I jabbed my thumb into the clay face of the sculpture, ignoring the powerful swirl of cobwebs that coated the sculpture as I twisted my thumb into the sculptured cheekbone. It might as well have been marble. The expression, however, altered. Clay Tenebrae looked like a fly buzzed into view, and it swatted the air, before glaring around.

"Safeguarded," said Guyer. "He's good. Something's baked into the connection that means only he can modify it. He felt something, though."

Clay Tenebrae's brows furrowed. Our guy was clearly pissed. I stared him down, tingles dancing over my hands and the air thick with spidery strands of magic that only I could feel. Could I shut it down? Turn him off? It would leave him on the street, disfigured and potentially unrecognizable. As it was, the simulacrum was a link to the man who'd murdered at least two people.

Clay Tenebrae tilted its head, then smiled and said something to its real world environment, clay lips moving soundlessly before us.

"What do you think it's saying?" said Jax.

"*Which way to—*" I broke off. "I'm not sure."

"Colin something?" Guyer leaned in, frowning. "I don't know. It's too fast."

It wasn't even like watching a surveillance film, where we could rewind and look twice to guess at a syllable.

"It's pointless," said Guyer.

"Maybe for us." I walked to the room's phone and dialed an outside extension. "But I'm going to bring in someone who's more experienced with this." When the line connected I did my best to sound chipper. "Hi Susan, is Doc Mumphrey in?"

While we waited for Mumphrey to arrive, we kept watch over Tenebrae's simulacrum, hoping for some indication of where he was. I called Gellica's office again, leaving more messages.

Mumphrey finally arrived, entering the apartment in a huff.

"Night before a holiday," he said. "It's a twice-damned madhouse out there."

I smiled. "Wait'll you see what's in the bedroom."

He humphed and turned to the others. He shook Ajax's hand and said, "I'm assuming that you're saying hello, young man."

Ajax's eyes crinkled in amusement, and Mumphrey smiled back.

Never shy, Guyer stepped forward. "Divination Officer Guyer." She held out her hand.

Mumphrey's smile dimmed. "I know the name," he said. And he did shake, but only with some sense of hesitation. "I've cleaned up after you on more than one occasion."

"Doc," I touched his arm and regained his attention. "We need your help with something."

"Lead on and show me what's so important."

We took him into the bedroom, and I watched his reaction to Clay Tenebrae. Doc's jaw dropped, and he took a half-step back. He would've crunched Jax's toes if the younger man hadn't been quick enough to sidestep. Clay Tenebrae was walking at a good clip, head turning, as if watching for surveillance.

Recovering quickly, Doc stepped forward, then looked to me. "He's not alive, is he?"

"Not as such," said Guyer. "But he's broadcasting all of Tenebrae's actions."

"He looks scared."

I grunted. "Good."

Tenebrae's eyes tracked someone invisible to us, and he flashed his winning smile. He said something to his conversation partner and stayed still.

Mumphrey grunted. "He's not speaking out loud, is he?"

"Not to us," I said. "Can you—"

"*Two for lunch,*" said Mumphrey, then pointed at the statue. "That's what he said."

"He's in a restaurant," said Jax.

Clay Tenebrae began walking again.

"Unless he's trying to fool us," I said. "I'll bet anything that bell was an alarm."

"He knows we've found his simulacrum," Guyer agreed. "We've got to assume he knows we're watching him."

"Get me a chair," Mumphrey said. We stared at the statue of Tenebrae, and Doc cleared his throat. "That was me. I'd like to sit down while I do this."

Jax fetched a chair for the doc as Tenebrae held out his hand and spoke.

"*Thank you,*" translated Mumphrey. And he and Tenebrae sat down. It was strange, watching the sculpture sit in midair, supported by the rods and pulleys built into the trunk, facing the pathologist perched on a physical object.

"Tell me we can use this thing to lure him in," I said. "Does he need to have this back?"

Ajax asked Guyer, "What about his security system? Can you break it? Allow us to mess with him directly? Even if we handcuffed him, or put a blindfold on him or something?"

"*I'll take a Teneyson on the rocks while I wait for my friend,*" recited Mumphrey. "*You know what? Make it two. She'll be here any moment.*"

My pager buzzed, and I fumbled it out, barely bothering to read its screen. I swallowed. "I'm calling the Bunker, gonna get a patrol car down to The Lotus Petal. He's been there before."

"Given enough time," Guyer answered Jax, leaning onto the dresser. "Probably I can break it, yeah. But we're talking days."

"You're a dumb-ass," said Mumphrey, staring at me instead of the statue. "That was from myself," he said. "Offering my professional opinion."

We didn't respond, and he scowled. "He needs it," Mumphrey said, before returning to watch Tenebrae. "At least to break the connection. If he lets us keep his imitation, we'll find a way to use it against him sooner or later."

As I walked to the phone I focused on the pager's display. Faded green on green showed Gellica's office number. I was afraid they were calling to tell me she had a lunch date. As soon as Jax was off the phone with the Bunker, I snatched the handset and called her office. Gellica's assistant picked up. I started to announce myself, but he interrupted me.

"Hold on," he said, and there was a rustle on the other end.

Clay Tenebrae sipped at an invisible glass of wine, then looked up and smiled. I'd seen that same radiant smile in person, directed at Gellica.

"My dear," Mumphrey recited.

There was a muffled, "Imp's teeth," in the phone's earpiece and hope filled my chest.

"Hello?" I said.

"Carter?" Gellica chirped in my ear. "Why is my office filled with a stack of messages from you?"

I let out my breath, glad for the rare turn of good luck.

Gellica asked, in a softer voice, "What's going on?"

Clay Tenebrae stood and made a motion as if he were pulling out a chair.

"I'm so glad you could make it," Doc translated. *"You look lovely this evening, Colonel."*

32

THERE WAS A LONG BEAT while we absorbed that, the only sound Doc Mumphrey's continued recital of Tenebrae's side of the conversation.

"*No need to apologize,*" he said. "*I've been waiting for this meeting for a long while. A little delay isn't an issue. Our third party should be here shortly.*"

"Carter?" Gellica's voice chirped in my ear.

Jax leaned closer to the statue. "Colonel Marbury? What's she doing with him?"

"Does he really look like that?" Guyer indicated the lean, muscled figure of Tenebrae's simulacrum. "Because I've got a good guess."

I leaned forward, getting Jax's attention. "Get on the horn," I said. "Call Bryyh, the mayor, anyone who'll listen. Tell them Marbury's in danger and we need to find her. Have them call in to the AFS military." I said it loud enough for Gellica to overhear, then spoke directly to her.

"Tenebrae's dangerous."

"Carter—"

"I don't have time to explain. If he contacts you, alert us immediately, okay?"

"Carter!" Gellica's call echoed in my ear again. "I know where he's supposed to be tonight."

The pigtail of the phone cord wrapped tight around my hips. "Where?"

"Listen to me," she said. "You cannot arrest him. Follow him, track him, don't let him get away. But don't let him know you're on to him. This blackmail plan he's got . . . If he releases classified information, he can do unimaginable damage to this town."

"Where is he?"

"I'll tell you, but promise me you'll wait to hear from me before you do anything."

"Gellica . . ."

"Promise me!" In her voice was the passion she felt for her work, for the programs and lives she believed rode on keeping Tenebrae's mouth shut.

Behind me, Mumphrey announced, "He's saying something about beginning—bargaining, maybe? I didn't quite get it."

"Fine, we'll play it your way," I growled, and placed a hand on Jax's shoulder, before he could leave and make those calls.

"Bryndel Grove." The relief in Gellica's voice was clear. "At some street festival. He's auctioning off his information to the CaCuris and Colonel Marbury."

Of course he was. It all flowed back to the 24th Ward, and the Titan's Day election.

I thanked Gellica and hung up, then relayed the information to everyone else in the room.

"You trust her?" said Guyer.

"As much as anybody," I said. Jax muttered to himself in Kampi, a swirl of high-pitched clicks and bass notes making it sound as if he were arguing with himself over some point or another.

"We can't have a patrol squad march into CaCuri territory in the middle of a rally without sparking a riot. Jax and I will head in that direction. If anyone gets a definite on another location for Tenebrae, radio it in, and we'll converge there directly. We'll radio all this in from the Hasam, agreed?"

Jax grunted his assent, looking at least a little happier.

I nodded to Guyer. "And you, try to focus on breaking whatever protection he's got on this thing. We'll need any advantage possible when we bring him in."

"*I'm looking forward to it*," said Mumphrey.

The bright banners in Bryndel Grove declared the night to be the Starlight Festival. The roads were closed, and tents were stationed down the middle of the street. The buildings were bedecked with strands of faintly flickering lights, made to look like stars, those semi-mythical things that Titanshaders could go a lifetime without seeing, hidden as they were behind the incessant glare of city lights.

Jax's head was on a swivel as we walked the festival. The closed-off streets and extensive parking had required us to abandon our vehicle more than a block away, and we strode down the middle of the road, peering into anything that could possibly be called a restaurant, while rubbing shoulders with residents and celebrants delighted to have a reason to party on an average Duoday night.

"Is every street festival like this?" Jax asked.

I sidestepped a pair of passersby gorging on jumbo fair snacks. "Pretty much." That was a bit of a lie. It was Imp's Night, the longest night of the year, and we had to pass through it before morning broke on Titan's Day and marked the return to light. The combination of street festival and annual holiday made for an even more happily inebriated crowd than usual.

Around us, people wandered from tent to tent and from open retail spot to open homes.

"Most neighborhoods have a handful of festivals a year," I said as we passed a pair of stocky men in modest sweaters, likely bouncers plucked from their usual perch at a bar and pressed into service as keepers of the peace among cotton candy and dunk booths.

The air buzzed with a thousand scattered conversations, words blending into whispering undertones that accompanied the eclectic swell of street music. There were musicians and performers at most every corner, hats set out for tips. Beyond them, tents were set up in the streets, luring in white-haired humans and Mollenkampi with faded plates to swig beers and play games of chance.

"Keep your eyes peeled," I said. "When we spot Tenebrae, or Marbury, or the twins, we'll separate, and come at them from the flanks. I'll do the talking, you watch my back."

"I know the plan," Jax said.

Farther down the street a news crew captured filler video to roll behind an anchor's description of the event, unless something more interesting happened to bump them from the evening news. We gave them a wide berth. I had a specific list of who and what I wanted to see, and the media definitely wasn't included.

Jax and I walked the streets and eyed the kids running along with poorly hidden packs of belca root that they were too young to buy. I'd run wild on the streets of neighborhood festivals when I was a kid. But the closer we got to the heart of the CaCuris' organization, the more the mood tilted from the pleasant buzz of nostalgia and toward anger and resentment. Silver and blue Titan's Day decorations were on display, but so were black and red banners with a stylized representation of the jagged peaks and ridges of the Mount above two lines of text: Titan First. Mixed in with these were black banners, apparently blank, but when the light caught them just right, the shiny sheen of the pattern showed up against the matte black of the banner fabric. A stylized hand clenched tight, an intimidating design that was new to me.

From down the block, a half-dozen Imp's Run celebrants dashed along with exaggerated, loping gaits, the long fur of their costumes waving in the air as they pushed and shoved each other down the street. There were the usual variations on imp costumes, and a sub-group with extra shaggy, white-streaked hair pulled themselves into a tighter knot and broke off down a side street, accompanied by the crowd's cheers and whistles.

"No guarantee that Tenebrae is in with the CaCuris." Jax exaggerated the swing of his shoulders as he walked, allowing him a slightly better than normal view of the crowd without broadcasting that he was looking around. "We don't know they'll be at the Paradise Parlor."

"I suppose not," I said. "But why meet Marbury in this neighborhood if it's not to see the twins?"

We drew nearer the Paradise Parlor, and found that a

stage had been erected at its front. Taking up most of the street, it was festooned in holiday decorations. The twins seemed intent on getting one last night of campaigning in before the Titan's Day special election.

A healthy distance from the stage a handful of protestors were cordoned off, placards leaning against their legs as they made small talk with the smattering of bored patrol officers walking the length of the barricades. I wished for a moment that we'd thought to requisition some backup off of that detail. But too little, too late.

Outside the Paradise's entrance, a handful of human teenagers milled about, playing dice or chewing belca root. Hopeful errand runners with dreams of gangster glory. If they kept chasing that dream, it'd probably be our job to find their killers. But not today. We brushed past them and their hostile stares as we entered the building.

Past the door was a small antechamber, occupied by a large man at a little desk. He pulled himself away from the pinup magazine in his hands just long enough to identify us as cops.

"Not in," the big man rumbled, turning to a new page.

"Yeah they are." I fished out a business card. "Send this back, and if they don't want to talk to us, they don't have to."

The muscle raised an eyebrow.

"Fine." He tossed the glossy magazine on the tabletop. "Wait here."

After he left, Jax whispered, "You're sure they'll talk to us?"

"No. But we gotta try, right?"

A few minutes later the bouncer or sub-boss or whatever he was returned and escorted us through a series of rooms decked out with overstuffed couches, recliners, and enough poker tables to stock a casino. There were side tables by the furniture, many of which held cocktails, their sides still sweaty with condensation. Whoever had occupied the rooms must not have relished the idea of being seen by a pair of cops.

Our tour ended in front of an imposing door, opened by the bodyguard to reveal a luxurious sitting parlor that was the closest thing to a throne room I'd ever seen. It was filled with ornate furniture, all of it antique or at least good fakes. A large television perched inside an entertainment center that dominated the far wall, but the centerpiece of the room was a big wooden chair, covered with ornate frills, its back draped by a pair of belts holding crossed daggers, the ceremonial weapons of salt plains clans. The room also had a single occupant: Thomas CaCuri.

Thomas wore yet another of the three-piece suits he favored, and he swirled a glass of liquor as dark as the gel that held his hair in place. He addressed the man who'd escorted us back. "Stick close. This won't be a long discussion." Then to us: "Come crawling around to join the revolution?"

Thomas punctuated his question with a menacing grin. The hulking gangster was a different species of predator than his sister. Thomas had no more ability to motivate men and women than a tibron beetle loose in the street. He might inspire people to run, but in one direction only: away from him.

"We're not here to hassle you," said Jax. "We're looking for a guy named Tenebrae. He around here?"

"Why would he be?" His emphasis on the words was off. I guessed that wasn't his first drink of the day.

I wasn't interested in playing twenty questions with him.

"We know what he's here for," I said. "And he's damaged goods. He's an amateur, who left thumbprints all over the cookie jar. Tell me where he's at and you'll get a gold star in the morning paper." I jerked a thumb over my shoulder, in my best guess of where the newly built stage lay. "That's what all this is about, right? Getting your sister elected?"

He seemed to think about it, pursing his lips and staring at the carpet. "They're at the Red Brick Ranch-House. Down the road." He lifted his head and added, "This was a one-time thing. Don't come back."

We turned to go, and Thomas called out to his lackey. "If those two show up again I want you to drag them into this room bloody and screaming, you got that, Marguiles?" The big guy nodded compliance without daring to look back. Thomas's slurred laughter was an echo of every schoolyard bully who pushed down and oppressed those more vulnerable than themselves.

Back on the street we shoved our way through the crowd, heading in the direction Thomas had indicated. Down the road, just as he promised, we found the Red Brick. We walked in the front door and took the lay of the land.

The Red Brick Ranch-House was modeled on an old-timey salt plains saloon. It was the kind of place where the walls were covered with historic re-creations and the servers were forced to wear costumes and greet customers with a loud, "Hey-howdy!" We walked through the place acting as if we were meeting a group of friends.

Toward the rear of the building a thick-necked tough squeezed into an ill-cut suit stood just inside a glass-doored private dining area. We walked past once, ignoring his glare as we glanced inside. Tenebrae was in there, as well as Katie CaCuri and Colonel Marbury. Never slowing our pace, we stepped into the corridor leading to the restrooms and paused, hidden from view near restroom doors marked *Buckaroos* and *Fillies*.

"We need backup." Jax's voice was quiet.

He wasn't wrong. But we also needed to move quickly.

"Did you notice his bag?" I said.

He shook his head.

"By his chair. Travel bag packed and ready to go. Whatever he's up to, he's planning to hit the road immediately after."

I exhaled a curse. Gellica needed time to pull things together, so she could make an honest attempt to escape Paulus's control. Everything she'd told me, all the things she'd trusted me with were on the line. But we couldn't let a man with at least two murders to his name simply walk out of the city. Whatever I'd promised Gellica, I had a prior commitment to Jane.

"You ready to do this?" I asked.

"We should at least call in Guyer," Jax said, a warning whistle behind his words.

I glanced back down the hall. The guard had moved farther into the room. Possibly in preparation for departure?

"Guyer's with that statue," I said. "She can probably do more there than anywhere else."

A man stepped past us, giving us a suspicious stare as he guided his son to the Buckaroos room.

"Let's do this fast, and prevent it from being a scene." I flipped out my badge holder and tucked it into my breast pocket, facing out. "Get rid of CaCuri and Marbury, then convince Tenebrae his best bet is to surrender and lawyer up. Unless you've got a better idea?"

"I haven't had a good idea since I moved to this city." He displayed his badge as well.

We turned the corner and returned to the private area. The thug at the entrance spun around and held up a warning hand.

I tugged my badge into his line of sight.

"Don't do something stupid." We didn't break our pace as we strode past him and approached the table. The trio of diners set down their silverware and watched us in silence. Tenebrae was closest to us, with Marbury to his right, and Katie CaCuri across from him.

Katie pouted in my direction. "What do you want?" Marbury stayed silent, staring at her place setting as she adjusted the fork to be at a right angle to the table edge. I didn't understand what the colonel was doing there. I could imagine her falling for Tenebrae's looks, but with her background and accomplishments, it seemed surprising she'd be so swayed by a pretty face that she'd saunter into a public meeting with CaCuri. Then it clicked. Gellica had admitted she'd been following Tenebrae to find out what he knew about the holdups at the manna well. Had Marbury been doing the same thing when I'd seen her at his party?

Tenebrae had funded his physical transformation by embezzling manna from his employer. And when he realized that couldn't last, he'd stolen secure communications from the AFS encampment as leverage. There were plenty of people willing to pay for that information, but Tenebrae didn't need cash. He needed manna. It explained why everyone he'd pursued since coming to town had been tied to the manna strike or snake oil in some way: Gellica and Paulus, Donnie and Micah, Marbury and the CaCuris. The gruesome collection of jawbones and teeth in his apartment? Tenebrae wanted to learn how Jane and Dale Turner had access to snake oil, even if he had to pry it past their dead lips. Now here he was, sitting at a table with two potential buyers he believed could provide the magical liquid he needed to maintain his condition. We'd walked into an auction.

I didn't know if Marbury was there with official AFS backing or simply to cover her own exposure, but either way the situation was far beyond a homicide investigation. And even I knew that a public showdown with a candidate for office and the head of the military encampment wasn't going to meet Bryyh's definition of "low-profile." Jax and I needed to wrap this up quickly and let the politicians sort it out later.

I put on my most winning smile, which admittedly I've been told is more of an unlikeable smirk. "We'd like to speak to your dinner guest," I announced, before turning to Tenebrae. "Just stay put and we'll get this all sorted out." The runes on his neckerchief flared, and I suddenly wished we'd put in that call to Guyer.

Katie turned her attention to Marbury. "Well, this will be interesting to read about in tomorrow's papers."

The colonel's jaw tightened, and she'd grown pale. Ignoring all of us, she stood and began to gather her things.

"I'm not going anywhere," Tenebrae insisted.

"Clearly not." Katie stood as well. "But we are."

"No." Tenebrae didn't shout, but his volume was on the rise. "No, you're not."

I'd had enough. "Tenebrae, it's over." I kept my eyes on him, pointedly ignoring Jax. If we did this right, we could secure him without too much of a fight. "We have your statue in our possession. Keep your hands where I can see them, and we can go downtown to talk it out." I stepped forward and he sprang away from the table, right into my partner's waiting arms. But Tenebrae was fast and strong, and he pivoted out of Jax's grip.

He was a full head taller than me, and had even more than that on Jax. He pushed past us, swinging elbows. One connected with my temple and my vision swam. I swung at his midsection, hoping to slow him with a body blow. Instead, it felt like I'd just punched the side of a train car. I thought of his apartment, and the metal supports draped with invisible cobwebs. He'd tied their strength to his clothes, a bond set to activate on sudden pressure, forming a lightweight armor.

Tenebrae dashed for the exit. The CaCuri muscle at the door stepped forward, eyes darting from Tenebrae to Katie. At a slight wave from Katie, the thug stood down and allowed Tenebrae to pass by untouched. I reached for my revolver, but pulling it in a restaurant would only cause panic and potential harm to bystanders. Instead I gave chase. I pushed past Katie and the colonel, with Jax a step behind me. Together we pursued the mad sorcerer as he ran toward the streets of Titanshade.

33

B Y THE TIME WE REACHED the entrance to the restaurant, Jax had passed me. Faster and more agile, he led the way into the bustling streets. I followed as close as I could, trying to keep eyes on Tenebrae's blond-tinted head of hair as he danced through the crowd of festival goers. He was headed back down the street, toward the Paradise Parlor and its newly constructed stage.

Assuming he was hoping to find sanctuary in the Ca-Curi stronghold, I angled to cut off his path. Flying past a cluster of festival-goers, I saw the cordoned-off protest area. Activists had already started to gather. They held signs declaring tolerance and restraint on the longest night of the year. At their front was Talena, her back to me as she coordinated and cajoled order from chaos. I ran faster, determined to intercept Tenebrae before he got to the crowd. But he surprised me, bypassing both the front door and the stage, heading instead into the narrow gap between the Parlor and its neighboring building. He briefly disappeared from view, and we slowed as we approached, wary of a trap. I considered drafting the patrol officers near the protest barricade for assistance, but there wasn't time. So we maintained our pursuit, and turned into the alley with caution. Halfway down the building, Tenebrae was climbing the suspended ladder of the fire escape. Already near the top, he swung a leg onto the stairwell. The ladder was a hook and drop design, and once it was free of Tenebrae's weight it began to rise away from the ground once again.

Jax pulled farther ahead, shouting at me over his shoulder.

"I can catch him!" He sprinted forward, leaping and catching the bottom rung. He clambered up the ladder and onto the fire escape. But he couldn't wait on me, and by the time I reached it, the ladder had ascended once more.

I jumped, but it was beyond my reach. I snarled a curse. Even if I had a bit more height than Jax, he clearly had a better vertical leap. Jax was already running up the stairs in pursuit, and calling him back might allow Tenebrae to slip away.

So I fell back on an old trick from my misspent youth. I took off my belt and held the tongue of it in my hand as I leapt again, swinging the buckle in an arc. It struck the bottom rung of the suspension ladder and hung there for a long beat. I crouched, waiting for gravity to win out. Finally the buckle slipped downward. I timed my jump to match the moment when the buckle and tongue were equally distant, the buckle headed down and the tongue headed up. I grabbed both then simply hung on, letting my weight do the work. The ladder came down with a rattle, and I scampered up, belt looped around my fist as I climbed first the ladder then the stairs of the fire escape.

I'd lost sight of Tenebrae and Jax, but the Paradise was a three-story, a little low for the neighborhood, and there weren't any options for hopping over to other rooftops or fire escapes. So I knew the roof was the only logical route they could've taken.

My legs pumped and my lungs ached from the chase, and in the back of my mind a memory tickled. There was something familiar about the cycle of ladder to stairs, but I didn't have time to ponder the connection. I ascended, revolver in hand, each step drawing me closer to the top of the building.

The fire escape terminated at an access point about a third of the way down the mountwise roof. It was a flat, hot-mopped tar roof, ringed by a waist-high perimeter wall. I peeked over the lip. Jax crouched a few strides down the wall, his back against the masonry. He held his service revolver in one hand and waved me over with the other. I joined him and scanned the situation.

Ahead a scattering of exposed pipes for plumbing and air vent stacks stuck up from the roof like oil derricks on the ice plains. To either side was open space, pocked by occasional piles of construction material from some long-ago project, stacks of I-beams and canvas-wrapped debris abandoned by contractors too lazy to haul them down to the street. No sign of Tenebrae. The biggest immediate danger was the far small hut to one side of the roof that provided stair access to the building below.

Jax tilted his head, indicating one side of the access door. I nodded, and headed in the opposite direction, spreading out from my partner in a pincer move. We made eye contact once more before we both snapped around the corner. To the right was a pair of water towers and to the left was Mitri Tenebrae.

He stood in the open, on the far side of the roof, peering over the edge and watching the sea of festival attendees mill around the stage three floors below.

I stepped forward, shoes grinding audibly on the silt and debris that collected in the windbreak of the access door. He turned at the sound, and I got a good look at him. The air between us swirled with the tingle of cobwebs, a sure sign that he was bound to something nearby. Corporate sorcerer, charmer, artist . . . whatever he'd once been, he was a cornered animal now. The pink tip of his tongue flicked in and out as his eyes danced over me, Ajax, the roof, searching for any way out, any way to find escape and keep his mad flight alive for another hour or day or week. To his back was the roof lip, and the alley that separated the pavilion from its nearest neighbor. It was a long jump, but conceivable for an athlete like Tenebrae or Jax. For me, it may as well have been the other side of the Mount.

My weapon was steady, trained on Tenebrae's center of mass. I couldn't let him make that jump.

"Stay where you are," I said. If we could get him prone, we could control the situation.

Tenebrae didn't move.

"Get down," I said. "On the ground, hands out in front of you. Do it now or I *will* shoot."

It was a lie. I didn't want to shoot him. I wanted him in front of a jury, humiliated and begging for mercy for what he'd done.

Tenebrae stared across the alley, to the far roof. He chewed his lips, clenched his fists, all signs of doubt. Doubt about whether he could make the jump, whether he was better off surrendering or taking the leap. Doubt was something I could work with. But I had to work fast. I took another step forward.

"You were searching for new manna," I said. "Desperate to make up everything you took from your corporate bosses."

He stared back at me, surprise clear on his face. Even with everything collapsing around him, the guy still had the ego to think that he'd somehow pulled off the perfect crime.

"So you came out here, and made connections, didn't you?" I put praise and admiration in my voice, playing to that vanity. "Smart. I gotta admit it was smart."

Tenebrae tilted his head. Even in an adrenaline-soaked panic, he couldn't resist a compliment. Then the bastard threw his head back and laughed at me. "You have no idea the pressure I was under."

Pressure is one of the things white-collar criminals cited the most. As if all the working-class parents struggling to feed their families had no idea what the obligation to make a luxury car payment could do to a man.

"I hear you," I said, slathering my words with as much sincerity as I could muster. "I can't even get my head around all the ways you played people. And the secrets you got hold of?" I whistled in admiration.

His laugh increased in pitch, threatening to turn into a maniacal giggle. "In here!" He tapped his head. "I got them all in here, and I can recite them at any time. You want to make your career? I've a record of every conversation, every plot and scheme run by the AFS."

Eyes wide, he stared over my shoulder. An amateur trying an amateur trick on a pro. I kept all my focus on him.

"That's when you found Jane."

Tenebrae's attention snapped back to me. His brows furrowed. "Who?"

"The woman in the alley." I fought the urge to scream. "The one you bought snake oil from."

"Oh." He was still shooting glances over my shoulder. I still wasn't falling for it.

"What was her name?" I slipped one more step closer to him. A wind was picking up, and it eased some of the sweat from my brow.

"The girl?" His eyes narrowed. "I have no idea. I'm offering you the entire conspiracy behind the military presence, and you care about the body of some whore in an alley?"

I almost pulled the trigger. But I moved a step closer. If he made it across the alley, I'd never bring him in. If he fell, he'd never face justice for what he'd done to Jane. I had to slow him down. I had to keep him talking. I raised my voice to be heard over the increasing howl of the wind.

"Did she have manna? Is that why you killed her?"

He blinked, looking puzzled. I pushed forward, and he took a step back. Dangerously close to the roof's edge.

"Her?" he said. "She was dead when I found her."

I struggled to process Tenebrae's statement—was it possible the video had shown Anson's reaction to someone else's presence, or was Tenebrae bluffing, lying about this like he'd lied about nearly everything else? Jax interrupted my train of thought, surprising me by interrupting my exchange with Tenebrae.

"Get down!" he ordered the sorcerer. "Step away from the ledge, then kneel down and put your hands on your head." There was a hint of concern in his voice, audible in the rising howl of the wind.

I finally looked behind me, in time to see Paulus in her black suit and silver-accented boots, her clothes untouched by the slightest breeze. Her lips tight, eyes locked on Tenebrae, she wore the same look of delight I'd seen in Rumple's eyes when he caught a stray mouse. She swung two fingers in a lazy circle, and a blast of wind bowled me over and stole the breath from my lungs.

The mopped tar roofing gave slightly as I struck it, the rubber-like surface warm and surprisingly yielding. It didn't do much to soften the blow as my head bounced off the ground. I lay flat on my back, body panicking as I struggled to breathe. I stared straight up at the cloud-streaked blackness of the sky and wondered what the Hells had happened.

All around me was the crashing and screeching of tearing metal. Realization set in as the first trickles of air seeped back into my lungs. Tenebrae had admitted that the AFS secrets were all safe in his head. If Paulus really wanted to keep them a secret, there was one sure way. She'd never let him walk away alive.

My lungs expanded, filling with oxygen, and I sat up with a jerk, only to be bowled over by a shockwave of heat and wind. Flat on my back once again, I felt for my revolver.

For a moment there was only tar and gravel, then the cold metal of the revolver's barrel was in my hand.

I secured my weapon and rolled away, coming up in a crouch. Jax was a short distance to my left, on his hands and knees as he fought to catch his breath. Paulus and Tenebrae were twenty paces in the opposite direction, fire and air warping and wrapping around them. It was a surreal scene, something I'd only read about in fairy tales and history books. An actual, true-to-the-Path sorcerers' duel.

I duck-walked to Jax's side, helping steady him in the onslaught of heat and wind vortex, when an echoing crash snapped my attention back to the combatants.

Paulus grasped a metal rod in each hand, each no more than the length of her forearm. She swung them as though conducting a diabolical orchestra, and for a moment she had the appearance of a storybook sorcerer, decked out with a magic wand. Across the roof, two large metal rails danced around Tenebrae, each taller than me and probably twice as heavy. The rails darted in the air, responding to Paulus's movements, mimicking the directions of her metal rods and allowing her to attack Tenebrae at a distance and in the process doing damage to everything nearby.

Tenebrae held up the most ludicrous thing I could imagine. A water balloon. He chanted, closed his eyes, and squeezed, forcing a portion to extrude into a straight line. Behind us, one of the water towers shook, rattled, and then burst open, an impossibly solid arm of water breaking free of its metal prison. The rest of the water tank fell away, revealing the thing that Tenebrae had created before his meeting. The water creature was fully twice my height, an egg-shaped puppet dancing to its master's commands. Matching Tenebrae's tiny construction, the water droplet formed tentacles and lashed out with rounded protrusions that held the weight of a small car and the force of acceleration imbued by Tenebrae's actions.

Beside me, Jax sighed. "Oh, Hells . . ."

The metal rails swung again as Paulus responded. Her aim was off, and the end of one railing caught in the roof membrane, tearing chunks of it up in a deep furrow. It slowed the railing but didn't stop it, and with a twist of her arm Paulus lashed out and hit her mark, plunging the massive metal rail into the shambling water shape.

Her strike cut through the water beast, disrupted the surface, and momentarily caused it to tremble. But Tenebrae's binding was too strong, and the water simply cascaded over itself, healing the wound. The water thing rolled forward, bending and twisting like the balloon in Tenebrae's grip.

As Paulus attacked, Tenebrae focused more attention on the rubber object in his hands. The balloon seemed abnormally thick, the contours of its surface more malleable, more capable of holding its form. Whether magically modified or simply a thicker rubber, the balloon didn't break under duress and Tenebrae was able to shape it, sculpt it, stretching and expanding the balloon and making the tons of water from the tower stumble forward like a drunken bruiser. No matter what Paulus did to the creature, it simply regrouped, conforming once more to the shape of Tenebrae's puppet.

The rails themselves had begun to glow. A scattering of red-rimmed circles appeared, consumed from within like steel wool burning in a slow fire. *Manna rot.* Paulus parried a swing of the creature's arm with one of the rails, but it began to twist, collapsing in on itself like the flower blossom I'd seen in Gellica's office.

The memory of Gellica's office triggered another thought. If I could affect the cobwebs, could I do the same to Tenebrae now? With Jax stabilized, I holstered my weapon and walked forward, hands outstretched. The winding strands of cobwebs grew stronger, and I focused on the tingling, biting sensation. It was stronger than when I'd encountered it with snake oil. This feeling was pure, more intense, like an undiluted whiskey that steals your breath even as it wraps you in a barrel-aged haze.

I tore at the threads, and felt the now-familiar sensations of hunger and cold, blended with pressure in my sinuses as the sights and sounds of the world seemed to slip slightly away. In the distance, somewhere off the roof, there was a growing buzz, as if the crowd below had begun cheering my name, like the crowd at the CaCuri rally. Tenebrae's water creature didn't move any slower, but he seemed confused, using his free hand to poke at his shirt.

I focused on breaking the link, trying to remember how it had worked before. "Dammit," I muttered, feeling the anger and frustration growing in me like a wild creature, and I grasped the threads and squeezed. "Dammit, dammit, *dammit*!" The cold and pressure lifted, and I looked around, hoping that I'd succeeded.

Across the roof, the water creature flew back and forth, reacting to Tenebrae's tiniest gesture like the flower in Gellica's office. My jaw dropped. Instead of reducing the magic, I'd boosted it. The hulking shape streaked across the roof almost faster than the eye could follow. Tenebrae tried to brace it by shooting out a pseudopod like a brake, but the combination of water weight and heightened acceleration proved too much for the roof. Tar and underlayment exploded outward from the impact, exposing the framing even as it, too, gave way.

The water creature wavered, and Tenebrae attempted to pull it back, causing it to swing one arm out and down, striking the roof beneath our feet and expanding the jagged crater. The combined weight and damage were more than the structure could bear. The creature toppled forward, falling through the hole in the roof. The structure gave out under my feet, and I followed Tenebrae's watery creation into the void. As we tumbled, I collided with its massive shape, and for a second the creature's liquid shell bent beneath my weight. Then the surface parted and I plunged inside it, absorbed into the creature as we fell.

34

INSIDE THE CREATURE, THE WORLD was blue-tinted and quiet. Surrounded by water, a cool chill spread across my body and a pressure built against my sinuses. I finally understood what connecting with manna felt like—being plunged underwater. For a moment, I was weightless. My arms and legs drifted and the sound of screaming was at a distant remove.

Then we hit the floor below.

We broke through with a rumble, as the massive weight and momentum of the creature propelled us on, through a room of terrified onlookers, and into the first level, where kitchen staff scattered deeper into the Paradise or out onto the alley through the back entrance. The solid slab of the ground floor finally proved too much for the creature to barrel through, and it dispersed, a water tower's worth of liquid creating a small tidal wave of destruction in the Paradise Parlor's kitchen.

Suddenly in air again, I gasped like a fish pulled out of an ice hole, dragged by a hook into a confusing new world and about to have my life extinguished. For two long, jagged breaths the water around me drained away. Then it began to reconstitute itself. Water flowed back together to form the creature. Puddles flowed upward from the tile floor, and droplets peeled back from the walls and ceiling where they'd splashed. I was no exception.

I clawed at a nearby worktable, pulling myself up onto unsteady legs. All around, CaCuri staffers and thugs ran in circles, baffled by what to do in the face of the impossible.

I was soaked to the bone, water dripping from my clothes as I got my bearings. A single drop gathered at the edge of my shirt cuff. But instead of falling to the floor, it hesitated, trembling, then dispersed back into the cloth. A heartbeat later, a bead of water gathered at the top of my shirt cuff, grew, then fell *up*, drifting away overhead. The enchanted water was responding as Tenebrae reexerted his control.

A second later the effect was all over my body. The water that had covered me began to pull off of my body. Moisture stripped away from me, drying my clothes and pulling free of my hair and skin, even from where it had gotten into my nose and mouth, a painful sensation like beads on a string being yanked from my sinuses. I cupped a hand over my mouth, but the water simply pushed out between my fingers. The pain was intense and claustrophobia-inducing. I swatted at the threads of spider silk leading back to the roof, where Tenebrae called the water to return to him. As I clutched at the threads the cold and hunger emerged once more, but before I could act, the threads were whisked from my grasp. The creature formed into a pillar of water and flowed its way back up through the crater, taking the threads with it. I was left partially dry, with some of my clothing still wet, where I'd managed to sever the connection completely. I stared at the retreating creature, ravenous and dizzy. That's when I realized that Jax was alone up there with Tenebrae and Paulus.

I had to find the stairs, had to get to the roof, had to stop Tenebrae and find justice for Jane. But something tugged at the frayed edges of my mind. I replayed Tenebrae's shocked denial. It sounded sincere, but for now I had to set it aside. Jax needed me. Chilled and damp, I stumbled forward, counting on the continued shouts and screams in the building to make the sight of a lone running figure seem ordinary.

I left the kitchen through a swinging access door and found myself in a large dining area. A little sit-down service for the CaCuris' best pals. I wove through the sea of round tables, making my way to the double doors at the far end of the room. I swung one open with as little noise as possible.

I entered the hallway with my badge miraculously still

tucked into my jacket breast pocket. Not that a badge
would get much respect here, but it might make someone
think twice about sinking a knife into my gut. I walked as
quickly as I could manage, gait unsteady after my multi-
floor plunge. Eventually I recognized one of the sitting
rooms we'd been taken through earlier to meet Thomas.
Oriented properly, I turned in a circle, surveying my options and eventually picking the most garishly decorated
hallway. I guessed the stairs wouldn't be too far from there.

As I crept forward, the sound of arguing voices echoed
from farther down the hall. The same voices I'd heard yelling at Donnie's, but now carrying even more vitriol and
anger. The kind of yelling that didn't end happily. I paused,
wondering whether to head back the way I'd come or try to
creep past unnoticed. But when an agonized moan drifted
out of the throne room I knew the CaCuris weren't alone.
Someone in that room had let out a wordless plea for help
that I couldn't ignore.

I crept toward the room at the end of the hallway and
peered through the half-open door. The building shuddered with the force of the battle raging overhead, and I
spotted Thomas. He'd shed his suit coat, and his shirtsleeves were rolled to his elbows. He was literally red-
handed with the blood of a thin young Gillmyn strapped to
the ornate throne. Thomas paced like a caged animal, back
and forth before his victim, occasionally reaching up to
check on the padded pocket of his waistcoat, where I suspected his pocket watch still sat tucked safely away.

Scenarios ran through my head of the best way to enter,
subdue him, and radio my comrades that I had Thomas.
When he hit the guy again I decided the Hells with it, and
burst into the room, drawing a bead on Thomas.

"Don't move!" I shouted the words, as if I could make
him surrender through sheer force of will. He froze, and I
considered it mission accomplished. Now I simply needed
to find a way to restrain Thomas, reach Jax, stop Tenebrae,
and get all of us out of the building before it collapsed.

I'd almost figured it out when a heavy hand clamped
down on my neck, twisting me to the right as my gun hand
was pulled backward. The bouncer from the front room
had me from behind. I hit the wall beside the door, cheek

pressing into my teeth, as pressure on my wrist forced me to release my weapon.

When I dropped the gun, my assailant released my arm and punched me twice. Pain exploded in my lower back as he targeted my kidney and then, with an uppercut, my groin. My face slid down the wall as he recovered my gun, and I heard the scrape of metal as he stowed my weapon behind his belt buckle.

Marguiles had one hand on my neck and levered my right hand back and up, keeping me stooped over and at risk of having my arm broken. I craned my neck to get a glimpse of the twins.

"It's the manna strike cop," he said. There was enough of a quiver in his voice that I knew he didn't like this setup. That was something to work with.

Katie stood by the chair, hand on its back, between the ceremonial knife belts, staring at her brother and the mess of a man in the chair.

"Thomas, what did you do?"

"Nothing that didn't need doing," he said, bottom lip jutting out like a petulant child. But when he looked at me he broke into a smile. A cruel child delighted to find a helpless animal to torment. He pulled out his pocket watch and absently ran his fingers over its face. "Nothing I can't do again."

I opted for the direct approach.

"Thomas CaCuri, you're under arrest for assault and battery," I glanced at the poor SOB in the chair, "of whoever that is."

Katie said, "Don't listen to him." But it was a whisper, more to herself than the blood-hungry Thomas.

Her twin sneered, speaking to me. "You come to save your little friend?" He shoved the palm of his hand against the Gillmyn's cheek, turning the victim's head so I could get a look at his face.

It was Weston, the eager Gillmyn who'd helped broker our meeting with the Harlqs. He was mercifully unconscious.

"We had eyes on them," Thomas said. "On the filthy Harlqs. And who goes waltzing in to talk to Anders? The ice plains hero. And after you and your throat-talker buddy show up in our house," he jabbed a finger at the floor, "who gets spotted at the festival, but Anders's right-hand man."

Weston wasn't anyone's right-hand man. He was a fool who romanticized gangsters. That wasn't a mistake that should carry a death sentence.

"Stupid," I said. Marguiles kept me doubled over, but I kept talking. "When I met the Harlqs I stared at them like my life depended on it. And that kid wasn't there. You grabbed some poor bastard who came here to celebrate the holiday and beat him almost to death."

The bloodied twin paused, considering my words.

"Well." Thomas walked in my direction with a spring in his step. He placed a large hand on my forehead and pushed, craning my neck back so he could look me in the eye. "I guess I'll have to finish the job, and then move on to you." He poked a finger against my forehead. "Put him in the chair, Marguiles."

"Got you red-handed," I said, panting as Marguiles tightened his grip. "You imbecile."

"Thomas," Katie's words grew in volume. "Listen to me . . ."

"Can't do nothing to me." Thomas slid his hand from my forehead to my ear, knuckles brushing over my cheek-bone before pausing to twist my earlobe, thumbnail pinching into soft flesh. "I got a whole organization that'll alibi me. I wasn't here, and I never said a thing."

"You know I didn't come here alone," I said. "Cop walks into your place of business and disappears? That's a strong lock." Tenebrae's denial resurfaced in my mind once again. "We've already got you on video," I said. "An-son on the fire escape, you in the alley."

Thomas grabbed my chin in his beefy hand and squeezed, forcing my lips into a pucker and bruising my jaw with fingers laced by gaudy rings.

"Shut your lying mouth," he said. Rumbling. Almost ready to burst.

"Thomas!" Katie sidestepped, trying to get her broth-er's attention. Thomas dropped his hand and stood back, responding to his sister's command, even as he kept his focus on me.

Katie pulled her lips back and let out a snarl. "Thomas,

wait. Once I'm elected I can do whatever I damn well want and the people will back me." She turned to me. "You know why? Because the feds are screwing over every one of us. And I've got proof."

Above us, the battle still raged on the roof. Sirens were approaching, though the street festival tents and crowds meant they'd be slow to arrive. I wondered if we'd finally met the requirements for Guyer's ARC squad to roll out. A particularly heavy blow shook the building once more. The lights flickered, dimmed, and then died.

Marguiles shifted, tilting off-balance, and I tucked my legs into my chest, allowing my weight to drag us down. He pulled back, putting even more weight onto his back leg, and I kicked out with both feet, slamming my heels into the side of his knee and bending it in an unnatural direction. We tumbled to the ground, limbs tangled, as Marguiles writhed in pain.

Katie practically screamed at her brother. "Thomas, let's *go*!"

The room was now lit only by the glow of the street-lights outside, and the other three were more silhouettes than people. My shoulders ached from being in Marguiles's grip, but I rolled in the guard's direction. When I bumped into him I threw a jab at his eyes. He pulled his hands up, and I grabbed my gun from his belt.

"No one move," I said. I had to find a way to restrain them, then I could get the guy in the chair to safety. Then I could get to Jax.

The building shook again, sending chunks of plaster raining down from the ceiling. Thomas snarled and moved toward me. I pulled the trigger.

The hammer fell with a damp *click* that sent a chill down my bones. The water from the creature—it had gotten everywhere when I was inside of it, and I'd cut off its connection to the creature before it got out of my cartridges. I had time to pull the trigger twice more as Thomas crossed the room, resulting in another pair of empty clicks. He backhanded my weapon, and it almost fell from my grip. I managed to hold on, but it now pointed uselessly across the room.

Thomas hit me, and it felt like I fell through another

level of the Paradise. He slammed me against the entertainment center as a crashing noise overhead told me that the battle had fallen down into a lower level yet again. A beefy hand snaked into my hair and pulled my head back, forcing me to look him in the eye.

"I don't care if you got home movies." His face next to mine, spittle flying as he spoke, his breath fresh. The kind of man who stopped for a breath mint between murders. "That candy in the alley was in the way. Like you're in the way. We're about to fix the world, and no whore or redback is gonna stop us."

"Thomas." It was Katie, standing in the darkness, speaking to her brother in a loud stage whisper, sounding like I suppose she had since they were children, attempting to calm her hot-headed twin. "He's too high-profile. We need him alive."

The building shook again, echoed by screams from outside. Whatever was happening, it was clearly drawing an audience. In the gloom I could see Thomas glance away, and I risked raising the forgotten revolver once more.

Click.

Thomas's attention snapped back to me. He released my head and grabbed my gun arm by the wrist, pointing the muzzle at the ceiling, increasing the vise-like tension even as his grin widened and widened. I pulled the trigger again. White light erupted, accompanied by the painful, cannon-roar of gunfire in an enclosed space.

The muzzle flash was blinding in the darkness, burning an afterimage of the twins in their throne room, their bouncer still sprawled on the floor. Thomas dropped his hands, no doubt pressing thick palms to his ears as I ran toward what I hoped was the door.

I stumbled across the room, the floor rolling in the combined blindness and deafening ring of the gunshot. At one point someone brushed against me. I pushed away and swung the butt of my revolver. I didn't connect but I did gain a little room. Confused and panicked, I pulled the trigger again. A second explosion of sound and light overwhelmed me, and doubled the intensity of the ringing in my ears. I stumbled further and found myself in the hallway. There was even less light there, and I picked a direction and ran blindly ahead. I had to regroup, and then figure the best way to find Jax, to hunt down Tenebrae.

I pushed through a doorway, and was thankful to have more light. The windows were illuminated by streetlamps and the lights on the twins' temporary stage. I'd reached one of the lounges with fine leather furniture and brandy snifters—now rolling madly across the floor—when everything around me shook with the largest rumble yet.

The far side of the building collapsed, masonry tumbling down and away. The now-missing wall revealed a street full of light, a cloud of dust billowing out and sparkling in the streetlights and Titan's Day decorations, spreading out over the rubble and debris scattered across the CaCuris' stage. The crowd had pulled back, screaming and pointing, while flashing lights signaled approaching first responders. I pressed a hand to my temple. I couldn't identify Talena anywhere in the fray. I couldn't believe that I'd somehow put her in danger once again.

The crowd fell silent. I tried to follow their collective gaze, but they were pointing at something far overhead, on the roof. I'd have to walk onto the stage to see what it was, and I chose to stay in the safety of the shadows. A crunching sound from above, and then Tenebrae's water creature landed on the stage with a rough grace. It was still imposing, but it was also leaking water. Two tentacle arms crossed its approximation of a chest, and they opened to reveal Mitri Tenebrae. He slid out of its grasp, the rubbercoated figure in his hands directing its motion. The water creature stood between us, leaving no way for me to reach Tenebrae without being crushed. He faced the crowd and waved, but there was something odd about him, almost transparent or watery, as if he'd picked up some of the traits of the water creature as well. He stretched the figurine, and behind him the water creature extended itself even higher.

"People of Titanshade!" he shouted. "Have I got some news for you!"

35

TENEBRAE RAISED AN ARM, THE other holding his puppet close to the chest. "The strike slowdowns are a lie! The manna flows like water, and it's being relocated and kept away from you!"

The assembled crowd began to make angry noises. I didn't let it bother me. What I was worried about was the destructive capability of the animated water creature, and making sure that Tenebrae didn't slip out of our hands.

"I can prove it," he said. "I have a full list of everyone who has communicated with the outpost, and what they—" Before the sorcerer could say more, a chunk of building hurled down from the roof, slamming into the watery being and cratering the stage on the other side of it. I craned my neck and spotted Paulus, dusty and blood-streaked, one arm propped around Ajax's neck for support even as the building's facade crumbled further beneath their feet. Even from that distance, I could tell she was seriously injured.

A predator's roar echoed against the buildings of Titanshade. On the edges of the battle, I noticed a large white cat pacing the perimeter. It was Gellica's transformed shape, but with all the witnesses in the crowd, I didn't see how she could get involved. Tenebrae worked his totem and the water creature responded, lifted the broken masonry and hurled it back at the roof. Jax grabbed Paulus and they both disappeared from view, I could only hope to safety. Tenebrae's monster began scooping and hurling debris, with no care for where it landed on the neighboring buildings, as the sorcerer himself backed in my direction.

Waiting, I let him take one more step into the shadows, then I dove. I hit Tenebrae around the waist, feeling his shirt react, but not with the same iron resilience it had before I'd drained its connection on the roof. I tried to wrestle him down, tried to knock the water balloon from his hand. But he was stronger and I was too physically exhausted to force him to the ground. He began to turn, and pushed my arm away, keeping his totem out of my grasp. But not the cobweb threads of manna. I clenched my fist and the strange lines flowed through me.

I immediately felt the chill grip my body, sliding under my skin and through my blood. The pressure was there as well, all sensations I now recognized as like being underwater. But there was also the other element, the hunger that grew stronger the more I ate. The buzzing song urged me on, demanded I consume, to take more of the magical connection.

As I pulled in the manna threads, the cold spread up my arm. I dragged in the power it held, but still hungry, I grabbed for more threads. The water creature's line was deep and rich. Tenebrae had woven a strong bond, and the threads were still fat from when I'd pumped energy into them earlier. I sucked that in as well. The pressure increased, more than it ever had before. I was full of the numbing cold. Manna rippled through my senses, overlapping my sight and hearing as the hunger grew ever more intense.

I was aware of Tenebrae beside me, struggling to escape. He dropped the totem, and the water simulacrum dispersed all at once, its remaining bulk breaking loose, pouring down the CaCuris' stage and spilling out over the streets with the force of a river. It struck the crowd of onlookers, a tidal wave rushing across the cobblestones, knocking the people to the ground, flushing them and the festival debris into the gutter. I paid it no mind. The hunger was overwhelming, and I wanted nothing more than to wrap my hand in more tasty cobwebs.

I fought for focus, but it seemed like there was no correct path ahead. I felt like I could be dragged down into the dark and cold. I could feel the cobwebs, could hear the whispered singing in the dark, but I had no idea what to *do* with any of it. I felt as useless and frozen as a statue.

My fists clenched, and I straightened. The clay sculpture in his apartment—it transmitted back to him, in some way. Even if he had turned off further modifications, there must have been some connection, otherwise he'd have shown the evidence of the accident that had started his downward spiral years ago.

I forced my half-frozen legs to move, but the lack of sensation, even the lack of emotion, meant that I barely budged. Desperate to find energy, I reminded myself that though the water creature's threads were gone, Tenebrae's link to his simulacra was thick with years of manna treatments. I thought of all the potential cobwebs with delicious, fat juicy spiders hidden away, and suddenly felt myself crouch and spring forward with strength I hadn't dreamed I possessed. Landing on Tenebrae, I snatched at the thread linking him to the clay statue. The roar of the song in my ears urged me to feed, but instead I pushed *out*. With a rush, the pent-up energy flowed out, leaving me as empty and exhausted as my worst regret-filled morning purge after a long night of drinking. The cold stripped away and I was suddenly coated in sweat, as the cobweb threads pumped and pulsed like living worms that burrowed into the stumps of my missing fingers. Tenebrae screamed and threw me aside. I found myself on my knees, gulping lungfuls of air as warmth flowed back into my extremities.

Tenebrae stood in the middle of the stage, one hand held at head height, staring as his flesh changed its tone and texture, color draining, becoming more and more gray, until it matched the clay of the sculpture back at the hotel. Horrified and transfixed, he touched the fingers of his right hand with those of his left. The digits pressed against each other, then *into* each other.

Tenebrae blinked, a slow process that mimicked two wet slabs of clay dragging across one another.

"Make it stop," he pleaded, not certain who to turn to. His voice gurgled, as if his lungs were congested with mucus. Or clay. "Please, make it stop!"

He was defeated. The patrol and the ARC would take him into custody, and we'd learn what had driven him to this madness in the first place. I reached for the cobwebs, trying to turn back the process, whispering to the threads, calming them. I never learned if it would have saved him.

Three stories above, Paulus made a darting motion, and a metal pipe shot out from the construction debris. Like the chunk of building masonry she'd thrown before, this one hurtled toward the stage. But now, with no creature to protect him, it pierced Tenebrae's abdomen, cutting through him like a straw through melon. He continued to transform, regressing into clay, the process slowing and stopping as his body died, and the manna link was no longer active. I suspected that he'd always have the shocked and terrified expression on his face, or at least until someone decided what to do with a corpse made out of clay. Maybe they'd wait till he dried out and break him into pieces to scatter on the Mount. More likely they'd send him back to Tele-scribe Communications in the big steamer trunk, a silent warning to the rest of the AFS not to step in Titanshade's affairs.

I ignored Tenebrae's corpse and faced the dark hole of the Paradise Parlor once again. I still had to bring in the man who'd killed Jane. If I didn't move now, the fire department would close the scene for safety's sake. I pushed away from the stage, turned my back on the crowd and the cameras, and returned to the CaCuris' den.

Smoke roiled down the hall. A fire had started, perhaps in the kitchen, perhaps in the damaged wiring.

I found them in their throne room, the twins and their henchman, Marguiles. Katie sat on the elaborate chair, the ceremonial knife-belts fanned out across its back, looking like the outlines of wings. Their Gillmyn captive had been dumped on the floor, West's breathing shallow as she rested one foot on his back. Thomas sat on the billiard ta-ble, nursing an injury to his arm that I wasn't sure where he'd picked up. Then it dawned on me—the final shot I'd fired blindly. I'd managed to hit the bastard after all.

The three of them faced me as I entered.

"It's all over," I said. "There's an army of press and cops outside. Come along quietly."

"Are we under arrest?" Katie said. "What for? Letting you destroy our building?"

I was exhausted, and we were all wounded in one way or another. Most people give up at that point, but I thought it better to be safe than sorry. "You're under arrest for murder," I said to Thomas. "You two," I pointed at Katie and Marguiles, "I don't have enough to book you on." It was a lie, but I hoped it would encourage the two of them to convince Thomas to comply.

Thomas's voice was thick. "Go to Hells."

"You're shot, there's a full complement of officers outside the building, and the news crews are filming everything. It's over."

Katie said, "Don't listen to him." But it was a whisper, more to herself than the blood-hungry Thomas. "We have to protect each other."

I couldn't resist one more comment. It may have been too much, but life was full of possibilities. That's what made it interesting.

"That's right, Thomas. Just like you protected your dear brother Roger."

Maybe it was my insults, or the invocation of his childhood crimes. Maybe it was simply his desire to ignore his sister's counsel. Whatever triggered Thomas's anger, it was enough to push him over the edge. He surged forward as more debris fell from the far wall, his steps matched by the rush of an explosion. Flames licked around the interior shutters as Thomas closed in on me, while I struggled to stay on my feet.

Then Katie was between us. Thomas attempted to stop, but his momentum pushed his sister into me. Katie's elbow was near my ribcage, as if she'd held something between her and her brother. Past her, Thomas stared down, then swayed slightly, revealing his sister's hand on the hilt of a thick-bladed ceremonial dagger. One of the pair that had rested across the chair at the center of the room.

Blinking in confusion, Thomas stared at the dagger, then back at his sister. His eyes showed stark shock at this betrayal of the natural order. Katie's were a swirl of sorrow and anger. The kind of look you might give a beloved pet who'd contracted rabies.

His mouth opened slightly. Katie put one hand on his lips and shook her head. The tears in her eyes were held in check, present but not falling. Then she twisted the blade, turning it in the wound and spiraling the point even deeper into her brother's body.

Thomas let out a long sigh as Katie released the knife, and I stepped away.

Katie's other hand still rested on her brother's pouting lip, silencing his cries. They held each other's gaze as a series of crashes and screams from the crowd indicated that more of the building had collapsed. Then she withdrew her touch, and Thomas teetered, fell to his knees, and slumped to the floor.

I stared at the dead man a long moment before I realized that Katie's eyes were on me. She was breathing fast, hands shaking as she absently wiped blood across her clothes. I wasn't sure if she looked horrified or thrilled at the death of the mad dog she'd controlled and sheltered for decades.

"I had to do it," she said. "He was going to kill you." She looked at her bodyguard and straightened her blouse. "Isn't that right?"

The big man struggled to find his voice, and Katie's command struck like a whip crack. "Marguiles!"

Marguiles nodded. His lips stuck together, but he eventually rasped out: "Yeah."

She leaned closer to me, speaking through clenched teeth. "I saved your life."

Somewhere down the hall, another section of the building toppled to the ground.

"We need to get out of here." Katie snapped her fingers at Marguiles, squaring her shoulders and blocking as much of her henchman's view of her brother as possible. "Get someone on the radio and rally the press outside." When Marguiles didn't respond, she snapped, "We built that stage, we're damn well going to use it."

Marguiles stepped away, unclipping a walkie talkie from his belt and demanding status updates. Katie walked out of the room. I considered following her, but instead I approached Thomas. Squatting over him, I felt for a pulse, half expecting it had all been an elaborate ploy. But no, the terror of the underworld was dead, gutted on the floor of his own castle.

"Get away from him." Katie had returned, a tablecloth from one of the dining area tables draped over one arm. She stared at me with fire in her eyes. "Don't you ever touch him again."

I stepped aside, and Katie draped the cloth over her brother's corpse. The bleached-white fabric hid his face, though its fringe bore a red handprint. Katie had collected it while still dripping with her brother's blood.

She stood there for a heartbeat, then pushed past me. I made no move to stop her. I didn't have the strength, and it wasn't like she was going far—I had no doubt she was headed straight for the stage. I thought of Glouchester's story about the twins' murdered older brother, and wondered if the reporter had gotten it wrong. Had Katie lied to protect her twin, or had Thomas taken the fall for his sister? Which one of them was the mad dog, and which one had held the leash?

From down the hall rescue teams called for survivors as they worked to clear the building. I signaled to them, and slipped an arm under Weston's shoulder, helping him to his feet. A moment later the first responders led the way outside, into the longest night of the year.

In the alternating red and white ambulance lights, the living were tended to while the dead waited their turn. I sat on the tail end of an ambulance, watching the medic walk away to another bus to check on Jax. The other occupants of the CaCuri stronghold were examined, triaged, and either sent to hospital or released. The wounded police went through the same procedure, but none of us were free to go home. Jax and Talena were a few ambulances over. They'd put up with my barrage of questions, until I was satisfied they were both okay. Now they sat side by side, sharing a blanket and a quiet conversation. It was one of the few pleasant things I'd seen all day.

Behind me footsteps crunched, expensive bootheels crushing the grit that hid in the crevices of the tar roof.

Paulus approached, slowing only slightly as she reached my side. She stared at Tenebrae's broken body impaled on the stage, and the team of halfhearted techs erecting a tent to shield it from the photographers and television crews.

"He was about to kill you." Her voice was light and mocking. "I saved your life." Then, louder and over her shoulder: "Isn't that right?"

From a shadowed doorway, Gellica emerged and nodded. Her lips moved, but if she spoke, I didn't hear it.

"See? I even have a witness, just like your little salt plains princess did." Paulus leaned in, hot breath whispering in my ear. "Everyone around you ends up dead sooner or later, don't they?" She looked me over and seemed to find me lacking. "You're bad news, Carter." She tipped her head toward Gellica, curled her lip, and added, "Don't go near my property again."

I said nothing, and after a moment Paulus hummed a note of self-satisfaction. "It's for the best," she said. "Though I'm not quite sure what happened to him before I put him out of his misery." She looked from me to Gellica and back again. The tattoos on her arms pulsed, creatures of ink slithered and bared their teeth in silent growls. "We'll speak more of that later," she said. "When we won't be overheard."

Paulus walked away, the click-clack of her bootheels tracking her departure. When they faded, it was still another long moment before I gathered the courage to look at Gellica, half expecting her to be gone.

Gellica stood with her hip pressed against an ambulance frame, blanket wrapped around her shoulders, head down, dangling hair hiding her face. As the emergency techs moved around us, I walked toward her. She didn't raise her eyes, though there was no way she didn't know I was there.

I took a breath, meaning to say "Hey" or "Let's talk" or maybe just whisper her name, but the life drained from the words, and their sound sat dead on my tongue.

Head still down, she said, "You promised me you'd wait."

There was a coppery taste on my lips, and I wondered if I'd bitten my tongue.

"But you didn't, and you put all those people who depend on me at risk. All those lives, and everything I've been working for, to finally find a way for me to be free. Flushed away." She raised her head, eyes red and wet, as if she were holding the tears back by an extreme act of will. "Why?"

"I had to."

She winced like she'd been slapped, mouth working, as if repeating the conversation to make sure she'd understood me. I wished that I could say something fast and funny and with precisely the right amount of remorse. I wished the whole damn thing hadn't happened. . . . Except it had. And I knew that if I were in the same position, I couldn't trust myself not to do it again. I'd never look a killer in the eye and let him go free, no matter how bad it hurt me.

But I hadn't only hurt myself. I'd hurt someone I cared for, someone who wanted to care for me in return.

"I didn't have a choice," I said. "Because—"

"Because you turn your back on the living," she said. "In order to serve the dead."

I flexed my hand, felt the reddened flesh of my face. Minor cuts and burns that would heal in a few days. Not like the pain I'd caused Gellica. I tried to sit a little taller, to find some way to explain myself. She watched and waited, but in the end I only fidgeted in place. Gellica let out a single, humorless chuckle.

"It's lonely being like us," she said. "The difference is, you prefer it that way."

I didn't have anything to say, and I'm not sure she had it in her to listen to my excuses. She turned and walked away, and I sat on the ambulance's tailgate, back against the door, and wondered if the flames in the building beside us would spread, and grow, and consume me where I sat, so that for once I wouldn't have to deal with the consequences of my decisions.

36

TWO WEEKS SINCE JANE HAD been killed, and the world went on like nothing had changed.

Titan's Day dawned. The sun came out ever so slightly earlier than it had the day before, and the city declared it a holiday. After the chaos at the street festival, Katie CaCuri sacrificing her brother to save a cop's life led the evening news and was the headline on all the morning papers. And Tenebrae's indictment of the military encampment didn't do the AFS faction any favors. The fact that an unidentified woman found in an alley off Ringsridge Road had found justice didn't make the papers at all.

CaCuri's supporters were already making the media rounds, appearing on morning talk shows trying to paint her as a martyr to the cause, a true patriot who'd put the good of the city ahead of everything, even her own brother's life. *And after all,* they said, *isn't that exactly who we need in office right now?*

When the talking heads on the news began declaring Katie CaCuri the projected winner at the polls, there was a loud knock on my door. I turned off the television and padded over to the door. A pair of burly Gillmyn stood in the hall. They had a delivery for me.

I can't say it was a complete surprise. After all, Gellica had told me what she'd do if she didn't want me coming to see her anymore. I tipped the deliverymen and they dragged away my old couch. I sat in my apartment, listening to records with Rumple perched behind me, idly tracing the quality stitching of floral patterns as Titan's Day faded to black.

The next morning was cold and crisp, with a surprising lack of mist slithering through the streets. I arrived at the morgue a couple hours after it opened and asked about Jane's remains. It seemed like the least I could do was to arrange for her body to be set to rest with dignity.

I was still massaging away my headache when the clerk told me that the remains had already been claimed.

"What do you mean *claimed*?" I said. "No one knows who she is."

The clerk poked the clipboard, as if it were the supreme arbitrator of all disputes. "First thing this morning," he said, a ragged thumbnail indicating a scrawled signature: *Allura Shade*.

"Alright," I said. "You got a phone I can use?"

It took twenty minutes of working my way through the telephone directory, but I finally found what I was looking for.

By the time I got to the guidepost, they'd already started the ceremony. I walked in, the only person in attendance besides the guide and the woman who'd claimed Jane's remains.

Lillian Moller stood alone, eyes downcast. Her usual outfit of black on black seemed slightly more subdued than the last time I'd seen her. Maybe there were fewer buckles on the jacket.

I stood next to her, and she gave me the briefest of dark looks.

"Fuck off, cop."

There was absolutely no fire in her voice. The anger and arrogance in which she tried to dress her words were merely distractions from what she really felt. That true feeling, hidden someplace deep and cold, was something I could relate to. After all, I'd spent decades with my own secret trove of regret.

So I didn't go anywhere; she didn't say anything else. And together we stood for Jane.

When the guide finished her speech, Moller collected Jane's ashes in the discount urn provided by the crematorium. She didn't look at me as she walked past. I didn't ask what she was going to do with them.

Moller had never said a proper good-bye to Jane. I'd never gotten to say hello.

Two days later I spotted the graffiti on a big building on Crater Road near Sullivan. It stopped me in my tracks, a pair of coffees cooling in my hands as the sea of pedestrians was forced to part around me. I stood before a newsstand, its wire racks filled with headlines screaming about the special election and stoking fears about possible secession from the AFS and threats of military intervention. But I didn't care about that. I only had eyes for the mural above.

It took up the entire side of the office building. A portrait of a beautiful Mollenkampi woman, head plates a startling shade of red, her eyes defiant and hopeful. The eyes of someone who saw more beauty in this town than it deserved. With a little help from Lillian Moller, it was Jane's last statement of love and hope and freedom.

My pager buzzed, calling to me from its resting place deep in my coat pocket. Farther down the street Jax waited by the Hasam. He'd probably already responded to the page, asking questions over the radio and jotting notes about another body found in an alley, or apartment, or abandoned car. It was another day in Titanshade, another step forward on the well-trodden path we all walk until we retire or get carted off in a hearse.

I took one step, then another. It was all I could do. It's all anyone can do.

Jane watched over my shoulder as I walked toward the Mount, my partner, my job. I was glad to have her blessing.

I figured we'd be needing it.

ACKNOWLEDGMENTS

I'VE BEEN TOLD THAT HAVING a second child is ten times as difficult as the first. I can't speak to that, but it definitely holds true for novels. This was a tough book to bring into the world, and I never could have done it without the support of many generous individuals. The full list is too long to include here, but here are some of the people I'd like to single out.

First, my parents, Jim and Maryann Stout. My mom has always supported me and cheered me on, even from my earliest attempts at storytelling, when she patiently wrote down the narrated adventures of my toys. And while my dad may be gone, I like to think he's smiling down at these books.

Mandy Fox is my best friend, partner in crime, and love of my life. A fantastic storyteller and teacher, she regularly consults with me on tricky plot issues, many of them two-pint problems that can only be resolved in our Over the Counter corner office.

My agent Nat Sobel, who suffered through my earliest drafts. His notes and efforts are greatly appreciated, along with the rest of the Sobel-Weber family: Judith Weber, Adia Wright, and Sara Henry.

Once again, I'm immensely indebted to my editor, Sheila Gilbert. Sheila was *extremely* patient as I found my way through this sophomore novel, and she has an incredible knack for knowing exactly what to bring into focus to make a story shine. And the rest of the DAW family never ceases to amaze me with their kindness and skill. Huge thanks to

Betsy Wollheim, Katie Hoffman, Joshua Starr, Mary Flower, Leah Spann, Jessica Plummer, Alexis Nixon, and Stephanie Felty.

Chris McGrath managed to bring life to Carter and Titanshade with another phenomenal cover illustration, while Katie Andersen and the DAW team's design work perfectly captured the book's aesthetic.

Massive thanks to the kind and generous beta readers who provided feedback and guidance during this drafting process. Thanks to all the members of Writeshop, especially Holly Bell, Matthew Cook, Sandra J. Kachurek, Jordan Kurella, Dan Lissman, David Palmer, Jerry L. Robinette, and Catherine Vignolini. Also, huge thanks to my Novel Buddies group: Jodi Henry, Stephanie Lorée, and Paul Nabil Matthis. (Paul is also the official Titan's Day music consultant.) Along with the Buckeye Crime Writers, these groups have been hugely helpful to me. If you're a writer just exploring the creative waters, it's well worth the effort to find quality in-person and on-line critique groups.

Special thanks to Elizabeth Vaughan for her continued advice and support, and critical insight into what makes the perfect eggs benedict.

The Debut 19 group kept me sane and focused during my debut year. I started to list everyone from that group who'd helped me out, but quickly ran out of space. So thanks to them all! The friendship and camaraderie I've found there has been invaluable.

I'm a little in awe of the bloggers, podcasters, book clubs, and reviewers who helped spread the word about this series. I'm moved anytime someone connects with my books enough to share their thoughts, and I do my best to read every one of them.

Lastly, thanks to everyone who holds this book in their hands. Stories are joint efforts, ephemeral things created by reader and writer in equal measure. Whether you picked this book up new, from a library, or in a second-hand store twenty years after its release, you are just as much a part of this story as I am. I hope you enjoyed it, I hope it moved you, and I hope you carry some small part of it with you going forward.

Thank you!

W. Michael Gear

The Donovan Novels

"What a ride! Excitement, adventure, and intrigue, all told in W. Michael Gear's vivid, compulsively readable prose. A terrific new science-fiction series; Gear hits a home run right out of the park and all the way to Capella."　　　　　　—Robert J. Sawyer

"Fans of epic space opera, like Rachel Bach's *Fortune's Pawn*, will happily lose themselves in Donovan's orbit."　　　　　　—*Booklist*

Outpost	978-0-7564-1338-5
Abandoned	978-0-7564-1341-5
Pariah	978-0-7564-1344-6
Unreconciled	978-0-7564-1567-9
Adrift	978-0-7564-1716-1

To Order Call: 1-800-788-6262
www.dawbooks.com

DAW 220

Edward Willett
The Cityborn

ISBN: 978-0-7564-1178-7

To Order Call: 1-800-788-6262
www.dawbooks.com

Tad Williams
The Dirty Streets of Heaven

"A dark and thrilling story.... Bad-ass smart-mouth Bobby Dollar, an Earth-bound angel advocate for newly departed souls caught between Heaven and Hell, is appalled when a soul goes missing on his watch. Bobby quickly realizes this is 'an actual, honest-to-front-office crisis,' and he sets out to fix it, sparking a chain of hellish events.... Exhilarating action, fascinating characters, and high stakes will leave the reader both satisfied and eager for the next installment." —*Publishers Weekly* (starred review)

"Williams does a brilliant job.... Made me laugh. Made me curious. Impressed me with its cleverness. Made me hungry for the next book. Kept me up late at night when I should have been sleeping."

—Patrick Rothfuss

The Dirty Streets of Heaven: 978-0-7564-0790-2
Happy Hour in Hell: 978-0-7564-0948-7
Sleeping Late on Judgement Day: 978-0-7564-0987-6

To Order Call: 1-800-788-6262
www.dawbooks.com

DAW 207